# purpose in her dreams

## IN HER DREAMS BOOK THREE

JOANNA REEDER

REED IT & WEEP

also by joanna reeder

DREAMWALKER WORLD:


In Her Dreams

Trapped In Her Dreams

Purpose In Her Dreams


In Her Dreams Trilogy Boxset

**Dream Walker Academy:**

Remember (Tessa)

Control (Sebastien)

Belong (Meg)


LEARN ABOUT JOANNA'S OTHER BOOKS AT:

joannareeder.com

Reed it and Weep

*Purpose In Her Dreams*
*Copyright © 2018 Joanna Reeder*
joannareeder.com

Cover Art by Angel Leya
**angeleya.com**

Edited By Katrina Beckstrand
editsbykb.com

*For Dan
For believing in my dream.*

## CHAPTER 1

# insomnia

*Fifty-eight deaths,* I read.

*Twenty—accidents,* which was broken down further. *(Nine— vehicle, Four— wagon, Five— falls, Two—smoke inhalation/burns, One—plane crash.)*

*Eleven—elements (Seven— hypothermia, Two—starvation, One—heatstroke, One—lightning.)*

*Fourteen—illness (Four—cancer, Seven—respiratory, Three—unknown)* I wasn't a doctor, so I didn't know about those last three.

*Five—murder* ~~*(One—poison, Two—gun, Two—knife)*~~ Yep, crossed those out. Because who really wanted the stats on that? Especially the girl who remembered most of the painful details. Really, sometimes I wondered why I even wrote it all down in the first place.

I couldn't sleep. Sometimes reading through my stats journal helped. A little psychotic, I know, because who wanted to re-live any of *that?* It might look like morbid stats to someone else— numbers next to different ways to die—but I had experienced *all* of them. Reading the numbers brought it all back. It was certainly fodder for an actual nightmare, but I hadn't had any of those in years. What I wouldn't give to have another one.

*Three—suicide.* Well, maybe that should technically be *two* because Carly wasn't dead anymore ... No, I'd still experienced it — the number would stay.

*Okay, moving on...* I flipped the page.

*One hundred seventy-nine birthdays.* I'd experienced one hundred and seventy-nine birthdays as other people. And yet I'd still managed to miss my best friend's birthday. Sure, I'd been in a *coma* at the time, but I needed to fix that somehow.

Flipping the page again.

*Two hundred and one parents splitting/announcing their divorce.* After one of those, Mom and Dad always got a ginormous hug and a string of threats about what I would do if they ever put me through that. It was a good thing they were still crazy in love and smart about their finances.

*Thirty-two proms, seventy-seven proposals, sixty-three performances.* Most of those were pretty fun, even though I was someone else. It wasn't *me* who had been asked to the dance, but I was there. It wasn't *me* the guy wanted to spend the rest of his life with, but I was there. It wasn't *me* who got a standing ovation. Then again, it wasn't *me* who got booed off the stage. (Okay, that had only happened four times, but it was still pretty awful.)

*Three hundred and forty-three times being bullied.* Some of those were almost as bad as the deaths, so I didn't linger on that page.

I kept flipping through my journal. The stats could be overwhelming if I lingered too long on any one page. What anyone else would see as a bunch of boring numbers held significant emotional weight for me. Reading the number three hundred and forty-three immediately flashed dozens of awful memories through my head in just a few seconds. It was too much.

I flipped to the individual entry portion of my journal. I was probably a glutton for punishment to even venture through those, but not all of them were bad.

· · ·

*September 21—Kelly thought no one liked her. But then nine of her classmates threw a birthday party for her. I think I was just there to help her contain her excitement. She's going to be okay.*

*September 22—Sierra found out her dad died in the war. Looked like WWII. Couldn't find her in the cemetery. Dead end.*

*September 23—Rochelle got lost at the zoo. She was five? Maybe? Felt like hours, but it was all over within fifteen minutes. Sang to her while she cried.*

That one made me smile. Rochelle was so scared, but I was fourteen (calculated by the date of the entry) so I knew that the people with name tags were employees. I told her to walk up to one of them and tell them she was lost. Her mom was a wreck—of course—when they were reunited, but she'd been proud that her little girl had known how to find help.

I flipped aimlessly several pages in, then froze on a page from last spring:

*Duncan kissed me! FINALLY! It's about time. **Smiley face with hearts for eyes***

It was in my handwriting, and I didn't doubt that I'd written it. But I had no recollection of writing it, no memory of any of the details about the kiss I'd apparently been anticipating for so long. In my memory—the reality where Carly died and I had no friends—I barely met Duncan last fall. This entry was from the reality I *didn't* remember. The one where Arianna never stopped being my friend and Duncan had been my official boyfriend for six months.

*Too bad I didn't think to read this journal sooner,* I thought. It would've saved me a lot of trouble when I woke up absolutely clueless. I flipped further.

*DUNCAN (MY BOYFRIEND... EEK!) AND I WENT ON A double date to the new Marvel movie with Duncan's cousin and Arianna. She's still smitten by Brian Nash (honestly, I think they'll start dating soon) but I think she had fun.*

I VAGUELY REMEMBERED ARI MENTIONING DUNCAN'S cousin at some point. I had just stared back at her blankly. I'd never met the guy. Well, at least *this* version of me hadn't. I'd never seen that Marvel movie either.

It wasn't a normal person problem—remembering different realities. Seriously, it would have been nice to know some of these details. Ever since I'd started dreaming of Lucy, I hadn't looked back at any previous entries. Now I wish I had.

I flipped ahead to one of the first dreams with Lucy.

*OCTOBER 14—ANOTHER LUCY DREAM. I ACTUALLY knew myself this time. I touched Andrew's ring at dinner and BAM! suddenly Emily was there. Lucy's fiancé, Charles returned. They're planning to have a ball announcing their engagement. (A Victorian ball could be super cool.)*

I SMILED FONDLY AT THAT MEMORY. IT WAS ONE I actually remembered. I glanced at Grandma's birdhouse that hung in my room. Painted pale yellow and decorated with tiny black birds that looked like vines crawling up the house and large black letters—or numbers—*VI* on one side. I missed Grandma so much. She had teased me the day after this entry. Somehow she'd known that I'd secretly wished Andrew had kissed Lucy that day instead of Charles. Even though he would have been kissing Lucy, not me.

*Lucy.* My heart ached thinking about her and where she most likely was right now. I flipped back a page, looking for my very first entry of her. *If I could only get back to her—*

But I froze.

*October 10—Nora Violet Harker. Born July 5, 1832. Died of <u>head injury</u> or drowning ~~or hypothermia~~ after falling through the ice on a river. February 12, 1849. She was only sixteen. Her brother, Colin William Harker, was there too. He looked like he was only about eight.*

But it wasn't Nora's entry that shocked me. It was the one that followed:

*Met a boy at the cemetery today. Luckily he showed up <u>after</u> the Nora Rose Ritual. (I can only imagine how strange that would have looked.) His name is Duncan something? (I can't remember his last name). Apparently he's known me for years. I didn't recognize him.*

I remembered writing that. At the time I didn't think much of it. I only wrote it down because it seemed odd. Odd that I didn't recognize him at all, but he seemed to know me.

But the writing survived the timeline change.

It shouldn't be there, right? Since Duncan was *technically* my boyfriend at that point, there should be another entry... *right?* Something like a study/make-out session with Duncan? Or my lamenting that he had football practice and I wouldn't see him until tomorrow? Something... *anything* like that?

How was this even possible? How was the entry still there?

I scanned ahead, back to October 14, *after* the entry when I finally knew myself with Lucy.

*DUNCAN KISSED ME TODAY! IT'S CRAZY, I'VE ONLY known him since... was it only Tuesday? But it feels like we've been friends longer than that. And I guess we're probably on our way to being more than friends.*

*OH, GIRL. IF YOU ONLY KNEW.*

Wow, this journal was crazy but *so* helpful. I'd have to remember that. And make sure I didn't miss a single day writing in it *ever*. It might be crucial someday.

# jumbo jets and sats

"Tell her I'm sick today," Genevieve says, rolling over under her silk sheets. Her head pounds like a jackhammer so it isn't entirely untrue.

*Ugh... she's hungover.* I've experienced the feeling plenty of times in dreams. I don't plan to ever touch the stuff in my waking life. Not. Worth. It.

"I allowed you to take the morning off, but you *will* attend to your studies today," Genevieve's father says from the doorway. "You will meet Miss Hattie downstairs in ten minutes. I will not have my daughter come to nothing."

Genevieve rolls her eyes at the wall. "No one this good-looking ever comes to *nothing,*" she says under her breath, not caring whether or not her father hears. "Perhaps I'll never finish my studies and never marry and just sleep all day if it suits me." But when she rolls back to flash the scowl she's meticulously placed on her face, the open doorway gets the full force of it.

Part of her wants to roll over again and sink back into sleep, but she knows that misbehaving won't get more attention from her father anyway. She struggles to sit up, dragging her heavy head upright, and brushes the nest of hair away from her face.

Twenty minutes later, she's bounding down the stairs, a smile creeping up her thin cheeks. *Andrew kissed me last night,* she muses, touching a finger to her lips. *Cornering him worked.* Pride swells beneath her two-piece blue frock embroidered with red cardinals. It gives her form a fashionable boyish figure. She hardly notices the disapproving frown on the pinched woman's face, who I assume is Miss Hattie.

I attempt to tune out her thoughts as they drift to future plans of "trapping Andrew." *Does he have any idea who this girl is?* I wonder. I make my own plans to warn him about her as she conjugates verbs and sputters through her French lesson.

Amazingly she pushes her headache to the background, through sheer focus—not on French, of course, but Andrew.

*Maybe I should feel grateful that Lucy never loved Andrew.* Genevieve's internal swooning over him grates my nerves like a fork caught in a garbage disposal. *Lucy loved Charles, but her thoughts of him never bothered me. Maybe I just don't like Genevieve.* That feeling makes me uncomfortable. I've never disliked someone I've walked. Sure, I've disapproved of some of their choices, but I simultaneously felt all their good intentions and naivete. I never disliked them. Not like I dislike Genevieve.

Reaching out my invisible feelers, I attempt to prod Genevieve's memories to find something to like. But all I come up with is a selfish-shallow rich girl whose father barely pays any attention to her. And her mother... well, all memories or thoughts of her mother are blocked. Her headache returns, so I stop searching and vow to look later. In the meantime, I attempt to endure being *her.*

Before Miss Hattie can move on to literature, a familiar figure catches my eye—all blond hair now and leaning in the door frame. I didn't think I would see him today, but my heart leaps in unison with Genevieve's.

"Andrew!" she sings and bounds from her chair, tipping it so far that it crashes to the ground. "Are you here to spring me?"

"Genevieve," Miss Hattie uses her scolding tone. "We have barely begun your studies, I do not think it is wise to—"

"Take me for a drive!" she interrupts and grasps his elbow, moving him in the direction of the exit.

He attempts to protest, but she shushes him, and we practically run to the driveway. Genevieve plants herself in the back of the car and puts her feet up. I cringe at the lack of seat belts. Andrew cranks the car to get it started, and before long we are going about twenty miles an hour down the dusty road. It feels like the car doesn't plan to go any faster, so my paranoia over the lack of seat belts diminishes slightly. The spring—almost summer — breeze swishes Genevieve's straight short hair along her collar. She keeps her eyes closed and her head up to soak in the sunshine.

She is strangely content, but I feel the cogs turning beneath her divided-brim turban that matches her frock perfectly. She lifts her neck to further expose her smooth white jawline in hopes that the driver notices. One foot is thrust out further than the other to show off a skinny white calf and ankle above her designer pumps.

I wouldn't know they were designer, but Genevieve has a running narration going through her head, and it's easy to eavesdrop.

*At this angle, if I keep my face relaxed and my chin upward, he'll see my smooth, blemish-free skin and imagine running his lips along it. And with my eyes closed, if he does sneak a glance, he will be free to look as long as he likes without worry of my notice.*

*I feel his eyes on me now, a quick glance at the rear-view mirror where I am in full view.*

*And if I push my foot forward, he will not only see my new designer pumps, but also my feminine legs and tiny ankles.*

Shoot me now.

I tune her out again. Does anyone actually think like that?

*When he pulls over I'll...*

STOP. I have to do something. I have to take control of this madness. She's clearly strong-willed, but I think I can do it.

"Where are we going?" I ask. Me. Not her. I'm pleased it worked.

He looks at me through the mirror. His face looks different.

*Of course his face looks different, Emily,* I chide myself and push the thought back.

"I thought we'd park at the grove of trees up ahead and walk around a bit." Another strange look.

"Perfect. She can't pose like an artist's subject if we're tromping through leaves and dirt. There will be leaves and dirt, I hope?" I try not to think about what leaves and dirt will do to her fancy pumps so she doesn't catch it.

His smile widens. "Emily." Did I notice tears prick his eyes before he blinked? "You're here."

"I'm here," I sing in Genevieve's gravely alto tone.

He pulls over and turns to look at me.

When he doesn't respond I ask, "How did you know?"

His sly smile makes its appearance. "You did not flash your pout face and complain about your designer hat or designer shoes getting dirty."

"Ah!" I try to push her back further. She resists at first, but recognizing how Andrew acts when I am present, she allows it. "Genevieve is fun, isn't she?"

He shrugs, then jumps down from the car and holds out a hand to help me down.

Wrapping my arm into the crook of his arm, he squeezes once. "She's not all bad. She is my way to see you." He kisses the top of my head, and we walk down the lane. "I've missed you."

"We talked last night."

"We did not. We talked about a month ago at her parent's party."

*Wait. But she said...* I gently tug his arm until he stops to look at me. "She said you kissed her last night."

The flash of guilt is instantaneous. "I hoped it would bring you out."

"How many times have you kissed her?"

The guilt face returns as Genevieve mentally squeals, *Six times! And here comes number seven!*

"You're dating her?" I am left to stare at his blond hairline because his eyes are trained on the ground. When they finally meet mine, they are flat and dark. Though they are the same chestnut color I remember, the gold specks that used to dance are absent. He almost looks like a stranger, but I suppose I can't complain. The last time he saw me I was a sweet girl with blonde curls and blue eyes.

I miss Lucy.

"She's my ticket to see you."

"And she's pretty smitten over you, so you are kind of leading her on."

"I don't want to talk about Ginny," he says, using the endearing name she loves. We begin walking again, slowly.

I drag Genevieve's pumps through the dirt slightly. Not in a malicious, I-want-to-ruin-your-fancy-shoes sort of drag, but more in a I-want-this-dream-to-drag-on-so-I can-talk-to-Andrew-longer sort of drag.

"What did you think about what I told you?" His voice is steady, though a little lower toned than Original Andrew$_{TM}$. There is a hint of stretched-tight nerves behind it.

"About you unnecessarily changing events in order to jump through time to get to me?" Yeah, I had thought a lot about what he told me. I'd also thought a lot about all his cryptic *"master planning"* hints before he jumped from Original Andrew$_{TM}$ to Andrew 2.0. And about my feelings and thoughts and moral beliefs about *"unnecessary changes."*

"You have thought about it." He read my face.

"Believe me, I am flattered," I say. Actually more than flattered. It is downright romantic that he is literally finding a way to change his whole life just so he might by some slim chance end up in the same century as me. But it feels irresponsible and impossible. Like trying to throw a rock from a jumbo jet and hoping it will land on the intersection between Center Street and Main Street, without any consideration of the danger to bystanders.

"A jumbo jet?" he asks, and I realize that I spoke the entire argument out loud.

"See!" I throw my hands in the air, effectively releasing my arm from his, and spin to face him. "Even if you could, even if by some miracle you end up in my century, you won't know a single thing about the culture or technology."

*I'm not touching him anymore. Why am I not touching him anymore?* Genevieve mutters in the background.

"Maybe I'll remember." He doesn't sound sure of himself as he says it. "Maybe you can teach me." A minuscule amount of hope is injected into his words, like that might be the answer.

"Okay, let's say that you do remember, or that I do teach you and am able to make you a functioning, normal, adjusted member of the twenty-first century society. Let's say it's no big deal and no one notices that you talk a little bit like a Jane Austen character. But who's to say that you won't overshoot and be born while I'm sitting in Chemistry class? What if we end up seventeen years apart? Or fifty?" He opens his mouth to speak, but I keep going despite Genevieve's threats to take back control. "Or what if you undershoot and you're a sixty-five year old new retiree who plans to spend the rest of his days on the ski lifts while I'm studying for my SATs?"

"SATs?"

"I'll tell you if you can tell me what a ski lift is." I raise one of Genevieve's eyebrows, albeit shakily because I regret the entire conversation. It was not contrived for her sake, but the action seems to calm Genevieve. At least enough to keep her from ripping the reins from me. Andrew is in 1925. He's an eighteen-year-old (I think) in 1925, and it's too late for him to go back to 1902 where Lucy and Charles are. It's too late for him to scrap the whole mission and return to life as he knows it. He's already done it once. He's already changed his entire life. He's a stranger in his own time.

"I thought you would be happy," he says to the road with his hands on his hips, parting the jacket he wears.

*Fix it,* Genevieve says sternly.

Feeling the tethers of control slip through my grip, I close the distance between Andrew and me and plant my pumps—well, Genevieve's designer pumps—in front of him.

"I'm sorry," I say and mean it. "I am happy." I mean that too. "But I'm scared." I didn't plan the words, but I mean them more than the ones before them. I close my eyes against the tears that threaten to build. Lucky for me, Genevieve doesn't cry, so her eyes remain dry.

His flat-dark eyes—without the golden flecks—search mine. His sly half-smile makes a small appearance and he says, "I am scared too. Just trust me."

"Okay," I say and stand on my toes to kiss him.

# weekend plans and ibuprofen

"So... I heard Scott asked you out again?" my best friend, Arianna asked as we stepped from her warm car into the icy school parking lot.

I let out a visible breath of annoyance that I'm pretty sure she didn't notice. "You heard right," I said, keeping the irritation out of my tone.

"And?" She shouldered her backpack over her electric-blue down coat and fell into step with me walking toward the building. "Did you say yes?"

I shrugged. "Honestly I was surprised he even asked me."

"But you two had so much fun at the dance!"

The dance. I barely remembered the parts of the dance with Scott in it. He was my date. He should play at least a supporting role in my memory, but the night was completely saturated with panic and anger at finding the capsule in my arm. And with then the pain of digging it out with a pair of hair scissors. The rest of the night was just a blur.

To Arianna, the rest didn't happen. At least that's how she acted.

"I said yes," I assured her.

"Yay!" She grabbed my good arm and laid her head on my

shoulder for a split-second in an excited arm-hug. "We should double!"

"Okay." That actually sounded great. Scott was a good guy, and I liked him enough even if he wasn't my first choice of a date. My first choice was beyond complicated, and not only because he was currently in 1925. Although that fact was extremely complicated.

Andrew was in 1925.

The thought still baffled me and left me in awe and swelling affection because he was doing it for *me*. He was jumping time, he was changing his past and his present, so that he could possibly one day be *here* in the twenty-first century with me. Yet I still didn't know exactly how I felt about it. I wanted to tell Arianna about Andrew's plans. I wanted to talk to someone, to anyone about it, but every time I brought it up, she changed the subject.

Another complication was that I wasn't entirely sure Andrew was my first choice. I shook my head of that thought. Either way, being with Arianna and Brian on my date with Scott would ease some of the pressure.

I stuffed my coat into my locker before absentmindedly squeezing the bandages on my arm underneath my cream knit sweater. Mom gave me some ibuprofen at breakfast to dull the pain, but it still throbbed uncomfortably. It had only been four days since Duncan's mom stitched up my hack job. Pain was to be expected for a while.

"What should we do on our date?" Ari asked. If she noticed me wince, she didn't show any sign. "Or should we make the guys plan it?" She winked.

I managed a genuine-but-small smile before saying, "Let's make the guys plan it."

"Done. I'll tell Brian." She blew me a kiss as she walked backwards in front of me. "See ya later then. I gotta talk with Mr. Tate about my make-up test."

"Later." I waved, then touched my arm again as she turned to continue down the hall.

"Have you tried Tylenol?" Duncan asked, coming up behind me. Hearing his voice without warning caused a mini heart attack inside my chest.

I took a deep breath before turning around to face him with what I hoped was a normal expression on my face. "Mom gave me ibuprofen this morning," I said, forcing myself to let go of my arm without wincing. The lack of pressure intensified my pain, but I ignored it.

"That's probably better." His eyebrows were knit in unconscious concern.

"Thanks again." I grabbed my arm again so I wouldn't have to grit my teeth against the pain instead. "For the other night."

He shrugged, his neck slightly coloring. "What are friends for?"

Friends. Duncan and I were friends. "Well, you were my knight in shining armor." I tried not to look at his gray eyes long enough to detect the hints of green in them.

"I was happy to help, but it turned out you didn't really need my rescuing."

"Yes, but I didn't know that." There had been a misunderstanding at the dance. In that I thought my parents let Dr. Shew inject a freaky capsule into my arm at the hospital. So I (briefly) ran away from home with Duncan's help. I later found out that my parents had no idea what my former psychiatrist had done. As soon as they found out, they called a lawyer. So running from home hadn't been necessary. I was beyond relieved that I could still trust my parents.

"Hey, Em," Clare said, closely orbiting Duncan until she pressed against his arm which he instantly drew around her.

"Hi, Clare."

"Any news on Dr. Shew?" she asked with an inappropriate smile that said I'm-totally-in-the-loop-on-the-biggest-gossip-story-of-the-century.

"Not yet," I said, "Mom and Dad know more than I do." It

was the truth, if not all of it. "They don't want me to worry about it much."

"Totally cool of them, and understandable. But if it were me, I'd want to know, you know?"

I shrugged. "I think I know enough. They want me to focus on my schoolwork and being a teenager." I didn't really want to explain my feelings about the malpractice lawsuit that took up every dinner conversation and movie-night chatter and passing-down-the-hallway comment and every single phone call and interrupted every spare peaceful second in between. My parents weren't keeping any of it a secret. They were just letting me focus on school. But I was already inundated with it just by hearing their conversations and seeing their stress.

And it had only been four days.

But my motto was, "Let the adults handle it."

It was endearing that they were going to such lengths, but honestly, it was a little overwhelming. I'd be glad when the lawsuit was finished and done with. Whatever the verdict. Either way, I had a hunch it would take a while.

"Well, we don't have plans this weekend if you want to do something with me and Clare," he said, instantly looking like he regretted it.

"Oh, I'd love to," I said, keeping my eyes trained on Duncan despite the daggers I felt coming from Clare's stare. I paused enough to make her squirm a little. "But I have a date with Scott this weekend." The plans weren't exactly set, but I figured it was probably the truth.

Out of the corner of my eye, Clare's shoulders visibly relaxed. But I hardly noticed as I tried to decipher the expression on Duncan's face, with no luck.

"You two really hit it off at the dance, huh?" he asked.

"Scott's a fun guy," I admitted.

He placed a friendly hand on my shoulder as his unreadable expression faded to the unconscious concerned one again. "Hang in there, Em," he said as his hand burned through my sweater.

Although the ibuprofen was starting to work and I'd released my grip when Clare made her appearance, I grabbed it again in self-consciousness. Duncan lowered his hand.

The first bell rang.

"Ooh! I gotta go!" Clare said and gave Duncan a meaningful look.

Duncan looked at me, silently asking if I'd be all right.

I nodded slightly. "Me too. I'll see you two at lunch." I flashed the best fake smile in my arsenal before walking away.

# past memories and future plans

Conflicting emotions swirl inside the unfamiliar body of a person whose physical dimensions are fairly close to my own. Similar height, similar frame, same hair color—though hers is a little shorter. Even her bra size feels the same underneath the loose pantsuit-like outfit she wears. I almost feel like I am actually in my own skin when I walk her. I half-expect to see my own reflection looking back at me anytime she primps in front of a mirror. My eyes are slightly narrower—and a different color—and her lips are fuller, but my teeth are straighter.

Still, we could almost be sisters if we weren't separated by a handful of decades.

But despite our eerie physical similarities, we are complete opposites in personality, which is why my emotions are conflicted when I flash into her head. Because she's strolling down a deserted alley with a blond-haired Andrew, her hand loosely looped through the crook of his elbow. They are touching before I even arrive.

I feel Andrew's uneasiness emanating through his coat sleeve, and I admit, it makes me feel slightly better.

"You worry too much," Genevieve says feeling it too. "We won't be seen, and the hidden door is just up ahead."

"Hidden door?"

She laughs then skips ahead, feeling along the brick wall with her fingertips. It's easy to feel the difference between the real brick and the flat wooden panel painted to look like brick. And although the artistry is good, it's easy to see the difference looking straight at it. I suppose only a casual glance down the alley would prevent the door from being noticed.

She reaches up into her hat for a brass key hidden in the faux flowers attached to the brim.

"I took it from Father's coat pocket," she says in what I can only describe as a villain's voice.

Andrew stuffs his hands into his pockets and purses his lips in possible disapproval. Maybe that's just my interpretation.

Genevieve swivels a round metal keyhole cover that's painted to blend in and reveals the lock. With flare, she inserts the key and twists until a hollow *click* announces the now-unlocked door. One cursory glance down the alley is enough to ensure we won't be seen, and in one fluid motion, Genevieve swings the door outward and we step inside. The door clicks closed behind us.

We stand for a moment, allowing our eyes adjust to the dim lighting in the narrow hallway before Genevieve grabs Andrew's hand and leads him to what looks very much like the backroom of a bar.

"What is this place?" Andrew asks. But judging by two dozen stacked wooden cases, several barrels, and glass bottles of varying sizes filled with liquid ranging from different shades of brown to clear, I know exactly what this place is.

"Did you just crawl out from under a rock?" Genevieve teases. "It is a speakeasy," she whispers though the room is clearly vacant.

When Genevieve instantly moves toward one of the bottles, I reach to take the reins. I don't want my thoughts clouded with alcohol just when I have a chance to speak with Andrew. I attempt to plant her feet, but she is determined and our movement surely looks like children playing red light, green light—moving fast then stopping abruptly. It must look very strange to Andrew.

"Emily?" he asks quietly, guessing the only logical reason for Genevieve's odd steps.

I want to respond, but she chokes my words and swivels with a scowl on her face. "My name is Genevieve," she growls. "Whoever this *Emily* is, I doubt you'll ever see her again."

Wait. Does she have any idea...? A pit forms in my stomach at her threat.

Andrew amazingly keeps his face neutral. "What makes you say that?" he asks suddenly careless as if he couldn't care less whether or not he ever spoke to me again.

She lowers her lids seductively. "First of all, you're here with me." She takes a step toward him.

Andrew keeps his stoic expression.

"And you have been spending more and more time alone with me." Another step. "And I am convinced that you will be having a conversation with my father very soon."

Wow. She's extremely forward, but Andrew doesn't flinch at her suggestion or even refute it. Is he falling for this?

"And that is why you've concluded that I will not see Emily again?" His face is skeptical, but with a touch of flirtation too.

She reads between the lines and takes the last few steps until she is directly in front of him. Until I am directly in front of him. Our breath mingles in the space between us, though we don't touch.

"Yes, and the fact that I've never seen this *Emily* girl. Whoever she is, *wherever* she is, she was a fool to let you get away. I will not make that mistake."

*Whew.* I practically sigh in relief. She has no clue who I am or *where* I am. She doesn't even notice that I pull one corner of her lip up in a smirk because she uses that moment to place a palm on Andrew's chest and I reach out to touch Andrew's ring-adorned hand with our other hand.

And I wrench control.

"You had me going for a minute there," I say, smiling full on.

He lets out a breath I hadn't realized he'd been holding. "Emily."

I don't move an inch, mostly to stay in contact with the silver ring that gives me more control of the situation. But being this close to him also results in the happy feeling of his heartbeat underneath layers of suit.

"Hi," I say staring at my hand and feeling a sudden thrill at the closeness between us. Maybe it's a result of the physical similarities I noted in the alley. Almost like he's seeing the real me. Almost.

"What is amiss?" he asks, the familiar lilting in his words reminiscent of Original Andrew $_{TM}$.

Without thinking, I remove my hand, but Genevieve fortunately doesn't cut in. "It's nothing," I say, keeping my eyes trained on his lapel.

I'm certain that he doesn't miss the lie, but he doesn't press me.

"Have you thought more about what I said? About what I am doing... jumping forward?" He asks softly like he knows the answer but doesn't want to hear it. It's a very different Andrew than I'm used to. His confident, almost arrogant attitude has vanished.

Then suddenly, out of the blue, a dream-walk from long ago flashes in my memory. Maybe it's the now-blond Andrew standing before me, although in the dream he definitely did not look like Andrew with bleached hair. But it was Andrew.

The Chevy Impala, the clothing that was clearly sixties or seventies, the utter confusion. My vision flashes, and I feel Andrew grab my hand to steady me.


*"WE'RE CLEAR," HE SAYS. "DO YOU THINK YOU CAN climb?"*

*With all of the will I can muster, I take three wobbly steps toward the bottom rung. There's no way she is staying down here, so* with my strength, I launch myself up and out. The suddenly bright light assaults my senses, but I feel the boy hook an arm underneath my legs and carry me several yards before gently putting me down in the cover of some green. When my eyes have adjusted I note we are among some trees on the side of a road.

I try to search her head for a name as a classic white Chevy Impala drives by. Maybe I can figure out a date by the cars. An old —no new—station wagon speeds in the other direction. Then a black Mustang. Sixties? I wonder. Or seventies.

"She wasn't saved, you know."

"Who wasn't saved?" I ask.

"You—er—Mary." He shrugs sheepishly. "Mary wasn't saved before."

I point to myself. "I... am Mary?"

He nods, then grins. "Seriously, Em, you really need to start wearing your ring all of the time." He looks back at the road.

Did I hear him right? Does he know my name? Or is Em short for Mary? "I thought you said my name was Mary?" I test him.

"Yeah, Mary Piper." He seems distracted watching the cars and doesn't look at me as he talks. He seems to be waiting for something.

"You just called me Em."

"Sorry, Emily," he corrects himself with a grin. "This one really disoriented you, didn't she?"

"So you know who I am?"

Finally he looks at me. "Is she, I mean Mary, present?"

I listen. She's checked out. Probably from emotional trauma and exhaustion. I shake my head no.

He smiles again. "Then yes, Emily Chandler, I know who you are." He chuckles softly. "How often have we done this?"

I don't answer, because I still have no clue what he is talking about. A small part of my head wants to believe he is who I want him to be, but it's impossible. You go backwards in time when you memory-walk, not forward. Unless he's about a hundred years old, there shouldn't be any Chevy Impalas.

*"So, why are you saving this poor girl, other than because it's a noble thing to do?" I play along.*

*He looks back to the road. "Because she was engaged to marry Matthew Harker before she was abducted.*

*My heart pounds again, but for a different reason. "Andrew?" I whisper.*

*"The one and only." He laughs then leans toward me and kisses me softly. "There's my girl."*

"Wow," I say when the vision clears. It's working. It's going to work. Andrew at least moves forward to the sixties or seventies. No, further than that because he's clearly having a dream-walk as the blond boy. My mind bursts at the implications.

Andrew's eyes are trained on me, concern pinching his eyebrows together again. "Did you have a flashback?"

I nod, then open my mouth to tell him that it's working, that whatever he is doing to move forward will work because I've been with him in a much later version of himself. But I close my mouth just as fast as a wave of fear washes over me.

What if he shows up tomorrow?

What if, when I wake up from this walk, he's waiting outside my front door? Or worse? What if he shows up *before* I ever meet Lucy? With grand declarations that we will meet and we will fall in love... but, oh yeah, he was actually born in 1882?

What if I wake up tomorrow and reality as I know it has shifted again?

"C-can you promise me something?" I ask, gulping down my sudden anxiety.

"Anything. Emily, you've lost your color. Is everything all right?"

"Yeah." I shake my head. "Yes, I just realized that when you make it to my time, a very-confused Emily is going to have a major breakdown when you—" I wave a hand at him—"suddenly pop into my life declaring who you are and how you came to be there." I can only imagine my five-year-old self throwing a fistful of sand at a five-year-old version of Andrew when he tells me his original birth date. Or worse, he shows up at my high school in his bowler hat and with his blonde—or red— hair and my life changes drastically. What if I'm suddenly a cheerleader who doesn't know how to do a cartwheel? Or back to being a loner loser girl who isn't even welcome to sit at the loner loser table? (Okay, maybe it wouldn't be so bad to go back to that life. But as frustrating as Arianna was, I wasn't ready to lose my best friend again.)

Maybe I'd get Grandma Grace back. I shake my head. No, he needed to show up at a later date as someone I have never met before and had no possibility of changing things before he gets there.

Andrew grabs both of my hands and leans closer, his eyes glistening with hope. "You said *when* not *if.*"

*Whoops.* I feel Genevieve's face color slightly.

"You believe that I am going to make it. Does…?" He pauses. "Does that mean that you *want* me to make it?"

I bite Genevieve's lower lip and nod yes.

In one motion his lips are on mine, in a kiss much like our first one. Passionate and relieved that we've both found someone who understands exactly who we are and the things we each have to endure. A kinship stronger than any other relationship. He's my people. And I am his.

"Yes, I want you to make it. And I believe you will." I still don't tell him about Mary Piper. "But I'm going to tell you a date. Remember this date because I don't want you to contact me and tell me who you are until then."

Realization shines in his features. "Of course, I do not know why I did not think of it before. Fortunately, I have not made the mistake as I have yet to reach your time."

Back to business. "June the ninth," I say, calculating in my head that it gives me four months to prepare myself to meet him and hopefully give him the time to jump forward.

"And the year?"

"Right." In all of the dreams I had been with him, I never told him which year I was born or which year I was coming from. It's a strange thought. It occurs to me that I could give myself years of preparation before I actually see him and he would be none the wiser until the day we actually meet.

But then he might show up as a seventeen or eighteen-year-old and I will have accidentally caused him to undershoot exactly as I said he might.

So, I tell him the year.

"And how old are you?" he asks and am grateful for not giving him a year far in advance.

"I just turned seventeen in January. A few weeks ago."

He smiles. "June the ninth."

Deep breaths. Only four months away. "It's a date."

# mama bear and supportive friends

"But you said it would only be a deposition process and that it probably wouldn't go to trial." Mom was on the phone with the lawyer again.

I chewed my cereal slowly. I hated the stress the lawsuit against Dr. Shew and the hospital was putting on my parents. Mom specifically. She seemed to be dealing with the brunt of it. But Dad had dark circles underneath his eyes most days too. Running everything at the cemetery during the day without Mom's help then coming home just in time for her to fill him in on everything going on with the lawsuit was draining them both. Physically and emotionally.

"So, what does that mean for us?" Mom asked then paused as she listened to the person on the other line. "It's just..." She lowered her voice even though she had to know I could still hear her. We were in the same room. "Emily is just a kid. I don't want to put her through more than absolutely necessary."

Pause.

"Yes, yes. Thank you..." Pause. "Yes. I'll talk with my husband..." Pause. "All right. Good-bye." She hung up and wrote something down in the notebook she carried with her everywhere. She noticed me watching her when she looked up from her notes.

"Can I get you anything, sweetie? I really need to teach you how to fry up your own eggs."

I shook my head quickly. "I should be getting *you* something. Mom, you're exhausted."

She dropped the pen she held and massaged her temples, elbows resting on the counter. "I'm sorry this trial stuff is taking up so much of my time lately." She ignored my comment.

"It's important, I get it." And it reminded me of something. "Hey, and uh... I'm sorry that I thought you and Dad—"

"For the thousandth time, Emily"—she threw her hands up in exasperation, cutting me off—"*please* don't apologize for that again. You were panicked. Doctors are supposed to ask the consent of a guardian. I can see why in your... in your panic... that you would come to the conclusion."

"I know... it's just..." The conversation was on repeat at the house. But the guilt I felt wouldn't back down. I couldn't believe I thought *they* were the bad guys.

"And we'd been pushing you to take the medication." Mom walked to me and drew me into a tight embrace. "Sweetheart, you've apologized enough."

I nodded into her shoulder.

"What Dr. Shew did you was inexcusable," she said when I let go. The mama bear in her came out whenever Dr. Shew's name flew from her mouth. "We need to make sure that she can never do the same to anyone else."

I nodded, though I didn't know of anyone else—well, anyone in *my* time—who had the dreams, so I don't know who else she could inject a mysterious capsule into. We didn't know what medication it was, but it effectively stopped the dreams altogether instead of merely making me forget them like my original medication did.

I still wasn't sure which was worse, but I was grateful the strain of me not taking my meds was gone. Currently no doctor was making me take anything.

"Is everything going okay at school? Do your friends know what's going on?" Mom asked.

"A few of them do." Although Ari refused to talk about it and Duncan was busy with his new girlfriend. "School is fine, Mom. Most of the kids don't even know what happened, so I'm not getting weird stares or anything." It also helped that it was still cold out and I could hide my bandages underneath a sweater or hoodie.

"That's good." She looked legitimately relieved at that fact. "And your friends who know are being supportive? You're able to talk to them?"

I shrugged like it wasn't a big deal either way. "I uh... I have another date with Scott this weekend." I forced brightness into my tone.

"The boy you went with to the dance?" Her eyes lit up.

"Yeah, I think we're going to double with Ari and Brian."

Mom's cell rang with the familiar Kansas ring tone. "That sounds like fun, sweetie. I want to hear more." Then she hit the answer button and walked out of the kitchen.

---

I WASN'T EXACTLY DEPRESSED WHEN I WALKED THE halls of the school building. But I shuffled my feet and lowered my head so it probably looked like I was. And it sort of felt like I was.

*Andrew was coming.* I knew he would make it. That fact wasn't depressing, but it was exciting and nerve racking at the same time. Andrew would meet me, Emily, after school ended for the summer. I wouldn't be able to hide beneath Lucy's curls. I'd never need to meet him in secret just to have a conversation. I wouldn't have to fight control with Genevieve just to get a word in edgewise or worry about why he was acting almost like he loved her. I wouldn't have to try to keep a nineteenth-century girl from throwing herself off of a ship all while being scolded by Andrew through a stranger's lips.

I'd see him and he'd see me. Without the masks.

Hopefully by then the trial would be over and my life could have some semblance of normalcy.

The trial.

Andrew's arrival.

And I couldn't forget about Lucy who was quite possibly in an asylum somewhere but I couldn't be entirely sure because I hadn't walked her since the day of her wedding. The day she was taken.

No, I wasn't depressed. I was overwhelmed and needed to talk to someone.

"What's up, Em?" Arianna asked as we waited in the lunch line together a few hours later. Her tone didn't say what's-wrong-tell-me-all-about-it, it was more of a what's-happening? I-see-that-you're-a-little-bit-down-but-I'm-going-to-ignore-it-and-force-you-to-brighten-your-mood.

I couldn't be mad at her for it. She often used that tactic after a bad memory-dream death or traumatic incident. Since I was unlikely—back then—to return to that person, her tactic used to help me get out of my current funk and move on with my life. Of course back then I also didn't know as much as I did now about my gift. Or curse, as I used to call it.

But she was my best friend. She would want to know if something was truly bothering me. So I started with the easier topic. "This trial is already getting really intense for my parents."

"I can imagine," she said, filling her tray with a bowl of fruit, a salad, and the meat of the day. "I don't see why people become lawyers at all. Everything they do is downright depressing."

I filled my tray to mirror hers. "Maybe they like helping people," I said, "Can you imagine if Dr. Shew just got away with what she did?" My heart pounded at the mention of her name. I realized that I hadn't talked to Arianna about any of it since Saturday night. And that was *before* I dug the thing out of my arm with her hair scissors. I hadn't even asked if she'd scrubbed them with Clorox or tossed them.

"Although I guess they do marry people," Ari said, taking a low-fat milk carton and moving on to the register. "And when my cousin was adopted, my aunt said the judge told them it was one of the best parts of his job. So, I guess they do have some good cases."

I got the hint. She didn't want to talk about the trial. We scanned our student ID cards then headed for our usual table by the tall windows.

But I couldn't let it go. I needed to vent.

"Andrew is jumping through time." I blurted before any of our friends joined us.

She looked at me with wide eyes that gave away the wheels turning behind them. I wanted to smirk. There was no way she wouldn't talk about this. It was too big.

"I talked to Brian," she said instead.

"Wait. I just told you that Andrew is jumping through time and you go and change the subject?"

She pointed at the lunch line where several of our friends were almost to the end. "I just wanted to tell you about this weekend before the guys got here."

"Why, is it a secret?" I didn't hide my annoyance.

"No, it's just... well..." She leaned closer like it was a secret, then proceeded to tell me not only that we were going bowling for our date, which totally could have been said when everyone else was around, but sprinkled it with some random crap about one of our classmates who worked at the bowling alley and had a crush on Scott and that he wanted to be nice to the girl, but also hoped that she'd get the hint that he wasn't interested in dating her.

In other words, Arianna quickly finished, would it be okay if Scott put his arm around me occasionally or held my hand, or anything else that would look like obvious flirting or togetherness?

"Howdy, girls." Scott scooted in next to me.

Man, I missed Duncan.

Who was sitting across from me with his fancy accessory at his right elbow.

"Did Ari clue you in on this weekend?" Scott leaned in close to ask.

"She did," I said trying not to focus on the happy couple in front of me.

"About... Lauren?" he whispered.

I nodded and took a bite of my salad. "Are you sure you aren't being mean to this girl? Because I'd rather do something else if that's what the plan is. Why can't you just avoid her?"

"Because she is relentless," he sighed. "Duncan, tell Em about Lauren."

Duncan blew out a breath. "She won't take a hint. She's been pestering Scott since homecoming. She's in his..." He looked at Scott for clarification.

"Spanish class," Scott finished.

"She's in his Spanish class, and he helped her with one tiny assignment at the beginning of the year. She's been attached to him ever since. Sending secret notes, hinting about certain movies she wants to see..."

"She asked me to the winter formal, but since I was going with you, I had a good excuse to turn her down."

I paused. "You turned her down? I asked you kind of late though," I reminded him. Truth be told, I never asked him at all. *Ari* asked him. At the last minute. This sounded very much like mean high school—kid stuff. My thoughts flitted to poor Jenny, a memory-walk I'd had a few weeks ago where an eighth grader got a mean note from her supposed friends saying that they couldn't be friends because it would hurt their social game and chances with certain boys. It was cruel.

Everyone at the table looked at me and at Scott, and then instantly turned to their neighbor and initiated an intense conversation.

"Okay, so she asked me early," Scott said quietly in our

suddenly private conversation. "And I kind of told her that there was someone else I wanted to go with."

"Who?"

"Do you really have to ask?" He flashed an isn't-it-obvious? look at me.

"You mean, me? You turned her down because you assumed I was going to ask you? While I was in a coma?"

"Look. After you and Duncan broke up I wanted to give you a minute to breathe, but truth be told, I had my eye on you long before that happened."

I wanted to sprint for the door. This guy was spilling his guts in the cafeteria about his feelings for me. *Ugh...* It had been quite a while since saving Carly, Arianna's older sister, and effectively changing many things in my life, but I was still surprised every time I discovered a new change. Scott had never even glanced at me, let alone had his *eyes on me*, in my old life.

"But still," I spoke slowly. "I. Was. In. A. Coma. You couldn't at least give her a chance? Play the part of the charming popular athlete you are and take pity on her?"

I wasn't finished with my food but didn't want to hear any more, so I stood with my tray. I don't know why it bothered me so much, other than the fact that I wasn't as interested in Scott as he was in me. I probably shouldn't be letting him think that I was. Was I leading him on?

Luckily, Scott didn't follow me. And neither did Ari, although I had a feeling that had more to do with her wanting to avoid any and all mention of my memory-dreams than a benevolent desire to give me space.

But Duncan did. He caught up to me in the main foyer. Alone. My knight in shining armor riding to the rescue again. I shook my head to banish the thought.

"Hey, what was that about?" he asked.

My mouth twisted into a frown as I tried not to cry. "Oh, they just want me to cozy up to Scott on our date this weekend so that poor girl, Lauren, can see that he isn't interested in her."

"You really should see this girl. She could use a hint." His smile was an attempt to lighten my mood, but it wasn't working.

"She might be blind to it, but it's still mean."

"And it has upset you this much?" He reached out to put an arm around me. "Hey, let Clare and I come with you guys. I'll talk to Scott and tell him that you don't feel comfortable doing it. If he tries to get too friendly with you for poor Lauren's sake, I'll put him in his place."

I laughed through the welling tears. "Protecting my honor again, Duncan?"

He squeezed my shoulder once more before putting space between us again. "I like to take care of my friends, so sue me. Oh wait..." he laughed at his jab.

"Hey!" I swung at him lazily and missed.

"That's what's really bothering you, isn't it?"

The bell rang.

I blew out a breath. "That and... other things." Maybe I could talk to Duncan about the stressful trial and maybe even some of the memory-dreams issues that were going on. Like Lucy.

But Clare found us right then. "Walk me to class?" She fluttered her fake eyelashes up at him.

"Yep!" He truly looked happy to see her and threw an arm around her waist. "It'll all be okay, Emily," he said and turned to walk away with his girlfriend.

In a last-ditch effort, I pulled out my cell and dialed Carly's number. She was in Italy on a study abroad program, but she'd told me more than once to call if I ever needed someone to talk to. And now I definitely needed someone to talk to.

"Hi!" Carly answered in her cheerful voice. "You've reached Carly. Leave me a message!"

Voice mail.

Hopefully Mom wouldn't ask about my *supportive* friends again anytime soon. I'd hate to have to lie.

# as if i never was

Genevieve presses her ear against a fancy—probably made of crystal—glass which she is holding up against a closed door. It feels very uncharacteristic—no, wait it would be very uncharacteristic for *Lucy* to be eavesdropping in this manner. It's feels right up Genevieve's alley. Why am I even surprised?

I miss Lucy.

The voices are slightly muffled but clear enough to decipher. I figure I might as well tune in since she is already listening.

"...pride and joy." It's her father's voice. "...only someone worthy." Part of me wonders if those are the actual words, or if Genevieve is only hearing what she wants to hear. She feels very pleased about the conversation. It's going exactly as she hoped.

Which piques my curiosity. *Who else is in there?* I passively ask, not expecting an answer.

"...intentions are genuine, I assure you."

*Andrew.*

My ears are so trained to his voice that I pick them out much easier than Genevieve's father. Plus, Andrew sounds closer to the door. "...premature, but I intend to have a very similar conversation with you in the near future." His tone is full of implications.

Genevieve covers her mouth to stifle her sudden giggle. Butterflies swarm inside her. *I guess he's giving up on that Emily girl,* she thinks to herself.

A surge of anger rushes through me, but I don't react.

The men pause for several seconds, leaving Genevieve—and me, by default—breathless, effectively extinguishing my sudden fury.

"...parents," her father says, "...highest respect...many years."

"...glad to hear it." Andrew is smiling. It's evident in his tone, but it sounds twisted somehow. Like it's fake.

"...intend to marry...?" Her father asks a question that don't need the filler words to interpret.

Genevieve lets out a high-pitched yelp from the back of her throat.

"I do." There is no mistaking Andrew's answer. It leaves a bad taste in my mouth.

Another pause.

"...Ginny stands to inherit..." Her father continues to speak in a lower tone.

Genevieve's mood darkens. She knows her father worries about gold diggers, unscrupulous men who might pretend to love her in order to gain her inheritance, but she is certain that Andrew is not like that.

"...my own wealth... know my parents..." Andrew says. My heart sinks with each phrase I catch. "...nothing to worry..." And finally, "...love your daughter."

He intends to *marry* her? Or does he intend to marry her the way he intended to marry Margaret?

Genevieve moves away from the door and walks down the hallway, satisfied by what she's heard. I suspect she feels my skeptical mood, but she ignores the doubt. At the end of the hall, she enters into a sort of greenhouse room. A conservatory maybe? It's hard to tell since my only frame of reference to a conservatory is from the board game Clue. She picks up a metal watering can on the floor and walks a few steps to water some purple orchids on a shelf. The air is thick with humidity and warmth, and the floral air banishes her subconscious thoughts that Andrew is being anything but genuine.

She doesn't realize that it isn't her subconscious. It's me planting the negative thoughts. It takes effort, but I squash my own negativity, reminding myself that I walk with those who need me for something. Genevieve must need me for *something*. Even though I don't like her much.

The door to the conservatory opens behind us, but Genevieve doesn't turn. She doesn't need to.

"Did Father unleash his full wrath on you?" she asks the orchids with a smile.

"Nothing I could not handle." Through the tone of his words, it's clear that he smiles too.

I want to unleash my full wrath on him, but I keep my emotions close. I half expect him to wrap his arms around her from behind. To kiss her cheek or move her hair aside to kiss her neck. She half-expects it too. Or at least hopes for it.

The feeling makes me want to scream.

Control. I need to gain control.

She turns to face him. "Can I ask what it was about?" she asks, a flirtatious smile plastered on her face.

*Oh, come on! You were listening!* I shout at her.

He takes a step toward her. "He asked what my intentions are regarding his only daughter." His smile matches hers.

"And what are those intentions?" She closes the gap between us and lightly touches the lapel on his jacket—her signature move, apparently—and looks up at him through hooded lids.

*He's going to kiss her.* My thoughts scream. *He doesn't even know I'm here and he's going to kiss her!*

She hasn't noticed my presence, so I wrench control then lift my head to narrow the gap between our lips.

He doesn't move and closes his eyes in anticipation.

"You're seriously going to let her kiss you?" I back away.

His eyes fly open. "Emily!"

"What's going on, Andrew? You told her father that you intend to marry her?"

"You know I don't."

"Do I? Because you are the right age and in the right decade to marry her. Why wouldn't you?" I fold Genevieve's arms across her chest when he moves to touch me. "What do you plan to do? What you told me or what you told Genevieve's father? Which is the truth?"

He raises his hands in surrender. "I am planning to jump. That is the plan. You know that is the plan."

"Then why are you doing this?"

His face turns serious, his charming air is gone. He focuses his dark eyes directly on me. "Genevieve's father is wealthy."

"Yeah, I got that." I roll my eyes.

"Emily, this is important."

I unfold my arms at his firm tone. "Okay, so he's rich."

"And powerful. And Ginny sits to inherit it all. In fact, she gets a significant portion when she marries."

"So... you do intend to marry her?"

"No!" Andrew runs a frustrated hand through his blond hair, mussing it in a familiar way.

"If I am to be close to her, close to you, she must think that... no"—he pauses with a shake of his head—"she must *believe* that I am planning to marry her."

My fire diminishes. "You can't just be her friend? You know... since you don't plan to stay forever?"

"I can't risk it. Besides, it's what she wants. She's wanted it for a while, but I pushed her away until you began walking with her."

I turn on my heel, walking further along the rows of exotic flora. "I still don't—"

He grabs my arm, stopping me. "She loves me Emily." He interrupts. "She *wants* to marry me. Trust me. It's the only way to be close to her."

"It's the only way? Or the easy way?" I wrench from his grip and water some flowers I don't know the names of.

"Why does this trouble you so?" His tone changes to match my frustration and anger.

"Maybe because it's cruel. Because you're leading this girl into thinking that you care for her when you don't." Truth be told, I'm starting to wonder if he truly *does* care for her. Maybe he is just making excuses about it to me. "Do you plan to stay here in 1925?" I have to ask again.

"A thousand times, no." He walks swiftly to me and takes the watering can from my hand before taking both of mine in his. "Why do you suddenly doubt me? I have come this far. I have no intentions of stopping until I get to you."

"Then why do this?" My voice is barely a whisper. His touch sends a shockwave through me. I am almost certain it affects Genevieve the same way it affects me.

"Because ultimately it won't matter."

I open my mouth to speak, but his words derail me with confusion.

"When I jump again, Genevieve will forget that I ever existed. I will not break her heart, I will not anger her father for leaving. It will be as if I never existed."

"I—"

"It was the same with Lucy and Charles." His features contort with brief pain. "They do not even remember that I existed."

He misses them. I don't know if the hurt expression is only for Charles and Lucy in a family-friendly way, or if leaving Lucy holds a deeper pain.

"Am I wrong?" he asks when I still don't respond. "You were at their wedding after I left?"

"I was. And you're right, they don't remember you."

The pain flashes in his eyes again.

"See? Genevieve's feelings for me and anything that happens between us before I jump will be nothingness when I am gone."

"It still doesn't feel right," I say, though my fiery ire is completely extinguished. "And you didn't know it would work to jump the first time. Yet you risked making things even worse for Lucy."

"I truly regret my actions then, but I know this will work. Ginny won't even know what she forgot."

I don't like it, and with everything I've seen and heard today, I am beginning to wonder how genuine he is. But what else can I do?

# tell me about your dreams

"What's the occasion?" I asked, taking a bite of my warm blueberry syrup and powdered sugar—coated French toast. Mom decided to take me to breakfast despite it being a school day. I couldn't remember the last time I saw that spontaneous look on her face, so I took her up on it.

She promised to write me a note for being tardy.

Mom set down her fork and chewed slowly before swallowing and saying, "I thought we both needed a little break from the chaos. And I wanted to talk about a few things."

"Oh yeah? What things?" I liked this new focused version of Mom.

"Well, first, I wanted to apologize."

"For what?"

"For everything." She sighed. "For what happened with Dr. Shew and the coma and that *capsule* that she injected into you." She spat the word capsule, like it was a swear word. "And don't you *dare* apologize for your reaction again."

I opened my mouth to speak but closed it again seeing her expression.

"And I am sorry for the litigation we're in now, sweetie, and that you might have to testify."

Dread filled me at the mere thought of talking to a court about things that I kept a secret from most everyone because of how crazy it sounded. Next to no one believed me, including my parents.

"But that's not set in stone," Mom added, "and it isn't what I brought you here for."

Slightly relieved, I ate a few more bites, waiting for her to continue.

"Tell me about your dreams." She said it in such a nonchalant, like-we-talked-about-it-every-day tone that I was completely caught off guard.

I paused mid-chew. "Wha—?" I asked with a mouthful.

"Tell me about them."

I swallowed. "Like my dreams and aspirations?" I didn't think that's what she meant, but I couldn't wrap my head around her actually asking about my *memory dreams*.

"No." She grinned like it was a common misunderstanding between us. Also bizarre. "Who have you dreamt lately?"

I took a sip of my orange juice before answering, "I thought you didn't believe my dreams were real. That they're just night terrors or something."

"Well, I'm taking a page from Grandma Grace's book. She believed they were real."

I blinked rapidly to banish any tears forming at the mention of Grandma. "She did," I agreed.

"Pretend that I'm her. What would you tell her if she were still here?"

I missed Grandma so much. I had hoped so many times that I would fall asleep and find myself walking with her. It hadn't happened yet. She had been gone long enough that I worried it never would.

"Well," I said slowly, getting back to the original question. "I haven't walked Lucy in a while. She's been sent to an insane asylum because of me, I think."

"Which one is Lucy?" Mom asked like it wasn't out of the norm for one of my walks to result in someone being sent to an *insane asylum* or wherever it was that Lucy actually ended up.

I needed to get back to her.

"She's a girl I used to walk every night." I forced my brain to focus on the good, and my memories were flooded with all of my walks with Lucy. "It was 1901 when I first walked with her. She had just got engaged. I was there for her wedding, but... but because of me being in her head all of the time..." I trailed off. "I worry about her, and I haven't been back with her since... in a while."

I half-expected to see a worried look plastered on Mom's face. An I-don't-believe-you look and I'm-afraid-we-will-have-to-commit-you-just-like-your-imaginary-friend-Lucy look. But there was none of it. Just genuine interest in what I was saying, like I was describing something fascinating I had learned in one of my classes. "So how will you get back to her?"

I shrugged, digging into my food again so I didn't cry. "I think about her all of the time, but maybe she's not ready for me to come yet. I don't know."

"Who else have you been with?"

*Really? She wanted to hear more?*

Genevieve was the most recent, but anything dealing with her would require a big long history of Andrew... and myself. And I'm sure Mom would just love to hear that I had a complicated relationship with a guy who was originally born in the late 1800s but was currently an eighteen-year-old in the mid 1920s.

"I walked a lot with Isabella while I was in the coma." Facepalm. Why did I have to mention that it was while I was in my coma? It was a sensitive subject. I *knew* that. I could have just said that I walked with Isabella a lot *recently*. Omit: Coma.

And it did affect Mom to hear it, I could see it on her expression. But she dismissed it and insisted that wanted to know more about Isabella and her voyage across the Atlantic.

So, I told her. In a lot of detail.

"And Mom, she was ready to throw herself off the side of that ship because she was in so much pain from breaking her foot. And didn't think that she'd survive the storm anyway. Plus, even if she did, she didn't think anyone would want to marry her, even though Nathan had said that he did. They didn't really know about mental illness back then, so she really needed me. She might have done it. But I helped stop her, and I think she lived happily ever after. Although I don't know what ever came of her injury."

"You helped her... want to live?" Disbelief shone obvious through her eyes. I think she wanted to believe me but was struggling.

"It was different than when Lucy was in that fire—"

"Lucy was in a fire?" she interrupted.

"Yeah. She was supposed to die in it," I said quietly, wondering when the shoe would drop and some intimidating people dressed in strange coats would storm the restaurant to take me away. Like how they took Lucy away on her wedding day. "But Lucy *wanted* to live, so I only had to worry about the physical danger. With Isabella, had I not been there..." I let out a whooshing breath.

Mom averted her eyes, swirling her fork around her leftover syrup on her plate. "Do you think Isabella lived long?" she asked me.

"I found her grave on Monday." With so many eyes watching me like a hawk, it had taken some time for me to check. But I had finally managed to sneak away while I was at the cemetery office with Dad last week. "She married Nathan and lived to be almost sixty."

"That was pretty typical for that time period."

I nodded. She had no idea the relief I felt when I saw that she married and lived many more years after I left.

We both sat in silence a few moments. It felt strange talking with Mom about all of this. I'd never talked so openly about my dreams to her. Ever. Until very recently I had run away to my grandmother's house for hot chocolate. For a long time, she was the only one I could talk to about it.

"Emily," Mom said in her we-need-to-talk tone, which was strange because we were already having a pretty serious talk. "I have to be honest and tell you that I still am not sure how I feel about your dreams."

I opened my mouth to speak, but she cut me off.

"Not that I don't believe you," she said quickly. "I still don't know the answer to that, but the trauma you are experiencing every night breaks my heart."

"Mom." I willed her to look at me, leaning slightly forward until she did. "It doesn't happen every night. I walked both Lucy and Isabella many times before the bad stuff happened."

"Yes, but it isn't always like that, is it?"

It had been so long since I had walked a different person every night. Back then it was extremely rare if I knew myself. It was strange to think about my life back then. Sometimes I was so anxious at night that I was terrified to fall asleep. I never felt that way about my dreams now. But those one-night dreams weren't nonexistent.

"No. Not always."

"I guess what I wanted to tell you," Mom began again, this time having no trouble looking at me, "is that although I don't *like* them, with everything that has happened with your former psychiatrist, I accept now that there is no way to safely stop them."

I wanted to clap my hands at that truth. She had no idea how relieved I'd been the past few days, not being forced to take anything or lie to her and Dad that I was taking medication to stop the dreams.

"And I want you to know that I am here for you," she continued. "If you ever need to talk about your dreams, I am here. And I will listen." She choked on her words. "Like your Grandma Grace did."

"Thank you, Mom. I..." I was about to tell her how much that meant since my friends avoided the topic, but I stopped myself. I didn't want her to worry about me more than she already did.

Our waitress brought the check, and Mom slipped a card into the black folder before handing it back.

"I wanted to discuss one more thing before I take you to school."

Her face had brightened, so I relaxed. Whatever else she needed to tell me was probably on the lesser-dark side.

"I think you need to see another therapist."

Okay. Maybe it was on the lesser-dark side in *her* opinion. I'd lost all trust in the entire psych community. I had implicitly trusted Dr. Shew. I had *liked* Dr. Shew, and she had betrayed me.

"She works in a different office, and her specialties sound more specific to your needs."

"Do I have to?"

"Could you at least meet her before you decide you're against seeing her?" she countered.

I rolled my eyes with my rarely used teenage attitude. "Fine. I'll meet her."

# stay a while?

"From this valley they say you are going," she sings. "*We will miss your bright eyes and sweet smile.*"

The tune sounds familiar, but I can't place it. The room is bright, with east-facing windows uncovered to let in the morning sunshine. But the white bedsheets that cover us and the other beds in the room make it seem even brighter.

"*Come and sit by my side if you love me,*" she continues.

I turn my head to take in our surroundings. Ten iron beds, five on each wall are occupied by seven other women of various ages. The oldest looks maybe sixty, and the youngest is perhaps fifteen. All wear the same bonnets and shifts. A few of them sing along.

"*But remember the Red River Valley, and the cowboy who loved you so true.*" Her voice is familiar, with a touch of sadness in it that I don't quite recognize.

Until a lock of golden hair, limp and dull, catches the corner of my eye.

*Lucy.*

My heart races, and she places a hand over it, the song caught in her throat. "Emily," she breathes.

*Lucy, I'm so, so sorry. This is all my fault—*

"Nonsense!" she cuts me off. "I will not hear another word of it."

"Nuuurse!" the woman in the bed directly across shouts to the doorway, lengthening her vowels. "Miss Luuuucy needs heeeelp!"

Lucy plasters her well-trained smile on the woman. "I am quite all right Nancy," she says, keeping her voice calm though her insides twist in frustration and fear. "Please do not cry out again."

Nancy looks straight at Lucy and yells, "Nuuuurse!" A new thrill of fear rushes through Lucy. Nancy's smile widens seeing Lucy's look of terror.

*What does she mean?* I ask. *What will the nurse do?*

"I've missed you, Emily," Lucy says aloud but quiet. She sounds relieved.

*Is this where... ?* It suddenly sounds stupid to ask if this is where she was taken the day of her wedding. This is certainly not her honeymoon. Or her happily ever after.

A robust woman wearing a long dress and nurse cap, looking quite the opposite of how Florence Nightingale must have looked to her patients, stalks into the room and toward Nancy.

"Nancy!" she shouts at the woman across from us with a finger raised to wag at her. "This is a hospital. You must be silent." She then raises the finger to her lips to illustrate.

Nancy cowers into her sheets but points at us nonetheless. "Lucy is talking to the voices in her head again."

*Again? But I haven't even been here until now.*

"I might have tried to talk to you. I hoped it would make you come sooner." Lucy explains. She talks quietly, but the entire room is silent at this point so everyone hears.

*You did what?! Lucy, I can hear your thoughts if you direct them. Please stop speaking to me aloud.*

"What was that, hon?" the nurse asks, now approaching our bed.

The youngest-looking girl, with stringy hair, pulls the sheet over her head without saying a word.

Lucy sits straight up, folding her hands in her lap and interlocking her fingers. "I apologize for Nancy's outburst. I am quite all right, Nurse Edith."

Nurse Edith narrows her thick eyebrows. "You are upsetting the other residents, Lucy. Do you need to be removed and taken back to your own room?"

"No!" she shouts, then stills herself into more poised control. "No. It won't happen again."

Nurse Edith stares at Lucy for several uncomfortable seconds. Lucy meets her gaze without flinching, although her insides are churning like an amusement park ride.

"Well, you're due for a visit with the doctor this afternoon," Nurse Edith says, her face finally softening. "I'll bring up the incident with him." She turns on her heel with flair and stalks back out.

The entire room lets out the breath it was holding, but the youngest girl keeps her head covered with her sheet.

I'm almost afraid to ask, but I have to know. *How long have you been here?*

*I do not know,* she finally answers only in thought. *I am happy you are here. Now I do not feel so alone.*

*Have any of your family come to visit? Your sisters? Or Charles?*

*No.* Her answer almost feels abrupt, and she immediately shields any thoughts connected with it.

*What about your uncle and aunt? Or Andrew?*

*Andrew...* She repeats the name. *You were looking for someone named Andrew before... at the wedding...*

Crap. I completely forgot he literally disappeared from her life. He won't even be born for a few more years. *Oh right.* I backpedal. *Sorry... I found him actually. He's from another memory walk, and I got mixed up and forgot that you didn't know him.* Being with her in a world where Andrew doesn't exist is so strange and disconcerting. He was such an integral part of Lucy's life. It is strange for her not to remember him at all.

I can't imagine how that must feel for Andrew. That look on his face at the mere mention of it... I shake the thought from my head. I know I would be a little bit upset if Lucy suddenly forgot who I was after everything we'd been through together. He saved her from the fire... well, I did the in the first version, but let's not split hairs. How did she remember it now? I didn't want to bring up the traumatic event to find out, but if she ever thought about it organically, I'd have to pay attention.

*How is your life here?* I ask, changing the subject but wishing I'd come up with a different topic.

*Good.* She starts to sing again, prompting the other women and girls to join in. "*From this valley they say you are going...*" *Stay a while?* She asks between lines.

*Of course.*

<hr>

I WANT TO FALL ASLEEP, LUCY'S LIFE IS SO BORING. Which is ironic because I have to *be* asleep to walk with her. She sings several children's and folk songs. The same women and girls sing along to each one, though Lucy seems to be choosing the songs from her head and unofficially leading them.

The ones who don't sing have this dead look in their eyes as they stare at the walls and ceiling. Everything is white and brown and iron. I wonder what a cheery coat of yellow paint, or a red armchair in the corner, or even a cheap replica of a Van Gogh or Monet hanging on the wall would do for the environment and the mood.

If I had the resources, I would do it.

Part of me wonders why Lucy sits in bed all day. Her mind seems intact for the most part. The boring monotony is clearly getting to her, but she feels hopeful. It's been so long since I've walked with her. I feel like I'm missing something. Why has she been pretending to have someone talking in her head when I am absent? Doesn't she want to get better and get back to her life?

To Charles?

If it were me, I'd run for it as soon as Nurse Edith turned her back.

That question is answered a while later when Lucy moves to use the chamber pot beneath her bed and I see that her right ankle is tethered to the bed frame with leather and chain.

I'm too shocked to even ask the question.

Soon the doctor arrives, all white coat with puffed-up shoulders and bald head held high and a condescending expression below his curling mustache aimed at the room. Lucy's heart starts pounding again. But she doesn't flinch as Nurse Edith removes the strap on her ankle, freeing her to follow the doctor down the hallway.

Lucy's legs are weak from lack of use, so she walks slowly, but I do my best to strengthen them and keep her pace steady to reduce the number of times she gets a hurry-up scowl from Nurse Edith.

We enter a smaller room with a strange, tall contraption sitting behind a wooden chair. My stomach drops. It looks like a strange version of an electric chair.

We are instructed to sit in the chair, but the doctor and Nurse Edith don't even move to touch the contraption.

*It's for electroshock therapy,* Lucy explains but doesn't elaborate. The doctor makes himself comfortable with one leg crossed over the other in an overstuffed chair in the corner.

"That will be all, Nurse," he says without looking at the woman. She silently nods and exits, shutting the door behind her. "Nurse Edith says you have been disturbing the other patients, Lucy."

"Emily came back," she says like it's a normal conversation. "She is with me now, actually. I..." She pauses. "I think I was surprised that she finally came back, and Nancy was worried..."

"Lucy." He leans forward, putting his elbows on his knees. "These voices in your head are not real people."

"Emily is a real person."

"You say that, and I have spoken to '*Emily*,' but... how do I say this...?" The doctor pauses, then stands and faces the wall behind him.

*He's spoken to me? That's not possible, I haven't been here.*

Lucy doesn't comment.

"Lucy, I do not believe that you have a mental condition."

*Well, he's right about that.*

"Let me explain, Doctor," Lucy says, using her hands to illustrate. "I lied when I told you Emily was here before, but the thing is, she has not been in my head since the day I was brought here." *The day of my wedding,* she thinks but doesn't say aloud.

The doctor turns. "Why would you lie about that? How do I know you are telling the truth now?"

"Because I could have her talk to you now. I just know that you would believe that she and I are two different people."

The doctor folds his arms over his chest, his face skeptical and clearly unbelieving. "Your new husband tried to visit yesterday, but you refused him. Why?"

*That can't be right,* I say. *Charles was here? Didn't they tell you he was here? Why would you refuse to see him?*

"I do not want him to see me like this," Lucy answers the doctor's question and avoids mine.

"And you have a lovely, quiet room with all of your favorite things, yet you choose to be in a room with the lower classes?"

"I was lonely." Lucy holds her head high, but I hear the lie in her voice.

"Just tell me that you no longer hear voices. Tell me that you were flustered with your upcoming wedding, that the stress caused a temporary derangement, but that your mind has calmed now." The doctor practically pleads with her. I realize that he doesn't really think she is sick. Of course, I know that she isn't sick, but I'm not exactly in a position to vouch for her.

"Would you like to speak with Emily?" Lucy asks. "She's still here, and she's spoken to people for me before. I know she will now."

*Why are you doing this, Lucy? It sounds like you could go home.*

The doctor stares at her for a moment before moving toward the machine behind us. "I will humor you," he says, "If 'Emily' as you say is residing in your head currently, let me turn on the machine and look for any differences that might explain what you say."

"Yes." Lucy leans back in the chair. "Yes, monitor my mind and you will see."

The doctor sticks what looks like ancient leads to different parts of Lucy's forehead, temples, and several places in her hair. She won't look, but we hear the doctor flipping switches and turning dials. I flinch with each switch expecting some electric shock to run through us, but Lucy doesn't seem nervous.

We sit like this for several uncomfortable minutes, hearing an electric whirring and the deep rumble of what sounds like a generator warming up. I feel like I'm in some torture charmber in a haunted house attraction.

But Lucy remains calm.

Suddenly the generator sound powers down and I feel the doctor's fingers in Lucy's hair, removing the leads one by one until all are removed.

The doctor holds some sort of printout of what looks like brain waves and studies it for a few seconds. "I will compare this to your other tests and see if I can find any differences."

Lucy nods. "Would you like to speak with Emily now?"

The doctor looks at us again, skeptical, clearly not expecting to hear anything he hasn't heard from Lucy before. He nods once, as if telling me to go ahead and talk.

*Say something, Emily,* Lucy prods.

I don't.

"What does Emily wish to tell me?" the doctor asks.

*Say something!*

*No.*

*Why?* she asks. *Please prove that you are here. I need him to* believe *that you are here.*

*No,* I repeat.

*Why?* I feel the real tears prick her eyes.

*Because if I don't, maybe you can go home.*

CHAPTER 9

*i'm sure*

I ate breakfast in an empty house despite it being a Saturday. Mom and Dad were off meeting an expert witness for the trial with our lawyer. Saturday morning was apparently the only time they could all meet on short notice. I guess things were moving at lightning speed for a lawsuit.

I sat on the couch with my bowl of cereal, still in my pajamas and wrapped in a blanket. Some generic rom-com was playing on one of the network channels, but I was only half paying attention. I half listened to the cheesy lines until my tears blurred my vision to the point that I couldn't see my *Froot Loops* anymore.

I was devastated. Lucy was in a mental institution in 1902. Because of *me*. And she had no desire to get out despite a very real option of leaving. I didn't even think getting out was possible in a place like that. But she didn't *want* to get out.

*Why?* I couldn't fathom why she wouldn't want to get out immediately. Besides the obvious, sickness was rampant in hospitals back then. It could be deadly.

I pulled my phone from the couch cushion again and dialed the number I'd already tried three times that morning.

"Hi!" Carly answered in her cheerful voice. "You've reached Carly. Leave me a message!"

Voice mail again.

*Where was she?* It was almost eleven-thirty. How late did she need to sleep?

I needed to talk to someone, but Ari would just change the subject if I tried and Duncan... well, Duncan was probably off at the mall with Clare. They were both out of the question. I'd see them both tonight on our triple date at the bowling alley anyway.

*Wahoo!* Insert sarcastic tone paired with a half-hearted high kick. I couldn't wait for my triple date with the following people: 1) a guy whose main goal tonight was to make it clear that he wasn't interested in another girl who was certain to be there; 2) my best friend who was pretending all of my problems don't exist; and 3) my ex who wasn't pretending my problems didn't exist but had a very clingy girlfriend whose main goal was to make sure he was too busy with her to care...

(Oh! And I had some very complicated feelings about said ex. Can't forget *that* detail.)

I couldn't wait. Again insert sarcastic tone.

And that's why I was eating sugary cereal at almost noon, still wearing my pajamas.

Moving on...

I wished I could speak to Andrew about Lucy, but there was nothing he could do. If she was still in the hospital in his current time, it was too late for her. If she even survived that long.

I suppose I could ask him if she had ever been released, but that was a moot point since the past could always be changed. There was no point finding out how things turned out in one version when I had a chance to change it.

*Ugh...*

I drowned myself in the cheesy lines on screen.

<hr>

Scott wrapped me into another hug after whooping about his spare. He was good at bowling and got a lot of strikes and spares. So even though I didn't get a single one the entire night, there was a lot of hugging.

I glanced at the shoe exchange area again. Lauren wasn't looking at us this time, but she also didn't look upset. In fact, she was wearing dark lipstick now, even though they'd turned the overhead lights off and the bright neon disco party had started. I had an inkling the lipstick was for Scott's benefit. The guys were right. She wasn't getting the hint at all. Or maybe she could see through me and could tell that I wasn't exactly into all of the hugging anyway. Maybe she thought we were just six teenagers having a fun Saturday night, not necessarily a romantic triple-date.

Except of course when Brian would lean over to kiss Ari, like the rest of us wouldn't notice in the dim lighting. But they were so cute about it that no one seemed to mind.

Clare tried to make Duncan kiss her too at one point, but he sort of pushed her away awkwardly. We all pretended *not* to notice for her sake, but I wonder if she noticed the way I smiled when I looked away.

"This is pretty fun, huh?" Ari asked when we snuck off to the bathroom for a minute.

"Yeah," I agreed, staring at the mirror as I washed my hands.

Out of the corner of my eye, I noticed Ari halt her primping in the adjacent mirror and turn to me with a hand on her hip. I glanced at her and saw the knowing half-smirk, half-sympathetic look.

"What?" I asked, my eyes flitting to the dingy bathroom tiles.

"It's pretty fun, but you wish you could switch dates with Clare?" Her eyebrow rose.

"I, uh..." I involuntarily shrugged, but she'd nailed it spot on. All night I'd been finding my eyes trailing to his face, his expression, his reaction to something funny someone said, or *anything* Clare did or said. Unfortunately, it seemed like he didn't notice me at all.

"Just talk to him," she said. "Tell him how you feel. Who knows? She might just be his placeholder for you."

I hoped she was right, but knew she couldn't be. Memories of our conversation only one week ago at his house was proof. He didn't feel that way about me. Not anymore.

"That's actually not what is bothering me," I lied. "I dreamt of Lucy again last night." Well, it wasn't a complete lie. I was worried sick about Lucy.

"Oh?" She turned back to the mirror. Her *'Oh'* was full to the brim with doesn't-want-to-hear-about-it filling. Her comments about Duncan were truly heartfelt and caring. This was the exact opposite. The difference was obvious.

I dropped it, defeated. "Maybe I will talk to Duncan," I said, steering back to a topic she cared about.

"Good." She smiled at me then led us out of the bathroom.

Mom called me right as we exited, so I slowed to answer my phone while Ari re-joined our group.

"Are you having a fun time?" Mom asked. I watched, horrified as Arianna leaned over to Duncan to say something then pointed at me.

"Yeah, bowling is great!" My tone pitched when Duncan's eyes found me across the dim-lit room.

"Good, hey..." She went on to talk about some meeting or other that her and Dad had early the next morning so they might not be awake when I got home later. And not to be late... or something. I kinda stopped listening when Duncan turned to Clare briefly before standing to walk toward me.

"I won't be late, I promise," I said. Duncan was only a few feet away. "Look, I better go. Love you." I hung up and looked at him expectantly.

"Arianna said you needed to talk to me?"

"She did... I... uh..." I shuffled my feet, suddenly experiencing extreme stage fright in front of my friend. Part of me wanted to tell him about my complicated feelings or even that I just didn't want him to be with Clare. But then he looked over his shoulder, back at our group like he couldn't wait to get back.

When he turned back, my nervousness was gone. "It's nothing," I said.

He reached out to touch my elbow, suddenly zoomed in on me. "Are you sure?"

*No. No, I'm not sure. At least not until things figure themselves out with Andrew. No matter what I may or may not feel about you.* "I'm sure."

# major problem

I immediately dump the contents of the glass into the nearest plant I can find as I pop in. I'm not a fan of intoxicated Ginny, but since she is slightly buzzed, I am able to take control immediately.

She isn't completely inebriated. She can still walk in a straight line—probably thanks to me—and her words aren't slurring (yet).

Briefly glancing around, I feel as though I've fallen into a Gatsby party. Ginny is chatting with a lady in the red flapper dress with matching red lipstick. Extravagance bleeds from the walls, from the chandelier, the plush furniture. The live band acts like a battery, energizing the mood of the entire room. But there's a calming effect as each guest holds a handblown glass filled with different colors of liquid, each sipping any anxiety, worry, any and all cares in the world... away.

"Has he asked you yet?" the redhead girl asks, leaning closer to keep the conversation more private.

Genevieve smiles. "Not yet, but he has spoken with my father. I expect it any day now."

"Do you think he'll do it tonight? At the party?"

"So public?" Genevieve places a hand to her chest, the dress cut so low that the majority of her fingers touch skin and not fabric. "If he knows me well at all, he'll do it at a public event. Just like this." She waves a hand at the energized party.

The lady sips her drink, her eyes falling to Genevieve's empty one. "Let's go refill your glass," she says, leading Genevieve away as I concoct another plan to keep it empty.

Then I spot him. "And here he is," I say, taking control and breaking from Genevieve's friend. "You will excuse me..." I scan her thoughts for a name but can't find it so don't finish the sentence.

"Good luck," the redhead girl says as I walk away.

He has just entered the party, his now-blond hair plastered smooth. I don't recognize the look on him, but he makes it look good. He makes everything look good.

I match my steps to the beat of the music, the live band's percussion vibrating my whole body. Sauntering slowly makes it easier to keep from stumbling or bumping into anyone in Genevieve's compromised state.

His smile widens when he spots us, and I wonder if the smile is for her or me. Then I remember he can't possibly know I'm here yet.

"Ginny," he says, taking the empty glass from my hand and placing it on a nearby table, then taking both of my hands.

"Hello, Andrew," she says, wrenching control and batting her eyelashes.

He leans close, and a shiver slides down the back of her neck all the way to her toes. "I want to show you something," he says, his vibrating voice tickling her ears. "Can I take you away?"

She pulls back to look at him full on. "Don't you have something you wish to ask me?"

A frustrated frown pulls at his lips, but he recovers quickly and leans close again. "Patience, my darling."

She closes her eyes in elation and bites her bottom lip. Opening her eyes wider, she stares into his and nods once.

Holding her hand, he leads her outside the house toward his car. She practically skips. The cool air clears her head almost completely, but the thrill of being alone with Andrew has a similar effect. She's fearless knowing that he is practically hers.

He reaches for the passenger-door handle, but stops. In one swift motion, he whirls us around until our back is against the car and his lips are inches away. Eyes searching ours for something he whispers, "Emily?"

Genevieve whirls away. "It's *Genevieve*," she spits, but she doesn't swipe his hand away when he reaches for hers again.

The metal ring against her skin is enough. I flash a sly smile that I hope mirrors the one I see on his face so often.

His chestnut eyes continue to bore into mine, willing me to come forward. He just doesn't know that I already have. I stare right back, waiting for recognition to color his expression.

But he doesn't catch on! *Ugh!* "Andrew, I'm here!" I say, "I'm here. It's me, Emily."

His sly smile finally makes an appearance. "Good," he says, then pulls the door open and helps me in.

We pull away from the mansion—not Genevieve's, but that's hardly surprising. A family like hers gets invited to other parties.

"I should have made sure you were here before whisking Genevieve away," he says after a moment.

"And why is that?"

"Because I want to show *you* something. Not Ginny. I just assumed you were with her."

"Have I been with her often? When you are with her, I mean?"

"Not as often as I would like," he says, looking over at me and squeezing my fingers limply resting in Ginny's lap.

"Where are you taking me?" I ask when he releases his grip to concentrate on driving. There are hardly any motorists on the road. I don't know what time it is, but back home I'd expect to see more traffic. Even at three in the morning. Different times, I remind myself.

"To visit an old friend."

My heart does a flip. "Lucy?" I blurt out?

He looks at me, surprised by my outburst, but shakes his head with regret. "No, not Lucy."

I almost spew the whole mess Lucy is currently in, stuck in an insane asylum. Or rather, *choosing* to be stuck there with no contact with family or her new husband. But I'm pretty sure there's nothing Andrew can do about it. And I don't want to worry him, so I don't mention it.

"You have been waking up in your own time, right?" he asks. It feels out of the blue, but I wonder if it's been on his mind often. "You aren't skipping from Ginny to Lucy without being Emily in between?"

"No, I've been waking up." Maybe that's the reasons for the infrequency of my Lucy dreams. Squeezing Emily time in doesn't leave much room for two other girls. Wearing the ring is supposed to control it, but with Andrew out of Lucy's time, I wonder if I am subconsciously choosing Genevieve more often. That idea floods me with loads of guilt. Genevieve doesn't need me as badly as Lucy does.

"Can I assume that it worked itself out?"

"Me being in a coma?" It feels strange talking to him about *my* life. "Actually it's a whole big mess with a malpractice lawsuit thrown into the mix, and friends who either don't care or don't want to hear about any of it. I mean, I guess they're supportive about the lawsuit, but I haven't been able to talk to anyone about my dreams in…" I blow out a breath, steeling myself from crying. "I don't know how long."

Andrew doesn't say anything, his eyes glued to the road. His jaw is clenched, like he is angry, but doesn't trust his words.

"Sorry," I mutter. "It's not your problem either."

He glances at me, his eyes glistening. "Let me come sooner," he says. "Tell me it's okay to come sooner. Clearly you need a friend right now. I suspect June ninth isn't in your immediate future."

I shake my head. "It's still a few months away, but it needs to stay that way. I don't think I could handle you coming sooner."

Terror fills me as I contemplate what messed-up memories I could wake up with when he finally reaches me. "I need to be ready for you."

He clenches his jaw again, but nods in agreement though I can tell he doesn't like it.

"Plus, I'm getting used to this new version of you. Seeing Andrew 2.0 makes me think we both need a bit of time before we finally meet," I tease.

"Two-point...?"

"Yeah, back there?" I hook my thumb back at the party. "Seriously 2.0. I thought you would've noticed I was here immediately." I honestly didn't know how he could know, but something about being in the car with him again lightened my mood.

He laughs, then takes my hand, interlocking our fingers and kissing the back of it.

A few minutes later we pull in front of a large home, not a mansion like Genevieve's, but not a cottage either.

"Where are we?" I ask as Andrew opens my door and takes my hand to assist me out.

He smiles warmly. "You'll see."

I hook my arm in the crook of his, and we walk up the path.

A balding man answers the door.

"Master Andrew?" the man says. "Did you forget something?"

"I promised the mistress that I would come back with someone I wanted her to meet."

*Meet? As Genevieve or Emily?* My palms begin to sweat as I'm not sure who I need to be.

The man backs away from the door and motions for us to walk inside. He leads us to a side room that's cozy and well furnished. A man and woman sit across from each other in high back chairs.

"Andrew, you've returned!" the man says, standing. He's portly, well-dressed, and looks like he's in his late forties or early fifties.

"I wish for you to meet someone," Andrew says, gesturing to me.

I curtsy, or something to that effect. I'm not sure what Genevieve would do.

"This is Emily," Andrew says, answering my earlier question. "She's my..." He pauses, then smiles. "Well, she's my future."

My heart warms. He introduced me as *Emily*! That could create so many issues in the future, but I have a feeling that whoever these people are, whatever happens, it won't matter.

"Are you two engaged?" the woman asks, standing to greet me. She looks vaguely familiar. Has she been at one of the parties? Obviously not the one tonight, but perhaps during my first walk with Genevieve?

I shake my head as Andrew says, "Not yet."

I feel my cheeks flame. Marriage has never been discussed between us. Besides his occasional engagements to women whom he claims he has no intention of marrying.

But I'm barely seventeen! Marriage is *far* from my mind. I still have a whole year of high school after this year, and hopefully several years of college before I begin thinking about marriage.

And that's when it hits me. I *know* this woman. She's more than twenty years older than she was when I last saw her, but despite the wrinkles around her eyes and mouth, indicating a life full of laughter and smiles, it is undeniably her. I'm baffled that I didn't notice sooner, but she acted so differently around Andrew the last time I saw her.

It's Margaret.

Lucy's best friend, Margaret. Andrew's former fiancée, Margaret.

The last time I saw her, she was in love with Andrew, holding onto every word that left his lips, clinging to him, and rightfully so because she was engaged to him.

But I see none of that now.

We sit for a while, listening as Margaret recounts the story of how she and her husband, George, met and fell in love. Then they ask us to tell our story.

Our story is exceptionally complicated, so Andrew concocts an excuse for us to leave with a promise to return soon to tell it.

We bid a heartfelt goodbye and are soon back in Andrew's car. I stare ahead, letting the conversation with Margaret and her husband sink in.

Andrew doesn't crank the car to turn it on right away and gets in to sit next to me.

"Emily?" he asks after a moment.

I finally glance at him. "She doesn't know you," I shake my head, swishing Ginny's short hair along my jawline. "I mean, she knows you clearly, but she doesn't remember who you were to her? Does she?"

He shakes his head slowly with a broad smile. "This is what I have been trying to explain. What happens doesn't matter when I jump."

I stare ahead again. "Yeah, I mean, I've seen the effect of you erased from Lucy's and Charles's memories but I guess..." I trail off, I'm at a loss for words.

"I did not break her heart. To her, I never existed."

I look back at him. "I guess that's what's important," I say, then open my mouth to say more, but stop myself.

"Say it."

"Hmm?"

"What you were about to say. Just say it."

"What if you can't jump? What if it doesn't work? Then you *could* break a heart."

His eyes widen with excitement. "Except I've just figured out how to make the next one."

"Oh?"

"My parents—my current parents—hate each other."

"So, you plan to go back and prevent their marriage since they've never loved each other?"

His mouth opens in surprise. "Spot-on assumption."

I shrug and almost comment that he may not always be so lucky. How far would he go? Would he prevent a marriage from two people who do love each other?

My pulse quickens, but I'm not sure why. I take deep breaths, looking around the car to see if there is some danger I'm sensing to cause the change in feeling.

"What is it?" Andrew asks, seeing my sudden panic. "What's wrong?"

"I don't—" I start to say, but she chokes my words. "You're leaving?" Ginny asks, almost in a shriek.

"I, uh..." Andrew's is clearly confused. He hasn't noticed her take back control.

"I thought you wanted to *marry* me? You had a conversation with my father! Why would you tell him your intentions if you plan to leave?" She begins to hyperventilate.

"Ginny," he shushes her. "Ginny, calm down. I don't plan to leave," he lies but she sees through the lie. She suddenly sees through all his lies. That he never intended to marry her, but wanted to get close to her for... she isn't sure why.

Which is good for me.

But we clearly have a major problem.

# sound advice

D r. William's office was on the opposite side of town as Dr. Shew's. Which was smart on her part because there is no way I would have walked in the same building or even driven along the same street to get there. Dr. Shew wasn't behind bars. As far as I knew, she had resumed her practice. She could be meeting with patients right now.

And that terrified me.

If there was *anyone* in the nearby area with the same dreams as me, I hated to think what she would do to them.

I was a bundle of nerves as Mom and I waited by the receptionist desk to meet Dr. Williams. I expected to see the twin of Dr. Shew. Perfect hair, perfect clothing, perfect smile that drew you in with false security. She'd pretend to care, and I'd believe her... and then I'd end up trapped in my dreams again, or worse—I'd never have them again.

Dr. Shew had done both to me.

But Mom promised she was different. I kind of hoped Dr. Williams was really old and stuck in the ancient ways of psychiatry and would just listen to me talk about my feelings. That she wouldn't try any of the new techniques or use me as a guinea pig because my "condition" was on the rarer side. At least I assumed it was on the rarer side. I hoped she would send me on my way with a prescription for Prozac, none the wiser about my dreams other than that they sometimes made me depressed.

Did they give Prozac to teenagers?

I bounced my knee as I sat in a cushioned chair in the waiting room. We were only a few minutes early, but those minutes dragged. My eyes trailed to the clock on the wall, ticking the seconds like they were minutes and the minutes like hours. If I hadn't been so nervous to meet the new shrink, it might have been hypnotic.

No one else was in the waiting room besides Mom, me, and the slightly overweight receptionist. I focused my attention on her to distract myself. The woman's fashion was the epitome of comfort. Her long flowing shirt was a calming blue color decorated with long-chained necklaces with flat metal pendants of different shapes. Her pants were also flowy—not in a lazy sweatpants sort of way, but in a sophisticated, comfortable slacks sort of way. Her hair was long and white and wispy, and a pair of purple square glasses teetered on the edge of her nose as she looked down at whatever she was reading. Part of me wanted to curl up against her and let her arms wrap around me like she was a long-lost aunt I should have had all along.

"All right," the receptionist said to her desk. "Shall we?"

I looked at Mom with a confused expression, who looked back at me with an identical look. We both looked back at the woman, who had stood and was watching us. She approached with an outstretched hand, and we both stood slowly.

"My receptionist called in sick today," the woman explained. "I am Dr. Williams."

Mom shook her hand, then I did.

"But you can call me Roberta." She turned on a heel and beckoned us to follow her down the hall.

I already felt that part of my wish had come true. Dr. Williams so far was *nothing* like Dr. Shew. I couldn't picture Dr. Shew filling in for her receptionist. And walking into her office—a cozy, but cluttered space—made me feel instantly at home. The orange leather couch was worn in places, and the rug was faded. Stacks of books took up the flat surfaces around the room. Though I never would have described it before, after seeing Dr. William's office, I realized that Dr. Shew's was sterile and cold.

I sunk into the couch next to Mom. I hoped that she'd be able to stay for this first session.

Dr. Williams took off her glasses before leading us down the hall. They hung around her neck, connected to a string of translucent multi-colored beads. With them off, I could see that her eyes were crinkly and kind. A friendly mud-brown color. She watched me for a few seconds, no sign of being uncomfortable or needing the crutch of a notebook or file to look busy while she gathered her thoughts.

"Can Mom stay?" I asked. I was understandably uncomfortable.

"Of course. Your mother can always stay. I imagine that you've lost all trust in my profession."

I nodded slowly. Mom took my hand and gave it a reassuring squeeze.

"Just promise me that you'll be honest." She tilted her head forward, like she was looking at me over the top of her frames, even though she was no longer wearing them.

I nodded again and pushed my glasses up the bridge of my nose in self-consciousness, grateful that I had worn them today as a security object. Since I preferred my contacts most days, it had been a while since I'd wore my glasses outside of the house.

"What would you like to talk about today?"

"What would I...?" I trailed off. Dr. Shew had always led our conversations. She'd always asked the leading questions. I couldn't remember when she'd ever asked what I wanted to talk about. "I don't know."

Dr. Williams didn't prompt me even a little bit, so I squirmed in my seat.

"What about—?" Mom began to say, but the slight shake of Dr. Williams's head silenced it.

She clearly wanted whatever we talked about to come from me and me only.

"Am I supposed to tell you about my dreams?" I asked, wondering how much of my history she knew and how much I needed to fill her in on.

"Do you want to talk about your dreams?"

I thought of Lucy and her predicament. I thought about Andrew and the crazy feat he was trying to accomplish. I thought about Genevieve... and didn't want to even think about her, let alone talk about her. "No," I said. I needed to trust Dr. Williams more before that happened, and I didn't know how long that would take. "At least not today."

"Then we won't talk about your dreams."

Another awkward pause.

I glanced nervously at Mom, who didn't give me anything this time. So, I did what Dr. Williams wanted me to do and thought about what I really wanted to talk about.

"I can't talk to Arianna about anything," I said. "I try, but she won't listen. She always changes the subject, so I give up."

"Do you feel that she is self-centered and only worries about herself?" Dr. Williams asked. "I assume she is your friend?"

"My *best* friend. And no, I mean, she listens when I talk about Duncan or Scott or *Clare.* Anything about school, but I can't mention my dreams or the trial without her shutting me down."

"Have you spoken to her about this?"

I didn't have to think long before answering. "Well, no. And I can't talk to Duncan because he's all occupied with his new girl-friend, and Carly said I could call her, but she's away on this awesome study abroad thing." I took a deep breath, then really got into it—talking about my dreams after all. About how help-less I felt about Lucy trapped in an insane asylum that she appar-ently wanted to stay in. About Genevive's selfishness, and how it was the only way for me to see Andrew. I omitted everything about Andrew's master plan.

When I finished, I unscrewed the water bottle Mom handed me from her purse and took a sip. Then I downed half of it.

Dr. Williams waited for me to finish. "It sounds like you are feeling like your life is out of your control. Why are you not taking action?"

I felt a little bit offended by that statement. "I do take action! I saved Lucy from a fire. *That* was *action.* I prevented Isabella from throwing herself off the deck of that ship. I freaking *saved* Carly from that train. I take plenty of *action.* "

"Those examples are all things that happened in the past."

"Isn't everything in the past?"

"But the struggles you mentioned are not from your past. They are things happening right now. And you haven't taken any action." Dr. Williams leaned forward so her elbows rested on her knees, and she clasped her hands together. "Talk to Ari. Tell her how you feel. Talk to Duncan. Take control of your life. It sounds to me that you are letting things happen to you, that you are afraid to act. Perhaps because of things from your past?"

*Perhaps.*

# they can't stop me from dreaming

"B ut I thought you liked the boy?" Father says, his eyebrows knit in confusion.

"But he's a threat. Father, I overheard him talking to the deputy. He says he'll reveal the location if they promise him immunity." Genevieve pinches the inside of her arm to produce tears in her eyes. "You can't go to prison, Father!" She throws her arms around him. "We have to stop him!"

Genevieve's thoughts are brutal, which is confusing. I look through her thoughts, and she hasn't overheard anything about a deputy or someone revealing something. Then it occurs to me that she is lying through her teeth—which she is very good at, by the way. I'd believe her if I wasn't inside her head.

Then it all clicks. She's doing this because Andrew said he was leaving and never intended to marry her.

*Oh no.*

Father quickly peels her arms away. "I don't understand," he says. "He was very clear about his intentions with you. I wasn't supposed to reveal it, but the proposal is happening tonight."

*Really?* Doubt creeps into her mind. *Perhaps I misunderstood. Perhaps he does intend to marry me... I might as well see it through first.* "Maybe I was wrong."

But Father is already thinking hard about this new information. "Unless he's using you as a cover." He stands and starts to pace. "Maybe he's just getting close to you. Maybe he intends to marry you so that when he reveals the speakeasy... all of the money will go to him."

Genevieve remains calm despite her rising panic. *What have I done?* she thinks, but her concern is fleeting and gone in an instant. "Maybe we should see it through. I'll marry Andrew and find out what his plans are."

I feel the sudden urge to take a shower...*shudder*... or two. She isn't lying now. She fully intends to marry Andrew and find out his plans like she says. She hopes he *does* plan to take her father's money, after daddy goes to prison for running the speakeasy and his other various indiscretions.

She just hopes that she is a part of his plan too.

She daydreams about their thousands of kisses for a moment.

*Okay, has it really been that many?*

She reminisces about Andrew gazing into her eyes, about his sweet words filled with promises and a future involving them both.

*How much of this is fantasy and how much is reality?* I wonder. I feel some relief at the realization that most of the conversations and intimate moments running through her head are ones where *I* was present and in control.

*Surely he didn't make it all up,* Ginny thinks to herself. *Certainly his plans include me in them. Even if he does intend to leave. I must've misunderstood the part about him not wanting to marry me.*

She's decided. She's convinced that whatever shady business Andrew is involved in—or whatever business she has imagined him to be involved in—she's on his side.

If Andrew asks her to go against her father, there is no question which side of the line she intends to stand on.

Firmly on his.

Genevieve's mood is much improved after the conversation with her father. And though she knows she's planted vicious suspicions into his thoughts, she doesn't care. Her plans have changed.

The party tonight will be epic, she decides, as she carefully combs through her dark hair. I try not to compare the similarities between her features and my own again. She slips into a white flapper dress—the finest one I've seen on her yet—and I'm suddenly feeling very much like I'm in a Fitzgerald novel. Even more so than I did at the last party. Gatsby had a party every night, right? I have no idea how long it's been since my last walk with her, but given Genevieve's anger toward Andrew, it must have been pretty recent. Maybe a few days ago? A week?

She pins an elaborate decoration in her hair with feathers and jewels—I suspect they are genuine rubies and sapphires—and applies a dark lipstick that sets off the paleness of her cheeks.

She is beautiful. And she knows it.

Genevieve and her father sit in silence as they ride to a nearby neighbor's house for the party. They must have been fashionably late because the place is already booming with piano notes and bass strings and a saxophone flitting a complicated and possibly improvised melody into the warm night air.

Genevieve effortlessly struts into the home, acting very much like the party can finally begin with her presence. She walks in on her father's arm, but immediately releases it when she spots the meticulously combed blond-haired man across the room and walks briskly toward him.

Andrew 2.0.

He is lost in conversation with his parents—Genevieve fills that information in for me—and hardly notices her arrival at his side.

"Andrew, darling," Genevieve says with a thick sultry tone. "Fetch me a drink?"

He looks at us with the briefest of annoyance before beaming and silently agreeing then walking toward the bar.

Genevieve pastes a fake smile, aimed at who I assume are the Harkers, while we wait for Andrew's return. She instantly regrets sending him away and not going with him because she has no idea what to say to his parents. I take this opportunity to confirm something I didn't know I needed confirmation on until this moment.

"Do you plan to travel this summer?" I ask, pulling an appropriate conversation topic from Genevieve's social tutoring.

"Mrs. Harker plans to stay where it's warm," Mr. Harker says in a nasally tone with no trace of affection. "Whereas I plan to embark to Siberia for a month or more. I have business there." He pauses, with a frown. "Unless a certain event forces me to return early." He looks Genevieve up and down, scrutinizing her.

Mrs. Harker has the same dull look in her eyes, nodding in agreement. It's clear that she cannot wait until his trip.

Andrew was right. His parents clearly can't stand each other.

I guess I can't fault him for planning to break them up. It doesn't seem fair to leave them stuck together for the long haul.

Right on time, Andrew returns with a round glass only filled about a third of the way with a light-brown liquid. Genevieve pouts at him. She wanted more but takes it and flashes a smile before downing it in one gulp. It burns as it goes down, but she hardly notices, watching Andrew's expression for a sign of... well, anything. That he is nervous about a proposal, or secretly planning to leave. Although she isn't sure what either might look like.

"Could I have your attention?" Genevieve's father's voice booms from the head of the room. It isn't his party, but he suddenly acts as host.

The room quiets. Genevieve's father is the type who demands attention and gets exactly what he wants.

"Could I have my beautiful, sweet, and only daughter join me?" He searches the room for her face and smiles genuinely at us when he finds her. It's the smile he only wears for her when he's on display at a party or charity event. She's never seen such a smile in the privacy of their home. But she's used to it and matches his when she feels the eyes turn to her.

The crowd parts as we make our way toward his outreached arm and tuck into his embrace. If someone snapped a picture it would look like a loving father-daughter relationship. They both play the part well. Only a well-trained eye would be able to spot the farce.

"And, Andrew Harker," he says. "Join us?"

My eyes instantly find Andrew where we'd left him standing. He looks sick. His face is pale, even from across the room. I see the glisten of sweat on his forehead.

Quickly, he gathers his wits and walks toward us, albeit slightly less graceful than Genevieve did moments ago. He stumbles a couple of times.

"It seems Mr. Harker has taken upon himself to enjoy the beverages early. Perhaps he needed a bit of liquid courage?"

The crowd roars in laughter. Genevieve's father is charismatic in front of a crowd. They are eating every word.

Andrew glances nervously at me when he arrives at Genevieve's father's other side. I give him a small smile, hoping he knows it's coming from me. It only lasts a split-second before Genevieve takes over, flashing a seductive look at him. Her father didn't warn her about this interruption to the party, but she has a strong inkling about what's coming.

"I had the pleasure of engaging in a very serious chat with this young man not long ago, and we decided that tonight would be the perfect setting to make it public."

Andrew's eyes widen slightly. Clearly that was not something they talked about. He is scrambling to find the best response.

"Mr. Harker?" Father waves a hand, giving Andrew the room. Andrew goes a shade paler.

"Do you have a question for my daughter?" he prods,

glancing at the crowd. They respond with enthusiasm and encouragement.

Andrew opens his mouth, and I fully expect him to go with the crowd, to propose to Genevieve right here and now. After all, he doesn't believe it matters what promises he makes here since they will all forget about him tomorrow—or so to speak.

But then he hangs his head. "No," he says quietly. "No, I do not have a question for your daughter."

Genevieve's father's face freezes in shock, but only for the fraction of a second it takes for him to snap and throw the scariest, he-might-just-kill-Andrew-if-he-doesn't-get-out-soon look. If the crowd sees the look on her father's face, they don't react. But the look is gone quickly, and a cool and collected expression replaces it.

Genevieve feels intense hurt, but she masks her face and looks to her father for something. He nods almost imperceptibly, then turns to a man behind him on his left silently signaling something. The man nods, then disappears from the room.

"I am sad to hear it," her father says, his voice also cool and collected. He turns to address the party. "I regret what I must tell you next. I fully anticipated protecting my future son-in-law, my future family, from the full force of what awaits him. But clearly he does not intend to become my son-in-law as he promised."

Andrew backs away, but two large men flank both sides, daring him to try to escape.

"I will give you one more chance," her father says. "Do you have anything to say to Genevieve?"

She is mortified that her father is dragging this out, but I step forward and gently grab his arm. "Perhaps I could speak with Andrew alone a moment?" I ask, making sure my eyes are pleading and innocent looking to her father.

"Of course, darling." He says and motions for Andrew and I to step from the party a moment.

"What are you doing?" I ask, when we are partially concealed behind a green velvet curtain. The two men who were ready to grab Andrew are watching him like a hawk, otherwise I'd suggest we find more privacy.

"I can't propose to her."

"Since when? You had no problem going along with being engaged to Margaret." That memory still stings a little. Even though I know now more than ever that it was all a show until he could set his plan into motion.

"This is different." He won't look at me in the eyes.

"How?" I put a hand on Genevieve's hip. A natural stance for her. Being with her makes me feel sassier than I normally am.

He grabs both of my elbows. "Because I don't love her."

"Did you love Margaret?"

He releases his grip and combs a hand through his hair, messing up the perfect way it laid. Instantly realizing what he's done, he tries to smooth it, but the damage is already done. "Of course I didn't love her." His darting glance at me urges me to understand, but I'm still at a loss.

"Did I ever tell you that I look a lot like Genevieve?" I try to smile, but it feels more like a grimace.

He just stares, clearly he wasn't expecting it.

"Yeah, um, personality-wise we couldn't be more different."

Andrew nods in complete agreement.

"And I have to admit, I don't really like her that much, but we could be sisters in appearance."

For the first time I can remember, he takes a studied look at me. His eyes trailing up and down Genevieve's form. I can't remember him ever doing that to her or Lucy even, at least not that I ever witnessed.

"We're about the same height, same hair color. My teeth are straighter, but our faces are similar too."

"Why are you telling me this?"

"Because I think things are going to get very bad, very soon, and you could maybe stop it by proposing to Genevieve."

"I can't... I—"

"Pretend she's me," I blurt out. "I mean, it's not a real proposal, but if you can't stomach asking her, pretend you're asking me."

He stares at me for several long seconds, weighing his options. But then he shakes his head again. "Genevieve, I can't."

"No, Andrew *2.0*," I say. "It's me, Emily."

His smile is small. "I know, and I'm telling you that I cannot do it."

"Why not?" My frustration rises.

"Because I don't love her." Andrew shakes his head.

The happy noises of the party turn into uneasy commotion. Glasses shattering, bottles clanking. It sounds like people are trying to stash the alcohol. Since we're smack dab in the middle of the Prohibition period, I can easily guess who has arrived.

"Mr. Harker is there," we hear Genevieve's father say in a booming tone. "He's the mastermind of the location we spoke of."

"Thank you, sir."

Four police men rush in passed the curtain and converge on us.

"You are here to take me away, I assume?" Andrew asks, his voice and posture calmer than it has been all night.

The leader grins at him and roughly traps his wrists in very primitive-looking iron handcuffs.

"Last chance, Mr. Harker." Genevieve's father grins wickedly. I suspect that he has these officers in his pocket. "Do you have anything to say to my daughter? Anything that could make this all a misunderstanding?"

Andrew aims an expression at me. Except I can tell he's not looking at *me*. "Genevieve, I'm sorry I don't love you. I cannot ask you to marry me."

Her heart breaks in two inside my chest, and it hurts as if he's said the words to me. I can't fathom why he couldn't just fake it. Why is he being noble or honest now?

"What now?" I whisper.

He winks at me. "Don't worry, love," he says in a low tone. The last word causing a thrill to run through me. "Wherever they're taking me, they can't stop me from dreaming."

I feel my eyes widen.

He smiles a knowing smile. "I'm jumping tonight."

# taking control

I was glad to be back. In all my years of dreaming, I couldn't remember ever feeling more grateful to be back, awake in my life. I mean, other than wanting the dying to end, or the pain to be gone.

Let me rephrase that.

I'd felt that way *many* times, but this was a different kind of wanting to be back. It was the first time I had ever woken from a dream and was grateful to not be *her* anymore. Genevieve was so selfish and manipulative. Until now I sympathized with all of my walks. I liked most of them. Heck, Lucy was one of my best friends. I loved her like a sister.

Just the thought of where Lucy was and that I was essentially helpless to help her made my insides twist. It made me sick and uneasy. I needed to find a way to get her out of that nightmare.

But I sort of loathed Genevieve. And if Andrew succeeded in jumping, I would never have to be her again.

I hope he succeeded.

Even though I was furious at him. What was he thinking? Why didn't he just do what they wanted and pretend to be in love with Genevieve and propose? I was walking her. How hard could it be?

What if Genevieve's goons killed him? He couldn't dream his way out of trouble if he were dead.

*The next time I saw him...*

I just hoped there was a next time.

I forced my mind from that line of thinking and glanced at my birdhouse. Well, Grandma's birdhouse. Seeing it every morning was bittersweet. It reminded me that Grandma was gone, that I couldn't call her or drop by whenever I needed to talk. So many memories.

How I wished I could talk to her about Andrew.

How I wished I could walk with her someday.

As I got ready for the day, thoughts of my conversation with Dr. Williams flooded my mind, washing away the strong thoughts of Genevieve, Andrew, and Grandma.

She said I should take action in my life. Talk to Ari, talk to Duncan. They were supposed to be my friends. They said they were my friends. Maybe they just needed a gentle reminder.

"Whether you like it or not, I hear that Lauren got the hint about Scott not being into her when we were all at the bowling alley," Ari said as she drove us to school.

"Really?" That was news to me. I'd been worried about Scott being too attentive and... affectionate, but the date felt like just a bunch of friends hanging out on a Saturday night. "Where did you hear that?"

She glanced uneasily at me. It was the you-aren't-going-to-like-what-I-tell-you-next-look.

"Oh no," I groaned. "What is it?"

She shot the look at me again.

"Just tell me!"

"Scott sort of told the entire school that you're his girlfriend now."

"Why would he do that?" I was shouting now. "He's Scott *O'Neil*. Resident player of the high school. Pfft," I scoffed. "Scott would *not* tell the entire school that he had a girlfriend. And if he did, it would *not* be me."

Arianna shrugged. "I'm just telling you what I heard."

I shook my head and folded my arms over my chest.

"Does it really bother you that much?" Ari snuck a glance at me when we were at a stoplight.

I unfolded my arms. "Honestly? It's really frustrating that for the second time in my life I suddenly have a boyfriend I never agreed to having."

"The second time?"

I glare at her. "Fine. Pretend that my dreams aren't real. Pretend that what happened to Carly wasn't real, but to me I woke up one day and suddenly Duncan was my boyfriend." I didn't exactly *mind* that Duncan was my boyfriend, but I didn't need to mention that part.

This was slightly different.

She stiffened the way she always did when I mentioned my dreams, but I didn't care. I was tired of keeping it a "secret" and pretending that they didn't exist when I was around her. Not long ago she would have loved to hear every detail. Who knows, she might've seen some qualities in Genevieve that I didn't? She would've liked the stories from the '20s at least.

"Well, maybe the girlfriend rumors are wrong," she offered. "I mean, I didn't hear it straight from Scott. Maybe he's just planning to ask you."

"Then I'll have to tell him no."

"But why? Scott is a catch! And he's cute!"

"But I have feelings for someone else."

"Duncan?"

Hearing his name made my stomach twist. "I'm not exactly sure how I feel about Duncan. Besides, he has a girlfriend."

Arianna seemed at a loss for words, which was frustrating. I knew her well enough that she couldn't resist insisting that I tell her more if I implied something. And if I had been implying that I had feelings for any other guy at our school (or in our time for that matter) she would have taken a bite without a second thought. But whenever I started talking about my dreams, she was suddenly not curious.

"I mean Andrew, you know," I said. *There. How's that for taking control and not beating around the bush anymore.*

We'd just arrived in the parking lot, and fortunately Ari didn't move to get out and force an end to the topic. Maybe she was finally curious.

"You might get to meet him soon," I added, hoping to tighten the trap.

"How? Why?" She wouldn't look at me though.

"He is moving forward in time." Okay, maybe I was saying too much, but I had to keep her interested. Force her to listen.

She looked at me with an eyebrow raised. "How is that possible?"

"Well, he's using memory walks to change who his parents are with the intent of moving forward."

She finally looked at me with an incredulous look.

With a smug smile I just couldn't help, I said, "He is currently in 1925." Currently? I had a dream months ago when he was already decades further. "At least he has been lately," I amended. "His plan is to make it here." And he might be finished with the twenties by now, but that was beside the point. I could catch her up more tomorrow if he succeeded. And if she'd still listen.

She raised a skeptical eyebrow. "Do you ever wonder if you made him up?"

"I—"

"Not like you *made him up,*" she rolled her eyes and smiled, as if trying to soften the blow. "But like you dreamed him up and he's not really real?"

There were no words. How many conversations did I have with her about believing my dreams were real memories?

"Or, okay, so he's real," she backpedaled, "but if he was really trying to get to our time, don't you think we would have known him this whole time?"

"I told him not to contact me until... well, until June ninth."

It sounded so lame telling her about it now. She had a point. And our conversation needed to end quickly. The first bell rang, and we were still in her car.

"And he's just supposed to wait until then? I mean, maybe you weren't playing in the sandbox together," Ari spoke quickly, "but what if he's already at our school? What if you've already met him? He's just supposed to hang around and do nothing until some arbitrary date?"

"He promised to wait," I said quietly. Lame. Lame. Lame. Who was I kidding? He wasn't coming. Yeah, he made it to the seventies or whenever, but something happened to stop him there. My heart lurched with the thought about who would be showing up at my doorstep on June ninth. Probably a sixty-something man who had contemplated all of these years the words he would use to explain to seventeen-year-old me why he never made it.

We got out of the car. Ari tried unsuccessfully to hide her smug look.

But the conversation wasn't over.

"Remember when we were like twelve, and we had that conversation about what we'd would do if one of us was diagnosed with a serious illness?"

We walked slowly, but Ari nodded, glancing at me out of the corner of my eye. "The green scaly, infectious disease?"

I couldn't help but smile at how well she remembered even the smallest details of our made-up disease. But this was serious, and I might not have the courage to bring it up again, so I dropped the smile. "You *promised* to be my friend. My *best* friend if something like that happened."

"And I would," she said.

"No. You've failed." Tears welled when she stopped walking and turned to look at me. "Twice." My voice shook.

Her expression was a mixture of disbelief and hurt.

"First, when Carly died—don't you dare look at me like that

didn't happen. It did, and I remember what the world was like without her."

Ari smoothed her features so I could no longer read them.

"You *broke up* with me back then because I told you that she put herself in the path of that train. That she *wanted* to die." Involuntarily, my voice lowered. "You didn't talk to me for months."

"Em, you might remember that, but I don't. Please stop punishing me for something I don't even remember doing."

"Fair enough, but now you are denying that my dreams are even real. That I don't truly walk with those in the past. With those who have died and are buried in Meadow Grove Cemetery."

"Can you blame me for not believing? Who are you to decide what I believe?"

Okay, this was not about belief systems, but I didn't want to argue that point with her. "So what do you believe? Do you believe that *I* think they're real?"

She hesitated a moment before nodding. "I do, but I could say the same thing about my schizophrenic cousin's hallucinations."

"Fine, but do you tell your cousin over and over that they aren't real?"

"Only if I think it will help."

"So if you *truly* believe that my dreams are all in my head as some sort of mental illness, is it helping anyone that you are now trying to convince me that they aren't real?"

"I guess not. Maybe that's a doctor's job?"

"Exactly." Although my new doctor seemed to believe me. "Be my best friend like you promised. Especially now when I'm dealing with something way worse than a green scaly, contagious disease."

The bell had rang several minutes ago. But the tardy was worth it. Maybe comparing my memory walking to a mental illness wasn't the best approach, but at least I could actually talk to her about the dreams now.

My chat with Duncan wasn't quite as successful. First of all, Clare interrupted us right when we were getting into it —surprise, surprise. And second, I became a blubbering, tongue-tied mess almost the instant I saw him. He had a new haircut, and it looked really good. He also wore my favorite green shirt that made the flecks in his eyes dance. Definitely swoon-worthy.

When Clare interrupted, I called it a fail and excused myself with as much dignity as I had left.

But when the final bell rang, I found him standing next to my locker. Sans-Clare.

I hoped he didn't notice the heat suddenly flood into my cheeks.

"Can I give you a ride home today?" he asked when I was a few feet away.

I nodded. "I'll tell Ari I don't need one."

His face split into a smile.

"Where's Clare?"

"She had a dentist appointment during last period," he explained. "She's already gone."

*Ah.* That explained the sudden availability to take me home. *Oh well.* I wouldn't complain.

Ten minutes later we pulled out of the parking lot and I was reminded of another time I sat in the passenger seat of his car: shivering with wet hair and clamping the gash on my arm with one of Ari's borrowed towels and her sweatshirt. Both of which were ruined and eventually thrown in the trash.

He really was a good friend who cared about me. Even if he was dating someone else.

"I thought about what you were trying to tell me earlier."

*Oh? How much did you actually get out of that conversation?* I wondered but didn't voice.

"Emily, you have to realize that I have a girlfriend now, and my loyalties are to her."

*Ouch. Wasn't expecting that.* I also didn't know how to respond. We sat in silence for several uncomfortable moments. I wondered if he regretted what he said.

"I like Clare—"

"I'm going to stop you right there," I said. I couldn't hear any more of it. And instead of hearing him say a bunch of things that would most likely hurt, I opted to continue taking control. I would take control. "I don't know what you *thought* I was trying to tell you earlier, but it had nothing to do with Clare and your relationship with her."

He opened his mouth to speak, but I cut him off and continued.

"You like Clare. *Fine. Great. I'm happy for you.*" I tried to squash the sarcasm, but it just flowed. "But the reason I confronted you is because once upon a time you believed in my dreams. You believed that I have this crazy curse-thing where I relive people's memories in my dreams. And most of them are not happy memories."

He hung his head slightly. "I know, I—"

"I wanted to talk to you because you are my *friend*. You don't actually remember it, but at one point in time you were my *only* friend."

I let that sink in until he pulled up to my house.

"I'm sorry if being my friend is messing up your relationship with Clare," I said softly. "But I'm dealing with a bunch of crap right now. I just needed my friends back. If that is really too much to ask, then fine. I won't ask again." I opened the door and got out without waiting for a response.

# creepy mustache

He doesn't look much different this time. His hair is closer to the brown I remember as Original Andrew ₜₘ, and though I can't see his eyes very well from my vantage point, there's no obvious blue or green to them. It looks like they've retained the chestnut-brown color of both Original Andrew $_{TM}$ and Andrew 2.0.

I take a deep breath. *This must be Andrew 3.0.* The thought is exhausting, and I'm not even the one planning and executing the jumps. But the gratitude I feel for no longer being with Genevieve is worth the mental exhaustion Andrew's little plan has had on me—a mere spectator.

Briefly I wonder if he's somehow dragged me with him in each of his jumps. After all, I never figured out what Genevieve needed my help with. Maybe I was only with her because she was the closest person to Andrew.

I close my eyes and shake my head slightly to clear my thoughts. Changing timelines was *crazy* complicated.

Ugh. But I hate the mustache.

Andrew is across the room talking with someone who could be his father. Or maybe the old guy is my father. I'm not sure if this is my house or Andrew's.

From the brown cabinets that look like faux-wood paneling, to the orange countertops and green carpet—even in the kitchen area—I have a general guess which decade I'm in.

I kick a leg out from beneath the table and glance down at wide bell bottoms of my pants. Based on the feathery curls around my shoulders and the floral billowy shirt that's gathered at my waist, the time period is even more clear.

1970 something. I think. I'll have to pull Andrew aside at some point to ask exactly when.

He glances at me as he speaks with the man. More so than when I first arrived. Perhaps he's suspected that I am here.

I shoot him a look, hoping it isn't something typical of her so he'll know I'm with her. It causes his eyes to widen. I smile. *He knows it's me.* I take a sip from the girl's coffee mug and wait for the conversation to end so that I can speak with him. I don't have to wait long before Andrew approaches.

"Mind getting me a cup?" he asks, sitting across from me.

I smile again, then stand and locate the still-hot coffee pot and bring it back to the table to pour him a mug.

"What was that all about?" the girl asks, surprising me with a thick southern-drawl.

"Oh, you know your father," Andrew says, also speaking with a slight drawl that lengthens his words. "Always looking for the next thing that will make him rich."

The girl shakes her head. "They never work."

Andrew shrugs in agreement but doesn't respond. Someone knocks at the front door, but he doesn't move. It sounds like her father opens it to greet the callers.

I glance at the open doorways and listen to the start of a conversation in the other room to confirm that Andrew and I will not be overheard.

"I'm glad to see they didn't murder you," I say. The girl attempts to push back, but she is more like a go-with-the-flow type.

Andrew almost spits his coffee. "Beggin' your pardon?"

"The mafia… er, mob guys." My eyes graze the ceiling as I speak, trying to remember exactly. "I guess it was technically the police who took you away, but I figured they were probably in her father's pockets and more on the dirty-cop side of things."

"Ah," he nods into his mug. "You're talking about 1925." He points at me. "Genevieve's father."

"Who else?"

His eyes turn serious. He glances over his shoulder, listening to the humming of the low conversation still happening in the other room before he leans forward, placing a hand on each side of my face, and cupping my jawline. His brown eyes—still chestnut—study mine for several seconds before he leans forward and plants a gentle kiss on my—on her—lips.

She pushes him away gently, but I can tell that she isn't unhappy about the kiss. "Things are over between us, Andrew Harker, remember?"

He chuckles and looks down at the table between us. "Things were never officially *on* with us, but that is not why I kissed you."

We both send him a shocked look. Hers feels more hurt, but he ignores it and becomes serious again.

"I've missed you," he says reaching forward so our fingers touch. Specifically, so my skin is in contact with his ring. Keeping me firmly in control.

*But we just saw each other.* I know that time between dreams can be vastly different for them than they are for me. There were times that I was away from Lucy for weeks, though I dreamt her night after night. There were also periods of time when I didn't dream at all. I wasn't entirely sure how that affected things.

"Did it take long to break up your parents?" I ask. "Were you in prison for a while before you succeeded?"

He chuckles again and meets my eyes with glistening ones. "No, it just took the one walk to get them to give up on their relationship."

"Okay," I say when he doesn't elaborate. "Thanks for missing me, I guess. But to me, walking with Genevieve was only last night."

He nods, still without responding. The voices in the other room raise in volume.

"I hated her a little, by the way," I say, ignoring the distraction. "Frankly, I'm glad to be whoever this is." I wave a hand at my current form. "She isn't calculating in her head about how to seduce you or get you alone."

He smiles at that.

"She doesn't sound as selfish in here either." I tap the girl's temple with my finger.

"Ah, Ginny wasn't all bad."

I roll my eyes.

"Emily," he says, blowing out a breath. "I've jumped twice since you've seen me." It comes out in a rush, like he's been wound up to say it since knowing I was here and has finally mustered the courage. He watches me for a reaction with his creepy mustache.

"Twice?" It's all I can think to say.

He nods. Suddenly weary and looking like he's aged a decade since I've seen him. "After I jumped from 1925, I landed in the fifties."

"And where are we now?"

"1973."

I was right about the decor and clothing.

"It took me a long time to get out of the fifties, but I finally pulled it off."

"So... not Andrew 3.0?" I ask, a bit hesitant.

He chuckles. Something I haven't heard since arriving here. It's an almost sad sort of chuckle. A tired one. Then he shakes his head. "Not Andrew 3.0."

*Andrew 4.0 then.* "Why do you think it took so long?"

He shrugs. "Because I had to bring two people together. Make them fall in love in order for the jump to work."

That seemed... *different.* And complicated, so I didn't ask more. "How long have you been here?" Someone in the other room shouts something I don't catch. We both glance in the direction, but the volume lowers a second later.

"Two weeks maybe?"

"You don't know?"

"It's just..." He runs a hand through his brown hair, mussing it up in his signature Original Andrew ᴛᴍ move. "I have a lot of the memories of this Andrew." He waves a hand at himself. "It's hard to know exactly."

"Really? It's never worked like that for me," I say. "I always only remember what I've actually lived. Not the current timeline."

He shrugs. Clearly he doesn't have the answer to why his memories in his timeline shift aren't following the rules that mine always have.

"So, when did you end the relationship with this one?" I point to myself.

His eyes don't meet mine when he says, "Two weeks ago."

My cheeks flush. He did it right when he got here?

"Maybe I shouldn't have." He winks. "But I know how much the engagements bothered you so I won't do it again. Even if you're walking her."

Wow. That's... super thoughtful. "That's why you wouldn't propose to Ginny?"

He nods slowly.

I almost make a comment that people don't generally get engaged at age seventeen in the future. But I chicken out. Because then he'd know that the thought had crossed my mind. Still, I should probably mention it before he makes it to my time or things could get awkward really quick.

But that idea makes me want to swoon.

Maybe I won't tell him.

All the voices suddenly go silent, and then there's a crash in the front room that makes us both jump.

The girl takes over and sprints to the front room.

"Daddy!" She rushes to see her father sprawled on the floor, but he quickly gets to his feet. A small gash above his right eye drips with dark blood.

The front door is ajar, so Andrew moves to close it.

"Daddy, what happened?" she rushes from the room to get a towel from the kitchen and returns quickly to dab at her father's wound.

"Mary, I'm fine. Really," her father says, shooting a meaningful glance at Andrew.

She holds the cloth to his forehead and looks at him expectantly.

"We just had a misunderstanding. That is all."

I raise an eyebrow at him since she won't. "And what would Mama say?"

Her father's face falls at the mention of Mary's mother who left when she was nine—I'm getting the 411 on that a little late.

"You mother does not have a say," he says. "Why did you even bring her up?"

I look to Andrew for help.

"She means her grandmother," he says. "We were just talking about her and how she felt like a mother to Mary."

I look back at Mary's father like that is what my intent was all along.

"Your Grandmother Piper would—"

She glares at him again, anticipating his upcoming lie.

"Fine! She would disapprove."

Mary's face falls into one of concern. "So, don't do it!"

"Mary, I..." He looks at Andrew again. "I can't get out of this one. But it's the last one."

"Promise?"

"I promise." He sounds like he means it, and Mary believes him, but I've met enough people involved in shady business. I can see the lie lit up like a Christmas tree.

*Poor Mary.* At least it seems that I'm with her for a reason. And what was her last name? *Piper. Mary Piper.*

*Why does that sound familiar?*
I look at Andrew again, trying to piece together a memory.
*Mary Piper.*
*There's my girl.*
The girl who gets kidnapped.
It just hasn't happened yet.

# total duh moment

"Carly!" I practically squealed into the receiver. "You answered!"

"Yeah. Sorry. I feel horrible that I told you to call and then became the hardest person in the world to get a hold of."

"But you're in *Italy!* That's amazing! It's like a once-in-a-lifetime experience. You get a pass for being hard to get a hold of." I couldn't help but think that she never would have made it to Italy in the original version of her life I remembered. The one where she died. Carly was the picture-perfect proof that anyone could find the will to live. "Is now an okay time to talk?"

"Absolutely. I'm just killing time. I don't have to be at the Uffizi for a few more hours."

"Uifi—what?"

"The Uffizi. It's an art museum. Like, a really, really cool museum." I could hear the total and complete awe in her voice and took her word for it. "What's up? I assume you need to talk?"

"Yeah..." I twisted the edge of my sweater sleeve around my finger. "I don't know where to start."

Waking up that morning, my first reaction was to be panicked that I was with Mary and it was clearly *before* her kidnapping. I didn't detect any PTSD or traumatic memories in Mary last night. Meaning, I might have to experience the whole terrifying ordeal from the beginning. And maybe the rescue will be a repeat dream. But it didn't add up that Andrew was himself, because in the original Mary dream, he was walking a blond-haired guy who was definitely *not* mustache-sporting Andrew 4.0. Either way, Mary was in for trouble. A lot of it.

But this was the reason I walked with them in the first place. I may have complained about being with selfish Genevieve, who didn't seem to need me at all, but Mary would definitely need me.

The way Lucy still needed me.

"A lot on your mind?" Carly asked.

"Yeah." But I decided not to talk about Lucy or Mary. "I sort of got into it with Arianna yesterday."

"Oh? What happened?"

"I told her she needed to be my friend. Whether she believes my dreams are real or not."

"She believes your dreams are real." There was no question in her tone.

"Not lately, at least that's what she's saying."

"Hmmm."

"Is she lying?"

"Probably," Carly said, sounding thoughtful. "She's probably saying that for another reason. Is that all she said? That she doesn't believe they are real?"

I shrug, though Carly won't see it through the phone. "She says that she believes that *I* think they're real, but I should quit trying to force the belief on her."

"Oh, Ari..." I imagined Carly shaking her head in disapproval. "It sounds like she's scared."

After a silent moment I asked, "What do you think I should do?"

"I think you should prove it to her."

*What?* I wasn't expecting that advice. "How?" Wait until June ninth when Andrew shows up and prove that he actually moved up in time? "How do I prove it to her?"

"Let her piggy back into a dream. Like I did."

Mind. Blown. *Why didn't I think of that?* I slapped a palm to my forehead. "You're a freaking genius, Carly! She would *love* that! At least I think she would."

I hear the smile in Carly's voice when she said, "Make her wear the ring. Tell her that if she truly doesn't believe in your dreams, it won't work. She won't join you in the dream. But if the dreams are real, she's in for an exciting ride."

# open mouth, insert foot

"**A**re you ready?" Andrew asks as I walk down the stairs.

*Ready for what?* I wonder, but Mary pipes up, "I don't know if we should go, Drew."

*Drew?*

"Why not, darlin'?"

She throws a hand on her hip. "Well, first off because you just called me 'darlin'.' When have you ever called me that?"

"Heard it in a movie, I guess." He shrugs. "Hey, I've got an idea." He winks. "Let's go to a movie at the *drive-in.*"

She lightly punches him on the arm, but she's serious. "I mean it, Drew. I don't think it's a good idea."

"Why not?"

She walks closer to him. "Because there's been some shady stuff going on around here."

Andrew crosses his arms. "What kind of shady stuff?"

"The kind that makes me afraid for my father's safety."

He unfolds his arms and leans closer. "Have those men been here again?" he asks. "I'm starting to worry about *your* safety."

*As you should,* I think. But I don't know if I'm supposed to tell Andrew I already know what's going to happen. How will he react to the news that I've already been a future version of Mary?

And that he was there, but he was someone else? So, I mention nothing.

"Maybe we should go," I say, taking over. "It'll get my mind off of everything."

His face splits into a smile, and he offers an elbow to me.

I take it. I can tell she wants to mention something about them not technically dating anymore, but she's hoping this is a rekindling of sorts. Apparently going to the drive-in used to be their favorite date night. Long before Andrew ever showed up, I suspect.

"What are we seeing?" she asks as Andrew pulls away from her house.

"*American Graffiti.*"

"Is it a double-feature?"

"Yes, but I can't remember the name of the other one."

"As long as it isn't *The Exorcist.*" She feels worried about that. And rightfully so.

"My parents won't let me watch that one even though it's so old," I add. "So I have to be home early if that's the one."

A flash of confusion flits across his face as he pulls onto the main road, but it doesn't last long. "Emily," he says. "When did you arrive?" He glances in the rearview mirror briefly at a car that has pulled onto the road behind us.

"While we walked down the stairs."

One quick glance at me. "You were the one to change her mind about coming after all."

"Guilty. I've never seen *American Graffiti.*"

He smiles again, then puts an arm around me. I scoot closer, although I am slightly nervous that the car doesn't have seat belts.

"How long have you known how to drive?" I tease after a few minutes.

He laughs. The booming laugh I haven't heard in I can't remember how long. "You know, I *do* have memories of my current time. They're just jumbled in there with the ones from my actual past as well as the past of 1920s and 1950s Andrew."

"That sounds confusing. I only remember what I've actually lived. Which makes timeline shifts tricky in a different way."

"I do not always remember everything," he says, then brushes it off. I suppose it's too late for that to be a problem. It's unclear if he could go back to his own time if he wished. "Let's just say that I remember how to drive."

I still wish the car had seat belts.

"I'm actually glad that you are here. I think I've figured out a way to accomplish my next jump."

"Oh?"

He kisses the top of my head, causing a thrill to run down my spine. He squeezes his arm around me in a hug. It feels like an unspoken, *I'm almost there. I've almost made it. Soon I won't have to concoct plans to jump any more. We won't have to meet in secret or worry about what horrible thing those we walk with are about to go through.* He moves his arm up and over my head to turn into the theater and slowly drives along the dirt and grass to find a good spot after paying admission.

After turning the car off, he looks at me full-on.

I resist the urge to bridge the gap and kiss him here in the privacy of the car. Suddenly I'm not repelled by the mustache.

"My current mother grew up in luxury while my father's family was extremely poor."

I nod and keep my eyes trained on his, forcing myself not to stare too long at his lips.

"They met by chance at a local carnival and fell in love in one night."

"That sounds like a plot for a movie romance," I say, swooning and glancing at the large screen that is currently playing a hot dog commercial.

"Plan A is to distract one of them so they never meet."

I hate the plan already.

"Plan B is to convince them that the economic differences between them are great enough that they could never make a marriage work." As he speaks, he sounds so technical. Like he's stating facts or merely talking about the best way to make a sand-wich. Like it's an everyday—needs to be done sort of task. *Mayo, mustard, meat, cheese, lettuce. Plan B: If you're out of meat and cheese, just make peanut butter and jelly.*

"Wait." I shake my head. "You said in order to jump from the fifties you had to bring two people together," I say. "That you had to *make* them fall in love in order for the jump to happen. Now you want to make sure that *doesn't* happen?"

He stares at me blankly.

I throw my hands in the air. "Won't it make you jump back-wards? Land you back in the fifties?"

Understanding flashes on his face and he smiles. "When I said I had to bring two people together to make the last jump, I never said that it was *my* parents I had to bring together."

"But... how...?" Now I'm really confused but when he opens his mouth to further explain I hold up a hand to stop him. "Never mind," I say. I'm afraid my brain might literally explode if he tries to explain the intricacies of his time-jumping. So I ask instead, "So, they love each other?"

He nods. "They do. I have hundreds of memories of being told the story of how they met and how they overcame their differences. But the amount of knowledge I have is enough to succeed in never allowing it to happen."

"Don't do it," I say in a rush. "Don't break up two people who love each other. I get why you would wanted to prevent the marriage of people who never loved each other, like the people who were your parents when you were in 1925. But this just feels *wrong.*"

He watches me. Searching for something. "Do you want me to come?"

I know exactly what he's asking. Do I want him to continue jumping forward? Do I want him to arrive in my time so that we don't have to be walking other people to be together? Do I want him to continue on this crazy journey that once upon a time seemed impossible because a century was between us? Now that the impossible is possible, has his allure vanished? Did I only want him when I couldn't have him?

"You never asked me if I wanted you to come in the first place," I say. I don't realize I've said it until I see the look on his face. *Whoops.* I did not mean for that to come out of my mouth. Or in that tone, that inflection. "Of course, you should still come," I amend. "You've made it this far, might as well go all of the way."

You know... since there's no possibility that he could just go back to how things were. I doubted he wanted to be stuck in the seventies knowing no one. Briefly I wonder how he is coping with that. By jumping he is changing *Every. Single. Thing.* about his previous life. But that wasn't what we were discussing, and I wouldn't, I *couldn't,* change the topic when this one felt so important. "I just wonder... is there another way?"

He closes himself off. I can visibly see it as the thoughts turn in his head. He is hurt. What I have said may be irreparable. If he ever does make it to my time, how many times will he wonder if he made the right choice? How many times will he look at me and wish he'd just stayed in his original time and married Margaret?

Margaret never would have said such a thing.

Even Genevieve wouldn't have.

"Y-your first jump," I stammer. "You told me once that you just went back and... Ahem, "I clear my throat, "interrupted?"

He smiles at that memory. The smile parts the clouds between us, and I smile with him.

"Can't you just do that?"

He shakes his head. "If they love each other... that much..." He raises an eyebrow.

"Ah... I see." How would he know which time to *interrupt*? "Good point." But I still don't like it.

The movie begins playing, and I sink into him, nuzzling in the crook of his arm.

About the time in the movie with a conversation about someone's mom's car—and a swoon-worthy young Harrison Ford—

we hear a loud commotion several cars down. We crane our necks to see what is happening but can't see a thing and focus on the screen again.

A few seconds later we both jump as someone pounds on my window. I don't recognize him, but he seems to recognize me. Well... he recognizes *Mary* obviously. Glancing at Andrew, I lean forward to crank down the window only an inch.

"I have a message for your father!" the man shouts. Some spittle flies through the crack in the window and almost lands on my cheek but I jerk away. I see more of it on the man's beard.

Mary's terror rises quickly. She's afraid he's one of the men who hurt her father the other night. I'm afraid he is too. We both suspect that her father downplayed the amount of trouble he was in.

"Tuesday. By noon."

"O-okay." Her voice shakes.

"He won't like paying interest."

# travel plans

"Everything okay?" Arianna asked as we walked out to her car after school. "You've been quiet all day."

"Just..." I sighed. "I have a lot on my mind." Normally I would leave it like that. Or at least lately. But I was tired of walking on eggshells around her. "My dream last night was a bit disturbing."

She sucked in a breath as she unlocked the car. "How so?" she asked as she threw her bag in the back and scooted in the driver's seat.

I mirrored her, getting in the passenger seat, then attempted to read her expression. She looked pained somehow, but at least she was making an effort. "Andrew is in 1973."

"Oh?" She sounded skeptical.

"Yeah. We went to the drive-in to see *American Graffiti*." I watched her face as I said it, waiting for the skepticism to melt away. "And yeah, I could have Googled movies that came out that year, but I promise I was there." Maybe I shouldn't have added that part.

She sighed again and turned on the car. "I know. I guess I'm just trying to convince myself that your dreams aren't real. For all of the things you know they must be real. Well, cultural things at least. You still only get C's in history."

We both laughed as she pulled out of the parking lot.

"Anyway," I continued, a bit more at ease. "Andrew and I sort of fought about some things."

"You sound like an actual couple."

That made me blush. For so long, the idea of him and me becoming a couple was impossible. Now, I might be mere months away from it happening for real. "I guess we've progressed past the getting to know each other part," I said. "Except the fact that he has no idea what I actually look like. It's like we're Internet dating through avatars or something."

"Except you know what *he* looks like."

"True. Although he was blond in the twenties. His features are similar in each version, but also slightly different. Still, I think I'll recognize when he finally gets here."

"What did you fight about?"

"For the next jump he wants to go back and break up his current parents."

"Isn't that what he's been doing to jump forward all along? At least I assume?"

"Not always. But this time's different. This time his parents actually love each other. I don't think it's right to keep them apart."

Ari blows out a breath as she turns onto my street. "That sounds like a great plot for a movie!" She waves her free hand, emphasizing the invisible words as she speaks. "Time Traveler tries to break up happy couple before they can become a happy couple. Will he succeed? Will love prevail? Find out in this romantic drama. Coming soon!"

"It does," I agreed, laughing at her movie trailer voice and noting that she and I jump to the same line of thinking all of the time. It was the exact thing I said to Andrew when he told me the story of how his parents met. That it sounded like a great movie plot. "Except in the movie you'd want the creepy time-traveler to fail," I added.

"Obviously," Ari said, rolling her eyes.

"And if Andrew fails, he'll be stuck. He'll have to live out his life where he's at right now. Which would make him about sixty years old."

"Ah, I see the conundrum."

"Wow! Expanding our vocabulary, are we?" I teased then we both laughed again.

Ari pulled into my driveway and put the car in park. We sat there after our laughing stopped, both in an awkward, we-want-to-repair-our-friendship-but-don't-know-where-to-start cloud of awkwardness.

"I talked to Carly yesterday," I said.

"Oh?" Ari looks truly shocked. "You actually got a hold of her?"

"Yeah, she had some time before she was going to ..." I paused, trying to remember the name of the museum. "To a museum I'm not going to pronounce right so I'm just not going to try."

"Ah, the Uffizi."

My mouth fell open.

"Give me some credit!" she lightly shoved my arm. "Mom's been practicing the pronunciation nonstop." Ari shrugged. "I just picked up on it."

I sank back into the bucket seat of the car. "I'm so happy for her," I said and again was reminded of this version of her life that almost never was.

"We should go after we graduate next year." Ari suggested.

Italy with my best friend? I couldn't think of anything better. I threw my arms around Ari, surprising us both, and squeezed tight. "Let's do it!" I said as I pulled back. "But I should probably learn how to say a few things first."

"*Grazie*," Arianna said.

I stuck my tongue out at her.

"That's how you say *thank you!*"

"Wanna hang out for a bit?" I asked. There was still one more thing I wanted to bring up but didn't have the nerve quite yet. "We could do that worksheet for history together... you know, so I can bring up my C average."

"Sure." Arianna smiled and shut off the car.

A few minutes later we were both sprawled on the floor of my room with our history textbooks and notes scattered around us.

"I seriously think that your dreams should help your knowledge in the history department at least a *little*," Arianna said when once again, my answer was wrong and she flipped to the page in the book to prove that I was wrong.

"That's not the reason for the dreams," I said, my tone very light. "Plus, half of the time, I have no idea what year I'm actually in." But when your sort-of-boyfriend/not-boyfriend is there too, he's more than happy to clue you in.

"Right," Arianna dropped her pen and leaned back against the foot of my bed. "You help people." I think she was trying to sound friendly and light-toned, but it didn't quite come out that way.

"What's wrong?" I asked.

Her jaw clenched. She was trying not to cry. "Do you want to know why I don't want you to tell me about your dreams?"

"I—"

"It's because they *scare* me. When you were in that *coma...*" She shook her head and closed her eyes.

I put my pen down too. Maybe now was as good a time as ever. "You know, when I talked to Carly the other day, she suggested something."

"Oh?" Ari crossed her arms over her chest after wiping at her eyes. It didn't seem intentional, but her skeptical attitude rose like a barrier.

"You know, she sorta helped me wake up from my coma. Now that you mention it."

"She wha—?" She dropped her arms and jaw in shock. "How?"

I shrugged like it was no big deal. Even though it was kind of a huge deal. "Did I ever tell you about Grandma Grace piggybacking into one of my dreams?"

"Piggybacking?"

"She had this ring…" I jumped up to get the ring from my jewelry box. "When she wore it, she would dream-walk someone in the same time and place as me."

"Wow. Really?"

"Yeah, she uh…" But the memory of the last walk she did forced my face to fall. I cleared my throat and concentrated on keeping my voice from cracking. "She walked with Andrew's sister, Tessa, once."

If Arianna noticed my sudden change in emotion, she didn't mention it.

"I'm pretty sure the fire we were in is what caused her heart attack."

Realization colored her features. "You mean—?"

"Tessa died in the fire. Grandma died in her sleep probably right when Tessa died."

Arianna frowned. "Oh, Em!" She threw her arms around me. "I'm so sorry!"

After a moment I pulled back and wiped a tear from my cheek. "That's not why I am telling you this."

"Right. Carly."

"Yes, Carly found the ring," I showed it to her. "She wore it and walked Andrew's *other* sister Rose."

"How many sisters does he have?"

"Four? I think?" *But not anymore.* "Well, he *had* four sisters. When I knew him in 1901 I really don't know if he has any now."

"In 1973, right?"

I nodded. "Anyway, while I was in my coma, your sister wore that and walked with Rose to tell me what was happening."

"You didn't know you were in a coma?"

I shrugged. "I think I noticed that I was walking in a lot of dreams without being *me* in between at some point, but I was so caught up with what was happening with those two girls—"

"Lucy and…" Ari cut me off.

"Isabella, yes. Lucy and Isabella."

"I don't think I ever asked about Isabella, but go on."

"I was so caught up with them, that I never thought about it long enough to worry. Until Carly showed up as Rose."

Arianna nodded, but didn't say anything.

"Anyway, Andrew helped me wake up, but if it weren't for Carly…"

We both let the implications on what that could have meant sink in.

My heart pounded as I contemplated what I was going to say next. "Carly suggested that you—" I held the ring out to Arianna, but she didn't take it—"piggyback into a dream with me."

I felt a little bit awkward just holding the ring out for her when Arianna wouldn't even touch it, so I dropped my arm. *Is she refusing because she still didn't believe me? Or because she is scared?*

"Or not, no pressure. They can be intense sometimes."

"No, I want to." She sat forward with her hand held out. I gave her the ring. "They scare me because of what they do to you. Let me experience one. Who are we walking?"

"I, uh…" I was a little bit stunned that she agreed. I hadn't thought that far ahead. I guess I never expected her to agree. Walking with Mary didn't feel like the best idea, since I didn't know exactly when the kidnapping would happen. And I wasn't sure how much control I'd have with her. "I'm not sure. Let me think about it. But maybe wear it tonight?"

"Okay," she said.

I thought about Lucy as I drifted off that night. I just hoped whoever Ari walked and whatever happened wouldn't give her nightmares.

# CHAPTER 18

## nurse mauve

My entire vision is white and water-damaged. Looking very much like a road map for a rural area, cracks in the plaster congregate near the edges. A few stray ones span the length of the ceiling.

The cracks and water spots are more familiar than I'm comfortable with.

*Lucy?* I say, a little hesitant. She's never been so quiet—inside.

*Ah, Emily. You have returned.*

…

…

…

*How are you?* I ask. I don't know what else to say. *How have you been?*

*I am well.*

…

…

…

We continue to stare at the ceiling. *Why won't you see your family? I think they'd let you go home if you just—*

"If I just what?" she says aloud, startling several of the other women in the room. She sits and shoots a glare at Nancy, daring her to call for the nurse. But Nancy cowers and stares off into space, not daring to make eye-contact.

*No, Lucy. You aren't going crazy. We aren't doing this!*

*What are you going—?*

"Nurse!" I shout in the best *sane* voice I can conjure up from Lucy. "Nu-urse!"

I'd expected the burly Nurse Edith to arrive, but am shocked by the petite, auburn-haired woman who enters instead.

"Yes!" The nurse sounds out of breath. "Is everything all right?"

I swing Lucy's legs over the side, the chains attached to her ankle clanking with the movement. "I need to take a walk. I need some air."

"Of course, right away, miss!" But she doesn't approach and rushes from the room.

*What have you done?*

*I'm getting you out of here!*

*Emily, I cannot leave this place. I need to recover.*

*You're getting sick in this place!*

A moment later, the nurse returns with a key. *Right. The restraints.* She deftly unlocks the cuff and helps us to our feet.

Without a word, we walk arm-in-arm with the nurse down the hallway, down a set of stairs, and out a side door into the summer air. But not without effort. Lucy has clearly been in that bed much longer than is healthy for anyone with working legs and lungs. It's slow going, but we aren't in a hurry for anything.

"Could you give me a moment?" I ask. I need to talk to Lucy without the prying ears of the nurse who—though she seems super nice and nothing like Nurse Edith—will probably report anything she observes during this clearly out-of-character venture outside.

"Actually..." The nurse pauses, her voice suddenly strange. "I would like to stay."

My eyes shoot to her, trying to decipher her meaning and sudden change in tone.

"I, uh…" The nurse darts her eyes around, self-conscious about… something. "I think…" She closes her eyes like she's trying to figure something out. "I think that you are Lucy." She opens them again. "At least I assume that you are, by your description and this… *nurse* has heard your name at least once."

*This nurse?* I narrow Lucy's eyes. *Do you know this nurse?* I ask her.

*Of course, she's the nice one. Her name is Mauve.*

"I do not understand your meaning, Nurse Mauve," I say in the best sweet tone I can muster.

"Oh man," she says, her eyes darting back and forth as she wrings her hands together. "You see, I'm looking for my friend, her name is Emily… She told me—"

I throw my arms around Mauve's shoulders, cutting off her sentence instantly. "Ari?" I ask in her ear, maybe a little too late.

She pulls back, relief on her face. "Em?"

I nod.

*What's going on?* Lucy asks.

"It's okay," I say aloud. "Lucy, my best friend, Ari, has been worried about my dreams lately. You actually met her sister when she walked with Rose."

"Ah yes, Carly was it?" Lucy asks.

"Yes, Carly suggested that Arianna come along for the ride to see what happens in a walk, I guess."

Mauve holds her hands up, examining them. "This is so real, so lucid. I half expect myself to begin flying or for the scenery to start folding in on itself like in the movie *Inception*."

"Well… this may be a *dream* for us. But the scene won't start folding. It is real life for Lucy and Mauve." Er, maybe this was a mistake. I'm beginning to question bringing Ari with me.

"Right." Mauve says but won't stop staring at her hands.

"Okay…" I say slowly. "Look, I really don't know when I'll get to be Lucy again," My thoughts flit to Mary and how many more dreams of her I'll experience before I'm back. I could be kidnapped before I'm back with Lucy. "I need to make this count."

Mauve nods, then sits down on the grass, now examining the blades in front of her and swishing a hand through it. "It feels so real," she says to herself.

"How have you been, Lucy?" I ask, trying not to let Ari walking Nurse Mauve distract me.

"I have settled into life here, I think," she says, her voice a little far off. Which feels strangely detached even though she uses the same lips to talk as I do.

"Don't you want to go home?" I ask. "To Charles?"

"But I'm sick. I have voices in my head."

"Only me," I protest. "And I've only been here one other time before now."

She hides her thoughts from me.

"I guess you got what you wanted," I say bitterly. "You wanted to remain here, make them think that you are crazy. You wanted *me* to speak the last time we were here to ensure that." I pause, listening to any sign of a thought. "Why don't you want to go home?" I ask softly.

She shrugs. Nurse Mauve's eyes have trained on us now, but I continue to ignore her. This is too important. I just hope that somehow Mauve sees the importance of not sharing this conversation between Lucy and I with anyone else.

"Because they already think I'm crazy!" she wails, and tears stream down her face. "*I* think I'm crazy!"

"But why?" Her tears make my words sound more emotional than they are. "You know why I'm here. You know where I'm from. You're not crazy."

"I cannot go home and spend a lifetime having Charles and my family look at me that way." She hangs her head. "It's bad enough that my hands are damaged and ugly. Charles probably wishes he'd never tied himself to me at all! What kind of wife am I? Sent off to an *insane asylum*. And now he's trapped. Married to me!"

"He's not trapped, Lucy." I make her voice firm. "He loves you and wants you to get better." I pull up the memory of their engagement. I never experienced it, but it is the first memory she recalled when I first walked with her and it kind of stuck. Strong enough that it felt like it could be my own memory too. "He said it himself the day you were taken away."

"The day of my wedding," she says softly.

"Yes. He said he wanted you to get better so you can go home."

Lucy doesn't respond.

"You're not staying here," I say, "I'm getting you out. You *will* have your happy ending."

She doesn't exactly agree but doesn't disagree either. It's progress.

"Hey, Ari?"

Mauve looks up from the fabric of her dress between her fingers, she's been examining it the past minute or so. "Um, yeah?"

I smile. *Definitely Ari.* "Do you think you could make it very clear...in here"—I point to Lucy's temple—"that Mauve shouldn't tell anyone about this conversation I've had with Lucy? You know, since it sorta looks like Lucy is having this entire conversation with herself?"

"Of course, aye aye." Ari salutes us with two of Nurse Mauve's fingers, then scrunches her face in deep concentration. After a few seconds, her face relaxes again. "No worries, we're good in here."

I pray that it worked.

# it always matters

"That. Was. *Awesome!*"

I expected nothing less from Ari when she picked me up for school the next day. "I remember Carly thinking it was pretty cool too," I said, getting in her car. "Although she got to see more than the grounds of an insane asylum. If I remember correctly, she was sort of fascinated by the furniture and wall paper."

"Yeah, I *need* to do that again!"

"Okay, okay," I said.

"When are you getting Lucy out of that place?" Her voice somehow remained at the same high-volume pitch. It was starting to make my ears buzz. "I wanna help!"

"I, uh..." I trailed off, not quite sure what to say. I may have succeeded in getting back to Lucy while Ari piggybacked, but Mary also had a pull on me. I doubted I'd see Lucy again that night, and I wasn't sure Ari should be experiencing any part of Mary's story. "Maybe give me a few nights?" I said. "There's this other girl I've been dreaming lately, and I don't really want you caught up in what she's soon-to-be going through."

"Soon-to-be?" Ari's voice finally lowered. My ears were grateful.

"How do I explain this...?"

"Explain it how you always do. Every. Single. Detail." She grinned with a reassuring look.

I was so accustomed to being shut down at the mere mention of a dream, I was out of practice gathering my thoughts to spill *every single detail*.

"Her name is Mary, in 1973—"

"—73," she said at the same time. "That's where Andrew is, right?"

"Yes," I said slowly, still reeling that Ari was not only listening now, but remembering what I'd told her when I thought she wasn't listening. "Andrew doesn't know this, but I've walked with Mary before. Right after my grandma died."

"Why doesn't Andrew know?" she asked, pulling down the mirror from her visor to check her lip gloss after we parked in the school lot. "Was he not there?"

"He was..." I hesitated long enough that she put the visor back up to look at me.

"You can tell me anything, you know that right?" she assured me.

"It's not that. It's..." I paused. "It's just a bit confusing."

The first bell rang, so we exited her car.

"The first time I dreamt of her happened *after* the dreams I'm having now. If that makes any sense."

"How far after?"

"I don't know, it felt like a long time after. She'd been kidnapped. Andrew saved her—er, us."

"She's going to be kidnapped?"

"Yeah."

"Do you know when?"

I shook my head.

"What's so confusing then?"

"Well, where I'm at now, Andrew is *Andrew*. He's jumped and he's... *him*. In other words, he isn't walking with anyone."

"But when he came to rescue you...?" Ari prods.

"When he came to rescue us, he wasn't *him*. He was walking someone else."

"Then he must've jumped again, and then gone back to save you."

"I guess it's not exactly confusing if that's the truth. But it's really, really sad," I said.

"How so?"

"Because that means he'll succeed at breaking up his parents."

Ari shook her head before we parted in the hallway. "I'll stick to dreaming Lucy's time with you. Just give me the signal!"

I couldn't help but smile as I walked down the hallway. Taking Dr. Williams's advice had worked. I had taken control of my life and invited Ari into my dreams, and it felt like thing were back to normal with us. She said I could tell her anything, and I believed her. The weight of carrying all of my worries alone lightened a bit knowing that I had my best friend again.

I needed to take control in a few more areas. And I had a very good idea who was next.

---

I BUMPED INTO DUNCAN DURING THIRD PERIOD WHEN I used the hall pass.

"Look, I—" we both said at the same time, then laughed.

"Where are you off to?" I asked him.

"The library," he said. "We have a sub today who decided a movie was the best way to kill time. I asked to be excused to get ahead on some homework."

"Smart!" I said. "I probably would've texted Ari through the entire the movie, but getting a head start on homework is the smarter idea."

"What about you?" he pointed at the large block engraved with the words: Hall Pass.

I stared at the block too. "I wonder if Mr. Maxwell would notice if I didn't come back right away..."

He shrugged. "I bet he's already gone off on some fly fishing story from his trip to Alaska last summer. He found a way to tie it into cosigns during my class. It took him twenty minutes at least."

"So, I have twenty minutes?"

"Give or take," Duncan said, then gestured toward a hallway that wasn't regularly patrolled by teachers or administration.

We sat against the wall in a corner at the end of the hallway. Our knees close and almost touching, although I doubted he noticed the proximity. I certainly did.

The silence was unusually comfortable, and we sat for several moments soaking in it.

"I feel like we haven't talked in a while," he finally broke the silence. I opened my mouth to respond, but he kept going. "But I think that's mostly my fault."

I closed my mouth.

"The last time we talked you mentioned that you wanted your friends back, what with everything that was going on."

I nodded.

"How are things?" he asked. "With the lawsuit and everything?"

I shrugged. "Mom and Dad don't tell me much. They're not keeping it a secret, but they don't want me to worry about it."

"That's... good, right?"

"Yeah." I had enough on my mind without worrying about the lawsuit. Between Mary's upcoming kidnapping and planning Lucy's escape from the insane asylum, I was booked. Even though those would happen while I slept, I still felt pretty swamped. "Things with Ari are better though."

"That's good. You two talk finally?"

I almost told him about the piggybacking but thought better of it. All I needed was my former boyfriend to be walking with... Andrew of all people—if that was even possible. I couldn't even *think* about all of the issues that would come of that situation. "We talked," I said instead. "I can talk to her about the dreams again. She doesn't shut me down anymore."

I worried that he'd ask about the dreams. But he didn't. "Well, I'm glad you two made up," he leaned over to nudge my shoulder. That small contact caused my heart to race. I was suddenly desperate to do something, anything, to make contact again.

I had to say something. I'd taken control and bridged my friendship with Ari. I had to try with Duncan too. "I miss you too, Duncan," I said to the linoleum tiles on the floor. "I get that you're with Clare and that you like her, but..." I lost my nerve.

"But..." he said, nudging my shoulder again and causing my insides to do flips.

"I mean look at us!" I pointed at the empty hallway before us. "The only way we can have an actual conversation without your girlfriend interrupting or putting in her two cents is to ditch class or get a ride home when she's in the dentist's chair." I shook my head. "I'm sorry, I shouldn't be complaining about her. You *chose* her. Your loyalty is to her."

He didn't respond.

I suddenly felt a streak of courage and went with it. "Wanna hear something crazy?" I asked but didn't wait for an answer. "I know that you and I dated for a while, like several months or whatever." I didn't dare glance at him for a reaction, it wasn't exactly coming out the way I wanted, but I kept going anyway. "You know my dreams change things sometimes, right? I mean, I'm sure I've blurted out something that seemed off from whatever you remembered, but do you want to know how I remember it?"

"Remember what?"

"How we first met."

"How do you remember it?" His tone sounded wary, like he was unsure how to respond. I didn't blame him.

"It was the day after I experienced Nora's death. *The first time.* I was in the cemetery paying my respects—"

"The Rose Ritual?" he interrupted, and my head snapped to him.

"Yeah," I said, keeping my eyes on his. He held my gaze, and for once I wasn't too scared or self-conscious to look away. "You kind of came up behind me." He averted his eyes, so I looked back at the white speckled tiles beneath us. "You surprised me. I didn't recognize you, but you knew who I was."

"Wait," he said. I looked back at him. "We'd been dating about six months when you first dreamed of Nora. I remember that day, I went to the cemetery with you and, man..." He let out a whoosh of a breath. "That was a rough one."

We stared at each other for over a second. It was a long second.

"That's not the way I remember it," I said, hoping he felt the truth in my words. "I kept all of that to myself for so long. Saving Carly changed everything."

"I thought that was just..." He trailed off and shook his head. "Never mind. Go on."

"Anyway, after that day we became... friends," I said. "I didn't have any other friends—"

"What about—?" he interrupted.

"Ari wasn't speaking to me back then." I also interrupted. "You were my new friend, but also my *only* friend."

"Why are you telling me all of this?" he asked, his tone laced with hurt that he tried to hide.

I shrugged. I didn't mean to hurt him by telling him this. I just wanted him to realize how complicated everything got. "The crazy thing"—I gritted my teeth to push back the tears that threatened to build—"is that we probably would have dated eventually anyway. I had a crush on you pretty soon after we first met, and things were sort of going in that direction. You even kissed me, I think." It was so hard sometimes to decipher my memories and what happened when and where. This I did know though. We met *before* I met Andrew. Falling for Andrew had been a whirlwind event. Immediate attraction, especially after finding out that we were both dream-walkers. And the forbiddennessness of our relationship made it go from zero to sixty almost immediately.

My relationship with Duncan was slow, but steady.

"So you broke up with me because...?"

"Because I felt like I didn't have a choice!" I blurted out. "Because we were almost there, but then I woke up one day and you had all of these memories about us... and I was way far behind..." I shook my head again. "I tried to keep up, but I felt like I was drowning in it."

"Why didn't you tell me any of this?" he asked, his posture very still, and his voice barely a whisper.

"Because I didn't know how," I whispered. "And now you're with Clare." My voice broke. "So, I guess it doesn't matter anymore."

"It always matters." His voice was so low I didn't know if I heard the words right, or if it was just what my heart wanted to hear.

## CHAPTER 20

# one more day?

I had hoped to just sit back and go along for the ride when I arrived with Mary. I could hardly concentrate after that conversation with Duncan. It ended with us saying an awkward goodbye in that deserted hallway because I'd been gone from my class too long. I hardly noticed the look I got from Mr. Maxwell when I walked back in.

But Mary is zoned out watching some television program on a small black and white. A cold, barely touched, not-appetizing-at-all TV dinner sits on the tray in front of her. Her father is snoring in the recliner, and she's lopped out on the floral couch, exhausted, but unable to fall asleep. I briefly wonder what time it is but realize after walking through her thoughts that it can't be later than seven at night. She's emotionally exhausted from every-thing that has happened lately. The attack on her father. Then the threat from that man at the drive-in.

Not exactly the best environment to sit back and *go along for the ride.*

The knock at the front door wakes her up faster than a cup of coffee, and she sits bolt upright. Heart pounding, she's afraid—and frankly, so am I. Is it the men who are after her father? I doubt the kidnapping would happen here with her father home, but I can't help but worry about that too. I do my best to keep that thought to myself since she obviously doesn't know about that upcoming trauma.

We glance at her father, still asleep and snoring. I am baffled that he can sleep with such stress and threats weighing over his and Mary's heads, but when I smell the faint whiff of alcohol even from here, it's clear exactly how he sleeps so soundly.

The knock comes again, this time more tentative. Relief fills me as I jump from the couch and let Andrew inside. I doubted angry criminal types looking for their money—or whatever—would knock tentatively the second time.

Mary places a hand over her heart as we lead Andrew to the small kitchen. "I was afraid you were *them*," she says before preparing a pot of coffee.

He removes our hands from their busy work and pulls us into a gentle embrace. I feel the cool metal of his ring against the back of my neck when he reaches beneath Mary's hair to tilt her head up to look at him. "Emily?"

I nod slowly. Mary's fear of the future overwhelms us both. I suppose I have good reason since I know what is coming. Again, I banish that knowledge from my thoughts.

He leans down to kiss me gently. Briefly. His weird mustache tickles my nose. "She's worried?" he asks.

"Yes. Those men rattled her, and I don't blame her for that."

"I suppose you now wish you still walked with a spoiled Genevieve whose problems were less than clear and less than terrifying?"

"Yes... and no," I say. "Mary needs me. That's why I'm here."

He doesn't respond and lets me get back to my coffee making.

"I may be jumping tonight," he says after a quiet moment filled only with the low hum of the television in the other room and Mary's father's snoring.

"You've decided to break them up."

"It is the only way."

"I don't think it is," I say, but won't look at him. "I think you should find another way."

"You won't talk me out of it." Andrew's walls go up immediately. "It's happening tonight."

I turn to look at him in the eyes. "I think it's important that you stay a while," I say. I don't know if I should tell him about the kidnapping, but suddenly I'm afraid that if he doesn't know about it, if he doesn't find out about it, he won't come back to save her.

"Look, I know that you don't feel it's the *right* thing to do, but it's for the best."

"You said so yourself that your current parents love each other. How is that *for the best*?"

"Because they're miserable! I can tell that my mother misses her former life and my father wishes he could give that to her. They both try to hide it, but it is clear that they would be better off if they had ended things when they were young so they both could find someone in their own worlds. Anyway, I've narrowed down a date. I have a plan. I think I can make it work."

I turn back to the now hot coffee and fetch some clean mugs from the cupboard and fill them before sitting at the small table across from Andrew. I take a couple of scalding sips, unsure what to say to make him stay as long as possible. "Could you at least wait a couple of days? Maybe even a week before you try?"

"Why wait?" His look is incredulous... and *exhausted*.

*Because I need you to know about Mary so you'll come back.*

"I am beginning to wonder if you want me to jump forward at all."

Here we go again.

"Emily. I am ready to stop. I truly am. Jumping and readjusting to a future life is utterly exhausting. But I thought it would be worth it."

"Andrew, I—"

"Say the word," he says, interrupting. "Say the word and I'll stay here."

"No! It's not that, I just…" I almost blurt out the dream I had so long ago that hasn't happened yet. But I don't want Mary to know. I don't want her to live the next *whatever* in fear. I'll be here when it happens, but I don't want her to know before. "Could you just wait one day? Please? One more day?"

He doesn't even finish his coffee or kiss me goodbye before he rushes out the door in a huff. He didn't have to say it again for me to know that he's jumping tonight.

Maybe I can stop it from happening.

Maybe I can go back and make sure his parents don't break up. It might be a good idea. It might buy me a bit of time for him to find out what is going on with Mary. And then he can jump, because I know he won't be himself when he saves her.

He just needs to know that he needs to save her.

*Crash!* The loud chinking of breaking glass stabs though the quiet house. I run to the front room to find Mary's father, now wide awake and too stunned to wipe the drool from his mouth.

When I follow his gaze, I realize—and so does Mary—that by the location of the gaping hole in the glass of the window, and the location of the large brick that sits on the shag carpet, it flew mere inches above his hairline.

# good news

I needed to keep them together somehow. I had to. Somehow.

But if I was going to succeed, I had no idea how, let alone *when*, to even attempt preventing Andrew from breaking up his current parents. It was impossible.

I groaned. It seemed like a good idea at the time, arguing him on the point, but I was an idiot to drive Andrew away before I gleaned any information that was useful about his plan. He could be gone by the time I was back with Mary. And then what?

Andrew had jumped from the fifties without me ever meeting him there. He didn't elaborate, but I know it took him a long time to get *out* of the fifties. Even though I went straight from Genevieve—where Andrew was Andrew 2.0—to Mary—where he was mustache-wearing Andrew 4.0—with only one waking day for me in between.

Time-travel crap was so confusing sometimes.

When I walked into the kitchen, I was met with two giddy expressions directed right at me that they tried unsuccessfully to hide.

"What?" I asked my parents, so surprised at their moods that my own current dilemma was forgotten. "What's with the smiles?"

"We have good news!" Mom said, clapping once.

I dropped my backpack to the floor and sat in the nearest chair. "What is it?" Their energy was infectious, and I felt myself feeling happy too, though I didn't know what I was supposed to be happy about just yet.

They exchanged a look before looking back at me. "It's about the trial," Dad said.

"Really?" Now I was *really* curious. "You're excited about something dealing with the trial?"

"You don't have to testify!" they blurted together, not quite in unison.

I lost all of the air in my lungs. "What?" I croaked.

"Well... possibly," Dad amended. "There is a taping of one of your sessions with her that might be incriminating enough, but the lawyers did ask if you'd be willing to meet with them for a few questions."

I nodded. What a relief! Testifying was the last thing I wanted to do, the last thing I thought I'd ever have to do. But if it would help prevent her from doing what she did to me to someone else, I was willing to help. And now all they needed from me is a little chat with our lawyers. I could definitely handle that.

That being said, I was in more than a daze when I walked into the school that morning while Ari jabbered on about something.

I was a terrible friend.

"Something on your mind?" Ari asked quietly after a silent moment. Like she read my thoughts.

"Yeah, I'm sorry, Ari," I said. "I'm just a bit distracted. Mom and Dad told me this morning that I probably won't have to testify against Dr. Shew."

"Really?" she whined like it was the worst thing ever. "Like, you don't get to sit up on the stand and talk about all of the horrible stuff that woman did to you? Will my hair scissors be evidence? They should be because that's what you used to..." She nodded at my still-healing arm.

I smiled. "You still have those?" I thought for sure she would've tossed them.

"I thought they might be needed for evidence."

"But I dug the thing out myself," I said. "Why would they need to be used for evidence against Dr. Shew?"

She shrugged. "Because you wouldn't have needed to dig it out if she hadn't put it there in the first place."

She had a point.

"So, what were you saying when we walked in?" I asked, "I'm sorry, my mind has been in ten different places this morning."

"I was just brainstorming how we're going to get Lucy out of that insane asylum."

That made me feel even worse. Poor Lucy. In all of the craziness of everything else, she was getting pushed to the wayside of my thoughts. I had to make time to walk her really soon. My control wasn't quite as good as Andrew's, but with practice maybe I could walk her more often on purpose.

"Any ideas?" I asked Ari when arrived at our lockers.

"Break her out?" she offered, as she spun her combination lock. "That place didn't seem like it was locked down too much. What if we just help her run?"

"But what if they put her right back?" I argued, pulling out my books for homeroom. "She can't go to Charles if she runs. We have to come up with something that gets her discharged and cleared of any mental illness. She needs to get her happy ending. She deserves that."

"So... we do that. We convince the doctors that her *insanity* was temporary and she's better now. That doesn't seem too hard."

"Easier said than done," I said, closing my locker. "It feels like Lucy doesn't want to leave. She won't even allow her family or Charles to visit."

"So... we go in and figure something out?" Ari was determined, and I loved it. It was nice having someone else thinking up solutions with me.

"That's a great idea." I smiled at her and we fell into step again walking to our classes.

"Yeah, and with me walking that nurse, I bet we can do it."

"I hope so." But first problems first. Preventing Andrew from leaving was first priority. He couldn't leave 1973 until he knew he had to come back. "Tomorrow night," I decided as the first bell rang. "I have to take care of something. I'm not even sure will work, but I have to try and it has to be tonight."

"Anything I can do to help?" She sounded hopeful.

It was tempting. It might be easier having someone else there I could trust. But I didn't even know if I could figure out how to get there myself. Or what I would be walking into. It could be dangerous. It could be painful. It could be traumatic, and I wasn't willing to allow that to happen to my best friend. "I can handle it," I said, even though it was probably a lie. Still, there was nothing she could do to help, so it probably was not a lie. "You keep brainstorming ways to get Lucy out."

I was afraid to see a disappointed frown on her face, but it never showed. Instead, I saw a different look. One that I think meant she was glad to be finally helping. One that I think meant she was glad to finally share this part of my life. This part of my life that filled me with such meaning and purpose. I helped people in my dreams. And now she was able to do the same alongside me. It was a good feeling.

"I'm on it," she said. "Oh, and while you were in your daze about not testifying against your old shrink, you probably missed the most important part of what I was telling you."

"Okay. What was the most important part?"

"That's how I knew you weren't listening. I knew it would snap you out of whatever was going on in your head once you heard it. And it's totally just a rumor, but I think it's for real. Like really real."

"And?" I asked, a bit impatient. She was definitely enjoying stringing me along with this information. "What's this rumor?"

"Seriously I think it's really real. And not just a rumor."

"Okay... what is it!?"

She moved closer and lowered her voice. "Duncan broke up with Clare yesterday."

# betty

*lick. Clack. Click. Clack.* The streetlights cast a strange glow as the rain streams down. She hugs the umbrella closer, trying to put herself as close to the center of its protective covering as possible.

*Click. Clack. Click.* Her expensive heels clack against the wet pavement as she hurries along, rushing home. *I shouldn't have stayed so late tonight only to be caught in this downpour,* she scolds herself.

I hang back and let events play out since I have no clue where or why I am here. Or even who she is. But I keep my senses keyed up for whatever is coming.

Her stockings are wet, and so is the bottom of her taffeta dress that peeks underneath her favorite red wool coat that matches her lipstick. (I take her word for it—I can't currently see her lips.) No matter how carefully she walks, her knees continue to kick the skirts out beyond the protection of the umbrella. It doesn't help that the rain is coming down at an angle.

How she longs for a nice warm bath and a glass of wine right now.

The street is mostly deserted at this time of night. Mostly.

Everyone has gone home to supper and are sitting cozily around the television in their dry homes watching *Father Knows Best.*

*Father Knows Best.* I rack my brain and try to pluck out a memory of when she has watched it. Maybe it will help me guess what time I'm in, but all I find is that she isn't going to be home in time to catch the show. Although she doesn't seem sad about that fact.

*Click. Clack. Click.*

A couple, who appear to be arguing, clog the sidewalk up ahead. *What could they possibly be talking about in this weather? And why didn't either of them think to bring an umbrella?* She wonders only for a second before deciding it must be a lovers' quarrel.

Casually, she watches them as we get closer. The woman is clearly crying. The man is talking in low tones, using elaborate hand gestures. Then he hangs his head and puts his head in his hands.

*Click. Clack. Click.*

"It might be best to cross the street," says a man leaning against the building next to me, hunching beneath the awning. "You know, let the heartbreak play out so they can go their separate ways." She is surprised that she didn't notice the amber glow of his cigarette, or him, until now. But huddled against the dark brick wearing a black trench coat and hat, he is easy to miss. She eyes his cigarette with envy. She hasn't had one since lunch.

She ducks underneath the awning next to him and closes her umbrella. She doesn't like to intrude on stranger's lives, plus, she really wants to smoke. "Mind if I wait them out here with you?" she asks, reaching into her bag for her own pack of Winstons. The man has a match lit and waiting before she pulls one out. *Smooth.*

I want to gag, but we stand in silence for several moments while they enjoy the calming cloud around us.

"Do you know them?" she finally asks, pointing at the couple.

He sucks in a drag slowly and releases it just as slowly before answering with a shrug. "Naw, I mean I've seen 'em around of course."

She glances down the street to see if she recognizes either of them, but with the haze of the rain and muddled street lamps, it's hard to tell. "Then how do you know it's a heartbreak?"

"Isn't it—isn't it obvious?" he stammers and points at them again. "Why would they be out here otherwise?"

She studies them again as a car passes by, making the woman's brown hair and purple coat flash in the headlights.

*Ella.*

"Oh dear," she says and stomps out her unfinished cigarette into the wet concrete. *Thank you, whoever you are, I say. Maybe I won't puke when I wake up.* She ignores my comment or doesn't hear it and says, "I should go to her, that's my friend—"

"I really suggest that you leave them alone," the man interrupts, placing a hand on hers before she can open her umbrella again. She looks at him, and something about his smirk, about the way his hair is tossed and the stubble on his chin, she knows immediately who he is though they've never met.

*The scum himself,* she thinks. *Ella's ex-fiance.*

And I am almost certain Andrew is behind the dark eyes of this man.

"*You* did this?" she asks, ripping her hand away. I try not to give away that I'm here. I can't let Andrew know, though I have no idea how I even made it here. *But I did it. Somehow.*

The couple down the block must be his current parents. And here he is, successfully breaking them up. I have to do something. And fortunately, this girl wants to interfere too.

"He needed to know."

"Look, it was her business not to tell him about you," she says. "They're *happy*. At least they were until you ruined things."

"*We* were happy," he retorts and won't let go of her hand.

"No, Ella was miserable." She wrenches her hand away. "Now if you'll excuse me, I must go save my friend."

He still has a grip of her umbrella, so she leaves it in his hands and stalks out into the rain.

Ella is now alone on the sidewalk, and we watch the love of Ella's life walking slowly in the opposite direction.

"Ella!" we call out to her as we rush her direction.

Her eyes widen in surprise at seeing her friend. "Oh, Betty!" she says, then bursts into sobs as we reach each other. Ella buries her sopping curls into the coat that gets more wet by the second.

"C'mon," Betty says, leading her friend around the corner, "Let's go to Pop's Diner and get you dry."

"What about you?" Ella's glistening eyes look up at ours, "What are you doing out in this storm?"

"Got caught late at the office again," Betty says. "And I forgot my umbrella." She squeezes the shoulder of her friend. "It's not a long walk."

Minutes later we are huddled in the booth nearest the radiator with their coats hanging and dripping side by side. The purple and red lean against each other, arm against arm, the same way they were hanging beside each other in the department store when they first saw them only months ago. Like they were made to be friends. Like Ella and Betty.

"He's back in town," Ella laments.

"Yeah, the little snake was slinking just down the block," Betty says as the jukebox changes tracks. "I ran into him."

"You *saw* him?" Ella is mortified.

"He was skulking like a vulture," Betty says. "Probably waiting until you were alone."

Ella shudders on the other side of the table as Frank Sinatra begins to croon the classic, "Young At Heart." Fortunately, our waitress arrives with our hot mugs. Ella huddles over hers for several moments, staring at the center of the table with red-rimmed eyes. Betty and I let her have her moment as we sip the hot cocoa in front of us even though we are both dying to find out what the exchange was about out on the street.

I have an inkling...

The door chimes, and Ella's eyes widen.

"You've got to be kidding me—" Betty begins to say as she turns around, but it's William Harker who walks in the door. Not *him*. She stops herself. Instead, she moves across the table to sit next to Ella, leaving the bench she formerly occupied available for Ella's beau. "I'm staying right here," Betty says quietly, squeezing her friend's hand before William joins them.

He looks worse than a drowned rat. Brown hair dripping streams of water down the side of his cheeks and along his neck. His shirt soaked and suctioned to his chest. He looks freezing, and his eyes are a light gray, but are full of warmth.

"I should've told you about him," Ella says, but then averts her eyes back to the table. "He wasn't good to me, Billy. He didn't have what we have." She moves to touch his hand but seems to think better of it and lifts her mug to take a sip instead.

He runs a hand through his hair, spraying some of the water out from it. I know that Andrew isn't walking him, but that one gesture makes me smile at the family resemblance. William's eyes dart to me, probably seeing the sneaking smile.

"Could ya give us a minute, Betty?" he asks.

"Lemme help," Betty says. "Bill, you gotta know that things are over between Ella and that... *snake.* They were over long ago."

He shakes his head.

"Yeah, their parents thought they'd be a good match, being business partners and all, but that man ain't nothin' like his parents. He's a waste of space if you ask me."

William shakes his head again. "It ain't about him, El." His eyes warm again when he looks back at Ella.

Her eyes meet his with the same warmth.

"It's about us." His tone lowers to almost a growl.

"W-what about us?" Ella asks, her voice small.

William makes a frustrated face and twists his mouth. "It's about where I come from and where you come from."

"Billy, I told you I don't care—"

"No!" he interrupts. "Money matters in the world, El, and

you should be with someone who can..." He pauses and stares at his rough fingertips. "Who can give you the things you deserve."

Betty is at a loss. She doesn't know what to say. She *agrees* with him. William Harker is poor. Like, *really* poor. And Ella comes from a wealthy family full of comforts and extravagance. When Ella broke off her former engagement, her parents didn't disown her as she had feared they might, but they made it very clear that she needed to find someone of the same caliber—or station. Or else they would.

I can't find a single memory where Ella ever voiced her fear to Betty, but she's read it in a thousand looks and conversations since Ella met and fell for William Harker.

"Look," I say, taking over. "You two were meant for each other. You two love each other." *You two are good to each other,* Betty wants to add but it doesn't come out.

The couple looks up from the table finally and at each other. There is clear and absolute adoration in their expressions. The feeling is palpable. Shooting streaks of invisible fireworks dart back and forth from his eyes to hers. Like Cupid's arrows as cheesy as that sounds.

No, these two ripped the arrows from the cherubim and kept them all to themselves, falling more and more in love with each passing second. If they could live forever, it would never be enough time to be together. It's gag-worthy. It's romantic. I have never seen two people more in love with one another than these two are. Romeo and Juliet were a couple of infatuated kids compared to these two. *Okay, maybe Romeo and Juliet were a couple of infatuated kids anyway, but that was beside the point.*

They cannot be ripped apart.

"Don't let a difference in how much *money* you have determine that you can't be together," I continue. "You'll work it out." I wish I had some stock advice to pass along, or a winning race-horse to bet on so they could make it big so that money was a non-issue.

He shrugs and smiles. He's caving, and I cannot help the broadening smile that splits my face to see it.

Ella looks hopeful and dares to smile too.

Neither of them can take their eyes off one another and suddenly both Betty and I feel like we are intruding.

We slide from the bench, "Now I'll leave you two alone," Betty says, retrieving her red coat.

William tears his eyes from Ella's face long enough to stand and help Betty with her coat. "Thanks, Betty," he says as she slips her arms into the still-wet sleeves. "Hey, and you deserve better too," he says quietly.

Betty's eyes begin to water as flashes of her horrible boyfriend flit through her memory. She looks at her friend still sitting in the booth. Ella smiles up and nods in agreement. I see through Betty's memories—the reasons for staying at the office so late, her volunteering for extra work, extra responsibilities, extra anything to keep her in the safety of her office building just a bit longer.

All so she can make the excuse not to see him. He sees it as being driven and ambitious though he doesn't have the qualities in himself.

But they've been together for so long. Everyone expects them to get engaged soon. Her family loves him.

But he's horrible.

*This is what she needs me for.* The real reason I am here.

"You're right," I say to Betty's friends. "I'm marching over there right now and ending it."

Ella jumps from her seat to wrap her arms around her friend. She's crying again. "Do it, Betty! You deserve to be happy too."

William looks worried when Ella pulls away and slides back into the booth. "Do you want me to come along? Wait outside?"

"Naw," she says. "I can do this." I file through her thoughts, making sure that she won't be in any physical danger. She seems confident, but I'm not quite so sure. "But maybe you could check in on me later? Say in twenty minutes?" I add, not knowing exactly what we'll be walking into.

William nods with a serious face. "El and I will just happen to walk by."

*Thank you,* she mouths at the happy pair before they go back to gazing into one another's eyes again. I only hope that they can look away long enough to keep track of the time.

We walk out with a smile on our faces. We did it. We made sure William and Ella wouldn't allow a small thing like money break them apart. Andrew will just have to find another way to jump. There *has* to be another way.

Normally I would bow out about now since my mission is accomplished, but I have to do something for Betty now. She needs me.

# freaking genius

For the first time in... I don't know, *forever* I woke up with a smile after a not-so-fun memory dream.

Betty's boyfriend was the *worst*. He was borderline abusive verbally and emotionally. It was hard to imagine how such a strong woman like Betty ended up with him in the first place. It made perfect sense that she tended to work late just so she wouldn't have to see him.

But I helped her break up with him, and she was walking on air afterward! Ella and William came by, but they weren't needed at all.

Maybe that's why I woke up with a smile even though the actual breakup was pretty horrible. Because I helped her. I had purpose in being there— besides the obvious/not-so-obvious need to keep Ella and William stay together. I helped Betty have the courage to do something. I was her moral support. Even though she didn't know I was there.

I stayed in bed for a while after I woke up. It was Saturday, and I had nowhere to go, so I stayed put and let my mind wander at leisure.

Ella and William were dreamily in love. It was so cute, and I was so glad that I helped convince them to stay together. Andrew would just have to find another way to jump up in time. There had to be another way. He would find another way. I was confident.

And that gave me time to let him know, or for him to find out about Mary's upcoming kidnapping. Ugh... I was *not* looking forward to that. I don't know what was worse, *being* kidnapped, or knowing that it was coming but not knowing exactly *when* it was coming.

But I had time. Maybe I could save Lucy tonight. I still wasn't sure how I'd save her from that place, but I would find a way. I owed that to her.

I stared at my ceiling as I considered some possibilities to help her, but my mind wandered more and soon an even bigger smile crept up my face.

*Duncan broke up with Clare.*

I hadn't seen him since Ari threw that that little bit of *ginormous* news at me yesterday, and I had no idea why he'd been absent, but at least now I had time for the news to sink in. I had all weekend to absorb and figure out exactly how I felt about that fact.

I considered texting him, but he'd been absent from school yesterday and I didn't know why. I didn't want to interrupt in case he didn't want to be bothered.

Maybe I should bother him, I thought. We were friends after all. *Yeah, I should text him and make sure he's okay.* He might need a friend right now. After all, he just broke up with his girlfriend. He's got to be at least a little bit sad about that right?

I sat up and reached for my phone plugged into the wall right as Mom walked in my room.

"Good, you're awake," she said. "We're meeting with the lawyers in an hour. They need to ask you some questions and make sure that they don't need you to testify."

My heart sank. "Why do your lawyers always want to meet on Saturdays? What kind of monsters are they?" I asked.

She shrugged and walked over to open my curtains, letting the morning light in. "The kind that will hopefully make sure that doctor will never practice psychiatry, or medicine for that matter, again." She walked back out of the room.

Begrudgingly, I got up to get ready.

---

Is tonight the night? I read the text from Ari covertly. Mom and Dad were doing the talking now, asking questions of the lawyers: an older man with a thick head of hair that looked suspiciously fake, and a younger man who looked like he was balding prematurely and couldn't be older than twenty-five. They were a strange pair. They had pretty much decided a half hour ago that I wouldn't need to testify. Again. Or I guess reconfirmed that fact. There was some incriminating footage of one of my sessions with Dr. Shew that was enough so they didn't have to put a teenager on the stand. But the talk about the upcoming trial still had to be discussed so I was stuck listening anyway.

*Let's talk. Come get me,* I texted back, then slipped a note to Mom asking if I could leave if I got a ride. She thankfully agreed.

Fifteen minutes later I was in the passenger side of Arianna's sister's silver car heading to the grocery store of all places.

"So, your mom's actually going to cook tonight?" I asked, a little baffled. All I knew of Arianna and Carly's mother was that she used to be horrible. She screamed whenever she found the light left on in the bathroom. She berated Ari and her sister on a daily basis. Ari routinely sought refuge at my house after school, and many times overnight, just to get a break.

Recently their mother had been more MIA than anything. She was *never* around. I think that's why Carly came home from school so often. She knew Ari spent most of her time at home alone. I tried to invite her to as many family dinners as possible, but with my recent coma and dream issues, I was sort of a really horrible friend to her lately.

*Ugh.* I felt awful. I'd even missed her birthday. I still hadn't made up for that. That would change. I made a mental note to speak with her boyfriend, Brian, at school Monday to plan a special surprise un-birthday party for her. It would be epic. It had to be. I'd make certain it was.

I made another mental note to get a hold of Carly ASAP to make sure the party was up to Ari's epicness standards.

"Yeah, she's gone through this whole rehab, anger-management training or whatever, and she suddenly has the urge to make stroganoff of all things." Ari was trying to sound nonchalant about the whole thing, but I could hear the excitement in her voice at a meal that required more than throwing a dish into the microwave and calling it dinner. "Do you think we should get the Hamburger Helper version? You know… since it's her first time making it?"

"Is that what she asked you to pick up?"

"No, she gave me a list of ingredients if you can believe that!" She gave me a sideways glance that was meant to look skeptical but didn't fool me. She was stoked.

We pulled into the parking lot next to the cart return, and I recognized another car just a couple of slots down that made my heart do a little flip. When we got out of the car, I eyed Ari to see if she also recognized his car. If she did, her expression didn't show it.

"So… tonight?" Ari asked as we walked through the automatic doors.

I scanned the immediate area for him, but he wasn't currently in sight.

"Em?" Ari asked as she grabbed one of the small carts.

"Oh, sorry," I said and shook my head. "Yeah, let's get Lucy out of that place tonight."

"Great!" She did a happy jump. "What's the plan? How are we going to get her out?" I could hear the excitement in her voice even without seeing the smile on her face. Walking in dreams for her was like an adventure. Yeah, she knew about all of the horrible stuff I'd experienced over the years, but she hadn't experienced any of it. To her, walking with that nurse, going back to help Lucy was like an eleven-year-old going to California to the mouse parks for the first time.

"The plan…" I said, repeating her word. I thought for a minute while she rifled through the onions like she knew how to pick a good one.

"Yeah, she's in there because of you, right?"

That reminder made my guilt alarm go off. "Yep. It's my fault." And that was one of the reasons why I had to get her out. It was my fault. "But even when I'm not there, she pretends I am," I said, lamenting a bit. "It's like she *wants* to stay there."

"Do you think that's why she's still there?"

Arianna was a freaking genius! "That's it!" I shouted louder than necessary. My thoughts raced with the obvious solution. "Why didn't I think of that before?" I awkwardly hugged my friend while Arianna gripped the cart. A mom with three kids in one of those carts with the cars in the front passed us by with all eyes on us.

"What did I say?" Ari's expression and tone were all confusion.

I used my hands to talk as we walked along the meats. "She's in there because of *me*. Because they thought she was crazy with voices in her head," I said. Ari eyed me with a strange look.

"Right…" she said slowly. "We sort of just went over that."

"So, in the past, I was able to take over for Lucy, you know… talk for her, act for her and so on."

"Why did you do that?" Ari asked, a little horrified. "Why *would* you do that? It seems wrong."

"I did it only when she needed me to." Memories of taking over to prevent Charles from walking out on her, or finding the words when Lucy couldn't formulate them herself. She'd done the same for me when I was at a loss for words around Andrew. I kind of missed those days. Now that he'd jumped, we'd never do that again. Lucy had forgotten that Andrew even existed. Lucy, Andrew, and I would never be in the same room ever again. I banished that sad thought from my head and continued, "And now she needs me to."

"Take over?" Ari asked. Clearly my line of thinking was not making any sense.

"Yes!" I shouted again. "If I take over Lucy, I think I can make her look... I don't know... *better?* You know, convince the doctor that she's better and doesn't need to be in that place anymore."

Ari's look was skeptical again. "And you think that will work?"

Now I doubted myself. "Well, maybe it won't work on the first try. But I can get the ball rolling. Maybe I can get her out in a few days."

Ari's expression changed again. "Do you think you can really do that?" Now her look was more awed. Like she was impressed that my abilities really reached that high.

Her look gave me renewed confidence. "I think I can really do that."

"Duncan!" Ari said as we rounded onto the next aisle.

# smiling hearts

"Oh hey, Arianna. Emily." Duncan dropped his tone when he said my name, although it was slightly melancholy to begin with anyway.

"Hey, Duncan," I said in a small voice and attempted to shake off my sudden awkward feeling. I glanced at his basket full of junk food.

"Are you having a party?" Ari asked, pointing at his basket.

He looked at it a little self-consciously. Was it all for him? He had a large bag of Spicy Nacho Cheese Doritos, Twizzlers, Starbursts, those gross orange peanut-shaped marshmallow things, three twenty-ounce sodas, and more that I couldn't see buried lower in his basket. "Not exactly," he said. "What are you two doing here on a Saturday morning?" He looked confused by the items in Ari's cart.

"Em asked me to spring her from the lawyer's office," Ari said. "And Mom's making stroganoff for dinner tonight, so I told her I'd pick up the ingredients she needed since I was already out."

"Spring you?" Duncan asked me. I was baffled that he was more curious about that than he was about Ari's mom actually planning to cook. He knew her history almost as well as I did.

I nodded. "They wanted to make absolutely certain that they

didn't need me to testify at Dr. Shew's trial, so we had a meeting with them this morning."

"On a Saturday?" he asked.

I shrugged. "I was surprised too."

"So do you have to?" he asked. "Testify, that is?"

I moved closer to Duncan to make way for an elderly couple trying to get by, then felt Ari's eyes move from me to Duncan. I could hear the smile in her voice when she said, "I'm going to get the rest of this list, Em," she said. "You guys go ahead and catch up."

I glanced at her briefly. "Okay," I said, then turned back to Duncan. We moved to the side of the aisle since it suddenly became busier. "No, I don't have to testify," I said, answering Duncan's question. "They found some video evidence, I guess? Of one of my sessions with her."

His eyes widened. "What was on the tape?"

"I dunno. They didn't show it to me."

"But aren't you curious?"

"I guess, but it's not like I said anything in those sessions that was super incriminating."

"But you talked about the—about your dreams in them right?"

"Yeah, so?"

"Aren't you worried about that getting out?"

"Why?" I asked, suddenly wondering why he was getting worked up about it. "Do you really think the judge or whoever is going to believe the dreams are real? And if they do believe, what does it matter?"

"It matters because I don't like the idea of other crazy doctors wanting to experiment on you." Duncan reached out to grab my hand with his free one and squeezed it gently. His hand was warm, and he thankfully didn't let go.

The sudden speed of my heart made my brain stutter though, and the resulting words that came out were fast and high-pitched. "I think Dr. Shew was the only doctor who wanted to experiment on me," I said. "I honestly don't think any other doctor would believe the dreams were real. That's what my parents have always thought."

"That they were nightmares?"

"I think *night terrors* is the word they like to use," I said. "But yeah."

Duncan set his basket on the linoleum floor and tested the shelves of uncooked pasta before leaning against it. He still didn't let go of my hand. Bravely, I moved even closer and leaned with one shoulder against the shelves too.

I supposed that Dr. Williams believed the dreams were real, but I didn't feel like mentioning it now. Not with something so delicate and vulnerable that was building between us in that moment. I didn't want to break the spell.

"What's all of the snack food for?" I asked, pointing to his basket, hoping it was a safe-enough topic that he'd keep holding my hand.

It wasn't.

"I, uh..." With his now-free hand—mine was suddenly cold from its absence—he moved as if he intended to pick it back up from the floor but decided against it. He wouldn't meet my eyes, though I kept mine trained on his face, trying to read him. "It's, uh..." he said, pausing again. Finally he shrugged as if defeated, and glanced at me briefly before saying. "Eating junk food is kind of how I cope when I'm having a bad day."

"Did...?" I hesitated, did he want me to pry? Did he want me to ask what was wrong or mind my own business? "Did something happen?" I ached to take back his hand. Heck, I ached to wrap my arms around him, here in the public grocery store next to the angel-hair and penne pasta. I ached to touch his cheeks and force him to look at me again.

He was hurting, clearly, and I had no idea why.

Briefly he glanced at me again, the green flecks in his eyes flashing against the gray like a strange lightning storm. "Not exactly." But he looked away just as quickly. "It's nothing really..."

He didn't want to tell me. That stung a little, but I couldn't blame him I supposed. I wasn't like his *girlfriend* or anything. He didn't have to tell me his deepest darkest secrets.

But we were friends. "Duncan," I said, moving my head in attempt to meet his eyes again. I got about one second before he stared at the floor again. "You know about my dreams, you know I've seen and dealt with some hellish things. Whatever it is, I might be able to help, or at least be a listening ear." Right then a shopper needed the specific brand of linguine noodles we were blocking, so we moved.

Duncan picked up his basket and walked down the aisle. I'm pretty sure he intended me to walk with him because his pace was slow and he didn't shoo me away or say goodbye. I fell into step with him as we passed by the marinara and alfredo sauces. I didn't miss the fact that he held his basket with his outer hand, leaving the one closer to me available. I was really, *really* tempted to take it. I even felt brave enough to do it, but was afraid I'd be too scared to bring up the topic again.

"You don't have to tell me," I said, hoping he would anyway.

"I know you've been through a lot," he said. "And I know you're tough enough to handle it... mostly."

"Mostly?" I said aloud but didn't mean to. I bit my tongue hoping my comment didn't deter him from continuing.

He glanced at me with a ghost of a smile. "Yeah, mostly. It's just, uh..." Another pause.

We'd reached the end of the aisle near the checkout counters. He scanned the lines then walked over to the self-check lines.

"Now really isn't the best time." We stood behind another couple waiting for one of the machines to vacate.

"Um, yeah, of course," I said a little more chipper than intended. "The grocery store isn't the best place to spill your guts."

The couple took the next machine.

He looked at me, finally looked at me, as if searching for something or wanting to say something but trying to find the courage to say it. It lasted at least three seconds before someone behind us cleared their throats. Another machine had opened up.

We walked toward it, and Duncan quickly rang up his processed food and sugar, then whipped out a twenty to pay for it all.

When he was finished, we shuffled to the front of the store to wait for Ari to finish, or perhaps for Duncan to say goodbye to me so he wouldn't be grilled anymore and could slink off to lick his wounds—whatever they were—in peace.

It dawned on me that he might be upset about the Clare thing and their recent breakup. *Of course! Why wasn't that my first thought?* I chided myself. *Oh that's right, because I always assumed he never really liked her.* I'd assumed he was still pining over me. How could I be so self-absorbed and stupid! I'd been told that he was the one to break it off, but that could be wrong. Maybe it was her! Maybe it was her and he wasn't expecting it or wanting it to happen! Maybe he was all torn up and *devastated.*

"I heard about you and Clare," I said, not even trying to hide the defeat in my tone.

He nodded once but didn't say anything. His body language revealed he at least intended to stand with me until Ari was finished, because he wasn't building up to say goodbye just yet.

"Is that why...?" I pointed to the bags he carried unable to finish my sentence.

"Oh! *Hell* no!" he said a little too quickly. "I mean..." His neck reddened. "Sorry about that... I mean, no, the junk food isn't because of my break up with her." He met my eyes finally without hesitation. "I'm over that. Besides, it was a mutual thing anyway." He was so flippant about it. It made my heart smile.

"Really?" *It was really mutual?* That shocked me.

"Yeah, she wanted to end things too."

"She did?" Still shocked. For a girl who was so intent on claiming what was hers whenever I was around, I was having a hard time believing *that.* "Can I ask why?" I said. "Or is that too personal? I'm sorry."

"No," he said, laughing for the first time since running into him. "She, uh…" another pause. "She could tell that my heart was elsewhere."

That made my heart smile and giggle and do a little flip similar to the one that happened in the parking lot when I first saw Duncan's car.

I couldn't help but let a smile spread across my face.

"Oh yeah?"

"Hey, so I'm getting this award *thing.*" He rolled his eyes like it totally wasn't a big deal to him, except I knew it was a big deal to him. I could hear it in his voice now that I was hearing him talk about it and not his girlfriend… I mean, ex-girlfriend.

"That's right!" I said, not even attempting to squash my smile that matched his. I almost added that it was Clare who told me about it, but thought better of it.

"There's a ceremony for it on Tuesday night."

I nodded. Yes, the one that Clare declared she'd be sitting at *Front. And. Center.* I doubted that was the case anymore.

"Wanna come?"

"I would love to."

"Perfect."

He hooked a thumb over his shoulder, though he looked a little sad about what he was about to say. "Look, I should head home."

"Yeah, of course," I said. "Nice chat."

"Call you later?"

My smile widened again. "Yes, please," I said. "Oh, and I've decided to throw Arianna a surprise birthday party. Help me plan it?" I winked at him. I *winked* at him!

"I would love to." He winked back.

# blind desperation

My thoughts are a jumbled mess when I pop in with her. Although I was exhuming confidence when Arianna and I finally fell asleep in my bedroom, a huge part of me is still worried. What if I joined Mary tonight? What if Ari somehow got mixed up in her upcoming kidnapping? Or maybe tonight of all nights I would be dreaming a new girl with new problems.

But it worked. Focusing all of my thoughts and attention on Lucy and only Lucy had worked.

Surprisingly.

After everything with Duncan—the grocery store, the phone call this afternoon that lasted two hours and fifty two minutes—plus wondering in the back of my head if I had really truly prevented Andrew's parents from breaking up the night before, I would have been easy to get distracted.

But I owed this to Lucy. I had to get her out and help her finally find her happy ending. Ideally a perfect ending that didn't include the sanatorium at all.

I was here. In this horribly, terrible establishment that sucked the life out of people.

*You are here*, Lucy says without moving a muscle. She is propped up in bed, eyes unfocused staring across the room.

*Yeah. How are things?* I ask tentatively.

She doesn't respond right away. She doesn't move other than to close her eyes against the depressing scene in front of her. *I feel like this is the end,* she says. Her thoughts so quiet I almost don't catch them.

*No! No, Lucy. This is* not *the end. I'm getting you out of here* today. *Don't give up on me now!*

She is coughing, a cough that is reminiscent of the illness she had during the fire. The core-racking, terribly-sounding, throat-scalding kind of cough.

She opens her eyes again, and I force her to focus. The room looks the same, but fuller. More beds have been added, and several people are lying on blankets in various places on the floor. Men, women, and fortunately only a few children sleep and stare. A few softly moan or talk to themselves or speak with one of the nurses —though there doesn't seem to be enough of them for the number of patients in the room.

My heart drops, but I don't dare even think about what the crowd means.

*Lucy, we're getting you out* today.

*Emily, just go,* she says. *I've lived my life. Just go.*

*No way.* If I could inject happiness and hope into my voice I would. *Arianna should be here too!* I say. *She'll be with that pretty nurse we talked to the last time I was here.*

*You mean the nurse who told the doctors she'd been taken over by other-worldly creatures and was hearing voices in her head?*

Oh no.

*She was dismissed that day.*

*Oh, Lucy, I'm sorry.* I scanned the room, wondering which of the miserable souls Arianna might currently be walking. A sick feeling bubbles up in Lucy's stomach, and I wonder if it's a physical thing for her. Maybe my increasing panic over Arianna is adding to Lucy's suffering. There's already so much of suffering here.

"Em?" says the young girl with the stringy hair. The girl who has been in this room across from Lucy since the beginning and has a tendency to cover her head whenever the drama in the room rose.

"Ari?" I whisper.

Tears begin to stream down her cheeks as she nods, breaking my heart.

I jump from my bed, temporarily forgetting that Lucy's ankles are usually strapped to the bed. Fortunately that's not the case anymore. I rush over to the young girl's bed and throw my arms around her.

"Shhh. It's okay, it's okay," I say softly. "We'll get through this. I can push you out if this is too much and you want to leave." I lean back to look into the dull, lifeless eyes of a girl I hardly know housing one of my favorite people in the world.

"No," she says, sniffing. "It's okay, I'll stay," Ari says. Clearly there is no resistance from the girl. Ari is completely in control. "You said you can do this, right?"

I nod. "I can do this."

"Then I'll stay."

I search her eyes, wishing I could give some of my strength to the both of them. But the sooner I get Lucy out of this mess, the sooner we can all go home.

Being so close to the girl I realize just how young she looks. Initially, I assumed she was at least fifteen, but now I can see she can't be older than eleven or twelve. My heart aches for her, and I try to memorize her face. Someday I'll have to come back to her and help any way I can.

"What's your name?" I ask.

She looks at me strangely, "Arianna," she says slowly. "I thought you knew it was me."

"Yeah, no, what's *her* name? The girl you're with?"

Arianna cocks the girl's head to the side as if she didn't understand the question.

*Her name is Caroline Barry*, Lucy says to me quietly.

I want to voice it. I want to assure Caroline that I'll be back to help her someday, but the words won't come. Not with so much hanging over my head.

Lucy first. I must help Lucy first.

"Where's the doctor?" I ask aloud, hoping that if Lucy doesn't know, Caroline might.

*He doesn't come in much anymore*, Lucy says conjuring up a picture of the doctor wearing a creepy Halloween-looking mask. She doesn't elaborate more.

"Then we'll just have to go looking for him."

"Emily, no," Lucy pleads aloud. "I just want to rest. I want to stay here."

"Okay, we'll wait a while," I say. *But we're going to look for him if he takes too long,* I say only to Lucy. Because we're finding him today. Who knows when I'll make it back.

Caroline scoots over in her tiny bed, and Lucy cuddles in next to her. We get some strange looks from around the room. But only a few. Hardly anyone notices what's right in front of them, let alone some out-of-character behavior from the spoiled rich girl who just had to room with the *commoners*.

I get the impression, by Lucy's thoughts, that most of her original roommates didn't like her. But their distaste was preferable to isolation.

Looking around, I only recognize a few of those originals. And clearly this room is co-ed now. And *damn* depressing.

It's like the life of the room—which wasn't much to begin with—has been completely sucked out.

That's it. No more.

"We're getting you out," I say quickly. I can't take it anymore. "This place is hazardous to your health." I stand up—a little shakily because she's been bedridden for so long—and head for the door.

I glance back at the stringy-haired girl hosting my best friend. "Are you coming?" I ask with a head nod.

She looks at me incredulously.

"Use your strength to help her, Ari," I say, hoping that she can. I don't like the idea of leaving my best friend alone in an unfamiliar time and place.

She hesitates another moment before scooting to the edge of the bed and testing her feet on the floor. When she stands, she's so frail and thin I expect her to break in half, but surprisingly she's sturdier and less shaky than Lucy. Either Caroline is stronger than I assumed or Ari is doing an excellent job steadying her.

Slowly, we shuffle to the exit and down the wide and dark hallway. The going is slow, and we pass several identical rooms filled wall to wall with hacking, crying, and moaning patients.

I try to remember the way to the room Lucy was taken to the first time I walked with her in the sanatorium, but we soon get lost, wandering the halls aimlessly.

We make our way down a few flights of stairs—both Caroline and Lucy double over in coughing fits after just a few steps. Lucy silently complains the entire way, begging me to return to her bed. She wants to go back to sleep and forget about this horrible life of hers. But I ignore all pleas and continue our search. *I'm getting you out of here.* You *will* have your happy ending, Lucy Harker. You have to.

Eventually we find ourselves outside what looks like a makeshift morgue. The smell clues me in. I step back and block Caroline from moving any further. I don't know what Caroline's life experiences have been, but I know for a fact that Ari has never seen a dead body. I don't want now to be the first time.

*Now what?* I ask. Her complaining and weary body is slowly wearing at my gumption to keep moving forward.

"Let's go back," Lucy says, taking over.

"Lucy Harker," a loud voice booms behind us. "And Caroline Barry."

We turn to see the doctor. We're saved!

"Doctor!" I say taking back control. Lucy's voice is a little bit hitched. "We've been looking for you everywhere." I take a step forward, but the doctor matches it with a sudden step back, so I remain where I stand.

He puts his hands behind his back and gives us a strange look.

*Emily, please,* Lucy begs. But I'm doing this *for* her, so I ignore it. She'll thank me later.

I glance at Caroline/Arianna, hoping for a reassuring look, but am met with only a blank and slightly confused stare. "I'm ready to go home," I say, trying to sound as mentally competent and formal as possible. Like the old Lucy I used to know. The person she was when I first walked with her.

The doctor cocks his head. "Excuse me?" he scoffs.

I raise Lucy's chin and straighten her back, then inject as much force and confidence into her words as possible, "Yes, I am feeling much more myself, and I'd like to go home and see my *husband.*" I emphasize the word.

The doctor smiles, not in a good way, and looks at the floor with furrowed eyebrows and a wide grin. "Lucy, do you remember why you came to us in the first place?" he asks, meeting me with a penetrating gaze. The smile is gone.

"It's Mrs. Harker, and yes, I remember why I came here," I say. Another coughing fit racks Lucy's poor body. The rib she broke coughing in the fire aches. But I regain her composure and continue talking, "I came because I said I heard voices in my head."

Even I hear the emotion in Lucy's voice when I say that. Emotion not from Lucy but from *me* and all of the frustrated and depressing feelings I'd felt ever since the dreams started in the first place. Of doctors and my parents believing that I had a mental condition. That the dreams weren't *real.* And here I was, arguing the same thing—that Lucy *didn't* have a mental condition—and the exact opposite thing—that the dreams weren't real. I was using some of the same words they'd used on me so many times.

Lucy slips up in her defenses. I can see that they have used those same terms and some worse to describe her condition.

*Lucy, why didn't you tell me?* I resist the urge to shudder.

"Now, now, *Mrs. Harker,*" the doctor says, backing away. "Let me find a nurse to help you back to your bed."

"No!" I practically shout. "Doctor, I am fine. And I want to go home." I grit Lucy's teeth and plaster a fake smile on my face, hopefully selling the fact that she can and should go home.

*Emily, stop. Please,* Lucy asks. *I have given up and so should you.*

*I'm getting you out of here!* I practically shout at Lucy in my frustration.

"What was that?" the doctor asks, eying me suspiciously.

"Em," Caroline/Arianna whispers to me. "You said that out loud."

"No, I didn't..." I shake my head. "There's no way..."

"Stay here for a minute," the doctor says, taking two more steps back but not looking away. "I will be right back." He then disappears around the corner.

I fold Lucy's arms across her chest. "Don't worry," I say smugly. "I've got this handled. He's agreed to talk to me. I'm sure I can convince him that Lucy is all right to go home."

"Emily!" Caroline/Arianna hisses. "Are you blind? Don't you feel it?" She gestures to her chest.

I shake Lucy's limp, greasy curls. "I'm getting her out of here," I say flatly.

"Who are you doing this for?" Ari asks. "Lucy? Or *yourself?*"

I ignore the question. A couple of minutes later the doctor returns with two burly men and Nurse Edith.

"Lucy, Caroline," Nurse Beth says. "Let's get you two back to bed."

"No!" I say, feeling frantic. "I. Want. To. Go. Home." I steel myself and put on Lucy's perfect genteel attitude. "I am fine." New tactic. "The voices are gone. It was simply a hysterical episode caused by the stress of my upcoming wedding. It has passed, and I would like to go home. Now."

When one of the burly men grabs Lucy's wrist, I lose it.

And get Lucy thrown into a tiny room by herself.

*Emily. You have done enough. Please go away.*

# quilt

"It's so weird," Ari said as we walked out of the chapel. "I know I was totally mad at you this morning, but I can't for the life of me remember why."

I shrugged. "I don't remember either, but I'm glad I dragged you here. Seriously, Ari, there's something about going to church that makes you forget about all of your problems."

"Yeah, I've never been a religious person."

"Maybe it's this building," I said, trying to rack my brain as to what exactly I forgot and what was so important outside. Maybe it just *feels* important when I'm outside, but at church, it was like it never mattered.

Arianna nudged me. "So, Duncan, huh?"

My face flamed. It *had* been a good run-in with him at the grocery store. I'd replayed that conversation in my head—well, the parts I could remember—over and over all through the sermons about faith and serving our fellow men.

The way he leaned toward me, held my hand, winked when he said he'd help me plan a surprise birthday party for Ari... The way he said he'd broken up with Clare because his heart was *else-where... Sigh.* It made my heart swoon.

*And then!* Our conversation on the phone that lasted almost three hours and consisted mainly of... well, I don't really remember. Maybe his upcoming award or sports? Oh, and the TV shows we were both currently watching. It was crazy that we were interested in the same TV shows and movies. We even set a date to binge watch a few seasons of that old show *LOST* together very soon.

"Yeah, Duncan," I said dreamily.

"Our get-Duncan-back plan really worked!" Ari said, hooking her elbow with mine so we walked arm in arm.

"Well, we're not like..."

"*Officially back together*," she said in a mock-voice. "Yeah, I know. But it's gonna happen, Ems. I bet you're his very serious girlfriend by this time next week. Maybe even by this time tomorrow!"

I didn't think she was wrong. (Well, not about the first part. I doubted it would happen today.) But I didn't want to jinx it, so I didn't say anything and just grinned a little too enthusiastically. And I might have let out a little yelp of joy.

We both practically skipped out of the double doors... and both about hit the pavement face-first.

Ari jerked her arm from me instantly. "What was that?!" she spat pointing at the doors behind us.

My happy feeling left instantly. Like so many times before.

*Oh man... I screwed up so bad.*

"It's what happens when I go to church," I said not even trying to hide the guilt in my voice.

"That's why you convinced me to come? That's why you practically *kidnapped* me to get me in the car?" Mary's future flashed in my head, and I cringed at Ari's choice of words.

"I didn't *kidnap* you," I said sheepishly.

Ari inhaled deeply and closed her eyes, placing a hand on each of her temples. "I get it. You come here to escape, I totally get it. And to be honest, I was intrigued when you said the surprise would be totally worth it." She opened her eyes. "But that doesn't change the fact that I'm still mad at you."

"What?" I felt myself getting defensive. "For trying to help Lucy? For trying to help and totally screwing up and landing her in isolation?" *Yeah, I felt absolutely horrible about all of that.*

"Do you not get it? Did you not see the blood spatters on her clothing? C'mon, you've seen enough movies from that time period."

"No," I said, shaking my head. It can't be true. "I've seen her grave. She lives a long and full life. She doesn't die a few short months after finally getting her wedding."

Ari crossed her arms over her chest. Spring was definitely on the way, but I didn't think the gesture was entirely because of the slight chill. "Have you seen her grave *lately?*" Her voice was eerily calm.

"No." I hung my head and almost asked if she had. But I didn't dare. I didn't want to know.

"Well, maybe you should. That hospital was filled with tuberculosis, Em. C'mon, you had to see it. You had to *feel* it."

"M-maybe she gets better? Not everyone who caught it died from it."

Ari raised an eyebrow at me. We both knew the odds of Lucy being one of those to survive it was a very slim chance. "You know, you always talked about your *dreams*," she said, waving a mocking hand. "Like you were being so *heroic.* You know, helping people, *being* there with people when things get bad. But you just like playing dress up!"

My eyes widened. And welled with tears. That jab hurt.

"You really screwed with that girl. Her life is *completely* in shambles because of you."

"I—"

"Don't try to defend yourself," she interrupted. "None of this ever would have happened if you didn't like prancing around in Lucy's dresses and seeing your *precious* Andrew so much."

*I mean, at least she wasn't stabbing me in the back... right?* I didn't stop the escaped tear.

"She would have died in that fire," I said softly after Ari

stormed off. I doubted she heard. But maybe I was kidding myself. Maybe she was supposed to die all along and getting thrown in an insane asylum only to contract tuberculosis was fate's way of finishing the job.

*No.* I saw her grave. I saw that she lived a long and happy life. If saving her from the fire had only prolonged the inevitable for a little while, wouldn't her headstone have reflected that?

I would still save Lucy. Yeah, I'd screwed up and landed her in an even worse situation. But I'd save her. Somehow.

# it was simple

Swirls of light flash across the hardwood floor around and around, hypnotically. I recognize the effects of a disco ball immediately. And though the song currently playing—"You're So Vain"—seems a little bit out of place, I figure that since there are only two people skating around the rink, the DJ can play whatever he wants.

Mary sips a Coke quickly and nervously at a table near the back corner of the room. Her eyes dart back and forth watching for someone. I'm tempted to try to calm her or buoy her up somehow, but knowing what I know, I can't help but feel anxious too.

A food attendant, who clearly has an acne problem, stares at the ground. His elbows are on the counter, and his chin is in his hands. He isn't even trying to pretend that he's not bored out of his mind. Seeing him makes me grateful to have a smartphone in my own time.

And what I wouldn't give to have one right about now. Pulling up my Kindle app would do wonders to calm the nerves. Honestly though, I'd probably read the same paragraph over and over, glancing up at every movement in my peripheral, until I gave up and either scrolled Instagram or put my phone back into my pocket.

I guess it wouldn't help that much. Maybe it's good my phone doesn't travel back in time with me.

I attempt to scan Mary's thoughts and ascertain why she is so nervous, but a huge part of me is afraid of what I will learn. As anticipated, it has something to do with that man who she saw at the drive-in, except she isn't thinking about that memory at the drive-in.

*I must have missed something. She must have seen him when I wasn't with her.*

I find a memory of her running into him in the grocery store parking lot of all places. Same conversation—he pounds on the glass of her vehicle and demands that she warn her father about a deadline. A different deadline.

It is confusing. Is something else going on? She is thinking about the man and how terrified of him she is, but she isn't thinking about the drive-in at all in connection to him. She's just thinking about that one run-in and what she's doing at the roller rink now.

*Where is Andrew?* I scan the room again as if he might suddenly appear. *Where is Andrew?* I wonder again, but direct the thought to Mary in hopes of an answer.

But she isn't thinking about him. At all. Every memory I have of seeing him in 1973 is either nonexistent (like the drive-in) or no longer features Andrew (like when those men attacked Mary's father at the house). Like he wasn't there when it happened.

*Oh no.* My heart sinks. I don't want to think about what has happened, but there is no denying it. Andrew jumped. He no longer exists in this world. In Mary's world.

Just like he no longer exists in Lucy's world.

Andrew is gone.

Before I can wallow, Mary makes a snap decision to get on the rink. She shoves her almost-empty glass to the center of the table before pushing herself up. She's already wearing roller skates and quickly enters the rink going clockwise, the same direction as the couple skating. Not that it would matter. I doubted she'd run into them if she went counter-clockwise and *tried* to hit them.

My mind immediately goes back to Andrew and what he had to do in order to jump ahead. Did his parents break up after all? Even after that talk with Betsy? They seemed so happy, like they wouldn't let anything get in between them.

Did Andrew come up with a different way to change things? Did he take my advice and merely find a way to *interrupt*?

Whatever he did, it doesn't matter. While I was royally screwing up Lucy's life and making my best friend beyond irate about my horrible choices and actions, Andrew was jumping ahead, unaware that poor, kidnapped Mary was about to need his help very desperately and very soon.

*What do I do now?* I wonder. *It's already happened. I already had the dream of when Andrew saved her, so I know it will happen... Unless everything's changed. Unless she won't be saved this time.* I know better than anyone that reality can be changed.

Carly is a living, breathing example.

Mary has absently been skating around and around for several minutes. I've lost count of the number of laps as I've been freaking out over Andrew's disappearance. We're both lost in our thoughts and distracted when another skater comes behind us and grabs Mary's hand.

We both try to jerk away, but the hand is strong and intertwines his fingers with hers to cement the connection. She looks at him and her heart—which was about to jump from her chest—calms almost immediately after seeing his face.

"Matt," she says, in almost a sigh.

"What are you doing here alone?" he asks, his voice hitched. There is clear affection between them.

"He said I had to be alone." She takes her hand back. He releases her this time, but I can feel her regret in doing it. "I couldn't risk you getting hurt."

"I can take care of myself, Mary."

When we get to the nearest exit, both Mary and Matt skate to Mary's table for privacy. She doesn't touch her Coke again, and I make a note to keep it that way. Knowing what's coming, it's not a good idea to leave her drink unattended. Absently I eye the acne attendant who is suddenly busy with the popcorn maker even though the only extra person is Matt. The couple on the rink left five minutes ago.

We sit in silence for several moments. Matt's eyebrows are knit in worry. He opens his mouth several times as if to speak but closes it again as if thinking better of it. But then his expression changes, and I can't help but smile. Still, I'm not sure so I ask a testing question. "What I wouldn't give for some of Mrs. Carter's delicious pecan pie."

"Pie?" he asks.

Okay, maybe I am wrong, but I need to make sure, "I mean, it was always Lucy's favorite, but I developed at taste for it too."

The familiar smirk appears on his face. "Except you only tasted it with Lucy's tongue," he jokes. "It might taste like mud, you know."

"Did it taste like mud to you?"

"Ha!" He laughs. "She was the best cook in the county! The best! It hardly tasted like mud."

"It is you," I whisper.

"It is me," he says, lowering his volume again. He takes one of my hands that rests on the table between us and moves his thumb over Mary's fingers, back and forth, massaging them. Mary is twitterpated by the gesture, and to be honest, so am I. Andrew has never shown affection in quite this way. "Why are you still here?" he asks, like it's a question he's wondered for years and is just now building the courage to ask it.

"Here?"

"Yes, here. With Mary."

*How do I explain this?* I wonder, still with the dilemma of desperately wanting Andrew to know but wanting to keep it from

Mary. "She still needs me," I say. If she listens at all, or is confused by this conversation, she can interpret that any way she likes.

"But you moved from Ginny right away after I left."

I roll Mary's eyes. "That's 'cause Ginny was spoiled and... *nevermind.*" I'm not really in the mood to discuss Genevieve, so I don't continue. "I still visit Lucy," I say quietly and release my hand from his, hoping desperately that he won't ask how she and Charles are doing. It would break his heart to know where she is. And I get the feeling that he has enough on his plate as it is.

That seems to explain it enough for him to drop the subject. "Look, I know you felt strongly me about breaking up my parents," he says, staring at the table again. "But if it makes you feel any better, I didn't succeed the first time."

My heart sinks, and I drop my hands into my lap. He said the *first* time. "So you did end up breaking them up after all?"

"The first time my mother's friend reconnected them shortly after, discounting everything I'd done to break them apart."

*Yes, right, I know all of this.* It had been me (walking with Betty) who convinced the happy couple not to let a little thing like money break apart something so real and worth fighting for. It honestly didn't take much nudging or convincing at all. I was half-convinced that they would have mended their relationship with or without her.

As we talked, the roller rink suddenly becomes busy. There are now at least twenty people in various stages of donning roller skates and falling in line with the skaters on the rink. Acne-counter boy is busy filling drinks and scooping popcorn. I guess he was making that popcorn was in anticipation of this. He must have known when the crowd would arrive.

"What did you have to do the second time?" I ask, although part of me doesn't really want to know.

He finally looks at me. "Made sure the friend didn't get in the way again."

My internal alarms went off. "What did you do to Betty?"

His eyes snap to me but lose their fire almost as quickly as it appeared. I wonder it if was my imagination. "It was simple," his voice is flat. "I made sure she left work on time and made it home to spend time with her suitor... or *boyfriend* as you seem to call them."

# pretending

"You did *what?*" Disgusted and enraged, I stand up and head back to the rink as quickly as I can skate. Hoping to get lost in the crowd.

Andrew really would do anything to get what he wanted.

I'm only alone for one lap before he's back at my side.

"I did not tell you her name was Betty," he says.

"How could you send that poor girl back into the arms of a man who was abusive?" I spat at him. I try to go faster, but he has no problem keeping up with me. "She was *miserable* with him!"

"I-I..."

"That's right. That was me, Andrew. *I* helped Betty convince William and Ella that they were made for each other, that they shouldn't break up because of such a small thing as economic status. And by the way, they didn't needed much help. Then I helped Betty waltz over there and break up with that horrible man."

"All right, so I didn't know about the boyfriend."

"It didn't strike you as odd that she liked to stay at work late?" I didn't even attempt to dilute the venom in my tone.

"I didn't know about the boyfriend!" he shouts over the very upbeat disco song that starts. The DJ turns up the volume as the crowd begins cheering at the familiar tune. Everyone but Matt/Andrew and Mary/me have an extra pep in their skate. "Why did you meddle at all?" he asks. Even with the noise there's no blocking out the hurt in his words.

"Because I thought you should try another way and you wouldn't listen!" It's a good excuse. It isn't the entire excuse—that I wanted him to know about Mary's kidnapping so he'd come back to help save her—but I still couldn't tell him that part.

"You don't want me to jump, do you?" he accuses. "You never wanted me to jump to be with you." He grabs my hand and jerks me to face him. He pushes me until my back is literally against the wall. Groups and couples pass us swiftly around the rink, some with concerned looks. "Now that it is possible, now that there is a way that I can actually see *your* face when I'm talking to you. When you aren't hiding behind Lucy's, or Isabella's, or Genevieve's, or Mary's, or whoever else's eyes, now that it is *possible,* you don't want a relationship with me. Do you?" His eyes are penetrating and full of pain. But he immediately masks it, and the only thing I see is anger.

I want to shout back that he doesn't *know* what I look like. That he might take one look at me and wonder why he bothered at all. I saw the way he looked at Lucy when he first met her. He even commented that Charles would have some hefty competition if Lucy wasn't already engaged. Lucy was blond. Lucy was petite and pretty and looked nothing like me. Andrew was obviously attracted to her. And he might not be attracted to me.

But it felt like a moot point.

A man passing us asks if I am all right and if Matt/Andrew is bothering me.

"Lover's quarrel," Andrew says, flashing a *don't bother us* look.

The man silently questions me to be certain. "I'm fine. Thanks for your concern," I say. When I look back at Matt, a flash of memory flits across Mary's mind. A proposal. *Of course. She was recently engaged before she was snatched.* That thought frightens me, because the snatching must be close. Looking back at the man I shrug and say, "We're arguing about the wedding date." I hold up Mary's hand with a simple ring on the fourth finger. I can't believe I didn't notice it before.

He buys it and skates away.

"It's just as well," Andrew says, his expression determined as he backs away and releases me from his prison guard stance. I can finally breathe again.

"What do you mean?"

"Well, I did it. I achieved the jump. I made it further ahead." His intensity is essentially vanished and is replaced by a stiff, proper posture. Like an Andrew I once knew. "It's pretty amazing, isn't it? I was bored with my life and the prospect...the *challenge* to jump was too enticing. After knowing that things could be changed, thanks to you," he says, flashing me an unreadable smile. "I wanted to see if it could be done."

Something in his tone and inflection suggests... *something*. Something uncomfortable.

"And look how far I've come," he continues as he looks past me, as if gazing into the horizon like the explorer he is. "The thrill alone has been absolutely worth leaving my former life behind."

*The thrill alone.* Is he saying what I think he is saying?

That he was never jumping time to be with me?

That's it. That's exactly what he is saying. The unspoken words cause literal pain in my chest. Stabbing, aching, and like a heavy boot has been placed on my ribcage with the 400+ pound man attached to it, kind of pain. Wow. *Owww.* I lean forward slightly at the physical pain I didn't know was possible. Unwanted tears fill Mary's eyes. "It was never to be with me," I say in barely a whisper as the roller rink crowd passes by in a conga line.

A hard lump forms in my throat when he doesn't answer, confirming my fears.

"Perhaps you should not follow me ahead," he adds, his brows furrowing. "Stay here with Mary a while." He waves a hand at her, and I feel the double meaning. Don't follow me now *or* into the future. "Help her with... whatever." His face finally changes into a caring expression. "And thank you for looking out for our dear Lucy."

All I can do is nod.

He rolls backward and turns to skate into the scattered, spinning crowd. He asked me not to follow. He doesn't know about Mary's impending trauma. He was supposed to come back to save her, but now I don't know if he will. I hope she can still be saved.

I'm frozen by the wall, wondering what I did to mess things up so badly. First Lucy and Ari, and now Andrew. Although I guess Andrew's anger over me interfering in his latest jump doesn't really matter. He jumped after all. No harm done. Plus, why should I care if he's angry about my meddling if he was only ever doing it for the thrill of it—the *thrill alone*—if he never even wanted to be with me?

I watch him skate near the rink exit by the concessions and expect him to walk out of the building and possibly out my life forever, but he continues around until he is heading in my direction again.

My heart dares to hope. He is coming back! He is coming back to fix things, and now I will have the chance to apologize too! I will tell him about Mary. I will tell him that she is in danger, and that he needs to come back to help save her. Because I have *seen* him come back and save her. I let the memory—*my* memory —flood my head and remembered that he'd called me "my girl." That was proof that we would make up, that this fight isn't the end for us. Because he already talked to me like everything was fine and okay between us. And that was his future. He wouldn't call me "my girl" if we hadn't mended things, right? And perhaps Mary should know. Maybe it would be better if she did.

His face is somber, eyes and expression full of remorse. That short skate was enough for him to realize and regret the things he said.

My guess must be right.

I look at him expectantly when he stops in front of me again.

This time not as a guard keeping me prisoner, but as an equal, ready to repair things together.

"I, uh..." he begins, staring at the floor.

"Look, I—" I say with a small smile, ready to spill everything first. "I'm sorry—"

"I am really sorry about Betty," he interrupts. "I had no idea." His expression is cool, but I can hear the regret in his tone. Regret about Betty. And only Betty. "Maybe... maybe you could go back..."

"I'll help her again," I say quickly.

This time he skates away and exits. After he's gone, I peel myself from the wall and make my way back to Mary's table.

A familiar man sits in the spot Matt/Andrew occupied not thirty minutes ago.

My stomach drops along with Mary's.

She smiles as convincingly as possible as he nods that she should follow him toward a heavy maintenance door in the far corner. She obeys, going over the speech she rehearsed in her head a thousand times over the past few days—though I am hearing it for the first time—it's an excuse of why her father didn't send her with the money for this meeting. She takes only a moment to unlace her skates and abandon them just inside the door before following him down the concrete stairs.

*Inside the door.* Where no one will see them and wonder who left them there. I try to scream at her that she should leave a clue, that she should leave her skates *outside* the door. I yell and shout. But she doesn't hear me the way Lucy does. I try again. But she doesn't feel my meaning and my intentions the way Isabella always did.

I recognize the room when we are only halfway down the stairs.

# maybe soon

"Hey," Duncan asked, catching up to me on the sidewalk. "You aren't riding with Arianna today?"

I shook my head slowly. "We sort of... got into a fight."

"What about?"

I waved a hand. "It doesn't matter. Girl stuff," I lied.

"What else is bothering you?" He could read me like a football playbook. For reals.

"My dreams are really screwed up, if that's what you mean," I said bitterly. "Or rather, I keep *screwing* them up. *Mea culpa* all the way." It warmed my heart that he cared so much. Especially since he seemed to be the only one—besides my parents—who wasn't currently mad at me.

"How so?" he asked but didn't really look like that was the question he wanted to ask.

"Never mind," I said, taking the hint. "What are you doing walking home?" *And in the wrong direction*, I wanted to add but didn't.

He shrugged and fell into step with me as kept walking. Part of me was afraid I'd screw things up with him too. I was definitely on an unlucky streak the past few days. First Lucy and Ari, and last night... *whew!* Andrew. There were no words for what happened with him. I hardly expected to ever see—*Nope! Not going to even think about it.* I blinked quickly to banish any forming tears.

"Didn't you drive today?" I asked, wanting Duncan to continue walking with me, but also wanting him to go away before I did something to push him away too.

"Yeah," he said with a shrug. "I'll get my car later. I'd much rather walk with you for a while."

I smiled at the cracks in the sidewalk.

"Plus, you said you wanted my help to plan a party for Arianna?"

"Yeah, that was *before* she was mad at me."

"Then what better way to make things right? Throw her a party!"

"What if she doesn't want to come?"

"Have you told her about it yet?"

"No."

"Then it's a non-issue. We'll make it a *surprise* party instead!"

"You've got some brains in there, Stewart." I looked at him and nudged his shoulder playfully.

"Since when do we call each other by our last names?" he teased then reached down for my hand.

Flames licked up my cheeks at the contact. My heart stuttered. And then they did it all over again, when after being well received, Duncan's fingers laced through mine.

*Sigh.* Everything about Andrew was essentially forgotten. Essentially. I could easily fall for Duncan. *Easily.* But there was a deep history and connection I felt with Andrew. Even though things were so crazy and we'd both done so many things to hurt each other, I didn't think I could ever be truly happy with someone like Duncan—*Okay,* not someone like him. *Him,* because who was I kidding? There was no one else.

But I couldn't truly give my heart to Duncan until I had some closure with Andrew. And that would have to wait until I saw him on June ninth. If he still planned to meet me then.

But in the meantime, Duncan's hand felt nice.

Our steps were slow. We walked in silence for several moments. Perhaps both lost in thought about where our relationship was headed. I couldn't break it to him that I still had to have a conversation with a certain time-traveling, heart-breaking, makes-me-furious-and-want-to-rip-my-hair-out-most-of-the-time guy who still held my heart hostage.

But I didn't want to talk about that now.

"So..." Duncan said, finally breaking our silence. "Arianna will expect something epic, right?"

I sigh. Maybe throwing her a party was not the best idea. I was not in an epic-planning mindset. Even at my best I doubted I could pull one off anyway. "Yeah, she will." Even I could hear how overwhelmed I was for the impossible task in my tone.

"Hey," he pulled my hand toward him, stopping my steps and forcing me to look at him. "Baby steps, okay?"

I nodded.

He smiled, and we resumed walking. "First off, location."

"The bowling alley?" I said. "No, Ari hates bowling. Maybe Retro Skate?" *Why would I mention Retro Skate?* Stupid, stupid. Roller skating was the last place I wanted to be after my walk with Mary last night. Thoughts of where she was, trapped beneath such a happy place, was tragic.

Not to mention the thing with Andrew.

I might never set foot into another roller skating rink again.

I was anxious to get back, but dreaded it at the same time. And who should I go to? Mary locked up or Lucy locked up? They both needed me, but I had no idea how to get either of them out. Probably Mary. Lucy currently hated me. It was better to stay away until I had a concrete plan—and an actual good one—to spring her.

"Retro Skate is fun..." Duncan said, but sounded like he wasn't sold on the idea either. "But wouldn't Ari enjoy something more formal? Make everyone wear what they wore to Sweetheart Dance or something?"

Now I was the one to pull his hand back so he'd look at me. "Duncan Stewart, you are a genius!" I let go of his hand to wrap my arms around his neck. There was no way I could've come up with that idea in my current state of mind.

His neck was red when I pulled back. He tried to shrug it off like it was no big deal, but I could see his excitement too. "My mom has connections with the hospital," he said. "I could see if she can get that big banquet room they use for fundraisers at the stadium?"

"T-that room where they host senators and do wedding receptions?" I doubted my meager savings from working at the cemetery for my parents would cover the base cost of that place. Especially since I hadn't worked in a while.

"Here, I'll call her real quick," he said and pulled his phone from his back pocket. We began walking again, he didn't take my hand because he didn't have a free one, but it was okay because my phone rang right then too.

"Emily?" It was Mom. She sounded a little breathless.

"Everything okay?" I asked, my radar going up immediately.

"Are you on your way home? Is Ari driving you?"

"Yes, and no..." I glanced at Duncan who was still on the phone. He smiled as he spoke, so hopefully he was hearing good news. "I'm walking."

"Tell me where you are. Right. Now." Her voice was firm. And panicked. "I'm coming to pick you up."

"What's wrong, Mom?" I asked.

"Please, baby girl?" She hadn't called me that since I was maybe five. Something was wrong. And it sounded like she was close to tears. "Please? I don't want you walking alone."

"I'm not alone." I glanced at Duncan again who had hung up and donned a concerned look. He pocketed his phone again and took back my hand. "Duncan is walking with me." I wonder if he heard the obvious affection in my voice when I said his name.

"Okay." She blew out a breath. "You're with Duncan. Good."

"What's going on?"

"You remember how Dr. Shew made bail?"

"Yeah, like right after she was arrested. Didn't she spend a total of two hours behind bars?"

"We've been told that she might be a threat."

"Since when—w-why?" I stammered.

"The police called and informed us that she hasn't made contact in over forty-eight hours. She hasn't been in her apartment in several days, and her car is gone."

"So maybe she skipped town?" I knew it wasn't the first time a criminal had fled. I'd seen the movies.

"They suspect she's still in town, but she's desperate, honey. And they're afraid of what she might do."

"Do you think she'd come after me?"

"Promise me you'll get home quickly?" she asked. "I don't want to scare you, but the last time she spoke with her lawyer she said she had something to prove. She said if someone didn't prove it for her she'd *'find a way'*."

"What does that mean?"

Duncan squeezed my hand, hearing the worry in my voice.

"They didn't think anything of it until they found notes of further experiments she wanted to do on someone with..." She paused. "On someone with the dreams."

"On me."

"Just... hurry home. Please."

"I will."

"What was that about?" Duncan asked when I ended the call.

"They think Dr. Shew might be after me," I said and filled him in on the conversation with my mom. He moved to the other side of me, putting himself between me and the street as if he expected an unmarked van to roll up any second and snatch me. He took my other hand and held it tightly. The gesture was endearing.

"Experiments?" Duncan asked. He sounded geared up and

ready for an attack at any second. "Like causing the coma? Like implanting that *thing* that stopped the dreams?"

I shrugged, trying to brush it off. I didn't want to think about it. "Can we talk about something else?" I asked. "What did your mom say on the phone?"

"About the party? Emily, I don't know if we should—"

"No!" I cut him off. "I can't halt my life because of some potential threat that may not even be a threat. Plus, it might be resolved by then. What did your mom say?" *And how much is it going to set me back?* I wondered but didn't ask.

"She said they owed her a favor and would book it for us free of charge."

"*Free!*" I squealed. "Now I can afford catering and maybe a DJ... or that local band that is totally washed up, but she still idolizes. What are they called?"

"The Silk Sheets?" Duncan laughed.

"When can we have the room?"

"Friday."

"*This Friday?*" That wasn't much time to plan.

"Yes, but I'll help you. We'll make it happen."

I let go of his hand and hugged him again. "I don't know what I'd do without you Stewart!"

"Again with the last name?" He asked into my hair. His voice was husky. "Whatever happened to calling me A— er, Duncan?"

I pulled away to look at him. I couldn't help the smile that spread across my face. Despite the fact that I should be afraid of being snatched by Dr. Shew. Despite the fact that I still hadn't found a way to save Lucy and possibly messed up Mary's chances of being saved herself now that Andrew was out of the picture. But I could mend things with Ari. And this party was the perfect way to do it.

And I had a friend to help me.

I watched the green flecks in Duncan's iris's a bit too long and wondered if he was about to kiss me. He looked like he might. But I looked away.

*Not yet. But maybe soon.*

I had to hope that Andrew would show his face at some point. He said not to follow him, but maybe I would find him in the 90s or wherever he'd jumped to. Then we could have some closure.

And then...

"You're a good friend, you know that?" Duncan said when I took his hand again. I wasn't ready for a kiss, but I could still do that.

I disagreed, but I would change all of that somehow. At least I had him.

And I could feel his implicit faith and trust in me.

CHAPTER 30

# wallowing

I spent half of Tuesday morning in bed with a "migraine." Although I didn't have to call it that anymore because Mom and Dad were fully on board believing that my curse was actually a real, crazy-awful thing that I went through every night. The word *night terrors* hadn't been spoken in a really long time.

And that was a good thing.

But Mom hovered. She was supposed to be helping Dad with some things at the office that had been neglected for too long, but she insisted that staying home with me. I blamed the litigation/trial stuff for taking all of their time. I wished it could just be over with. At one point I made a suggestion around the dinner table that they drop the lawsuit because it was creating so much stress, but the fire in my parent's eyes and the way they both became emotional about making sure Dr. Shew saw justice was enough for me to never mention it again. With that and with the potential threat of Dr. Shew being missing, Mom refused to leave the house until I convinced her that I was fine. She insisted that she take me to school, even though I really didn't want to face the crowd today.

Still, it was better than her hovering.

My feet dragged as soon as I walked in the building. I'd spent the night soothing a terrified, cold, and very uncomfortable Mary. They hadn't started drugging her yet, but it was only a matter of time. I'd experienced it in Mary's near future. And frankly, I hoped it happened soon because then I'd be that much closer to saving her. *Saving her.* Yep, still didn't have a plan for that.

Or Lucy.

Could anyone blame me for dragging my feet and hanging my head underneath my hoodie? I caught a glimpse of Arianna before I walked into class, but met only a dagger-stare. She was still mad at me. The only thing that helped me get through my class before lunch was the prospect that at least I could eat with Duncan if I was temporarily banished from my usual spot. And he'd be certain to cheer me up with more birthday-plan details for Friday.

Friday couldn't come soon enough. Everything would be okay after Friday. It was only Tuesday, but I could make it. Just a few days.

Duncan wasn't at lunch though. I caught Scott before he snuggled up to his new girlfriend on the opposite side of the cafeteria and asked if he'd seen him.

"You two get back together yet?" he asked.

I couldn't help but smile. "Not quite."

"Well, hopefully he'll text you the next time he skips school. That seems like something a boyfriend should do." He winked.

"But he's not—"

"Teasing, Emily," he cut me off. "He said he was taking a personal day."

I rolled my eyes. "That's not exactly a thing you do in high school."

"Really? I thought it was brilliant." Scott laughed. "I plan to use it the next time I catch wind of a pop quiz in American History."

It was about then that Allison Duke, Scott's brand-new girlfriend, showed up to sit with him.

"I'm sure he just spaced telling you," Scott said. "The only reason I know is because we had back-to-back dentist appointments this morning and he mentioned that he wasn't coming today."

I didn't want to play third wheel to the new couple, so I implied that I was heading to my regular table and went instead to eat my lunch in the front foyer.

A large group of choir and band members ate in the foyer near the mascot statue, but I sat against the wall on the other side. I probably could've joined them, they were all nice enough, but I chose to be alone as I wallowed about my mostly screwed-up life. Hopefully the current sucky status was only temporary.

It reminded me of how life was after Carly died and the months that followed before I saved her and changed everything. This wasn't exactly the same, because Duncan was still my friend and I had a plan to fix things with Arianna. But for one small moment, I pretended I was back there again. It was a comfortable, familiar feeling. I still remembered that version of my reality, and therefore I knew exactly how to act. Sure, I was grateful for all the awesome parts of *this* reality, but it felt like I deserved to feel this way at least for a little while. So although the thought crossed my mind, I didn't try to call Carly for some encouraging words. After everything I'd said and done to Lucy, to Arianna, and to Andrew, I embraced the feeling.

Mom picked me up from school that afternoon. Thankfully she didn't ask why Arianna wasn't speaking to me or why I wasn't walking home with Duncan. Her and Dad didn't even ask what was wrong or attempt to take my temperature when I announced I was going to bed early that night.

# worst. friend. ever

I had to force myself to go to school the next day. Things were getting bad for Mary. Why had I been in such a hurry to get to bed early last night? I spent the whole night strapped to a chair, ankles and wrists aching from the cords that were too tight and feeling like all of the sand from the Sahara had sucked the moisture from my mouth. It had not been restful. It had been a long night.

I should've stayed up late watching mindless TV with my parents.

I told my parents I was getting a ride with Arianna and walked instead. The lie was totally worth it. Twenty precious minutes alone to walk and think felt like a godsend. Plus, I doubted Dr. Shew was staking out my school route this early in the morning. If she'd taken the time to stalk me, she would've learned that most days I rode with Arianna. And unless she'd seen my fight with her on Sunday, she wouldn't have any reason to think differently.

Honestly the whole thing with Dr. Shew felt like an unnecessary precaution. I doubted she was actually a threat to me anymore. Why make the situation worse for herself? She'd probably already skipped to Cuba by now. If not, she'd quietly disappear after the trial and sentencing were over with. And from the talk I'd heard between Mom and Dad, there was a 99% chance she'd never practice psychiatry again. Well... not legally anyway.

I walked, not to ponder about Dr. Shew and her travel plans, but to let my mind rest. I needed to shake off the horrors of Mary's experiences and brainstorm a plan to rescue her, sans Andrew. And Lucy too. I needed not one, but two, awesome rescue plans. Like right now.

Still, by the time I walked in the doors, I felt much better than I had yesterday, even though my night had been exponentially worse. Fresh air and thinking through my problems usually dissipated my anxiety a bit.

Also, I could barely admit it to myself, but I was a little giddy about seeing Duncan.

And he was standing by my locker! *Eek!* His back was turned as he was talking to one of his football buddies.

*Football buddies.* There was something I was supposed to remember...

I pulled out my phone that I'd thrown into my back pocket without really looking because I was in a hurry when I'd left the house. It wasn't in my nature not to look at my messages, but my mind had been elsewhere.

Wednesday. It was Wednesday. *Wasn't I supposed to remember something?* But it wasn't on Wednesday.

I had 5 unread texts.

All from Duncan.

*Tuesday was...* My stomach dropped. I stopped in my tracks and ducked behind the fire extinguisher on the wall with my back turned toward him to read the texts.

6:13 PM

DUNCAN: hey, sorry I missed you at school today.

DUNCAN: had a lot on my mind with the ceremony thing tonight

. . .

FACEPALM. DUNCAN'S SUPER-BIG-DEAL-FOOTBALL-award-ceremony-thing was last night. And I went to bed early.

6:32 PM

DUNCAN: saved you a seat. no rush. Doesn't start until 7

*OH NO. WHAT HAVE I DONE?*

7:01 PM

DUNCAN: still hasn't started yet, but you haven't answered. Everything ok?

7:10 PM.

DUNCAN: are you coming?

WORST. FRIEND. EVER.

DUNCAN: (...)

I DOUBTED HE WAS STILL TYPING IN HIS PHONE, BUT the animated dots indicated that he'd been writing another text at some point. Possibly after I completely blew off his football ceremony. I could only imagine what might've come next:

DUNCAN: I TAKE BACK WHAT I SAID ABOUT YOU BEING a good friend. Don't bother talking to me today. Or ever.

· · ·

Or...

DUNCAN: HOW COULD YOU FORGET? I'M THERE FOR you in all of the crap you go through, I'm freaking helping you plan a party for Arianna because she's mad at you! And you go and forget about this?

Or...

DUNCAN: SELF-CENTERED MUCH?

Or...

DUNCAN: I'M DELETING YOU FROM MY PHONE.

WORST. FRIEND. EVER.

Should I chicken and head to class? I didn't know if he'd seen me yet, but the fact he was waiting by my locker had to mean something. I decided to face the music and get this over with. When I turned around he was standing inches away.

"Duncan, I..."

His mouth twisted in a mixture of fury and hurt. "Eh." He mock-shrugged. "No biggie. It was just a *football* award. It just means I'll get a full-ride scholarship if I can pull off even half my stats next year. How could you?" His voice went scary low.

"I know!" I shouted. "I'm the worst friend in the world, and I just happened to make all of the wrong decisions lately to alienate everyone I care about!"

"Go ahead and twist it! Go ahead and talk about how horrible your dreams are and how you have to deal with... *stuff* that makes you mad depressive. Go ahead and make the excuse that if it weren't for the curse you have, you'd be a halfway-decent human being!"

*Ouch.* Again the physical pain at the words. Except this time the words actually came out. I never wanted to hurt him. I really wanted to go to his football thing. I was *honored* that he cared so much about me being there.

This couldn't all be about a football award. Could it?

Was something else going on with him?

I mean, I was still pretty awful for missing it.

*Stupid. Stupid. Stupid.*

"I-I didn't mean for it to come out like that," Duncan said.

"No, I deserve it. I have no excuses for missing it. I forgot and went to bed early." I hung my head and stared at my hands as I spoke. "And for that I must be a horrible friend and human being. Because who forgets something so important to someone she cares deeply about?" Okay, hadn't meant to be so gushy with the *deeply* talk, but I also didn't regret saying it.

"Duncan!" Scott said as he passed by with an arm around Allison. "Our girl Emily finally found you! And congrats last night!"

"Thanks, man!" Duncan said pumping Scott's fist as he passed before turning back to me. "I'll still make sure you have the room for Arianna's party," he said in a low voice. "But I need a few days. Are you all right to plan it on your own?" It was a question, but not in the way that my answer would change anything. He wanted distance. He couldn't even spend time with me to plan a party. I was on my own.

"W-will you still come?" I couldn't bring myself to look at him.

"I'll come, but let me be clear. I'm coming for Ari."

I nodded and didn't even look up as he walked away.

# one of our favorite games

"Am I dying?" she asks.

I conduct a well check. No pain. No blood. She can breathe. She can see and hear. Her thoughts are clear and... *happy*. Very happy.

*You're not dying*, I answer her though I don't know if she'll hear it. I absently wonder who I'm walking.

"Good." She holds a hand to her heart and retrieves a familiar mug from its hook.

*I have a mug just like that*, I note.

"Do you use it to make hot chocolate on cold winter mornings?" she asks.

*Did she just answer me?*

"When little voices speak to me in my head and make comments, I figure I might as well answer them."

*Wow.* She's only the second person to be so aware of me inside their head. Lucy would be the other and it took several walks, not several *seconds*, to achieve that connection.

*Who am I with? What's your name?*

"Let's play twenty questions," she says as she spoons one more scoop of chocolate powder than the canister recommends before stirring in the hot water. "I'll ask you a question, then you can ask me one."

She's comfortable. She's happy. And so am I to be here, especially after expecting to go back to Mary. *Okay.* It sounds like fun too. *You go first since I'm the one intruding.*

"All right. Let me think... And no names yet."

*Deal.*

"How are you here?"

*Easy. When I sleep, I experience the memories of those who have passed on.* I hope I put that delicately enough.

"So, I'm not dying, I'm dead?"

*Hey, it's my turn to ask the question, but no. You aren't dead now.* I think hard about a question I can ask. *You feel happy today. Is something special happening?*

"As a matter of fact, yes. My granddaughter is being born today. My daughter is in labor, and I expect a phone call any minute now."

*That's pretty special.* Part of being a guardian angel was to be with people on their happiest days. I guess it was a sort of reward-type thing for also experiencing the bad stuff.

"You're my guardian angel?"

Wow. She even heard my thoughts not directed to her. *I guess I am. Is that your question?*

"So, if you are experiencing this moment with me now while you sleep and you only experience memories with those who are dead, you must be from the future. Right?"

*Yes.*

I could feel the giddiness build inside her. She was clearly a mature woman—I mean she was becoming a grandmother today, so I suppose that was obvious—but it felt like she was young at heart. It reminded me of someone. "I have so many questions, but I will play fair. Your turn."

I had to think. I could ask her if she knew me, but that would require telling her my name. Maybe I knew her granddaughter? *What will your granddaughter be named?*

"They haven't decided on a name yet. But I put my two cents in."

*And what was that?*

"Nope. My turn," she said, but I could feel the playfulness. Still, she was ruthless! "How old are you?"

*Seventeen. You?*

"Fifty-six. But you're seventeen in the future so you might not even be born yet in my time."

*Correct. I've experienced the memories of many people who died long before even my parents were born. What year is it currently?* I ask.

She tells me.

*That's funny. That's the year I was born.*

"Really? What month were you born?"

*January.*

"January the what?"

*Hey, rule-breaker! My turn again!* I tease. There is something so familiar about her. I like her. It could be because of the general atmosphere and the feeling of being with her. There is no pain or sadness. I feel like she could be a very good friend. Almost like a— *Wait. What's today's date?*

She smiles and hides her thoughts. "January 13."

*That's the day I was born!*

"What is your name?"

*I thought we weren't doing names!*

"I know, but I want to know if they took my suggestion, Emily."

*Grams?* I want to cry.

"So, they did take my suggestion? They named you Emily?"

I nod, which makes her nod because I've accidentally taken over. *Yes! You're my Grandma Grace! Mom and Dad said that you had a hand at naming me. Although I've always wondered, why Emily? It's really common.*

"Your parents never told you why I suggested the name?" She suddenly gets choked up too. "Before I married your grandfather, I had a baby out of wedlock whom I placed for adoption."

*I have another aunt?*

She nods. "I have not seen her since she was a baby, but her adoptive parents named her Emily."

*Does Mom know?*

"No, she just knows the name is very important to me." She wipes her tears. "But this is a treat! Meeting you like this, my dear Emily. Although it could just be me lost in my own happy thoughts. Are you really here?"

I felt like she believed what was happening when I first told her. But she's also not the first person to question who I really am.

*Read Grandma Cole's journals. She has the same gift as me.*

"Oh, how I still miss her! How did you find out about her journals?"

*You told me about them. In fact, you believed in my dreams—the way that I experience other people's memories—sooner than anyone. It took my parents a long time to finally come around.*

"I'll read them but not for proof. I'll read them to help you."

*Thanks, Grandma.* I want to tell her how much I miss her and how much I wish I could call her up and tell her all about the woes of my current life. She'd be sure to have advice about how to patch things up with Lucy and Ari, Duncan, and maybe even Andrew. But if I tell her any of that, then she'll know that she doesn't even make it to my seventeenth birthday. I can't do that to her.

"So how does it work?" she asks. "The dreams, I mean?"

*Oh! Well, you are the one who told me that I am like a guardian angel who visits people.*

"Guardian angel, huh?"

*Yes, I am with people when they experience their most painful, or scary, or heartbreaking experiences. Heightened emotions. I also get to experience the good stuff too, but still, heightened emotions.*

"Like the birth of a new granddaughter," she says with a smile.

*Yes. Exactly.*

We sit in silence for a long while. I'm just happy to be here with her, and she feels content just having me with her while she waits for the phone call from Dad. Too bad I didn't remember what time of day I was born to give her a heads up. Either my parents never mentioned it or I forgot it.

After she finishes her super-rich hot chocolate, Grandma moves to the front room to stare out the window. "You seem troubled about something, dear. Would you like to talk about it?"

*Wow, Grandma. You haven't even met me yet and you sensed that?*

"I feel a kinship with you. Different than your cousins. Tell me, do you have siblings?"

*No. Only child.*

"Is it because of your dreams? I suspect that could take a toll on a person's psyche."

*No, they couldn't have any more after me. But you're right. It has been rough. You were the biggest help to me for a long time—* I want to bite my tongue for implying that she isn't alive anymore.

"Don't beat around the bush. The fact that you dream of dead people clued me in immediately that I won't be seeing you graduate."

Oh right. *But in the future, when we talk, just please don't tell me... don't tell me that we met like this. Don't tell me that you're not going to be around very long. Please?* I ask, realizing the implications. That she *knew* my entire life that she would die before I was eighteen.

"I promise," she says. "And please spare me the details of when or how."

*I won't. I promise.* I'd experienced enough death that I completely understood not wanting to know what was coming.

"You've experienced death? Oh, sweetie! If I could hug you right now."

Wow. She heard me again. *Yeah, I... Grandma, you were—you are wonderful and you helped me so much and I'm so—*

I feel her tears prick with my emotion.

*I'm so happy that I finally came to see you again. I hoped it would happen.*

The sun rose above the trees right then and illuminated a familiar—though perhaps newer object that currently hung in my bedroom—the birdhouse.

*How long have you had that?* I ask.

"A young man sold it to me about a week ago. He was selling them door to door."

*In January?*

"Strange, I know. He had kind eyes, and a smirk that would make the strongest girls swoon."

*Did you catch his name?* For a while I'd had a feeling that I knew who sold that birdhouse to Grams, and she swore that she didn't remember the man's name, but if he sold it to her only a week before...

"He said his name was Andrew Harker."

Gram's breath caught, but it was all from me.

"Is he important to you?" she asked.

*Yes... we sort of got into a fight—Andrew and I—and I don't know what will happen between us, but, Grandma... I... I...*

I what? How exactly did I feel about Andrew even after everything? Even with the way things were going between Duncan and I—I mean, before my total screwup? How did I really feel?

*Grandma, I'm in love him.*

She smiled at that.

*But things are definitely complicated.*

"Oh, I'm sure things will work out."

I wasn't so sure. *Did he tell you what the roman numerals on the side meant?*

"Roman numerals?" She craned her neck to get a better look. "Yeah, I guess that's what they could be. I always figured they were the letters V-I."

*You told me you thought they were Roman numerals!*

"So, we've had this conversation?" She was clearly amused by this. So was I.

*It was one of our favorite games, trying to guess what it meant. He didn't tell you then?*

"Sorry, he did not tell me. Maybe you can ask him?"

*Maybe.* If I ever saw or spoke to him again. He told me not to follow him.

The phone rang.

*I bet that's Dad!* I say.

Grandma's heart races with excitement. "See you soon, dear."

*Love you, Grams.*

# CHAPTER 33

## there's your answer

The little family reunion with Grandma gave me hope. She always knew how to make things better even though she didn't know the whole mess of it. Yeah, I'd royally screwed up in so many ways and had alienated so many of my friends, but I was going to fix it. All of it. *Somehow.*

And I was starting that right now. Today.

Unfortunately, I still didn't have a plan to save Lucy, so I'd keep that thought in the back of my mind and hope for some inspiration.

Duncan needed time to forgive me for missing his special night. But Duncan was amazing. He'd forgive me. Even though I probably didn't deserve his friendship. But the very thing he asked me for, *time*, meant that by *not* calling him or seeing him was doing something about it.

Then there was Andrew. *Oh, Andrew.* I could hardly even think about him. *If* I ever saw him again... well, let's just say I had no idea what would happen if I saw him again. I didn't regret what I did in 1956, trying to keep his parents together and helping Betty. That had nothing to do with trying to stop him from moving forward.

But he had sold Grams the birdhouse the year I was born, and she described him as a *young man*. He'd done it. He'd jumped again. He only had one jump to go. That thought made my stomach lurch. He would make it. I had no doubt now. The idea that I would soon be able to ask him about that birdhouse myself... well, it made me go crazy if I thought about it too much.

Pushing all things Andrew from my head, I decided on a plan. I'd start by fixing things with Ari. It would probably be easiest to work things out with her anyway since I hadn't hurt her directly. Throwing her an epic birthday party would hopefully do the trick and persuade her that I wasn't a total fraud. *Right?*

Life actually looked a lot like it did before the timeline shift when I saved Carly. Like for real now, not just pretending like it did at lunch the other day. Although back then I didn't have any friends. Now, I had friends, they were just all angry at me.

Also back then, I didn't have a surrogate older sister to call.

I dialed Carly as I walked home from school. Alone again. I hoped no one would notice and call my parents.

"Emily!"

I blew out a sigh of relief. *She answered.* "Hey, Carly, I was hoping to get your advice on a few things."

"Sure! Can we talk tomorrow? I fly in later tonight."

"You're on your way home?"

"Sadly yes, but I have missed being home."

"I've missed you too!"

"So... tomorrow?"

Tomorrow would be too late to plan the party of the century. "Actually, it's kind of time sensitive. Do you have a minute for me to pick your brain right now?"

"Um... my flight's not for another hour..." It sounded like she was shutting a book or laptop decisively and loudly. "Sure, yeah, I've got a minute. Is it about one of your dreams?"

"No, I'm throwing a belated birthday party for Arianna tomorrow. You know... since I was in a coma *on* her birthday."

"Oh, she'll love that! Let me help!"

"But how...?"

"Do you have a place?"

"Yes." I sighed. "But nothing else." I hadn't even started spreading the word. Duncan was the only one who knew about the party at the moment. "Carly, I'm not good at this kind of stuff. I can't believe it's taken me this long to finally do something for her." Not to mention that she was mad at me for something completely unrelated.

"Well... tell you what," she said. "You work on getting the invites out tonight, I'll call around for some caterers while I wait for my flight, and I'll help you set up the place in the morning."

"You are a lifesaver."

"Do you have music? Or any sort of entertainment?"

Right. I was supposed to see if I could get that band... what was their name? "No," I said, defeated.

"Okay, hang on," she said and went quiet for a minute.

"Carly?" I asked.

"Just a sec, I'm texting Zeke." It sounded like she put me on speaker. "Perfect," she said about thirty seconds later. "He owed me a favor anyway." Now it sounded like I was off speaker again.

"Who is Zeke?" I asked.

"He's the drummer for that awful band, The Silk Sheets. Ari loves those guys."

"The Silk Sheets! How did you get them?"

"I used to work with Zeke. I covered for him all of the time when he had gigs," she said. "They'll be our entertainment."

"Carly, you are amazing!"

"Anything for my little sis. She deserves a good un-birthday party."

"Yeah, she does," I said guiltily.

"Hey, don't beat yourself up over it. You've been dealing with a lot of crap lately. Give yourself some slack. I'm sure she'll understand."

"I don't know if she does," I said. "You know, Ari walked in a couple of dreams with me lately."

"Oh yeah? How did that go? I have to say I'm a little jealous. I might have to join you one night after I get home."

"The thing is... Carly, I totally screwed up." I proceeded to tell her the whole mess Lucy was in. The fact that Lucy was in that sanatorium because of me and I'd made it worse while trying to get her out and now she was in isolation. Dying of tuberculosis. And that Ari was mad at me because she thought I was a complete fraud—I claimed my dream-walking was helping people but I was really just meddling in another person's life and playing dress up. "The party tomorrow will be a surprise," I continued. "I don't know if Arianna would show if she knew about it." In fact, I hadn't figured out the part about how to get her to the party. I made a mental note to ask her boyfriend Brian's assistance on that one.

"The party will help, I promise," she assured me. "Ari knows what kind of person you are. She knows your intentions with Lucy are good." But even she didn't sound so sure. "Do you have a plan to help Lucy?"

"No!" I lamented, throwing my free hand out as if she could see the gesture. "I don't know what to do!"

"I'm sure that saving Lucy will help mend things with Ari."

"I had the same thought," I said, though my tone was defeated. I'd racked my brain for days now and nothing had come. Too bad I couldn't bring myself to ask Grandma's advice when I talked to her last night. But I didn't want to ruin her perfect happy moment.

Carly was silent for a moment but then said, "You know, we never really talked about you saving me except that one time when you came to my dorm room."

Strange change of subject. "True," I said. Did she really want to re-hash this?

"Why did you come that day?"

"What do you mean?"

"Why did you come to my dorm room *that* day? I mean, you'd saved me months before that. Why did you come that day?"

"I, uh…" I couldn't remember how much I'd told her, but the day everything changed was so disorienting. I probably didn't explain much because I was just so happy that she was alive. "Well…" I paused. The memory of her dying was painful, even though she wasn't my blood sister like Ari was.

"I'm a big girl, I can handle it."

"No, it's not that. It's just that, uh…" I paused again. "Carly, in my memory, you died that day."

"No," she said. "You *saved* me."

"The *second* time I saved you." I took a deep breath. "The *first* time you died and I went to your funeral. That's why I dream-walked you in the first place. Because you were already dead." And then Ari stopped being my friend, but I didn't bring that part up. "You were gone for about six months. Then I dreamed you again."

"*Again?*" Her voice was barely a whisper.

"I must've been thinking about you, because I relived it." I held out my hand to study the Harker ring. Duncan had given it to me before that second dream, and I wore it that night. Andrew once told me that thinking of a certain person while wearing the talisman would cause me to dream that person.

"You went through that twice?"

"Yeah, except the second time…" My voice cracked. "You were saved."

There was silence on the other line. For several moments. I didn't think that she had hung up, but I checked my phone again just to make sure the call hadn't dropped.

"You can go back," she finally said.

"Go back?"

"You can go back and repeat a dream?"

"Yes." With Carly, with Nora, and with Lucy during the fire. I'd walked all of those memories two times each.

"Then do that. There's your answer for Lucy. Go back."

"But how? Where? At what point would going back make a difference?" I wanted to cry, I was so frustrated. I felt like she was on to something that might work, but the answer was just out of reach. "I've dreamed with Lucy so many times. There were so many mistakes. Changing just one might not even make a difference. How do I pick one?"

"Maybe Lucy isn't the answer."

"What do you mean?"

"Maybe someone *else* needs to save Lucy."

That felt like the answer. But who? *Think, Emily. Who could help Lucy?*

"Do you know of anyone who is Lucy's contemporary that could help?" Carly prodded.

Not Charles. Andrew is gone. Maybe Margaret? But I'd never dreamt of her, and even if I could, she'd just get thrown in with Lucy anyway. Who could help her?

"Maybe a relative?" Carly asked.

"Her relative?"

"Or yours."

"I visited my grandma last night," I said, realizing that though I'd been wanting to talk to someone about it, Carly was the only person on the planet who I could tell at the moment.

"Really? That's awesome!" she said. "Was it awesome?"

I nodded, suddenly getting choked up. "It was," I managed to say.

She paused as if waiting for me to say more. But I didn't. "Your grandma probably wasn't around back then though, I suspect." Her tone held regret. But she was right.

"No, she wasn't." Relative. Another relative. "There's Grandma Cole."

"Your grandma or Lucy's?"

"Mine... well, my great-great-grandmother. Juliet Cole."

"And she could help? She was alive at that time?"

It was coming slowly, but it was coming. That could be the answer. I could possibly ask for help from my ancestor. "She was a dream-walker like me, so, maybe?"

"So, if you found her and walked with her..."

"She'd believe me. And maybe she could help me help Lucy and convince the doctors, or someone, that Lucy isn't crazy and doesn't need to be in the sanatorium."

"There's your answer, Emily."

"Thank you, Carly."

"I'll see you tomorrow."

"Thank you for helping make Ari's un-birthday party epic," I said.

"I wouldn't call The Silk Sheets *epic*. But Ari will like it."

# yul-ette

I stayed up until past two o'clock in the morning reading Grandma Cole's journals. I'd spent my entire afternoon and evening texting and messaging out invites to Arianna's party —and donning my thick skin because everyone was a little annoyed that I was calling so last minute. I got more than one lecture about being more organized when I planned things. Which was kinda funny coming from teenagers. I'd recruited Ari's boyfriend, Brian, to bring her to the party.

By the time I was satisfied that the party wouldn't be a flop, people-wise, I was exhausted. I told Mom and Dad I was going to bed, then set to work finding Grandma Cole *tonight*. I hoped reading her journals would help give me a sense of her so I could find her. If I could walk her, or walk with someone who was close to her—somehow—I felt that I could finally figure out a way to help Lucy.

And it had to be tonight.

I needed to have a plan in place so I could tell Ari tomorrow. The party wasn't enough for her to forgive me for everything. I had to have a plan to right my wrongs.

Grandma Cole was born in 1879, so she was twenty-two

when I first began walking with Lucy. It was perfect. I hoped. She was already married to Samuel Cole, a doctor, by then. My plan was formulating. I just hoped I could walk her and that it would work.

When my eyes burned with dryness and I struggled to keep them open, I made sure the Harker ring was secure on my finger and even wore the piggyback ring that Ari had given back to me Sunday in hopes that the two combined might give me even more control.

Light off. Head on pillow. But before I sank into unconsciousness, I repeated her name over and over in my head. *Juliet Cole, 1901.* Hopefully that was the way the dreams worked, that I could just pick a date. I shot for an early one just in case. Lucy was taken to the sanatorium in the summer of 1902. If I could get there long before, maybe I could prevent a few things from happening. *Juliet Cole, 1901. Juliet Cole, 1901. Juliet Co—*

---

*PRETTY FLY. PRETTY FLY.*

Run.

Run.

*Hmph.* Fall down. Look at Mama.

Her smiles.

Me smiles.

Mama helps up.

Run. Run.

Pretty fly goes up. Hands in air.

Feel so sad.

Cry. "Mama!"

"Oh, sweetie," Mama says. Holds me. "The butterfly flew away."

Still cry. Feel so sad.

"That makes you so sad." Mama pats head. "But that's what butterflies do. They love to fly."

Grass is soft.

See white fuzzy. Happy.

Grab it.

Put in mouth.

*Yuck. Yuck!* "Eh! Eh!" Out! Out! Use hands. Wipe mouth.

"Oh, Hazel!" Mama says. "Those aren't for eating."

Mama gets yuck out. "De-do." Thank you.

"You are welcome, my sweet. Now, watch this." Mama grabs white fuzzy.

Mama funny face. White fuzzy flies!

"Oooh!" Point.

*What the... Where am I?*

"Meh!" Point at white fuzzies.

*Yeah, a dandelion,* I say to her, but the white fuzzies flying away are so fascinating. I must try it myself. Run. Run. *These short legs are so slow.* Grab another. It's tricky with these hands. Doesn't matter. Puff up cheeks like Mama did and *spit.*

Now they're all wet. It didn't work. My eyes fill up with tears again.

"Try again," Mama says, hugging me. I love her so much and feel better right away. She holds the partially wet dandelion and shows me how to puff up my cheeks.

Blow. They fly. "Mo!" Point. Look at Mama. "Meh! Eh!"

So happy.

*Wow. It's hard to concentrate.* I've never walked a toddler before. She can't be older than two. If that. My experience with toddlers is virtually nonexistent. I'm not the babysitting type, and my cousins live in a different state. And thankfully no toddlers have ever needed my help. Though I'm sure toddlerhood isn't dandelions and butterflies for all kids. That thought made me sad.

And we cry. And cry.

So sad.

Look at Mama. Holds me.

"What is wrong, sweetheart?" Mama holds and rocks me. "Are you getting tired? Shall we go in for a rest?"

*No! She can't go to sleep yet. I've got to figure out where—or more importantly* when *I am.*

Jump off Mama's lap. Smile at Mama.

Look for white fuzzy.

"A few more minutes, my sweet. Then it is time for a rest."

Find white fuzzy and pick it. Blow. White fuzzies fly. Watch. "Da. Da. Da."

*Man they are so cool! They just float up there like—* Concentrate, Emily! *I chide myself. Who knew it would be super hard taking control while walking a person so small. I rack my brain for the time I was aiming for when I fell asleep. I was aiming for a* when, *right?*

Think. Think. Think.

*Ooh! Another fuzzy.*

1901. I was aiming for 1901.

Pick it.

Why? Why was I coming here?

Blow. They fly. "Ohhh!" Point and look at Mama.

She wears clothes that look familiar. Like a dear friend. *Lucy.* She wears a dress like Lucy wears. Or wore. Before she was sent to that awful hospital.

Lucy. I need to save Lucy.

*Butterfly. So pretty.*

Run. Run!

These legs won't go faster. Need to go faster. Want to catch it.

*It's gonna fly away. It's gonna fly away. But the black and yellow so pretty. So pretty.*

It flies away.

So sad. Not cry. Not cry.

*Emily! Get a hold of your thoughts!* I shake her feathery curls. They tickle my cheeks and make the world look so funny. Shake head again. Laugh. Laugh.

Laugh.

Shake hard. Fall down.

Laugh. Look at Mama. She smiles.

I smile.

She looks a lot like... *me.* I sober immediately. Hazel's mama looks exactly like me, *Emily Chandler.*

Hazel cocks her head to the side. Probably trying to decipher these new thoughts that have invaded her head.

This mama, who looks just like me and is wearing a dress that is scarily similar to Lucy's.

Lucy.

I have to save Lucy.

I concentrated on coming to 1901 for help. I needed to find Juliet Cole, my great-great-grandmother.

"Yul-ette?" I say.

Her face changes.

Not like.

Me frowns.

Mama picks up and hugs. "Did you just say my name, Hazel?"

"Yul-ette?"

Her eyes widen and frighten Hazel again.

We bury her head into Mama's dress.

"Sweetheart, I am not angry." She hugs us.

*It is her! It has to be! I'm here! I can ask for her to help save Lucy.* I am relieved and... *yawn.* Suddenly so ready to go to sleep.

Lay head on Mama's shoulder.

"Let us go inside for a rest."

"Mama," Hazel says, sleepily turning mama's face with her hand. "Mama."

"Hazel," Mama says.

"Mama. Yul-ette Co," I say.

Mama stops walking and pulls back to look at me. I just want to lay back down. I just want to sleep.

"Gray-gray-gramama." Not the way I wanted that to come out. I point to her. Hazel puts both hands on her face again. "You. My." I point to me with chubby fingers. "Gray-gray-gramama."

"No. I am your Mama."

"Yes. Mama," Hazel says.

"In." I point to Hazel's baby curls. Juliet has the dreams. I'm hoping that she's familiar enough that she'll catch on. I have no clue how I would talk to her if she didn't have some experience with it. "Me. Emmee."

"Emmee?"

Nod. Smile. Wave hands. "Eeek!" Scream. Happy.

But it's confusing Hazel. "No. Hay 'Zel." She points to herself.

"Yes, your name is Hazel."

*Ugh. This isn't working. Plus, I really want to sleep.* We lay our head on Mama's shoulder again. She walks again. Up the steps.

"Emmee," Mama says to herself.

"Yes! Emmee!" I say sitting up again. Turn Mama's face with hand. "Mama. Me. Emmee."

Hazel forces our head back to the shoulder and refuses to budge. I resist closing her eyes. I have to get through to her somehow. I have to get a message through.

Hazel keeps her head on her mama's shoulder the whole way to the nursery, where she sits in a rocky chair. *Rocking chair.* And begins to sing a lullaby. Hazel's favorite.

"Emmee," she says, stopping halfway through. "Gray. Gray. Gramama."

I sit up and nod. "Yah. dah. Gray-gray-gramama."

"Grandma?"

I nod energetically. "Gray-gray!"

"Great-great?"

"Yeah. Yeah."

"Are you visiting my daughter? Are you dreaming with her?"

Nod slowly. Angry eyes.

"Is something about to happen to her?" Angry eyes.

Shake head. "No. 'Appy."

"Happy?" No more angry eyes. "Hazel is happy?"

I nod fast again. "Yah. Dah."

"And I am your great-great-grandmother?"

"Yah. Dah."

"Is Hazel your great-grandmother?"

Shake head. "No. Meh." Holds hands out. "Eye-zuh."

Her eyes widen. "Eliza?"

Nod.

"I don't have a daughter named Eliza, but I've always want-ed..." she trails off. "And your name is Emmy?"

"No. Emm-ee."

"Emily?"

"Yah. Dah."

"You have the dreams like me," She says to herself. "That must mean it passes through generations. Does anyone in your family have the dreams?"

"Yul-ette." I point to her. "Meh." Point to me.

"How did you know?"

"Gamma Ga-se," I say each syllable slowly.

"Ga-se?" She pauses and thinks. "Grace?"

"Yah. Dah."

"My granddaughter."

"Yah. Dah."

Hazel feels my happiness that I'm conveying at least some-thing to Grandma Juliet and we wrap our arms around her. "Ma-moo, Mama."

"I love you too, sweetheart," she says. "Can I talk with Emily for just one moment?"

"Yah. Yah," Hazel says.

"Meh. See! You," I say. Man this is hard! "Vi-ssit."

She smiles at us. "Hazel only says a few words. You are saying more than is typical for her. How old are you, Emily?"

"Sev..." I pause, twisting Hazel's mouth in a way she's never done before. "eeeen."

"Seven?" Her voice is panicked.

"No. No. N-eeen."

"Seventeen?" Mama's voice is normal again.

"Yah. Dah."

"And you tried to visit me?" She points to her head.

"Yah. Alp." I sound it out again. It feels like Hazel has already passed out in exhaustion. I'm not far behind her. Little bodies need a lot of sleep. "Elp. Ap."

"You need my help?"

"Yah." She is good at translating the babbling of a not yet two-year-old. But my voice isn't as enthusiastic. My head rests in the crook of her arm.

Juliet sits us up again. "I imagine Emily will be upset if she doesn't tell me what she's come for. Am I right?"

I nod sleepily. "Yah. Dah."

She lowers her head to look right into Hazel's eyes. "Do you think you could write it? Of course Hazel cannot write, but if you focus really hard, I think you can do it."

I nod. My eyelids getting heavier by the second.

Juliet stands up from the chair and carries us to a different room. She retrieves a paper and quill, then helps fold Hazel's small, uncoordinated fingers around the quill.

"Emily," she says, willing me to look at her. "Take a deep breath."

I fill Hazel's lungs. We giggle because some hair goes into her mouth.

"Concentrate." Mama smiles.

I try to focus.

"And maybe this will help." She slips off a ring and puts it on the thumb of Hazel's other hand. It's much too big even for the thumb, but I recognize it. It's Grandma's ring. The piggy back ring I currently wear.

*Now what to write?* I don't know how long Hazel will be able to do this so I skip some of the vowels.

"Lucy Harker?" Juliet asks when I've finished.

"Yah. Dah."

"Emily, sweetie, I am not acquainted with a Lucy Harker."

*Ugh!* I concentrated on making it to 1901. She's not Lucy

Harker. Not yet. But we don't have time for a long drawn-out guessing game. Hazel wants a nap. Like five minutes ago. I pout.

"Let me think, sweetie." Mama pauses. "I do know a Harker family though. Lets see... Hazel's papa has had some business with a young Charles Harker."

"Yah. Yah!"

I write three numbers. Well seven to be exact.

"Six, eighteen, 1902."

"Yeah. Dah." I point. "Meh. Eh."

She scrutinizes the numbers.

"Eh. Eh." Point. Point.

"June 18, 1902?"

"Yah. Dah." I point at Lucy's name again.

"Is that when Lucy was born?"

"No!" I move Juliet's face with my hand again and point her at Lucy's name, then the date. Lucy's last name. Then the date. *This is so frustrating!* Maybe there was a good reason people didn't remember their toddler years. It was certainly a very trying time.

"She becomes a Harker on June 18, 1902?"

"Yah! Yah!" I squeal loudly.

"Does she marry a Harker?"

"Yah! Dah!" I move her head to look at me. "Yul-ette."

She smiles and says, "I did hear that Charles is recently engaged..." she pauses and looks away. "To a young lady named Lucy Rhett!"

"Yah! Yah!" I squeal again. Then scream. *She's getting it!* "Elp. Alp." I point to Lucy's name again.

"Help Lucy?"

"Yah! Yah!"

I write another word. It's easier—surprisingly—than saying it.

Mama turns her head to read it. "Asylum?" she whispers. A quiet terror in her voice.

"Dah," I say quietly.

"Is she there now?"

"No." Point at date again.

"On her wedding day?" She sounds appalled. "Why? Why did she get sent to an asylum on her wedding day?"

I point to Hazel's tiny chest. "Meh. Vi-ssit." I point to her curls.

# reject roses

Working alone in the banquet room, my mood went from okay to dismal within a few hours. I'd taken it upon myself to decorate the banquet room Duncan's mom had reserved for Ari's un-birthday party by myself. Carly couldn't help until later and I was panicked that if I waited, it wouldn't be done in time. I wanted it to be magical and epic, but all I'd managed so far was to turn a classy blank slate into a bad rendition of one of the high school dances held in the gym. The ugly, boring kind, not the kind decorated by someone with Arianna's eye.

What I wouldn't give to have her turn my mess into an elegant non-mess. But it was her party, I couldn't ask her to help. And she probably would've said no anyway since she was still of the opinion that I was a liar and a person who enjoyed ruining people's lives. Specifically, Lucy since she'd witnessed that major screw-up. She no longer believed I helped anyone else in dreams or otherwise.

Duncan was supposed to help me, but he wasn't talking to me. Again, my fault for being a horrible friend and missing his award ceremony thing.

Dad was busy with some issue with one of the diggers at the

cemetery, and Mom was dealing with a client at the mortuary about transferring their loved one from another state, so they couldn't help either. Although, honestly, I didn't dare mention needing help anyway. I was certain that Mom would pitch a fit about me being alone since she was still convinced Dr. Shew was after me.

I doubted I was in any actual danger. I'd been working with streamers and limp balloons (blown up myself—I should've rented one of those helium tanks) for over three hours and hadn't seen so much as a mail carrier.

My phone rang. It was Mom.

I took a deep breath, faking an optimistic tone and plastering a smile that I hoped she'd hear when she answered. "Hey, Mom! Get everything worked out for that family?"

"Yeah, um…" She sounded distracted. "Yeah, I took care of that this morning. How are you feeling? You sound better."

"Yeah…" My face colored. Fortunately, there wasn't anyone around to see it. "It was just that crazy dream last night." My walk with Hazel had messed with my language abilities that morning. I still had no idea whether I'd successfully conveyed Lucy's desperation to Grandma Juliet—and I had no idea how she *could* help for that matter. But Mom had been inches away from taking me straight to see Dr. Williams this morning because I couldn't stop talking like a baby.

Thankfully, the baby talk had worn off after a few hours.

"Well, we should probably get you in to see Dr. Williams soon anyway." She sounded like she meant it, but I doubted it would really be anytime soon. Between work stuff and lawyer stuff—which felt like it was taking *forever*—she had a very full plate.

"Yeah, probably," I agreed anyway.

"Hey, uh, Detective Ash just called. And I don't mean to scare you or anything, but there still aren't any leads about where Dr. Shew is… Although I guess we don't really need to call her *doctor* anymore. But they still haven't found her."

"Mom, I'm fine," I assured her. *Here we go again.* "I promise no one followed me, and I've locked myself inside. She doesn't know I'm here." I still doubted she was even *looking* for me, but Mom still couldn't be convinced.

"Wait. Where are you?" Mom's voice rose a few notes.

*Crap.* "I'm decorating for Ari's party, remember?" I said, trying to play it off like she should've known where I was all along. Like she'd been the one to drive me here. "But I promise I've locked myself in."

"And you're alone?"

"Yeah, but Carly will be here soon." Yep, probably should call her to make sure that was the truth.

There was a pause on the other line. "Okay, so you're locked in?"

"Yes, Mom. I'm fine." It was true in the sense Mom was worried about. On the other hand, I was pretty sure the party would be a disaster and that I might end the night with even *more* people angry at me. But I couldn't dwell on that. Not while Mom was using her super-human mama-bear ears for any change in the tone of my voice. "If there weren't any leads, why did Detective Ash call?" I asked, in attempt to change the subject.

Mom didn't speak right away. She'd spent so much time shielding me from everything that dealt with the trial she had a hard time talking about any details at all. I think she was afraid they might break me. "Well, there aren't any leads pointing to her *location,* but they found some of her early medical journals that are giving more insight into her motive." The mama bear growl was barely audible, but there.

*Wow. They were really digging deep.* "What did the journals say?"

"Besides the part where they think she might be a clinical psychopath," she said, muttering under her breath, "Shew learned about someone with the dreams several years ago while in medical school... A roommate, I think? Anyway, she became obsessed with the idea. Not the fascination with what it was, but with becoming famous by publishing her findings and research about such a person."

I gulped. A growing fear planted itself at the bottom of my stomach. "What happened to the roommate?"

"Um... nothing bad. That I know of. I think they said the roommate was actually lying, that it was actually a friend or family member of the roommate who had the dreams. Either way, Dr. Shew never met them. But after that, she was sort of waiting for someone with dreams."

"And then I came along."

"And then you came along. The point is, honey, her research plans sounded pretty..."

"Torturous?" No need to beat around the bush. Mom still had no idea the things I was capable of handling. I'd been through a lot.

"Possibly—" Her voice caught. "Dangerous for sure."

"I'll be careful."

---

AFTER HANGING UP WITH MOM, I PUTTERED AROUND the hall for a few minutes until my imagination got the best of me. Dr. Shew was lurking around every blind corner and shadow, waiting for the right moment to snatch me and take me to her lair. I imagined a place like the horrendous room where Mary was being held, with a cold surgical table in place of the hard chair she was strapped to.

Poor Mary. At least I knew that she'd get out. Sort of. I didn't know how my recent falling out with Andrew would affect her escape. But she would get out? Right?

Thinking about Mary naturally led to thoughts of an also-trapped-but-in-a-different-way Lucy. Stuck in that place. Hating me. And dying. And that one was all my fault.

At least Mary's kidnapping wasn't my fault.

I intended to visit Lucy tonight. But maybe I should visit

Mary? At least where Lucy was, nobody wanted her dead. Except tuberculosis, of course.

But Mary's captors might actually resort to something awful.

It was an impossible decision.

On the other hand... they both lived in the past. And the nature of my dreams could put either of their predicaments on hold while I saved the other.

I'd messed up the most with Lucy. I needed to make that right. And it could be tricky because I needed to somehow go back and visit an earlier Lucy who wasn't dying of tuberculosis—as Carly suggested—and somehow save her. I wished I could have made some more concrete plans with Grandma Juliet in that respect, but I had to move forward either way. I had to save Lucy somehow. Tonight. I would save Lucy tonight.

And then I'd go back for Mary.

But first things first. I had to mend things with Ari at her party tonight. And I planned to grovel at Duncan's feet if he showed up, but only if things with Ari were good first.

*Whew!* I had a lot on my plate.

Looking at the clock and seeing that it was past three, I immediately dialed Carly. She said she'd be home around three and I could call. I definitely needed her help. Like in a huge way.

"Does the place look amazing and you're calling because you want to go get mani-pedis before the party?"

"Um... not exactly."

"We'll make it fantastic. I'll be there in five."

"Thanks, Carly."

We walked into Brewster's Floral twenty minutes later. The familiar ping of the door flooded me with nostalgia. I hadn't walked into this flower shop since... I glanced at Mr. Brewster behind the counter and smiled.

"Emily!" he said, rounding the counter to greet me. He even pulled me into a half-hug. I don't remember him ever doing that. "I heard about the lawsuit." It was a nice hug. Like from a favorite uncle or grandpa.

I hugged him back. "Really?" I had no idea the lawsuit was general knowledge to the community. I mean except my classmates. A lot of them knew about it.

"Hello, Carly," he said, releasing me and pulling her into a tighter embrace with both arms.

I also had no idea he and Carly were so close. Or even knew each other. At all.

"I keep him updated," Carly said, shrugging as they pulled away from each other. "Mr. B and I are tight like that."

He winked at her and went back to the counter to answer the telephone.

"He was one of the people who pulled me back," she said in a quiet, sober voice when he was occupied. "You know..."

"Really?" Again, surprising news to me.

"He's a volunteer for the teen suicide hotline."

I nodded. It was explanation enough.

"Yeah, if it weren't for him... and, well, *you* of course," Carly said and pulled me into a half-hug. Another surprise. "I wouldn't *be* here today. Like literally."

I shrugged. I knew. I'd lived the literal version of a world without her.

Mr. Brewster hung up the phone and walked back to us. "So, what brings you girls in today?" He looked at me. "Not a white rose?"

I smiled and shook my head.

"She's throwing my sister an un-birthday party. We were hoping you had some discounted reject flowers we could buy and turn into masterpieces." She waves her hands when she says the word *masterpieces.*

Mr. Brewster did us one bigger. Since we were two of his favorite customers/girls who he'd saved in different ways, and the store was slow, he brought us to the back and created seven masterpieces out of the *reject* flowers as Carly called them. Although I couldn't see how any of them were *rejects.* Sure, some had brown petals, but he just plucked them off; and others looked a little mashed on the top but were still beautiful. He threw in some lavender tea-light holders with *Ethan & Bethany* engraved on them. (Apparently either Ethan or Bethany or both got cold feet.) Artfully, he positioned each one into the arrangements so the names weren't visible among the petals and leaves.

When Carly took the first load to her car, Mr. Brewster said, "Haven't seen you in a while, Emily. Are things... better?"

I stuck a faded pink rose in the spot he pointed at then shrugged.

"I don't mean to pry. We just have not seen you in a while. I've had an overstock of white roses as of late."

"No, it's not that." It was a good question, and I had to think. When *was* the last time I'd come in for a rose for my Rose Ritual? Mr. Brewster kept extra white roses just for me. They were always meticulously wrapped in clear cellophane and were just the thing I always needed right after a death. That's what I used them for. To decorate the grave of someone I'd experienced a death or particularly painful memory with. I'd place the rose on the grave and have a last final flashback, which ultimately eased the mental and emotional pain of the bad memories.

And surprisingly it had been Dr. Shew's idea. So she had gotten something right.

But when was the last one? Nora's death last fall.

No wait, I had needed a rose more recently when Tessa died. *When Grandma died.* But someone had mysteriously placed a white rose, wrapped just how I liked it in my mailbox, saving me the trouble of walking all the way to the floral shop that day. It had been a bad day. And it was before I knew Grandma and Tessa could not be saved.

Still a hard question to answer. It certainly wasn't an indication that I was getting better at this gig. But an interesting thought. I shrugged again. "I guess I just haven't needed one in a while."

"That's good news?" he asked, seeing the look on my face. Just because I hadn't experienced a death and needed the Rose

Ritual to cope did not mean I was finished experiencing death or pain. "Well, I'll continue to keep some on hand."

"You don't need to do that. I don't want you to lose money because they're going to waste."

"Trust me, nothing goes to waste." He waved a hand at the seventh finished product made with the *rejects*.

"They turned out beautiful," I said, picking up two of the arrangements and adjusting them in my arms to take to Carly's car. "Okay, but maybe don't keep an overstock of white roses anymore. I kinda like the rejects... you know, for next time."

# definitely thawing

Mr. Brewster let us borrow a helium tank for the afternoon, and Carly bought some of those expensive silver and metallic-blue balloons, so we popped all of my limp ones and added bunches of two and three balloons to go with each Brewster-masterpiece arrangement. In thirty minutes, Carly and I managed to make the place look a thousand times better than it had looked after my three hours of work. And when the rental guys arrived with their fantastic lighting to go along with it—Carly had called and got us a fabulous last-minute deal— the place looked better than prom.

Everything was falling into place.

I texted Brian while Carly drove me home to change. His plan was going smoothly—he'd lied about dragging Ari to some family wedding.

BRIAN: ALMOST CANCELED ON ME, BUT I CONVINCED her to come. We are good. Picking her up at 6.

. . .

BRIAN WAS THE BEST. IF ANYONE COULD CHANGE HER mind, it was him. I briefly wondered why she almost cancelled, but I didn't dwell on it long.

I rushed into my house and had just enough time to don my fancy dress—the one I wore to the recent Sweetheart Dance with Scott O'Neil: full-length cream satin, overlaid with a burgundy lace that melted from light at the bodice to a dark rich color as it met the floor. There wasn't time to dwell on the memories I'd experienced in said dress. I would have worn something else it if I had another option. But I didn't. A quick touch up of my makeup, but not enough time to do anything with my hair other than leave it in the messy bun it had been in all day. But what could I do?

*Lovely as always.* The thought jumped in my head, and my eyes pricked with tears. That was the compliment Andrew always gave Lucy—long before he knew who I was. I suddenly wished I could talk to him, but I hadn't seen him since *before* Mary was taken captive. When we had that ginormous fight. Because he thought I didn't want him to jump to my time. And he made it very clear that he was only jumping for the *thrill alone.* His words.

I held a hand to my chest, pushing against the suddenly potent and strong ache there.

I loved him. I fell in love with Andrew Harker while I wore someone else's face, and there was a very real possibility that I may never see or talk to him again.

But I couldn't think about that now. I had a party to get to and a best friend to win back. And if I was lucky and could find the right timing and the perfect words, I just might gain someone else's forgiveness tonight too. And that other person was a very big reason why I hadn't thought much about Andrew until this moment. I could see and talk to Duncan again.

Hopefully tonight.

Carly waited for me in the car—she couldn't go home and change until Ari was out of the house to avoid suspicion—and we drove back just in time to let the caterers in.

Seriously, Carly had *connections*! We paid half price for Ari's favorite BBQ place with yummy smoky brisket, pulled pork, and roasted chicken. Plus all of the delicious sides: baked beans, potato salad, loaded mashed potatoes.

I hoped we had enough napkins. Having everyone show up in their finest to eat BBQ maybe wasn't the brightest idea.

But it would be okay. It would be an epic party, the party of the century.

I hoped.

As friends began to arrive—all wearing the requested attire— my nerves both rose and eased. Somehow I had managed to pull it off. With Carly's help, of course, and Duncan's connections to get the place. And I hadn't drained my savings completely, so that was a plus too. It had come together, and it would be fabulous. My nerves eased.

But it was almost game time to fix things with Ari. And Duncan. But Ari was priority tonight.

Brian sent me a text when they were five minutes away. We gathered around the entrance of the room a minute before go time. The Silk Sheets were poised to play their signature song the moment she walked through the door.

Her emotions were as expected. Confusion. Shock. Realization that it was all for her. Excitement. Squeals (mostly for The Silk Sheets). Jumping around the room. Hugging all of the guests. Well, all except me. In her defense, she probably just thought I was another guest. The decorations and food—and everything for that matter—screamed Carly. Not Emily.

Carly had somehow managed to leave, dress, and get back in record time *before* Ari arrived. She was a wonder woman. It was getting harder and harder to remember the Carly I'd walked twice. There was almost no resemblance.

When Ari hugged her, Carly whispered something in her ear. Then Arianna finally looked at me and made a beeline toward me with tears in her eyes.

"You did this?" she asked.

I shrugged. "Carly helped a lot," I said. "She has all of the connections."

"But, *you* did this?"

"Look, I'm sorry I've been such a flaky friend lately. With my, um..." I didn't finish the sentence. "But it's no excuse. I should've been a better friend to you. To everyone really." I said the last part quietly as three other faces flitted through my head. One of whom I'd hoped would be there tonight but I had yet to see. "I wanted to make it up to you," I said as she hugged me. "I may hate birthdays, but you don't."

"Yeah, and you went all-out," she said pulling back and admiring the room.

"We got some good deals," I said and shrugged again. "But is it epic enough for Arianna Swartz?" *And do you still hate me?* I wanted to add, but chickened.

"It's better than *epic*, Emily Chandler. You are the best friend a girl could have!" She turned to oogle at the band again. "And you got The Silk Sheets!"

I'd tell her later that Carly should take the credit for that one and nodded instead. "So... are we good?"

For the first time in my life I couldn't read her expression. "I've, uh... I've been doing a lot of thinking about... *things.*" She paused. "*Lucy,*" she whispered. "And I wanted to talk to you about it."

"Okay?" I couldn't tell if it was a good thing or bad.

She hugged me again. "Let me mingle a bit, then we'll talk?" When she pulled back, she had a smile on her face. "Hey and, uh..." She used her eyes to point at the entrance. "Duncan is here."

I nodded and she walked away.

Deep breath.

By Ari's tone and expression, it felt like things were on the way to being mended with her. And maybe not even because of the party. We would talk tonight. But now I had to face someone else.

I turned in the direction Ari had pointed, and my knees immediately turned to Jell-O. He was wearing the suit he had worn at the dance. The one he wore when he found me hiding and crying, when he comforted me, when he found the injected drugs in the capsule in my arm and offered to take me home.

It was the suit he was still wearing when he picked me up after I freaked out at my parents. I cringed at the memory and how I'd acted. And maybe he thought I was crazy and wrong and out of my mind, because I totally was, but he still rescued me.

I'd slept on his couch that night.

But back then he had an almost-girlfriend who wasn't me.

And now he was unattached.

I took another deep breath and slowly walked toward him. He hadn't looked at me yet, and I didn't want to spook him. He said he was only coming for Ari, but I hoped he wasn't as angry as he'd been on Wednesday.

Sure, it had only been two days, but a girl could hope.

"Hey, Duncan," I said tentatively.

His guard was up instantly when he looked at me.

"Thanks for coming. Really," I said, my heart hammering in my chest.

"I told you I would." His tone was cool. *He's still mad.* I could see it on his face and hear it in the tone of his voice. But I couldn't blame him.

"Look, I—" I held my hands out in surrender. "I'm really so sorry for the other night. Really," I took a step closer and he thankfully didn't back away. In fact, it was either my imagination or I swear his look was thawing. "I've been a horrible friend, and that football award ceremony was important to you."

He nodded once. Definitely thawing. "I appreciate that."

"Is there anything I can do to make it up to you?" I dared take another step closer. "Because I really am sorry."

He looked down at my dress, then back at my face. He was going to forgive me! He was going to say that everything was okay and that one little misstep of mine was forgotten! I could see it in his expression, in the tiny movements of his face as they projected the emotions underneath.

But then he shook his head. And looked at the floor. "I need just a bit more... time," he said and clenched his fists at his side. "I hope you can understand that." He looked back at me, then took two steps back.

I nodded. Afraid any words would come out shaky and broken, it was all I could do. I nodded again and he walked away.

Time. He just needed time.

# CHAPTER 37

# MEMORIES

"Emily Chandler, that party was amazing!" Ari said as we divvied up the floral arrangements a few of the girls had begged to take home. Ari couldn't fit seven in her bedroom anyway. She gave me a side-hug since I currently had two of the arrangements cradled in my arms. "Seriously, thank you!"

"Only the best for my BFF!" I leaned into her to return the hug, then headed out to the parking lot while she followed with the last an armful of decorations. It had been a long, but fun night.

"Sleepover tonight?" she asked, surprisingly tentative.

"Yes! Please!"

A half hour later we were propped up in my bed, shoulder to shoulder, scrolling through the pictures taken at the party. One of the Brewster masterpieces spilled over the top of my dresser, another was downstairs on the kitchen table. Mom's eyes practically bugged out when I brought them home.

"I have to say, Ems," Ari said. "I'm impressed." She waved a hand at my dresser. I'd already explained all of the ways Carly and I—mostly Carly—had made it a perfect night, and I didn't forget to mention Duncan's huge involvement either. "No offense, but I didn't think you had it in you."

That stung a little, but it was the truth. "Seriously, Carly had all of the connections and most of the ideas were hers. You should've seen the place before she got involved."

"Your talk with Duncan didn't last long." Ari said as she scrolled passed several pictures with Duncan smiling with an arm around Scott. Allison (Scott's new girlfriend), Clare (Duncan's ex-girlfriend) and a couple more of Duncan and Scott's teammates were also in the picture. Clare looked smug, but at least she wasn't next to Duncan in the picture. "I expected you two would be inseparable all night."

"He said he needed more... time," I said and filled her in on my major screwup with Duncan earlier in the week.

"You've done all kinds of friendship damage lately," she nudged me. "Haven't you?"

That little nudge spoke volumes. She was right. I'd managed to make everyone I cared about mad at me, but she'd forgiven me. Granted, she was angry because of what I had done to Lucy. But still, it was encouraging that fences were being mended.

"I visited my great-great-grandmother the other night," I said. "She's a little bit older than Lucy, and I hoped she could help."

Ari put the phone down and blacked the screen. "Can she help?"

"I don't know!" I lamented and threw myself back on my pillow with my arms covering my face.

"What did you tell her?"

I peaked at her between my arms and an unwanted smile snuck out. "You're going to laugh."

"What happened?" She moved my arms away from my face. Then laughed. She was already laughing.

I sat up again. "I concentrated so hard that night. *Juliet Cole, 1901. Juliet Cole, 1901.* I said it over and over. I read her journals until my eyelids slammed shut, just so that I could hopefully have a memory-dream where she was."

"So, you didn't make it?"

"No, I made it. 1901. And Grandma Juliet was there." An embarrassed smile crept out again.

"What?" She pulled my hands away because now I'd covered my face.

"I didn't walk with Juliet."

"Then who?" She shook my shoulders.

I laughed. "I walked with her daughter, Hazel."

"And why is that embarrassing?"

"Because Hazel..." I paused and blew out a breath. "Wasn't even two."

Ari's eyes widened. "She wasn't, like, even two *years old?*"

I nodded.

She tried to hold it in, I could tell that she tried really hard, but the instant she went to open her mouth she burst into laughter.

That lasted at least thirty seconds.

Mom even poked her head in the door to see what was so funny.

"Did you know?" Ari asked Mom between giggles. "Did you know Emily dream-walked a baby?"

Mom smiled and Dad poked his head in behind her. "She talked like a toddler for about an hour that morning," Dad said.

I glared at him.

He just smiled at me. "You have to admit it was pretty funny, Emily."

I gave in and shrugged, then finally joined in the laughter.

Mom and Dad asked about the party. Ari jumped up to show some of the pictures that conveyed some of the ambiance of the lighting and decorations. They all congratulated me on a party well done. I focused the praise back on Carly and Duncan. Then they left to watch a movie downstairs.

"So, I gather you weren't able to talk to your grandmother?" she asked.

"No, I did. I just don't know if she will be able to help."

"You mean, as a *not-quite-two-year-old*, you were able to talk to your great-grandmother?"

"Great-great-grandmother," I corrected. "But yeah, I mean, she has the dreams too, and when her daughter began speaking words she shouldn't know she figured out really quickly that someone was walking her daughter. Or *visiting* her, as she called it."

"So you wrote Lucy's name and her wedding date. That's it? That's not much to go on."

"I know," I wiped my hands over my face.

"How does Lucy's wedding date help anything?"

"It was the date she was sent to the sanatorium."

Ari pauses for a long moment, probably absorbing everything I've told her. "But Lucy was dying. Even if we go back and your... Even if Juliet is able to do something..." Ari paused. "Lucy will probably still die of tuberculosis."

"I know. That's why I plan to go back *before* she gets sick." And before I mess everything up with the doctor.

"You can do that?"

"I've done it before. I hope to go back to the first time I visited her in the asylum while her spirits were still up and before she became infected."

Another pause. "Well, I don't know if you heard, I said *we*. I'm coming too."

I smiled. "I heard."

We resumed scrolling through pictures when I came upon one of a not-so-happy Brian. I hadn't spent a lot of time with him tonight, but he did look a little on the morose side. In every. Single. Picture. And now that I thought about it, he did leave the party in a tail-between-the-legs sort of way.

"What was with Brian tonight?" I asked.

Ari shrugged. She stared at the picture and not at me. "We... broke up."

"You broke up? Why?"

She glanced at me briefly, but then became very interested in her cuticles. "It just felt like we..." She blew air upward, scattering the blonde hair that hung near her face. "Like we weren't meant to be together."

"Did he do something? He's always been a good guy. Did he end up being a major jerk?"

"No, no, no." She finally looked at me. "Nothing like that. *Always the perfect gentleman,*" she sang. "Just not for me."

I just stared at her. This didn't seem very like the Arianna I knew. But it did kinda make sense why she almost cancelled on him, thinking she was going to a family wedding.

"Do you... do you still *like* him?"

She frowned. She did. I could see it on her face.

"Then why breakup? Is there someone else?"

"Nope," she said, twisting her mouth.

"Then why?"

"I dunno, Em!" Ari threw her hands in the air and stood up from my bed to walk toward the window. "It was just one of those *it-felt-like-the-right-thing-to-do* sort of things."

"Huh." I didn't know what else to say.

"Look, you said that something happened with Duncan, right?"

"Yeah..." I said slowly, though I had no idea what that had to do with her and Brian.

"The thing with you two is..." She turned back to look at me. "And it's crazy that neither of you can see it yet," she said, looked at the ceiling. "Or rather that *you* haven't seen it yet. I'm pretty sure he is well aware."

"See what?"

She removed one of the pictures on my bulletin board. One of Duncan and me from a memory I didn't remember. "That you two were *made* for each other. That you're perfect together. That if you'd been born in the 1300s or 1400s—or whenever Shakespeare was around—that the Bard would've been writing sonnets and romantic comedies about you and Duncan."

*Really?* It was a strange thought. Mainly because of our

biggest obstacle. "You think that even after everything I've told you about Andrew?"

"What, that he's stuck in your dreams and you can never actually be with him?"

"Ari, he's moving forward." I omitted the part that he wasn't actually moving forward because of me, but I couldn't deny that my connection with Andrew had a lot to do with the fact that we were kindred spirits who endured the same types of terrors. And if I got a chance to talk with him, if he suddenly became available to me in my own time, things could change drastically for me.

And Duncan could be collateral damage.

Maybe it was a good thing Duncan was currently mad at me.

"Well, I guess things will get interesting when he gets here," Ari said, then laughed once. "I'd like to see the two of them duke it out. But for the record, I'm on Team Duncan."

"Noted." I smiled. I was kind of on Team Duncan at the moment too. I was just having a hard time letting go of Andrew.

"Remember this day?" she held up the picture. In it Duncan and I were soaking wet and covered in green slime. I didn't remember the day, but fortunately she just continued talking. "It's when we were Jell-O wrestling last fall—you know with the tarp out on Allison Duke's back lawn?"

I nodded like I remembered. It sounded fun. Probably more fun than whatever I actually remembered doing that day. Because I didn't remember.

"You two had recently started dating, and he made some Freudian slip about some girl who would love Jell-O wrestling, if only because it tasted good."

"Ew!"

"I know."

"Who was the girl?" I tried to ask in a I-am-merely-curious-and-not-at-all-jealous type of way. But I half expected her to say Clare Pickett, his recent ex-girlfriend. I wasn't sure if I could hide my jealousy if it was her.

"It was like an herb-name like Thyme or something."

"*Thyme?*"

"I dunno." She yawned. "Maybe *Rosemary?* Or *Basil?*"

"Seriously? Basil?" I laughed, but then yawned too.

"I can't remember! No wait... Sage! He said Sage. Anyway, I thought you were going to flip out about him wanting to be with some other girl. Except you didn't."

"What did I do?"

"You stared at him. First you were confused, then you had this cryptic conversation about his sister."

"His sister? Duncan doesn't have a sister!"

She shrugged.

I let it go and laid down on my pillow, suddenly very tired. It had been a long day.

"And then you said a random guy's name. It wasn't anyone I knew."

*Wow. What had gone on in my previous past I didn't remember?* So strange. "What was the name I said?"

Ari returned the picture back to my board, "Adam? Maybe?" She grinned. "Maybe it was Andrew!" she said with a wink! "Or maybe that's just the name my memory is filling in, because it really wasn't the name of a person I knew."

"Huh. *Weird.*"

"I know," she said.

I couldn't help but compare the vast difference between our barely *acquaintance*-ship that day Arianna invited me to be in her Hamlet group last fall and our *best-friend*-ship now. She'd invited me in their group out of pity after months of not speaking, and now we were discussing my memory-dreams and the success of her birthday party—well, and boys. I couldn't deny that a large part of our conversation had revolved around boys tonight.

She didn't remember ever *not* being my friend.

But I did.

And I couldn't help but feel sorry for that past Emily who was a loner and had lost her best friend. I was so happy. Sure, things were still screwed up in a lot of ways. But I had my best friend back and that made everything else seem less *bleak.*

"Look, that party was am-azing, but I am beat," Ari said covering another yawn. "Now, where's that ring?" I smiled and pointed at the jewelry box, where she easily found it. "Let's go save Lucy!"

One best friend back. Now to save the next. "Yes, let's go save Lucy."

# bright future

"From this valley they say you are going," Lucy sings. "*We will miss your bright eyes and sweet smile.*" *What? No apology?* She asks only to my thoughts, but there is a bubbling excitement that doesn't match her words.

*I, uh...* My heart hammers. Despite the strange energy, of course she would still be mad at me. I'd just hoped to come earlier before the sickness and before the isolation. *Look, I'm sorry for what I said. I'm sorry for taking over and making things look so bad—*

*What do you mean?* she asks, then continues her song. "*Come and sit by my side if you love me.*" It's the same song she was singing the first time I came.

I turn my head to take in our surroundings. The room is bright, with east-facing windows uncovered to let in the morning sunshine. There are ten iron beds and only eight of them are occupied by Lucy and the seven original women. We're back in the group room. *Whew!* So no more isolation. And the extra beds crammed between them are gone too. Strange.

A few of the women sing along with Lucy. Like the first time I visited here. The oldest looks maybe sixty and the youngest is...

*Caroline.* The eleven or twelve-year-old whom Ari walked the last time. I hope Ari isn't walking her this time.

*Wait.*

"*But remember the Red River Valley and the cowboy who loved you so true,*" Lucy sings.

*It can't be. Did it—?*

"Well? Emily?" Lucy asks aloud. "Are you going to apologize for getting me into this place?"

"Nuuurse!" the woman in the bed directly across shouts to the doorway, lengthening her vowels. "Miss Luuuucy needs heeeelp!"

It's the original memory. The one I lived with Lucy before. I fill her lungs with air. No more sickness. It worked. I came before the tuberculosis outbreak. I can get her out! I hope. I have no idea if my little trip to Great-Great-Grandma Juliet helped. But I'm getting my re-do.

Lucy plasters her well-trained smile on the woman. "I am quite all right, Nancy," she says, keeping her voice calm though her insides twist in frustration, but not fear. That's different. "Please do not cry out again."

*It'll be okay,* I say, even though it doesn't seem like Lucy needs buoying up. I try to remember exactly what happens next. *Ugh.* There was that horrible nurse. Nurse Edith? Was it?

"Nuuuurse!" Nancy looks straight at Lucy when she says it, but this time the fear doesn't increase. Lucy is really just irritated.

"I've missed you, Emily," Lucy says aloud, but quietly. She is comforted by my presence. It's a stark contrast to the way she felt about me the last time we talked. "I really cannot stay angry at you for long."

*Only because you don't remember all of the ways Andrew and I messed up your life,* I wanted to say. But I was desperate to keep my thoughts to myself. *You definitely had strong feelings about him.*

But Nurse Edith doesn't enter the room. Instead the petite,

auburn-haired nurse arrives instead. The one Ari walked what seemed like ages ago.

"Ari?" I whisper as she walked over to Nancy and speaks with her quietly.

The nurse then walks over to us. "I am sorry if Nancy has disturbed you. Is anything amiss, Lucy?" she asks.

I scrutinize her, looking to see any sign that my best friend is behind those kind eyes.

"What? Do I have something in my teeth?" she asks in a very twenty-first century teenager way. She then proceeds to pick invisible food remnants from her front teeth.

Ari. Definitely Ari.

"You know that's really gross, right?"

She sticks her tongue out at me.

Lucy feels confused so I fill her in. *My best friend Arianna is walking with this nurse.*

*Nurse Mauve?* Lucy fills in the nurse's name that has fled my memory.

*Yes, with Nurse Mauve.*

"But why?" she asks aloud.

"You are going home today, Miss Lucy," Ari/Mauve says with confidence. "Em and I are here to help that happen."

I shoot her a glare. My overconfidence the last time I walked with Lucy—well, in the future for her—was really the reason Ari was so mad at me for screwing everything up. Granted, here we had a sort of second chance at things, but there was still no guarantee it would work. We didn't even have a plan.

"Trust me," Ari/Mauve says. "Now, let's get you out of bed. The doctor will see you now."

"Now? Is the doctor even here?" I ask. The last time I lived this memory with Lucy, it was a very boring several hours until the doctor arrived in the late afternoon.

"Of course he's here. And he wanted to see you the instant Emily was walking with you," she says in a low tone, although by the glances around the room—none of which are directed at us—I doubt anyone heard. And if they did... well, look where we are.

I wait expectantly for Ari/Nurse Mauve to remove the ankle straps, but she just looks at me. Impatiently, I remove the bedsheets and see that my feet are free. In fact, there aren't any marks on her ankles or other indications that Lucy has been strapped in at all.

*Something has changed,* I say, mostly to myself, but I have no idea what that could be.

We follow Nurse Mauve down the long hallway that somehow seems brighter. Maybe it's the absence of sickness? Lucy is calm without any anxiety about what is coming next. Also different.

We enter the same room with the machine I remember Lucy being hooked up to, when she pleaded for me to speak up and talk with the doctor to prove that she was hearing voices, but Nurse Mauve doesn't turn it on and merely leaves the room for a moment before returning with the doctor.

A different doctor.

Whose smile brightens the room even more. The twinkle in his kind eyes make any uneasiness within me—Emily, not Lucy—disappear. He has a full head of hair and looks young, like maybe twenty-seven? Twenty-eight?

"A-are you the doctor?" I ask. Despite his kind smile, I still have some trepidation. Although I don't know if it is the anticipation of whatever happens during Lucy's examinations or the pressure to get her out of the sanatorium.

He scrutinizes my face. "Lucy Harker, you know I am your doctor," he says. "Which means that you must have a *visitor.*"

*Visitor?* That's the exact word—

"Yes, Dr. Cole," Lucy says. "Emily is with me today."

"Finally!" He claps his hands, making me jump.

"Cole?" I say. "Your name is Dr..." I pause. "Dr. Cole? As in my..." But I can't finish the sentence.

"As in your great-great-grandfather? If I'm not mistaken?"

"But how?"

"Did you not know that I was a psychiatrist when you came to us for help?"

"I, uh... no, I had no idea," I said. "I just knew that Juliet... er... that Great-Great-Grandmother Cole had, or *has*, the dreams like me. And being a contemporary of Lucy, I hoped she could help somehow."

"You thought right." He puts his hands behind his back and looks at the floor thoughtfully. "In fact, it was *after* your visit to Hazel that she finally opened up about her *gift.*"

"Really?" *He didn't know before?* I guess I never gathered that in her journals. Perhaps she didn't tell him for the very fear of ending up in a place like this.

"Yes, if not for you, I do not know if she would have ever told me."

"And how is Hazel?" I ask, deflecting the attention from me.

He laughs. "She is a very energetic three-year old now, and I think she'd like another visit from her *Auntie Emily* as she calls you."

"She remembers me?" I laugh too. "I'll have to visit her again someday. Except *technically* I think she's like *my* great-great-aunt."

"What has Lucy told you about our research here?" He asks, taking Lucy's wrists to feel for her pulse and motioning for Nurse Mauve to turn on the machine. It whirrs as the motors warm up and makes a zapping electrical sound. This time there is no foreboding about what the machine might be used for. Although there never was for Lucy, even back when it was Dr. Baldy and Nurse Intimidating.

"Nothing really. I didn't know you were doing research."

"Well, now that you're here, we can run some tests with you present. Then Lucy can be discharged as soon as we have finished."

*Really?* I asked Lucy silently, not daring to hope.

He nods and smiles, then focuses his attention on the nobs and switches of the machine.

*He knows about the dreams. He believes that it isn't a mental condition. He says there is no reason why I cannot lead a normal life.* She says to me while we wait.

*That's good since... well, I suspect* everyone *has guardian angels. You are just more* aware *of me than most people are of theirs,* I say.

*Exactly.*

*And Charles?*

She smiles. She feels very happy. *Charles has been to visit many times. He and I agreed that I would remain here until Dr. Cole could get a reading with you present. He wanted to bring me home sooner, but I didn't want to miss the chance to complete the tests.*

Great-Great-Grandfather Cole attaches the ancient-looking leads to Lucy's temples and into her hair. "I hope that with this research, those who have the dreams, and those like Lucy who are more aware of their visitors, will be better understood."

"I wonder how that will affect the future," Ari/Nurse Mauve says.

"You know, Ari," I say. "You know what happened to me after Carly was saved. I don't remember all of those memories that happened."

Nurse Mauve looks at me with slight surprise on her face. "So, when we talked last night? About the Jell-O wrestling?"

"I don't remember that happening," I say. "At all."

She shakes Nurse Mauve's head. "Well, that's going to change," she says. "At least the part of you not knowing about the good times. I'm going to dig out my journal."

"That you write in once a year?" I tease.

"Or look at the calendar on my phone," she amends. "And fill you in on everything you missed."

I smile at her. "That sounds great," I say. "I can't wait."

The machine makes more whirring sounds while Great-Great-Grandfather Cole reads the machine and makes notes in a file. He directs Nurse Mauve to some tasks of turning dials to specific numbers and writes more notes. It takes maybe fifteen minutes total, then he turns the machine off and removes the leads from Lucy's hair.

"That's it?" I ask.

"That is all," he says, then his face turns sober. "Emily, I have seen the look on my wife's face after a bad... *visit*. And it pains me to think a young descendant of mine suffers the same fate."

His words bring tears to my eyes. He has no idea how hard this *fate* is on me. Or Juliet. But he loves us and wants to ease our suffering. He *loves* me. I can see it in his eyes. He loves me. He has never met me in this life, but he loves and cares about me. And he wants to somehow help, to somehow ease *my* suffering.

"Now, I may not be able to make a huge difference for my Juliet, but I intend to make this my life's work. Hopefully my research will be continued after I am gone. If I succeed, by the time your dreams begin, I hope there will be some ease to your suffering. Maybe there will be better understanding and more effective help for you."

"Thank you," I say. "You have no idea what this means to me." I wrap my arms around him, not knowing if I will ever speak to him this way again. "Say hello to Grandma Juliet and *Aunt Hazel* for me?" I ask.

"Of course," he says, squeezing Lucy tight. Squeezing me tight. "Now let's get Lucy back home!"

"Yes. Please," I say, letting out a sigh of relief.

"Hey, and Dr. Cole?" Ari asks, tentatively.

He releases me to look at her.

"Could you take care of Caroline?" she asks. "She shouldn't be in here. She just doesn't have a family."

He smiles at her. "I will see what I can do." And I believe he means every word.

"Better?" I ask Ari.

She nods rapidly. "You did it! I'm sorry I was so mad."

I shake Lucy's head. "I messed up. I'm just glad we could fix it." I feel Lucy's unasked question and confusion. *I'll tell you later*, I say and mean it. I will definitely visit Lucy again.

She smiles.

"Well, I can't wait to see how this affects the future!" Ari says.

"Me neither," I say and give my ancestor one last hug.

# i'm famous?

It didn't surprise me that Ari was gone when I woke up. In fact, I really hoped that the now-missing beautiful arrangement of flowers on top of my dresser from last night meant that I had been a better friend in this version—the version of reality changed by Great-Great-Grandpa Cole's research. (I should really look up his first name). Hopefully I never needed to throw Arianna an un-birthday party. Hopefully I threw her a fabulous, thoughtful party closer to her actual birthday.

No party means no sleepover, so she probably didn't spend the night.

I wondered if this version of me experienced the coma. In the reality I remembered, I was traipsing with Lucy and Isabella *on* Arianna's birthday several weeks ago. Did that actually happen?

I skipped downstairs, smelling my favorite breakfast of fried scones wafting throughout the house. My mouth watered.

"What's the occasion?" I asked, brightly.

Mom turned from the hot oil with a not-as-excited-as-she-should-be-for-Saturday-morning-scones face. But seeing my smile, she matched it. "You're happy this morning. Any good dreams?"

"Yeah," I said and breathed a sigh of relief. It was amazing how much better I felt with the burden lifted. I had Arianna back,

Lucy was saved from dying a horrible death in a sanatorium, and Duncan was still mad at me but that couldn't last long. The only person I didn't know how to make amends with was Andrew. But a big part of me expected to see him when Mary was saved, and hopefully soon. There wasn't anything I could do about him while I was awake, so I banished that train of thought from my head.

Wait. Maybe Duncan *wasn't* mad at me. If I'd changed something, maybe that meant that I hadn't miss Duncan's important football award ceremony a few days ago.

"That good, huh?" Mom teased when I didn't elaborate on my answer to her question since I got lost in thought.

She asked about my dreams, so she must know about those. "I fixed something. A mistake," I said, not knowing exactly how much Mom knew about my dreams in this new reality. "Hey, did I go to a football ceremony thing for Duncan this week?" I was itching to know if he was still mad at me or if I could text him after breakfast without an angry I-told-you-I-needed-time! response.

She watched me strangely. "No..."

My stomach dropped. What did that look mean? *No* I didn't go? Or *no* who was Duncan and what was I talking about? I panicked. How should I proceed? What should I say? I mean, this was Mom, but did she even know about the dreams? Did I somehow erase Duncan? "I had some flowers on my dresser last night," I said, hoping it was safe territory. "But they were gone this morning."

Mom smiled and shook her head. "You changed a timeline again," she said, turning back to the scones. "You really need to be careful about that, Emily." If I wasn't mistaken, I could hear a tenseness in her voice.

Well, at least that was still my name. *Emily*. And she knew about the dreams, clearly, and that I sometimes changed a time-line. And she didn't seem mad, just... *tense*. So maybe Great-Great-Grandpa had done some good. Like major good.

"Who gave you the flowers?" she asked, busy in the hot oil. "Duncan?"

*Whew.* "He does exist," I said quietly, feeling immensely relieved. "Why did you look at me strange when I asked about his ceremony thing? Does he not play football or something?"

She laughed, then using her tongs, placed the recently fried scone onto a plate and turned to push it toward across the table. "Oh, he plays football," she said. "But you didn't go to his ceremony this week."

"Why?" I reached for the honey butter. I could tell she was having fun toying with me. "Are we not friends? Does he hate me for some reason?"

She didn't put on any more dough to cook and looked at me.

Dad walked in right then and sat next to me after scooting his iPad over to show me something. "Another article, Ems," he said lightly.

Mom made signals at him to stop, waving her hand over her throat.

But Dad didn't get the message. Dad never got the message. I couldn't help but smile as I looked at the article that he'd pulled up.

The headline read: FUNDRAISING SUCCESS FOR DREAM TRAVELERS.

I looked at Dad. "What?"

Mom cleared her throat. "She changed a timeline last night, hon," Mom said, sternly to Dad.

"Oh, *oh!*" He pulled the iPad away and blacked the screen before I could read more.

"What is going on?" I ask. This secrecy was getting irritating. I stared at both of them. They looked like they were at a loss. "Look," I said. "You know about my dreams, correct?"

They both nodded.

"And you believe they are real?" I closed my eyes. I had to ask. It felt like they did, but all of this would be for naught if they didn't believe me. It would be too discouraging after all of our recent progress.

When I opened my eyes again, they both looked dubious. "Did we not believe you, *before?*" Mom asked, like there was no way she would ever *not* believe they were real.

I shrugged. "You called them night terrors until very recently."

"But you're the Lucy-Walker, Ems!" Dad said, "You're famous. Everyone knows—"

But he was cut off by another glare from Mom.

"I'm... *famous?*" I asked. "W-why?"

Mom turned off the hot oil then sat next to me. I still hadn't touched my food. "Let's start at the beginning," Mom said. "What was your dream about last night?"

"Lucy," I said.

That response didn't surprise either of them, and they both urged me to continue.

"She was in one of those sanatoriums." I didn't add that she was in there because of me. "I met with Great-Great-Grandpa Cole—"

"Yes, Dr. Bartholomew Cole," they said in unison in a way that sounded like the name was spoken often. At least at home.

I made a mental note to remember the name *Bartholomew* but had a hunch that wouldn't be necessary.

"He said he was going to start researching the *dreaming* because of me and well... Grandma Juliet."

"And that happened last night for you?" Dad asked.

I nodded, but my frustration was building. I hated being left in the dark about my life. I had dealt with it alone when I saved Carly—well, mostly—but why now? "Look," I said. "If you know about my dreams and you know that sometimes I change time-lines, you must know how confusing it is to wake up to a new one."

"We do," Dad said the same time Mom said, "Yes."

"So, please fill me in. There's a lot I'm afraid I don't remember."

"Right. Where should we start?" Dad asked.

Mom shook her head at him. "There's a reason we have rules about this," Mom said through gritted teeth.

"Rules?"

"Oh, right," Dad said. "Sometimes you get too... what's the word?"

"Overwhelmed," Mom finished for him.

"Yes, sometimes the changes are too overwhelming," Dad continued. "And fortunately, it's a Saturday so you don't have to go to school, but we have to limit how much to tell you."

"Yes, we learned this the hard way," Mom said. I couldn't help but stare. This was so... *different.* "We can't answer all of your questions today but you can ask more tomorrow."

"But what if I change the timeline again tonight in my dreams?" I asked, a little bit annoyed that they planned to purposely keep things from me.

"If you do, whatever you didn't learn today won't matter tomorrow anyway."

*Good point.* "Okay," I said. "What can I ask?"

"What's your first question?"

"Um..." I didn't have to think long. "I'm famous?" I pointed at the iPad.

# benevolence

"Yes!" Dad swiveled the tablet back toward me and pulled up article after article about the ongoing research into the "Dream Travelers." It went clear back to 1917.

"This is a lot of reading," I said. "Could you give me a summary of all of this?" I waved a hand at the screen.

"Yeah, uh... you said you visited Grandpa Cole?" Mom asked, apparently giving in and going along with telling me stuff. "That's so strange to call him that, although I guess he is our relative."

I nodded. "He was really nice too," I added. "Hopefully I'll see him again. And Grandma Juliet."

Mom stared at me wistfully. Was she envious of my *gift?* Never in a million years would I ever think that was possible. First, she believed the dreams were real—it seemed that she believed all along in this reality—and now she was looking like she wished she could have them too? Maybe I'd have to let her piggyback someday.

I shook my head in disbelief.

"Dr. Bartholomew Cole was the first to research Dream Travelers," Dad began. "He spent his entire life investigating the phenomena."

I smiled. Great-Great-Grandpa had kept his promise. "Did he see Lucy more than that one time? Or do you know?"

"Yes, Lucy and, of course, your *Grandma Juliet*"—Dad said her name strangely, like it wasn't what he was used to calling her —"were his first subjects. Lucy as someone who was aware while she was being visited or walked, or whatever term you prefer. And Grandma Juliet as someone who traveled in the dreams herself."

"Lucy was visited her entire life by one person," Mom continued where Dad ended.

"By me," I said, my voice catching.

Mom nodded.

*Wow.* That was a relief. So many times I'd felt like I should say goodbye to Lucy, that she didn't need me anymore and I was causing more harm than good. And perhaps that was true in the past—especially when Andrew made such a mess of things. But he was gone in the future now, or the past. I wasn't exactly sure where he was at the moment. And Lucy would have more bad times in her lifetime. She'd have bad days, and good. And I would get to experience all of them with her. "She's like my best friend," I said.

"I know," Mom said and pulled me in a hug. "She always said the same about you."

"She did?"

"You two sort of grew old together," Dad interjected. "Well, I guess that *you'll grow* old while you keep visiting her."

That made me happier than words could express.

"Only a few people know the name of the person who walks with them," Mom continued. "And even those that do aren't supposed to reveal their name of their walker because of complications in the future."

"Why?" I asked, though I guessed I'd need to have that conversation with Lucy soon.

Mom and Dad looked at each other as if wondering if they should tell me.

"C'mon!" I said. "I knew why before? Didn't I? Why shouldn't I not know now?"

"Lucy left you an... inheritance," Dad said.

"An *inheritance?* Like money?" I asked.

"Yes, it was meager to begin with, but over the years with the compound interest..."

"It's a substantial amount," Mom finished Dad's sentence. "Even though she didn't start it until the 1920s."

"You can't touch it until you turn twenty-one," Dad said. "But as you can imagine, a lot of people went to great lengths to try to convince the bank that they were the *Lucy Walker.*"

My head was reeling. This was a lot to take in. I'm glad we had *rules* about how many questions I could ask after a timeline shift. But seriously, I needed to stop making changes that were so drastic. A big part of me was pretty terrified about what else I would learn tomorrow. *If I didn't shift things again, of course.*

"How did I prove that I walk Lucy? *When* did I prove it?"

"That was the hard part," Dad said. "By the sixties, people began to suspect that the *Lucy Walker* might never be proven because so many people knew her story and anyone could pretend to be that walker."

"But it turned out to be relatively simple," Mom said. "There was a letter written by Colin Harker dated 1901. It was addressed to you."

*Letter. Why would Colin have reason to—?* Wait. The letter. That letter! The letter I read during the fire. The letter Colin wrote and I was never able to finish! "W-where is the letter now?" I ached to read the rest.

"Well, until a few years ago It was hidden underneath a rock beneath a bench behind the remains of St. Sebastian's church in Old Town," Mom said. "The one that was re-named and used to be called St. Marie's. You told them to look there."

"Yes," Dad continued. "Everyone knew Lucy left a clue in her will about her *favorite place in the world.*"

Of course. The bench. It was *my* favorite place in Lucy's

world too. But St. Sebastian? I couldn't believe I never knew the connection.

"Anyway, the lawyers at the bank had it authenticated after it was found," Dad said.

"And you confirmed the details Colin spoke of in the letter," Mom said.

"It took some historians some serious research to verify everything," said Dad. "There were some obsessive people who were determined to claim the money, so they had to make sure you weren't a really good forger and liar."

"Yes, but ultimately you just took one of them to piggyback with you, so speaking to Lucy while you were there was the ultimate and final proof." Mom laughed when she finished speaking. "It was pretty simple in the end. We all wondered why we hadn't thought of it sooner."

"Wow." It's the only word I had. "Wow."

Mom and Dad just nodded.

"So what's with the *fundraising success?*" I asked, pointing at the iPad again.

"Oh!" Dad said, pulling up the original article. "After you declared to everyone what your intentions with the money were, several groups began fundraising campaigns to add to it. Everyone realizes that you're only seventeen, but a lot of people are pulling to get the process started."

"What did I declare?" Really, who was this *other me?* What sort of thing would I announce to the world that I wanted to do with the money? Seriously my first thought was to finally have my own car. Maybe save some for college? That didn't seem like the type of thing that people began fundraisers for.

"What do you think you would use it for?" Mom asked, quietly. Maybe wondering herself if I was the same person she knew yesterday, or if this version of me was vastly different and less selfless.

I had to think for a minute.

"You came up with it only a few months after the dreams

started. Even before you became the *Lucy Walker*," Mom said. "You knew what you'd do with the money if you were the one to get it. Does that help?"

Honestly, I'd spent a lot of my time in those early months with the dreams believing that they were exactly what Mom and Dad said they were: *night terrors*. But *if* they had believed me from the beginning. *If* I'd had the help to cope with them and talk about them without scrutiny or strange looks, where would my head have been? What benevolent purpose would I have for a large sum of money that I inherited?

*To help people like me.* To help those whose parents *were* nonexistent or couldn't afford the piling psychiatrist bills. Because even if the curse was known and the whole world knew about them, it was still a lonely curse, something that a person dealt with almost absolutely alone. "To help other dreamers," I said. I knew that's what I'd said, although I had no idea what that would entail.

Mom came around the table to hug me and kiss me on the head. "To help other dreamers," she repeated. "They've started support groups with some of the money raised. It's not exactly what you said you wanted to do with it, but that'll take time and a few years."

"Until then you said you want to finish your schooling," Dad interjected. "And be a young adult for a couple of years."

"What's my grand plan?"

"To start a center essentially, a home, a school, a sanctuary. Specifically for dream-walkers."

And there it was. My future laid out right in front of me. And it was exactly what I'd pick in any of my realities.

To help other dreamers.

The idea had never blossomed in my head until that moment, because how could I help others when I was struggling myself? When I was constantly butting heads with my own support system? But with a family who suddenly believed it all and even had *rules* to protect me when a timeline changed... It made perfect sense.

And with the funding taken care of, it was possible. No, it was *highly likely.*

And with Andrew moving forward... No, I couldn't think about that just yet. So I let my mind travel back to another question.

"What did the letter from Colin say?" I asked. "I only got to read a small portion of it back when I actually read it."

Mom turned the hot oil back on. "It was water damaged and decayed. Mostly unreadable besides a few names and dates."

"That's too bad," I said. The condition of the letter would be better in Lucy's time. Maybe I'd get to finish it after all.

# the letter

*I am so happy.* It is the first thought that enters my head.

It smells very... floral, I note, as I take in the surroundings. It's a warm, late-summer morning in the Harker Manor gardens. At least thirty people leisurely talk and sip their cups of tea and bite their finger sandwiches. I wave a hand over the spread of food laid out next to me recognizing the same sandwiches Lucy served to her friend, Margaret, at the luncheon when she announced she was engaged to Charles. Also pastries, pecan pie—that certainly must have been provided by the Harker cook —tea, and various food items I do not recognize.

Smiling at the guests, I note that all of the women wear pastel-colored Victorian dresses with ruffles and lace, while the men look a little bit uncomfortable in their suit coats. By the lighting it can't be noon yet but feels like it will be a hot day.

*What's this?* I ask her.

*A garden party,* she says, smiling again. *Charles planned it for my return.*

*How long have you been home?* I ask. Her good mood and happiness is spreading throughout me. She hasn't felt this way... well, *ever.* The last time that came close was that first morning I walked her. But back then she had the air and thoughts of a self-centered rich girl, who mostly had a heart of gold, but her entitle-ment muddied that a little bit. Now, after everything she has been through, the fire, the sanatorium, that self-centered part of her is vanished. And what is left is a more *refined* heart of gold.

*Only a week. And even though the world doesn't understand yet, Charles has stood by my side. My family believes that I have not lost my mind and that you are truly a real person.*

I inwardly laugh at that.

"Darling," Charles says, approaching us. "Is everything all right?" He puts an arm around her waist and pulls her close.

"Fine, sweetheart," Lucy answers, then whispers, "Emily is here."

"Ah," he says, smiling sweetly down at her beneath the brim of his straw derby hat.

"Mind if I slip away for a moment?" she asks. "I promise not to be long."

"Of course." He kisses her on the head and walks away to speak with another guest.

Lucy slips away down a side path of the garden that leads around the house. I half expect her to walk to the church, to sit on her favorite bench, but that would go against her promise to Charles.

Instead, we venture into a more-secluded area of the garden. I recognize it as the place where I first spoke with Grandma Grace as she walked with Tessa. It's a bittersweet memory, but I banish it before it seeps into Lucy's very happy mood.

"Why did you laugh a moment ago?" she asks, no longer speaking to me in thought now that we are alone.

*Because you said the world doesn't know about me walking with you yet.* I, however, vow to be respectful and not take over her voice, even though we are alone.

"And what was so amusing about that?" she asks, her lilting tone thick now that her depression I felt with her in the sanato-rium is gone. How I've missed that.

*Well, the world knows about me in my time!* I almost mention the inheritance she left me, but don't want her gift to me be because of a suggestion or hint that I gave her. It didn't feel like the right thing to do.

"Is that... *good?*" she asks.

"Yes!" I say aloud, then quickly and wordlessly apologize. *When I woke up yesterday, my parents had accepted it. I no longer get those* looks. *And it's not just that they've accepted it. When I woke up, my whole reality shifted because of Grandma and Grandpa Cole... and you... In my world, people have known about the dreamers for decades. My parents have known about it and accepted it and helped me through it since the day my dreams started.*

"That's wonderful!" Lucy claps her hands.

Of course I don't remember any of that, but at least my present is better. Still, I don't add that.

*I hate to bring this up, but during the fire... Hannah gave you a letter from Andr— from Charles's grandfather, Colin.*

"Yes?"

I take a deep breath. *Do you have it?* I ask. And even though the future is proof. Even though I know Lucy placed it underneath that bench for me to find over a hundred years later. Yet I still struggle with the hope that she might have it.

"Yes," she says. Her heart is full of happiness and the desire to make everyone around her as happy as she is. When she reaches into her sleeve to pull it out, I realize that she's been carrying it with her for this exact purpose.

*But how?* I ask. *How did you know I'd ask?*

"Because of the name it mentions," she says. "When I returned home and found it amongst my things, I recognized a name you once asked about. And besides that, it is addressed to you. I have carried it around for you ever since."

*What name?* I ask but know the answer. When I first read the letter, I only made it about a third of the way through it and was unable to read the rest. *Andrew?*

"Yes, it speaks of Andrew."

*Can I...?* My breath catches. I can barely breathe. *Can I read it?*

Without another word, she carefully unfolds it:

*Dearest Emily,*

*Yes, I mean you, Emily Chandler. I know who you are. I know what you are. But I thank you. I thank you for being with my sister in her last moments. I thank you for taking over her lips. Her lips which never spoke a word in her entire life until that fateful day she ordered me off the ice.*

*Something strange happened. I have two memories of that day my sister died in the frozen river. I know which one really happened —the one when my sister did not speak. When I almost fell in myself and drowned. I know you were there with her for both.*

Yes, I remember this. He talked of Nora. I couldn't save her, but he was with her... *twice.* Colin was saved twice. I'd already read that part, and now I could finally read the rest. Now that I wasn't at risk of letting Lucy die in a fire. Now that she was safe and living her happily ever after, I could finally finish this letter. The letter that mentioned a person she did not know.

Another deep breath. *In... and out... Breathe in... and out...*

*I suppose that is the curse from being in a family of memory walkers. Even those of us who do not have the gift can sometimes remember when something was changed because of the choice of a walker.*

· · ·

WHAT? EVEN THOSE WITHOUT—? WAIT. WHEN I SAVED Carly and changed so much of my life, Grandma Grace also felt the effects of that. Could that be what he spoke of?

*BY NOW, YOU MUST KNOW THAT MY GRANDSON, Andrew Harker,*

MY BREATH CAUGHT. MY HEART SPED. LUCY'S EYES welled up. *Andrew Harker.* Colin wrote of his *grandson*, Andrew Harker. Andrew Harker who was no longer his grandson. *How is this possible?* How did this letter survive in a reality where Andrew no longer exists?

It's just like my journal.

"I do not know," Lucy says. "You once asked me where *Andrew* was." She says the name like she doesn't know him. Like his lips had never kissed hers. Like she and he never had a million conversations. Like they'd never talked about their past, like he'd never seen her cry over her parents' graves, or that she'd never listened while he lamented about his *curse.* Like she never made it possible for him and me to talk, like he never overstepped the boundaries and almost messed up her chances of marrying Charles—because of wanting to be close to me. Like she never hated him. Like she never *knew* him. "This is the Andrew you were looking for?" She points at the letter like it's the answer to the mystery of all things Andrew.

So innocent and hopeful and *convincing.* It's depressing. *It's a good thing Andrew isn't here,* I say. I immediately wish to take it back so she doesn't hear it, but she takes the hint and doesn't answer anyway. So I continue reading.

*BY NOW, YOU MUST KNOW THAT MY GRANDSON, Andrew Harker, is also blessed with the gift. Although he considers it a curse. His experiences have jaded him in a way. And I cannot say I fault him for that, but I am concerned. You see, he is planning something dangerous, something I'm not sure will even work, but I don't want him to even try it because of what it might mean. For I will surely lose him if he succeeds.*

HIS GRANDFATHER KNEW ABOUT HIS PLANS TO JUMP ahead... Mind. Blown.

*I'M SURE YOU ARE AWARE OF THE POWER OF WEARING A talisman as you have been aware of walking Lucy more than once. I could see it in your eyes that first day we met. You can tell when someone is being walked if you know what to look for.*

*Andrew's talisman is especially powerful in that he has found a way to gain control in deciding who to walk.*

*It is clear that he has strong feelings for you.*

HEART SWOON.

*I DO NOT MEAN TO CAUSE YOU PAIN, BUT I FEEL THAT some of that love for you stems from his attraction to Lucy as well as the fact that you are like him.*

HEARTBREAK.

*I knew it.* Andrew *fell* for me because of our kinship but only because he was already attracted to Lucy. He loved *Lucy* first.

*I ASSUME HE HAS DONE THE NECESSARY RESEARCH AND preparation, but I am wary of his initial plans to drag you into a walk with him.*

*ISABELLA.*

*BUT BRINGING YOU INTO A SPECIFIC WALK WITH HIM will be his testing ground for what he plans next.*

*The future holds so much wonder for him, as anyone, and he declares that his feelings for you go beyond Lucy's pretty face. He plans to change his lineage and hop through time and get to you.*

*I am afraid of his failure or success. If he fails and becomes desperate, I fear what he will do. If he succeeds, then he will no longer be my direct grandson and will be obliterated from my life— and possibly my memory.*

*And if he doesn't succeed in hopping, he may erase his existence from all times.*

*Please, if you care for him at all, dissuade him from this. Stop him in any way you can.*

*TOO LATE.*

*SINCERELY,*
   *Colin William Harker*

"I FEEL YOUR TURMOIL," LUCY SAYS AFTER A MOMENT. "When I read this letter alone, it was baffling, but after reading it with you... it feels almost... *painful.*"

*Yes,* I say, but cannot even form more words in my thoughts to elaborate.

"Tell me about Andrew," she says.

# plot twist and happily ever after

*h-what? Like... everything?*

"Absolutely," Lucy says, her lips pulling into a smile.

And so I do. I tell her *everything*. About our first meeting when he barged in to introduce himself, our first outing, our trip to the church grounds, and all of her confusion before she knew about me. That when I was gone, they felt only a brotherly feeling toward each other. But when I was present, Lucy felt strange, inexplicable feelings for Andrew which he reciprocated.

She smiles and comments that at first, she suspected she was going mad. She was mostly alone when I visited her—besides the occasional dinner or outing with Margaret—but sometimes *she* felt different, like she was not alone.

The thought makes me sad. Not only because she was alone more often now that Andrew was gone, but because she never got to know Andrew. In my memories, she loved him too. It was different than the way I felt about him, but she truly cared for him—despite how much he irritated her at the end.

But then I tell her more. I tell her about Isabella and Nathan. Then I tell her about Andrew moving forward in time. And the last time I saw him. The fight we had at the roller skating rink after he jumped. My fear that I might never see him again.

And how it all happened right before Mary was taken.

He said he was doing it for the *thrill alone* and not for me.

We are both quiet for a time. It is probably about time to get back to the party, but it feels like she has something important to say, so I wait.

"Emily, dear," she says. "Andrew lied to you."

*What?*

"About not loving you," she says, guarding her thoughts about something else. "He lied about that."

But you don't know him, you weren't there—I want to say, but I don't. *How can you be so sure?* I ask instead.

"I just know," she says.

*But you never knew him.*

"T-that is not exactly true," she says leaving me stunned.

*How? What do you mean?*

She pauses a moment. If I could tap a foot, or fidget without Lucy doing the same and feeling my increasing impatience, I would. One of the cons to sharing a body with someone as I experience their memory.

Two words. She says two words and everything becomes clear and incomprehensibly complicated at once. A relief on the one hand and pure terror on the other with all of the implications and all of the varying ranges of emotion and confusion and depression and elation it brings. That it *will* bring when it happens to me.

"The fire," she says, then floods my mind with the memory of *two* versions of what happened that day. Of the *two* times that I lived it with her. It was almost a year ago for her, but it happened to me just last fall, mere months ago. The agony and terror of it that hasn't faded. It is once again fresh in my memory with the impressions and feelings of *both* our memories and of *both* fires melting together as one.

*You remember?* If I were speaking I would choke on my words. *You remember...?* Then panic sets in as I vividly remember one of the biggest reasons—besides trying to save Grams—of why I went back.

"I remember my sister dying," she says, her voice catching slightly. Of course she lived it with only a fraction of time compared to the final result of actually saving Hannah. But I remembered that initial pain of learning Lucy's beloved sister was dead. It was tragic. It was devastating.

It was the way I felt about losing Grams and not being able to save her by going back.

*You remember both realities.* I am absolutely in awe. And I want to ask her how, but I doubt she has the answer. *Which means you remember Andrew's part.*

"Yes, but it did not come instantly. It was only very recently, while I was away in that... *place*... that the memory of losing my sister came back to me so vividly." She pauses and moves to take a seat on a nearby bench, her legs and lungs weakening from the emotional strain. "I believe they would have kept me in the sanatorium longer if Dr. Cole hadn't explained why I had two conflicting memories of one event. For a moment I believed I had truly gone mad."

*Wow.*

"But it's not just *two* memories," she says then fills my head with a third. The final and actual memory she lived in *this* line of reality. It's similar the other two. She locates Hannah in time and the two of them get out and fall on the back lawn. And again, Tessa—being walked by Grandma Grace—is nowhere to be found, much like the second memory I have.

It's surprisingly anticlimatic. Almost like it was too easy. Too simple. For all of the drastic changes the dreams have caused in my life, this felt like the universe was attempting to keep the actions of what happened the same. Or as close to it as possible.

Lucy patiently waits as my thoughts tumble and snowball. She pushes down any spiraling thoughts, but I don't dare bring up any of the hopeful, happy possibilities.

But I have to ask, *Was Charles's cousin Tessa there?*

"There? During the fire?" She almost seems confused until she remembers the conversation with Tessa in the first memory. "I apologize," she says. "There is so much to keep aligned. But no, Tessa was not in town until the wedding. She did not come to visit before."

My breathing quickens. Which in turn causes Lucy's breath to quicken. We stand and pace a few steps. I note that Lucy is wearing her favorite blue dress. The one she wore that first time I visited, but I almost cannot appreciate the bookend fabulousness of it because of where my thoughts have turned.

Grandma might be alive! All day yesterday I asked silly questions about being famous and about the things Grandpa Cole accomplished and left the biggest question unasked. I might be able to call her again. To go to her house and be hugged by her again, to sit and sip hot chocolate while I relate the recent happenings of the life of a teenage memory-walker.

I rack my brain for the memory of my room. I noticed the flowers from Arianna's party were gone, but was the birdhouse there? I feel like I would have noticed if it had been missing.

A huge part of me wants to wake up right then and there. To push myself out and find out. But another part of me is afraid of what else I might find out. *Not just yet,* I tell myself.

*So do you remember more about Andrew?* I ask. *The parts where he almost caused Charles to cancel the wedding? Or the parts before?*

"No. But the fire was traumatic. Perhaps that is why those memories returned? Perhaps the others will return with time?" she asks, though I don't know the answer. "The memories of the fire came several months later. I expect I will gain more and more memories of your Andrew over time as well. Have you ever recovered the memories of another time?"

*No.* The first timeline shift I caused was saving Carly last fall. It was in October, I think. But that gives me a thought. *When you remembered the fire, how much time had passed since when you remembered?*

"Nine months? Perhaps ten?"

It had only been about five months since saving Carly. Maybe I would still recover those memories of the previous six months. If it worked that way. The idea gladdened and terrified me all at once.

It was another question to ask when I woke up.

*We should get back to your party,* I say.

"But I feel your desire to go," she feels immensely sad suddenly.

*Yes, but I'm not ready to face my world just yet.* There was so much unknown. *I'd like to stay in your world a while.*

That makes her smile again. "I'm glad," she says in a way I might say it. The change in her inflection surprises me, and it makes her laugh. "You've influenced me too," she says, "and I'm going to miss you."

*But why?* I ask. Doesn't she know by now that I always come back?

"Because now that I have achieved my happy ending, you are no longer needed."

Oh. She doesn't know. *So, in my time, in the future,* I say, *turns out I'm kinda famous.*

I feel her confusion, but she doesn't voice it.

*Because I'm the* Lucy-Walker, I say. *Lucy, they told me that I get to walk with you the rest of our lives. In my time, the Lucy Walker walked with you regularly until you died.*

A bubbling happiness seeps into me as we walk back toward the party.

"So, you will be back," she says. "Do you not wish to go and find out about your grandmother?"

*I do,* I say. *But I'd like to stay with you a while.* I want to soak in her happiness. I want to revel in it. I want a front-row seat to the beginning of her *finally* happily ever after.

# fear the worse

I jerked awake despite such a joyful, leisurely dream. It was the first Lucy dream *ever* where I sat back and enjoyed the dream for the pure sake of reveling in Lucy's happiness. And only Lucy's happiness.

There were no stresses. Well... besides hoping there was enough food for the party and that the guests wouldn't melt in the heat.

But there were no major stresses. No wishing to be with someone else, or worry about running into that someone else, because he was no longer in her time. No drama about being caught in the wrong situation at the wrong moment with Andrew. (Although seriously, Charles had the *worst* timing.) As she ate her finger sandwiches, there was no fear of a fire that was supposed to kill her—a fire which I repeated more than once to get it right. There were no worries that Lucy's wedding might be called off, no sanatorium, no isolation cell, no tuberculosis.

Yeah, getting her thrown in isolation hadn't been my finest moment. But to Lucy, it had never happened. She was happy and healthy.

All of that was in the past. Lucy got her happily ever after.

I jerked awake despite such a joyful, leisurely dream, because I had to find out one hugely major thing. Something that might've changed in my life by not only saving Lucy, speaking to my ancestor, and becoming famous. Grandma Grace might be alive.

The one object that I expected to be vanished from my room, along with the arrangement of reject flowers, to prove Grandma was alive still hung in its place of reverence. The birdhouse. Grandma's birdhouse painted a pale yellow with the blackbirds flying across the roof and down the side like a vine. And the large black number, *VI.* The Roman numeral six.

My heart sank, and I dragged my feet down the stairs to breakfast.

"Why the long face?" Dad asked when I scooted into a chair, he was cooking bacon. It was Sunday tradition. "Did Mom tell you?"

"Did Mom tell me what?" I asked but then blurted because I *needed* to know. "Did Grandma die?"

He looked at me strangely. "Grandma Grace?"

I nodded.

"Heavens no!"

"Then why is the... is *her* birdhouse in my room?"

"She gave that to you for your birthday," Mom said, walking into the room and seating herself next to me.

"So, she's alive?" I repeated.

"Honestly, I think that woman might outlive all of us," Dad said, then laughed. "I don't think she's going anywhere anytime soon."

I sort of glared at him.

He raised his hands in mock-surrender.

"Yeah, maybe not the best thing to joke about if Grandma was dead in her last reality," Mom said and matched my scowl aimed at Dad.

"Okay, okay. No joking about Grandma Grace's lifespan," Dad said, getting back to his bacon. "Noted."

"Can I call her?" I asked, still not believing. "Can I talk to her? I've missed her so much!" My voice cracked at the end.

"We're going to visit tonight for dinner. Is that soon enough?"

I wanted to say yes, this version of me should've been able to say yes, but the version of me I remembered lost her grandmother months ago and couldn't wait another minute now that she knew she was no longer dead. "No, I can't wait. Can I take the car?"

They both nodded as I grabbed two pieces of bacon and bounded upstairs to quickly get dressed. In my haste, I knocked over a box partially hidden beneath my bed with a bunch of articles and scraps of paper. I had no idea what it was, but I could wait. It could wait.

Fifteen minutes later I pulled up to the familiar driveway, with the familiar red door and tree out front where I once broke my arm. I didn't knock and barged right in.

"Grandma?" I said, a little loudly and hoped I didn't wake her.

I heard her familiar chuckle before she rounded the corner into the front room looking... exactly the way I remembered. She held her arms out to me and I ran to them, sinking into her embrace and weeping. I wasn't at all surprised by the waterworks.

"Your mother gave me the heads up," she said moments later when we pulled away. I followed her into the kitchen for a mug of hot chocolate. The water was already hot. She knew I was coming.

"She told you that I had a timeline change?"

She nodded. And poured us each a mug, letting the steam from the chocolate fog my glasses. "You died last fall," I said.

She nodded again. Almost like she didn't know what to say. Which was strange. She was always the one who knew what to say, she was always the one I spoke to about my dreams... although back then had I called it a curse.

"Do you want to know how?" I asked, a little irritated that I had to bring it up.

She cringed. "Do I?"

"It was my fault. Well... I dunno. It's complicated."

"How so?" Grandma leaned forward to move a stray lock

behind my ear. "You know you can always tell me things. I assume it relates to the dreams?"

"Yes, I wanted to save Lucy from a fire she was supposed to die from, and you wanted to keep things the way they were. You said it was bad to change things."

"That sounds like a different me."

"Well..." I paused. "Maybe because back then you were the only one who believed the dreams were real. The world didn't know about them."

"Not even your parents?" Grandma had the same expression Mom and Dad had yesterday when I asked if they believed they were real. Like how could they ever believe the dreams were *not* real? Like that was crazy talk.

"My parents thought the dreams were night terrors."

Grandma cringed again. "This recent timeline shift was a big one!"

"You're telling me! You're alive!" I couldn't help myself and hugged her again. "Grams, I've missed you so much."

She didn't let go until I did. She was great like that.

"How did I attempt to keep things the way they were supposed to be?" Grandma asked when I finally pulled back and took a sip of my cocoa.

"You piggybacked and walked with Tessa," I said. "Tessa died in the fire. And you died of a heart attack in your sleep."

She studied me for several moments. "And how do you count that as being your fault?"

I shrugged. The dreams were mine, so I'd always felt responsible. "So, you never walked with Tessa?" I asked.

"Charles's cousin?" She shook her head. I hadn't mentioned the relationship, but she clearly knew who Tessa was. "No, but I remember seeing her at the wedding." She seemed hesitant to mention that.

"You were there?"

She nodded.

"Who? How?"

"I was with a mature woman by the name of Lady Frighil."

"Who?"

"Oh, she was a peacock of a woman." Grandma chuckled. "I remember she wore a velvety purple hat with white feathers to the wedding. She was very proud of that hat."

Ah, yes, the description did ring a bell. "But that was..." I trailed off.

"Right before Lucy was taken away. I know."

But something didn't add up.

"What's wrong, sweetie?" Grandma asked.

"I don't understand." I took another sip. "Tessa was in the fire because of you, and because of Andrew."

She choked on her hot chocolate.

"Okay," I said, smiling. "So you know about Andrew."

"I do." She winked. "But do you?"

I shook my head, "I can't deal with that just yet. And for the record as far I know, Andrew isn't in our time yet. He's currently somewhere in the nineties, I think." That was my best guess, assuming he could walk as far back as '73.

"Okay, no talking about Andrew."

"But Andrew began jumping several weeks ago—at least in my time—but you just came back ... yesterday, I guess? Why didn't you come back after Andrew did his first jump?"

"The *mysteries of the dreamers*," Grandma said, as if it was a well-used term. "Scientists have studied it for decades."

"And that's the best they've come up with?" Honestly, it sounded like a cop-out.

"Basically, whatever changes Andrew made by jumping time didn't save me from my fate," she said. "You said I died of a heart attack?"

I nodded.

"Then I still died of a heart attack even after he changed things," she said. "The thing that saved me was the change *you* made."

"I still don't understand," I lamented. My hot cocoa was getting cold, so I downed the rest of it.

"I understand you were not the famous *Lucy Walker* in this previous timeline?" she asked.

"Nope. I mean, I walked her all of the time, but only a select few people even knew about the dreams."

"So *something* else gave me that heart attack. If it wasn't from walking with Tessa when she died in a fire, maybe it was the overall stress of worrying about my granddaughter who didn't have the right support for her gift."

"Huh." That actually sort of made sense.

"And when you changed things and woke up as the famous *Lucy Walker*, you had the correct support of your parents and doctors and scientists. Putting my heart at ease."

I shook my head. It sort of made sense but still baffled me.

"I wish I could have seen you yesterday," I said after a moment, realizing that she was alive and well and I'd spent the whole day being self-absorbed and wanting to learn about my famousness.

"Your parents set those rules as a protection. They've seen what happens when you have to deal with too many changes at once. And they have no idea what those changes could be, so the rules are the only way they know how to protect you from the mental and emotional trauma."

"But still..." I whined.

"Hey," she said, her tone suddenly firm and parental. "You've been sent to the hospital after a drastic change. They only want to protect you."

"Okay." I almost said, *I know.* But I really didn't know. This was all new to me. I almost wanted to ask what change had put me in the hospital, but I didn't dare. What if it landed me in the hospital again?

"Are you going to church today?" Grandma asked, her tone back to her normal grandmotherly sweetness.

Right. It was Sunday. "Um..." I checked the clock. It was in twenty minutes, but I was in no hurry to leave.

"Or at least to the candlelight vigil—" she said, but then stopped herself.

"Candlelight vigil?" My heart sped. That usually meant something bad had happened or was happening. "Who is it for?"

Grandma's eyes widened. She was cornered. She didn't want to tell me. She had accidentally dropped the pretense and gone straight to a familiar conversation of two people who were fully aware of all of the events and people surrounding them.

"Just tell me," I said. "I'll find out eventually." A huge part of me didn't want to know and wanted to go back and be with Lucy in her happy ending. Where it was safe.

She sighed and her shoulders fell. Taking my mug and hers to the sink she muttered a name underneath her breath. But I heard it. I suddenly felt sick, the rich chocolate suddenly churning in my stomach.

"What happened?" I whispered. "What's the vigil for?"

She turned to look back at me. Defeat on her features. "Arianna has been missing for weeks now. And they..." She paused, taking another breath. "And they fear the worse."

# devastating and dangerous changes

"Arianna's what?" I nearly shouted. "But how... why?"

Grandma shrugged. "Mental illness runs in their family—"

"What about Carly?" I interrupted. "Is Carly okay?"

She furrowed her eyebrows like I should know the answer. "You saved Carly. In one of your dreams."

I sighed with relief. "Okay, that didn't change." But then my heart palpitations sped. "But Ari's gone? And they don't know why?"

"They think she ran from home. That she became depressed and..." She might as well have actually said the words, the implications in her tone were so thick.

"That she left to... to *kill* herself?" I whispered the forbidden word. "No! Ari wouldn't *do* that! She's fine! Sure, Carly was depressed but she's better now! Right? Carly is better now?"

"She is."

"And yeah, mental illness runs in their family, but..." Tears welled.

Grandma looked at me with that pitying expression, and even though I thought Grandma was dead yesterday, even though I *mourned* her last fall and went months missing her because I was still in mourning, I suddenly needed to leave. I needed to get away from that *look*.

Luckily I had a car. I grabbed the keys and headed for the door.

"Emily!" Grandma said, following me.

"I just need time to think," I said. I didn't want to hurt her. I just needed to get away. To be alone for a while. "I'll see you tonight." I shut the door behind me and sprinted for the car.

It wasn't in me to drive aimlessly since my vision was getting increasingly blurred as the tears ran steadily down my face, so I found myself at the only place I could think of for sanctuary. I should've gone somewhere else because someone was certain to find me there. But I didn't care.

It was my place.

It has always been my place.

"Why didn't they tell me yesterday?" I screamed at the dash after parking behind one of the big poplars on one of the dead-end streets of the cemetery.

Obviously, I knew why.

They didn't know what I knew and what I didn't know. If I had asked, I'm sure they would've told me. But I didn't know to ask, because it wasn't something that was in my reality before everything changed at the sanatorium with Lucy that day.

Before I was famous.

Before Grandma Grace was alive.

Before Arianna wasn't missing and was safely sleeping in my room after a very eventful, very awesome, and fantastic birthday party.

I got out the car and walked to sit underneath the poplar tree. I picked the spot because it wasn't near anyone I knew. How crazy was that? I was avoiding the graves of the long dead as if they'd interrupt my solitude if I got too close.

They would if I had a flashback.

Lucy and Nora were a couple of streets over, and Isabella was in the section of old white headstones that had only names and dates. Hers and Nathan's were actually carved out of a pretty, dark-grayish stone, so theirs stood out. I had yet to find Mary, and since she supposedly married a Harker (as Andrew informed me once upon a time), I assumed she'd be close to Lucy and Nora but she wasn't. I had no clue where Genevieve was. I was tempted to try and walk her again and find out what she needed me for, just so I didn't dislike her as much, but I wasn't in a hurry. I had other pressing matters.

I sat and tried to clear my mind. I couldn't think. I didn't *want* to think. Because if I did, I was doomed to feel overwhelming guilt.

I pulled out my phone to scroll through Instagram, but my head wasn't in it. My thoughts drifted as I gazed past dance pictures and memes of cats without actually seeing them.

Arianna went missing the second I saved Lucy and met my great-great-grandfather. When I woke up as the famous *Lucy Walker*, she was already gone. I couldn't wish Lucy back in that place to get my best friend back. But it was the very act of saving Lucy —

my other best friend—that had caused her to flee. Or whatever. *She didn't run away.*

Grandma said Andrew's act of moving forward in time didn't prevent her heart attack. It didn't make sense, but somehow something I did in Lucy's time had saved Grandma. I suspected Ari's disappearance was also connected, but there was no way to know what that was. There was no way to know what, if anything, I could go back and change to bring Arianna back.

And even if there was something I could do, even if I knew how to fix it, I couldn't risk harming Lucy. She finally had her happy ending. After everything I did to cause her misery, she finally had that. And she deserved it.

"Emily Chandler! What the *hell* are you doing here?!"

I jumped from my skin when he shouted at me. My heart pounded out of my chest. I pressed a hand against my ribcage and dropped my phone on the grass next to me. "Duncan! You scared me!" I said but didn't move from my spot.

He paced in front of me, fuming. *Oh no. What else do I not know?*

"What are you doing out here alone? With—"

"I'm gonna stop you right there." I interrupted firmly. He disobeyed and opened his mouth to continue his rant. "No! Stop talking!" I shouted. Slowly I stood up from my tree and brushed off the back of my jeans. I folded my arms across my chest to mirror him. I could almost see the steam rising above his tousled hair. "I changed a timeline two nights ago," I said, assuming he knew what that meant. "So, I don't know why you're mad at me."

His arms relaxed and fell to his sides. His jaw went slack for a second before he caught it. "Okay," he said slowly. Calm, but his posture was still wary. "What do you know?"

I dropped my hands too and put one against the tree's bark— maybe to steady myself? "I know that I'm the *famous Lucy Walker*," I said a little bitterly.

He nodded. Almost like he assumed that one.

"I woke up and my grandmother is no longer dead, but my best friend is missing."

Duncan cocked an eyebrow. "And what do you know about me?"

I stared at him for a brief moment as if his face could tell me his thoughts.

"That I missed your football ceremony and you are *really* mad at me about that."

"Eh," he shrugged, "you probably had a good reason."

"Maybe in *this* reality. In the last one I missed it because I *forgot* and went to bed early."

"Okay, I get why I might be really mad at you over that," he said, trying not to laugh. "But I was probably just being a dumb teenage boy over it anyway."

That was a strange way to put it.

"So you aren't mad at me." It wasn't a question. I was *so* glad it wasn't a question.

"And what about you and me?" he asked, tentatively.

"We used to date," I said, but didn't add that I'd never made that choice because it was due to another timeline shift—but that would probably be too complicated to mention or explain. "We broke up and you dated Clare Pickett for a while."

He made a face that made me smile.

"But we've never stopped being friends," I said slowly, gauging his reaction, "and you've been my knight in shining armor a couple of times recently." I felt my cheeks flame, so I turned my head to study the bark on the tree. I'd never told him that before. "And lately we've been... *reconnecting.*"

No response. My stomach dropped. *Did he* hate *me in this reality?* No that couldn't be right. Otherwise why would he care enough to track me down and demand to know why I was at the cemetery? I looked back at him to decipher his silence, but he was looking over my shoulder, around the tree at something with wide eyes.

I moved to look, but he shouted, "Don't!" stopping me. "Don't turn around."

"That's right," a deep voice said slowly from behind. "Don't turn your head."

"What's goin—?" I started to say, but then felt the cold steel of a knife underneath my jaw.

# how did you know?

*I*n *through the nose.*
*Out through the nose.*
*In through the nose.*
*Out through the nose.*

*Concentrate.* If I don't think about it, the putrid rag shoved halfway down my throat won't make what little is left in my stomach come out. The rag is so much worse covered in bile.

*In through the nose.*
*Out through the nose.*

The sticky tape stretched across my face pulls at the skin and tiny hairs near my hairline. It hurts.

And it keeps me awake.

But so does sitting on the wobbly wooden chair with my ankles strapped tightly to the legs. They were smart pulling my pant legs up this time, since I shimmied out of the bonds and kicked one of them yesterday. Or last week? My sense of time is so screwed up.

Being locked in a dusty, dingy basement with rusty pipes, no windows, and only a naked light bulb hanging from a cord has really messed with my circadian rhythm.

But I suppose the drugs did that too.

*Click.* The door unlocks, whines as it swings open. Heavy footsteps enter the room.

My heart jumps in my throat, then pounds in my head as adrenaline rushes through my body. Part of me is surprised I have any of the hormone left.

I close my eyes tight. Pretending to be asleep. Or high. Maybe they'll leave me alone this time.

I jerk back at the pressure at my wrists, ready to swing or claw at whoever is untying the ropes. My eyes betray me and fly open, always too curious to see which one it is.

But I don't recognize him.

Ash-blond hair. Young. Maybe a year or two older than me.

"Whoa," he says, startled by my sudden motion. "Easy there." His smile is kind. But a kind smile can always be faked.

He raises his hand, and in one swift, painful instant, the duct tape is gone. I almost gag as he extracts the rag, but I don't miss the opportunity to sink my teeth into his last finger before it pulls away from me.

I expect a yowl and smack in the jaw, but instead he merely hisses, shakes his hand, and squints his eyes.

He's trying to be quiet.

"What was that for?" His eyes are still shut tight, and he holds his injury tenderly.

I don't answer. I never do.

A moment passes, and he opens his eyes to look at me. "What did they do to her?" he asks almost absently, but still directed at me.

I cock my head to the side. An old habit when something does not compute.

"I'm trying to help you. Remember?" He motions to my wrists, his eyebrows asking if it's safe to continue untying. I don't tell him it's not. "I can see that this is a hard one for you." He resumes, though carefully, unknotting the cords.

"Am I—?" I croak. Weeks with a rag in your mouth will do

that to your voice. I clear my throat, hack up some gunk, then spit it on the stained linoleum next to me.

The guy tries not to show his disgust.

"Am I supposed to know you?" I ask.

"Seriously?" He looks annoyed. "You died in a fire in another life." A strange thing to say with an irritated tone. Seeing no realization on my face, he goes on, "You saved your friend's sister from killing herself?"

But then everything flashes purple. Then blinding white.

And I know myself.

I've been here before.

I've been with her in this exact moment before.

And I know who walks with *him*.

I push back the sudden urge to cry. "Go on, keep going," I say. "What else do you have to say about me?" I don't know why I'm suddenly mad, but after so long it all spills out. "You dragged me on a boat with you... where we fought and argued. You nearly broke up a happy couple who were very much in love—all for lies. You used a selfish girl, pretended to love her for heaven knows why—because it sure as *heck* wasn't to be with me. I have no clue what happened in the fifties, except that when you got here..." I waved a hand at the glorious year of 1973. "You thought it best to go back and break up *another* very-happy-very-much-in-love couple in 1954, was it? But of course, *I'm* the bad guy for trying to prevent that one."

"There's my girl," he says, then leans forward to kiss me.

I jerk back. "What are you doing?"

"I, uh..." For the first time *ever* the person Andrew walks looks absolutely baffled.

"And why aren't you with Matthew? You would've avoided that—" I pointed at his bitten finger. "If you'd been someone Mary knew."

We hear footsteps above. *Right. Need to get out.* No time to argue.

He makes quick work of getting the rest of the bindings loose.

"Let's get you out of here before someone realizes you are missing."

I nod. "You read my thoughts."

"Can you stand?" he asks.

"*Pfft.* Can I stand?" I scoff, and immediately push off of the chair, but my knees instantly buckle in weakness. *Right. That happened before too.* He catches me under the arms before I crash to the floor. Then half-drags, half-supports me to the back of the room.

"How did you know about the door?" I ask.

"I scouted the building in my current time, asked the owner the right questions and they showed me this door," he says, while concentrating on the puke-green wallpaper. "It's a nuclear bomb shelter, built next to the basement of the roller rink. Not a very good one, but a bomb shelter nonetheless." He feels around then finds a button painted the same color as the wall and pushes it, revealing a small door next to it. It slides open to reveal a dark tunnel. "How did *you* know about the door?" he asks.

I shrug and rush through. He slides the door back, and we are enveloped in darkness.

We race in silence, as quickly as my weakened legs will allow.

Left, then right. *Yes, I remember.* I'd memorized the turns the first time I was here. Another sliding door leads to a dimly lit cylindrical concrete room with ladder.

And blinding sunlight bleeding through the cracks.

I can't help but smile. Mary's rescue day is finally here.

"I'll check first," Andrew says, breaking the silence. "Make sure no one is guarding above."

"No one is guarding above," I say with confidence then lean against the cold concrete to support myself. She's weak and needs to rest anyway.

"How do you know?" he asks but still scurries up the metal rungs and takes a deep breath before pushing up the round cover. "How did you know?" he calls down to me after scanning the area above.

"Because this isn't my first rodeo." With all of the will I can muster, I take three wobbly steps toward the bottom rung. And once again with *my* strength, I launch myself up and out. The suddenly bright light assaults my senses, but I feel Andrew hook an arm underneath my legs and carry me several yards before gently putting me down in the cover of some green. When my eyes have adjusted, I note we are among some trees on the side of a road.

"I am not familiar with the term *rodeo.* How did you know?" Andrew asks as the classic white Chevy Impala drives by. Then a black Mustang. "How did you know there wouldn't be anyone up guarding the exit?"

"Because I've sort of already lived this memory."

"Sort of?"

"I never finished it," I say. "I lived it soon after the fire... well, soon after the fire for *me*." I give him a meaningful look.

"What do you mean?"

"It was right after the fire, but you were *here,*" I said, waiting for something to click. "It was confusing because you were back in your time the next time I visited Lucy," I say. "I couldn't figure out how you dream-walked *forward* in time."

"So... when I told you I was jumping forward..." He trails off like he's still trying to piece the puzzle together.

"I actually didn't really figure it out until I met you as Ginny. You were jumping forward and dream-walking backwards. So I knew you made it at least this far because I had already seen you in 1973."

"You knew all that when I was Andrew 2.0?" he teased. "And you still didn't believe I could catch up to you?"

I shrug. Then shake my head. "I don't know. It's complicated." I wave a hand at him. "The last time I saw you was when you tried to break up Ella and William in 1954. Where are you now? And again... why aren't you with Matthew?"

He watches me, as if he's studying me, but I know he's

processing something. "You knew Mary would be kidnapped," he says at barely a whisper.

"*Yes*," I say a little exasperated.

"Why didn't you tell me?" Did his voice break?

"Because..." I can't look at him. I'm a mixture of emotions. Grateful that we're finally here, that Mary has been rescued and I don't have to guard my thoughts so much to protect her. That I don't have to stall Andrew in his jumping. *Not that it ever mattered since he was never doing it for me anyway.* "Because I didn't know how to tell you without panicking her."

"Of course," he laments, throwing his hands in the air and speaking louder than he should. "And that's why you tried to prevent me from breaking up Ella and William... correct?"

I nod, and hold a finger to my lips. We really need to be quiet and should get moving again, but I'm grateful he's giving Mary a rest. "I still wish you had found another way, but, yes, " I whisper. "I was trying to stall you until she got kidnapped, so you'd know to come back. I mean, you weren't *you*, or Andrew 4.0, when Mary was saved, so I knew you must've been walking someone else. I knew that you were somewhere in the future."

"I was always coming back," he says, his tone warm and inviting.

It makes my heart swell.

"She was engaged to Matthew Harker, but she died," he says, looking over the branch to see if anyone is looking for Mary yet. The coast is clear so far. "I figured if I saved her, she might become my grandmother and give me that one final jump."

My heart drops. I turn my head and put the heels of my hands against Mary's eyes to push back the burning tears that threaten. He didn't come back for me. He didn't come back for Mary because he cared about me and wanted to see me. He came back because of his *plan*. Because of his need for adventure. Somehow he'd learned about Mary's kidnapping and death and decided to save her for his goals. For the *thrill alone.*

I still don't understand why his final destination is my time. If

I ever meet him—correction, *when* I finally meet him—I'll find a way to convince him to vanish from my life as well. It'll be better if I forget him. Just like Lucy and Charles have.

Like he'd never existed.

I want to say goodbye right now. I want to tell him to leave and that I can get Mary to safety on my own, but she is so weak I don't want to risk it. So I steel my heart and push myself to my hands and knees. "We'd better keep moving," I say, attempting to hide the catch in my voice with a cough. "She's seen their faces, and they didn't seem like the type to leave any witnesses."

"Right," he says. "Oh, and I'm walking Adam Harker currently." He points to himself. "Matthew's brother. I figured Mary would recognize him, but she's obviously never met him." He looks once more to make sure we can venture out of hiding and continue moving.

That name sounds familiar. *Adam Harker?* I shrug. Probably just because it's close to the name *Andrew Harker.*

"Matthew blocked me somehow. I could not walk with him," he says. "Let's go."

# leisurely stroll

My heart pounded. The man's breath was hot against my ear. It smelled terrible. I had to resist the urge to gag for fear of what the knife against my throat would do if I did.

Duncan held his hands palm up. "Listen, man," he said, "you don't want to do this."

"Stop talking!" the man shouted in my ear, making my eardrums buzz. I wanted to cringe but didn't dare move. "You're coming with me," he said at a normal tone, then huffed a huge sigh. "And I suppose you are too," he said to Duncan, clearly irritated by that fact. "Get in the car. Both of you!"

*Car?* The only car nearby was my parent's car underneath the poplar tree.

Duncan must've walked.

I had no idea how the man had gotten here.

I hesitated, causing him to pull the knife tighter. It was sharp. It hurt.

"Now!" he shouted, releasing his hand long enough to point at the car I came in and pull the keys from my pocket in one motion.

Duncan practically skipped backwards and went for the driver's side.

"No! The back!"

Duncan opened the back door when the man clicked the fob to unlock it and slid in. The man shoved me practically on top of Duncan, who scooted over to make room for me.

*We'll just jump out at a red light,* I thought to myself, but then the man switched the child locks on my door before slamming it shut.

*Now what?* My mind went a million miles an hour, trying to come up with a way to escape.

That's when Duncan opened the opposite door and grabbed my hand pulling me out faster after him than I thought possible. Something small and hard hit my shin and landed on the floor of the back seat as I scrambled out, but I couldn't look back to see what it was.

We sprinted across the uneven road, me in flip flops, gripping Duncan's hand tightly to keep from falling. It felt like it took thirty *years* to gain speed. Just one crack or some loose gravel would land me on my face and close the distance between us and our pursuer.

But we lucked out, and I didn't trip.

I didn't hear him following us either.

At least not on foot.

The engine of my car turned over but I don't dare look back. Some sickening crunches told me that he'd cracked some headstones as he barrelled toward us over the grass. In a car, he wouldn't have to wait for me to fall on my face. He'd be on us in seconds.

*Think. Think. Think.*

*The gate!*

I pulled Duncan's hand and suddenly stopped in my tracks, veering to the left. Duncan looked over our shoulders, but I didn't have to. The car was right on us!

Since I'd parked in the back of the cemetery, we were close to the backyards of the homes bordering it. One of which had a gate that the owners never locked. I couldn't believe I remembered it in my adrenaline, running-for-my-life, can't-think-of-much-else-than-getting-away-from-that-knife-again brain.

We rushed through the gate as the man slammed the car into park and hurled himself out. But he must have thought better of his ability to pursue both of us because before we'd reached the front yard, I heard the car door slam again. My car peeled away.

---

IT IS IMPOSSIBLE TO MOVE FASTER THAN A LIMPING gait, so Adam/Andrew and I dart across the street the speed of a leisurely stroll. Not the ideal speed when you're trying to escape with your life. *Well, Mary's life.* But still a valuable life. And on top of that, we're out in the open where anyone can see us.

It's terrifying.

I hope that Mary's captors haven't noticed she is missing yet and sent out the search hounds.

"Are you all right?" Andrew/Adam asks.

"She's weak," I say, my tone laced with annoyance. But I'm mostly frustrated at the fact that I can't move any faster. "They were horrible to her."

We are only two steps across the street when a car careens around the bend. Between the new adrenaline rush and my own strength, I manage to dart into the parking lot of the diner on the corner and slide behind a car.

Andrew/Adam gets there seconds before I do.

It rushes past. A green El Camino with missing rims. I wish my eyesight were better, but after being locked in a dingy basement, Mary can't make out the license plate for the police.

I assume our destination is the police station.

My heart screams underneath Mary's ribcage, and my lungs

ache to get more oxygen. My head spins with the adrenaline mixed with the absolute exhaustion Mary is feeling. Fortunately, she is completely checked out at the moment, just like she was the last time I went through this with her.

We've never made it this far before. I was woken up by a neighbor's car alarm going off in the middle of the night last time. I never saw the rescue and escape through to the end. I couldn't get back afterward either. It filled me with guilt at the time.

Andrew/Adam reaches for my/Mary's hand. "Let's go into the diner," he says. "They'll expect us to be moving and perhaps we can use the phone."

"Okay."

He helps me up, but it's like trying to lift a mountain. I assist as much as I can, but Mary's body is spent and there are several new stinging scrapes on her elbows from the pavement. I hiss at the movement. We hobble into the diner, and Andrew nods at a waitress before we make our way to a booth near the back window. Perhaps not the best place if we need to run again, but Andrew unfolds a couple of menus for us to hide behind and plan our next move.

"How are *you* doing?" he asks, worry lines etching his features.

"I told you, what they did to her…" I trail off and shake her head. With the movement I can feel the grease in Mary's hair by the weight of it. One of the perks of dream-walking with someone *before* they are kidnapped and not allowed a shower is that I know her once-feathery curls are in desperate need of a shampoo. Seriously, her curls rivaled Farrah Fawcett's. "She's actually not even conscious, as far as I can tell," I say. "So that's good. Adam would've been carrying her if I weren't here."

Andrew doesn't have to remind me that Mary didn't make it, that Adam *didn't* carry her. She was only being saved because of our intervention—Andrew's and mine. Mostly Andrew's. It felt like the only thing I was contributing was my ability to keep her body conscious enough to move. And I struggled even with that.

"I did not ask how *she* was doing," he sighs before looking over his menu at the approaching waitress. "I asked how *you* are doing."

"Can I get you two anything?" the waitress asks, her order pad and pencil ready.

---

"C'MON," DUNCAN SAID. "LET'S KEEP GOING. HE'S probably going to call for backup and corner us on the next street."

"W-who is he?" I asked, a little breathless and a lot embarrassed that I was out of breath but Duncan wasn't. *He is the quarterback,* I reminded myself, but it still wasn't an excuse. I could benefit from some running and exercise. *Not the time to be worrying about that!* I told myself.

"His last name is Shew too. I think he's Dr. Shew's brother," Duncan said. "I remember seeing something about him on the news recently. He got out of prison a few weeks ago. Five years for aggravated assault."

We rounded to the front yard of the house—hopping the fence because *that* gate was locked—and then immediately reached for each other's hand. We were *not* letting go. We hurried to the sidewalk where we slowed to a walking speed. No need to draw attention just yet.

My eyes darted back and forth for a hiding spot just in case. If a car rounded the corner and spotted us here, we were in broad daylight. There was no way they wouldn't notice us.

"Dr. Shew," I said. "How is she involved? Was I in a coma in this timeline?" It was weird to ask, but I had to. "Do you think that guy is trying to take me to Dr. Shew?"

"Maybe? And, yes, you were in a coma," he said, then his expression turned thoughtful. "Ari actually went missing only a couple of days after you went into that coma. A lot of people thought that was why she fled. Because she was torn up about what happened to you."

"Ari has been gone that long? And I went *weeks* without knowing about it?" Panic flooded into my veins. I just found out *hours* ago that she's been missing for—*Wait.* "You mean, she's been missing for over a *month* now?" I did the calculations in my head.

"Yeah, it was in mid-January."

My stomach felt sick. I mean, it already felt sick, but now I felt *really sick.*

*Hold it together. It's going to be okay.*

But is it? Really? C'mon, subconscious, let's get real about things. One step at a time. Let's not get snatched by some crazy relative of my former—very possibly insane—psychiatrist.

"Why do you think Dr. Shew is after me?" I asked. "She's already on trial for what she did to me, wouldn't this make things worse?"

Duncan shrugged. "Shew's been saying she needs to talk to you. In person. You haven't told me all the details, but you have a theory." Duncan kept a brisk speed. It was a feat to keep up with him and speak at the same time. For me anyway. "Well, you *had* a theory. Before your timeline changed."

"I... *what?*" I huffed. "What kind of threats?"

Duncan looked back and forth up and down the street, but there were no cars, so we crossed quickly and walked between two homes where a path led to the park on the other side. I only recently learned it was there. I wouldn't have remembered it without Duncan to guide me.

"You kept finding notes from Shew in your locker, in your backpack. *Under your pillow.*" He sounded exasperated. "There were a few text messages too, I think."

"Why didn't I tell anyone?" I asked. It didn't sound much like me. Especially after everything that woman did to me. "Why didn't I call the police?" *Why don't we find a way to call the police now?*

"I've been trying to get you to call the police for weeks, but..." He paused, like completely. He stopped on the pavement and turned to look at me. "Shew said she'd kill her if you went to the police."

"I don't understand, Duncan," I said. "Kill who?" I couldn't even enjoy the way the shadows of the trees played along his face as the breeze rustled the leaves. I couldn't enjoy how good it felt to have his hand in mine. Locked together, with our fingers intertwined. *I was not letting go.*

"I don't think she, or *they*, ever expected you to wake up from that coma." He paused. It was that ominous hard-to-explain-feeling you get before you're about to find out something really, really bad. "You told me you suspected Dr. Shew was involved in Ari's disappearance somehow."

Words completely escaped me, but he had to see the confusion on my face.

He shrugged as an answer. Seriously, he was no help in this situation, but I cursed my alternate self for not telling him more information. "One of the notes said she had Arianna."

"That's a little bit more than suspicion!" I let go of his hand and grabbed fistfuls of my hair. "Damn it, Duncan! Why didn't you say so sooner?" My voice rose despite my attempts to keep my cool. "That's evidence! We should call the police. Right. Now." I reached into my back pocket for my phone, but it was gone. I must've left it on the grass at the cemetery. "Do you have your phone?"

He patted his pockets looking relieved that I finally wanted to get help, then his face fell. "I must've dropped it somewhere."

My heart sunk. That was probably what hit my leg as we scrambled out of my car.

A car passed on the street behind us, so we sprinted toward the park.

"Two coffees please?" Andrew/Adam asks the waitress.

"And a turkey sandwich," I say, inadvertently making her eyes look at me.

"Oh, honey!" the waitress says in a patronizingly sweet tone, not even bothering to write any of our orders down. "Are you all right?"

*Facepalm.* I haven't had a chance to glance in a mirror. Mary looks awful, I'm sure. Not counting the greasy hair, I'm certain there are bruises and dried blood from cuts all over her face. Her face feels tight, so definitely dried blood. But Mary is so *hungry*, and I thought it would be good to boost her strength.

*Stupid, stupid, Emily.*

But there really wasn't any time for that between escaping captors, keeping hidden, and trying not to pass out from pain and exhaustion all at once. There is no make-sure-you-don't-look-like-you've-been-held-captive-for-weeks-before-you-escape on the to-do list of *Escape from Kidnappers.*

"We're fine," Andrew says quickly. "Just the coffees and the sandwich please."

Our waitress looks at him suspiciously, and I get the strange sensation of familiarity in her features before she walks away, still with the pencil and pad in hand.

She never wrote down a thing.

*Why does she look familiar?*

"She must think you're the reason I look like this," I hiss at Andrew. Mary's stomach probably won't even be able to keep anything down anyway. *What have I done?* "She has suspicion written all over her."

"Then maybe she'll call the police, and we won't have to keep running."

We sit—still hiding behind our menus—hearts pounding and hands sweating despite sitting absolutely still and trying to look calm on our bench. I hate that we are sitting next to a window because I can't stop looking out it for signs of well... *anything* that means they're after us.

*Why does she look familiar?*

My heart stops when lightning strikes.

"We've gotta go," I say, pulling Adam/Andrew's hand and sliding from the bench.

"Wait, why—?" he says but stops himself and follows me out.

The waitress momentarily has her back to us—she's on the phone—so we slip out.

I let go of Adam/Andrew's hand and link arms with him right as Mary's legs buckle.

"Why did we have to leave?" he asks.

"Because I recognized the waitress," I say, very out of breath. Suddenly I get a stitch in my side.

Sure enough, the green El Camino speeds back down the street. I worry it's too late, but Adam/Andrew rushes into a small copse of trees only half a block away from the diner, dragging me behind him.

I fall, crashing hard, scraping Mary's arms and hands again. Fortunately, Mary is wearing pants, but the fall is hard enough that I feel scrapes on her knees now too. Her head spins, probably from dehydration and low blood sugar. They didn't feed her much in that basement.

Adam drags her further and quicker than both Mary and I would like because it *hurts*. But we make it behind one of the larger trees by the time the El Camino passes by and pulls into the diner parking lot.

We keep our breaths shallow as if the men clambering out of the car and stomping into the diner can hear us from here.

"Who was the waitress?" Andrew asks.

"I dunno..." I say between labored breaths. "But she looked like she could be the sister of the guy driving that car."

"One of them?"

I nod, holding a hand to the painful ache in my side. It's a good thing I never got that sandwich, because it would have been food for the trees about now.

"We need to keep moving," Andrew says sympathetically. "It won't take them long to realize we're gone."

I want to cry, to curl in a ball, and just let them come and get me. But I can't do that to Mary. I *will* save her. So I nod and let Andrew drag us out of the trees.

# it's them

I t probably wasn't even him, but we were both on edge and sprinted when we heard the car peel out. We didn't stop running until we were in sight of the playground. It was just after noon on a Sunday, but the weather was nice and there was a family with three small children playing.

*Too bad there aren't more kids,* I thought. We could probably hide on the playground if there was a crowd. But at the same time, we wouldn't want to risk putting anyone innocent in danger by our presence. Who knew how desperate Dr. Shew and her *brother,* or whoever he was, were to get me.

*Wish I'd listened to Mom.* Yep, too late to be wishing for that.

We forced ourselves to slow after several steps, and I took Duncan's hand again so we played like two teenagers in love—as opposed to two teenagers running for their lives—in case the parents of the kids were watching. And I admit, it made my heart stutter when Duncan pulled me playfully into his arms, spinning me around and looking into my eyes with a sly smirk on his face.

I dove right in and dreamily looked back into his storm-gray eyes and melted into the green hints—the flecks that danced in the sunlight.

He leaned forward and kissed me surely and firmly. And I kissed him back.

Duncan smiled when he pulled back, and we continued walking in an albeit more leisurely stroll.

I admit, the whole charade *definitely* calmed my nerves.

*But was it a charade?*

*Not the time, subconscious!*

*Wait! Maybe the parents of those kids have a phone?*

Brilliant!

I let go of Duncan's hand and approached the mom. "Excuse me?" I asked. "Do you have a phone we could borrow real quick?"

She looked at me like I should know not to ask such a question, then shrugged, "No screen time on Sundays," she said. "We left our phones at home. Sorry." She didn't *sound* sorry.

*Figures,* I thought, but muttered a polite, "No problem." And rushed back to Duncan to reclaim his hand.

When we reached the opposite street and crossed, Duncan's spell over me still hadn't lifted—despite the condescending mom at the park. I stared at the pavement, attempting to get a hold of myself. It really wasn't the time to be daydreaming about Duncan. We were supposed to be staying alert.

*C'mon, Emily. Keep your head up. Pay attention.*

I followed my own advice and scanned the area. We were on another residential street. I'd driven down it maybe once? But I wasn't super familiar enough to know if there were any other paths hidden between houses or other good escape routes. We might have to jump a fence again if the need called for it. But even that was risky. What if the yard we escaped into had backyard fences higher than we could climb? Six-foot vinyl fencing wasn't as easy to jump as chain-link, and the idea of jumping chain-link didn't sound much better. Definitely a bad idea if the fence housed a Rottweiler.

*Just keep walking.* Okay, that sounds good. Let's stick with that plan.

A red Camaro was parked in the driveway of a house across

the street, but I admit I only noticed it because Duncan ogled for a minute. All of the houses were the same cookie-cutter design, just with different colors. One had a door painted the same color as Grandma's door.

*I should've stayed at her house this morning.* Again, not the time to think about *should've.*

A green van sat next to the house up ahead. It was one of those carpet cleaning ones with the windows painted green too. It made me wary, so I slowed my steps. Duncan did too.

"Emily!" A chill went up my spine when I heard my name from that familiar voice.

She was right behind us.

I guess I didn't need to worry about the van.

I turned around slowly. "Dr. Shew..."

---

MARY IS WAKING UP NOW, MAKING US HOBBLE EVEN slower. She's disoriented and confused and jerks her hand away from Adam/Andrew's.

"Let go of me!" she shouts at him and attempts to run forward. But it turns into more of a stumble, and Adam/Andrew reaches forward and grabs her elbow to keep us from skidding into the pavement again.

*Quiet!* I shout at her. *He's helping us!*

Adam/Andrew lets go after we're steadied, holding his hands up, his face full of confusion, and he looks behind us to make sure her shout didn't draw attention.

I pray we didn't draw attention.

"Give me a second," I tell Andrew.

He nods and walks a few feet away and toward the curb to peer down the street from where we'd come.

We are only two blocks away from the diner. Not far enough. We had to duck behind some shrubbery when the green El

Camino sped by a few minutes ago, but we'd gone undetected so far.

Thankfully.

*Mary,* I say, deliberately and forcefully. This is not the time for her to misunderstand my talking to her as her subconscious. *Those men want to kill you. Adam is helping us.* I try to come up with something quick that would help her trust him. I want to smack myself for not thinking of the obvious immediately. *Adam is Matthew's brother. He can be trusted.*

I don't know if she heard, but she seems to calm. The flight reaction in her is fading. She allows us to walk back toward him.

"We're going to the police station, right?" I ask.

"Yes. I stashed a car over there," he said. "It's at the arcade, just another block. I didn't dare park at the roller rink."

"Why didn't you say so sooner?" I want to sprint. Mary is on board too, so we grab Adam/Andrew's hand and pull him in the direction we were headed with a bit more enthusiasm.

But then we freeze on the sidewalk.

The men are on foot now. Walking *toward* us.

"It's them!" Mary whimpers.

---

"Now, if you will kindly come with me," said Dr. Shew. "I will lead you to your friend."

"Do you have Ari?" My voice came out as barely a whisper. "Where is she? Is she okay?"

"Just... get in the car," she said and waved a hand. My car came into view at that moment and pulled up next to us.

Two men were now in my parents' car, one in the driver's seat the other on the passenger side.

We were outnumbered.

"Get in!" Dr. Shew said through gritted teeth when we didn't immediately move.

The men open the back doors and clicked the child locks on both doors. The one on the street side slammed the door again.

I looked at Duncan. *What do we do now?*

He stared back with the tiniest shrug, then took two steps to whisper something that confused me a little.

"In!" Bad-breath-Shew shouted next to my face and yanked me away from Duncan. I want to retort something about finding himself some mouthwash but reminded myself that he still had that knife.

I scurried to clamber in the near side, hoping they only meant for me to get in. If they left Duncan, he'd be safe. Then maybe he could get help.

"All. The. Way," said Bad-Breath-Shew, shoving me.

I obeyed and had the privilege of being even closer to him as he slid in next to me. The other guy, a typical burly bodyguard type, shoved Duncan in on the other side, then slammed the door.

So much for Duncan finding help.

The burly guy got back in the driver's seat and Dr. Shew took the front passenger spot before we sped away.

***

ADAM/ANDREW JERKS US TO THE SIDE, THEN PUSHES US down and underneath a trailer parked in a vacant lot. As long as they look down, they won't see us. It doesn't give me much comfort, but Adam/Andrew leans against the trailer and pretends to be impatiently waiting for someone.

The men get closer.

My heart pounds faster.

Mary hyperventilates, making our head fuzzy.

Only a few more feet and they'll pass us. A few more feet. A few more. I close my eyes tightly, like a toddler who thinks if she can't see mama, then mama can't see her.

A few more...

"Hey, fellas?" Andrew asks throwing my stomach into my throat.

*What is he doing? Don't draw their attention!* They will almost certainly see my hiding place if they get any closer.

"Do either of you have the time?"

One of them mutters something that I don't catch.

"Thanks," Andrew says. "Y'all have a nice day."

The trailer above me muffles their voices, and I can't make them out any words in their response.

"Can't say that I have. A young woman, you say?" Andrew pauses and Mary breathes so fast I'm afraid we will pass out. "Nope. I've been waiting forty-five minutes for this guy, and I haven't seen a soul until y'all came along."

The men grumble something incoherent. Then they *walk away!*

My breathing calms.

My heart slows.

My mind clears.

A thousand seconds later, Andrew reaches a hand down to help us out.

We sprint toward the arcade.

# heartbreak

"W-where are you taking us?" I managed to ask despite my terror. After what Duncan told me, I had little hope that Arianna was okay, or that she was even alive. If they've killed her for whatever reason, what was stopping them from handing Duncan and me the same fate?

What he said back there was right. It wasn't like I was Isabella or Mary or Lucy and would wake up safely in my bed if something happened. This wasn't just a walk for me. This was *real*.

*I can't believe this is happening. I can't believe that something so terribly horribly awful is happening to me.* I hadn't had a chance to let that sink in until now. I'd been through *hundreds* of awful experiences with others. All of them with very real, very painful and emotional consequences for me. But none of them actually happened to *me*.

*You've got this, Em,* my subconscious seemed to say. It was weird. But it calmed me down.

"Calm down, Emily. I just need you to come with me so I can run a few more tests," Dr. Shew said, "just to tie up loose ends. Once I finish my research, everybody will understand what I've been trying to explain."

"Where is Ari?" Duncan asked.

"The Ari situation is... regrettable. But it's not my fault. *She* came to *me*. We were both trying to help Emily."

Bad-Breath-Shew mentioned that maybe she shouldn't talk, but she shushed him and shouted something about who was the smart Shew and who wasn't.

That shut him up.

My nose wanted to thank her for that if nothing else. It smelled like he had just eaten fish. Except it had been rotten. Mixed with sewer water. And topped with decomposing garlic. *Yuck.*

I tried to sneak a glance around Bad-Breath-Shew at Duncan but couldn't get a good view. "Arianna came to you for help?" I asked, since keeping her talking was probably the best strategy at the moment. I hoped that Duncan was paying attention to our destination and coming up with some sort of plan. Because I certainly wasn't.

"Yes. It was her idea," she continued. "When you went into that coma and no one could figure out what was wrong, she figured it out."

"Figured what out?" Duncan asked. *Did I ever tell him about Isabella or Mary?* That comment he whispered before we got in the car had me suddenly wondering.

"That perhaps Emily was stuck in her dreams." Dr. Shew's tone was so thick with condescension, I had a sudden totally-not-like-me urge to slap her in the face. I didn't. "She suggested that she piggyback into your dreams," she said, now directing her attention to me again. "And find a way to pull you out."

It's exactly what Carly eventually did. Only she came weeks later when I'd been in that coma for almost two weeks. So what was different? "How did she plan to piggback?" I asked, knowing that Carly used the ring.

"She promised me that if she could just talk to you..." she said, ignoring my question and shaking her head. "It seemed like a good plan. She was very insistent. And I was only trying to help."

"How did she do it?" I repeated. "Did she use the ring?"

"Ring?" she asked, but her confused look was revealing. "I don't know anything about a ring. I warned her it could be dangerous, but she insisted on helping you. She begged me not to contact her parents, to keep her involvement confidential. She was determined to go through with it. I really had little choice."

I wasn't very good at reading people, but even I could tell she was lying.

---

YEAH, SPRINTING ISN'T THE BEST WORD. STILL hobbling. Still moving *super* slow and painfully. But we make our way to the arcade parking lot where Adam's car awaits.

We had barely ducked into his car when the El Camino passes by again, slowly. We crouch down, hoping they aren't looking *inside* the cars as they scan the near-empty parking lot. The odds aren't exactly in our favor.

"Emily, I want to apologize," Andrew says, Adam's face inches from Mary's.

My pulse quickens for a different reason.

"Before, I was trying to ask how *you* are doing. And if you hate me now." He won't meet my eyes.

I count to four Mississippi before saying, "I don't hate you."

He lets out a breath I didn't realize he'd been holding.

"We've been through too much for me to hate you," I say. "We have too much history."

"Look, what I said the last time we saw one another. While I walked with Matthew?" he says. "I didn't mean it. Any of it."

"You mean—?"

"When I implied that the only reason I was jumping forward was for the thrill of it?" He looks me in the eyes—Mary's eyes—and my heart stutters again. "That was not true. The thrill is part of it, but a very small part. I wouldn't have even considered it if my pull to be where you are—*you,* not Lucy, not Isabella—*you.* Emily Chandler. Who maybe looks a little bit like Genevieve." He smiles, then grabs Mary's hand in our crouch. Which is uncomfortable and awkward the way we are positioned, so I count to four Mississippi and then pull away.

"We should go," I say.

Andrew nods, then looks out the window to make sure the El Camino isn't in the vicinity, then starts the car and pulls out of the arcade parking lot.

---

"So what happened to her?" Duncan asked, incredulously. "Arianna's been gone for over a month. Where is she?"

She looked back and forth between us as if still trying to decide whether or not to spill. "I ran some tests," she finally said. Her voice was scarily nonchalant.

"What kind of tests?" My voice caught.

"Jessica," Bad Breath Shew said under his breath, using her first name. His eyes were murderous.

But she ignored him and forced my gaze. "Might as well tell her," she said, decidedly. "She deserves to know. It's not like she'll ever dream again. *Such a waste.*"

I heard Duncan suck in a breath.

I felt her meaning but ignored her comment. One thing at a time. "What. Kind. Of. Tests?" I asked again.

Dr. Shew stared at me with those eyes I trusted so much. Her makeup was perfectly applied and flawless as always, she wore a pressed suit as always, but some strands of her hair were beginning to unravel from her normally perfect bun. "Well, as soon as we had everything ready to go, she started second-guessing herself, kept saying she had to go get a ring first."

"But you didn't let her," Duncan said.

"No. That would have been... unwise. I couldn't let her go, not after she knew of my involvement in Emily's coma. So I improvised," she said. "And it worked. I knew it would work. A non-dreamer was actually in the dreams! It was incredible!" she said, with a crazy smile that met her eyes.

"I don't understand," I said. "Arianna never piggybacked in those dreams." But I remembered too late that I'd had a recent timeline shift. It was very possible that Arianna *had* piggybacked while I was with Isabella being tossed around on that ship. I just didn't remember that she had.

"You had a timeline shift, didn't you?" Dr. Shew asked, reading my thoughts. She looked more excited than I would've liked. "You don't remember any of this, do you?"

I didn't dare open my mouth to confirm or lie.

She clapped her hands once.

"What happened?" Duncan asked, his tone firm and forceful. It made me nervous since he was on the other side of Bad-Breath-Shew who still had a knife.

"You mean your girlfriend didn't tell you?" she asked. "I wondered why you both acted like you knew nothing. Maybe I won't have to kill you after all."

I kept my face neutral.

"Actually, no I probably will."

*Get her to focus,* my thoughts directed. "You said it worked," I said. "So where is she?" Maybe she was still in a coma. Maybe she could get out. I would find a way to get to her and out of the coma.

"She died the day you woke up."

---

ANDREW DRIVES THE SPEED LIMIT WITH HIS EYES GLUED to the road. I watch him from the corner of my eye, watching his expression. He clenches his teeth. I can see the tightness in his jaw. His Adam's apple bobs every fifteen seconds or so as he swallows, holding back his tightly wound emotion just underneath the surface.

"Andrew, you hurt me," I say, finally breaking the silence. "When you said what you said at the roller rink, it hurt."

"I know—"

"Just," I cut him off. "Just let me talk."

He nods and closes his eyes briefly.

"But it wasn't just that," I say, glancing out the window to hide my own tears that form in Mary's eyes. "You were reckless. You lectured me about not being responsible with Isabella's life, but you disregarded Lucy's."

He opens his mouth to say something, but I stop him again.

"And don't spout about how it doesn't matter what happened to Lucy since she doesn't remember you anymore," I say. "Because you didn't know if it would work, and even though it did, things were pretty messed up for her for a long time. And I feel like part of that was due to what happened when she knew you."

"What are you trying to say?"

If I am being honest, I don't know exactly what I am trying to say. But his question suddenly makes things crystal clear. "I am saying that I do want to see you... in the future. But you and me... *together?* I just can't." Perhaps we could be friends, I thought. Maybe he could be a part of my plan to create a center for people with the dreams. Certainly, he could be an asset in that aspect.

"Because of what happened in the *past?*" he asks, anger in his tone, probably hiding the hurt. "Emily, I will change, I *have* changed!"

"Andrew—"

"No!" he shouts. "This is not the end for us! You'll forgive me. And I'm not the only one at fault for things that happened in the past."

"I know, but—"

"I do not think you do! Emily, I—"

"There's someone else!" I blurt out, and it silences him immediately. I didn't plan to blurt it out. I didn't even know it was a decision I had made or that I'd finally sorted out how I really felt.

"From your time?" he asks, his voice low and ragged.

"Yes," I say. "And I'm ready to meet you. I think we should meet sooner."

He nods, staring out the windshield with gritted teeth again.

"There's a meeting, a *support* group, for dreamers." I give him the exact date and time. "Meet me there. We'll talk." Perhaps that would give him time to get over it. Maybe when I finally see Andrew as himself—well, he'd be Andrew 6.0 at that point—hopefully enough time will have passed for him that we can be friends.

---

MY HEART BROKE. LIKE *LITERALLY*. IT WAS PHYSICALLY painful. I could hear my heart wailing. It was quiet, but audible.

"She... *died?*"

"Yes," Dr. Shew said so clinically. So matter-of-factly. So cold. "That's why I've been sending you messages to meet."

"You mean *threats?*" I asked, although I hadn't actually read them so I didn't know what they said. But it was the word Duncan had used. Suddenly I remembered that box underneath my bed that I kicked this morning. *Wow, that felt like forever ago.* The notes or *threats* must've been in there. I tried to compartmentalize the wailing of my heart that got louder, but almost sounded far away. But it was near impossible to block it out.

"*Messages,* not threats," she said. "I need to know why you woke up and she died. And of course, I couldn't *say* that she died in my *messages*, so I merely *asked for your help*." She looked at Duncan. "I hoped you could help too."

*What?*

"Don't you get it? She died because she *doesn't* have the dreams and you experimented on her!" Duncan said. He was angry. I couldn't remember *ever* hearing that tone from him. Toward anyone. "The thing that threw Emily into a coma is what killed Arianna."

She scoffed. "Are you wishing you'd said yes, now? And spared them both?"

"Said yes?" I asked.

Duncan glared at her in a stare that spoke volumes.

"Said yes to what?" I asked again.

"To taking the same medication." Dr. Shew's attitude was flippant. "I asked him first, after all."

"Why would he—?" *WHAT?*

"He never told you?" she asked.

The wailing got even louder and then lights began flashing.

She looked back at Duncan. "You never told your girlfriend that you're a dreamer too?"

There were lights in front *and* behind us. We were surrounded.

Somehow the cops came.

CHAPTER 49

# that's impossible

When we rush into the police station in the middle of the day, everyone looks bored out of their minds. Several patrol officers eagerly rush out in search of the men driving the green El Camino the second we give them the description. Andrew pointed them to the diner, hoping they were doubling back at some point.

I crash Mary's body into a chair, exhausted and dehydrated and broken. And finally safe. She checks out, and it's all I can do to keep her conscious until the ambulance arrives to take her to the hospital. Which is also en route. And her father has been contacted to meet her there.

She won't need me anymore.

Adam/Andrew recounts Mary's whole ordeal to the very attentive detective while we wait. He is very familiar with her story. There is an active missing person's report on Mary. The men who took her posted ransom for her father to pay by Friday —only two days away—or else they'd kill her. And he hadn't managed to come up with the money so without Adam/Andrew's help, and I suppose maybe mine too, she would've died.

I reminded myself that she did die in another version of reality.

Unfortunately, Matthew Harker was caught in the crossfire. He was found murdered in a ditch one week ago. The detectives suspect he found out where they hid Mary. He was probably trying to rescue her.

I brace myself to comfort her when the emotion hits, but it doesn't come in the way I suspect. At least not in the same way Adam is taking the news. Luckily Andrew is with him.

Mary loved Matthew in a way, and she is sorry that he was killed—she isn't completely unfeeling and feels horrible for Adam's sake—but Matthew was merely a means to get out of this small town. She was hoping to convince her father to leave with them and get away from all of their troubles. To start over somewhere far away.

Although, the way Mary looks at Adam now—safe and sound in the police station—stirs something in her that she never felt toward Matthew. I have a feeling she will be all right. And since Adam is also a *Harker*, I suspect that Andrew's plan isn't entirely thwarted. If the future plays out the way Mary dares to dream about, she and Adam will likely be Andrew's grandparents.

When the ambulance arrives, and I am finally able to crash on the gurney, I bow out of Mary's life one last time.

*Goodbye, Mary,* I say, though I doubt she hears.

---

I KEPT CHECKING MYSELF FOR KNIFE WOUNDS BECAUSE Bad-Breath-Shew had dug his weapon into me in one last desperate attempt for... I don't know. But I was fine.

And I was fre-aking out. But one thing at a time.

The three suspects were in the back of patrol cars on their way to county jail at the moment, and the paramedics had finished giving Duncan and me a once-over. They assured me we didn't have a scratch on us.

We were fine.

Well, physically.

Duncan refused to let go of my hand as the police questioned us and got our statements. Somehow, Duncan had covertly picked up his cell off the floor where it had fallen and turned on his record feature while simultaneously sending a message and our location to his brother, who called 911.

It was brilliant. He was brilliant.

While we waited for our parents to arrive at my car, I had to ask him the question. I had to get the answers.

"You're a dreamer?" I asked. I'd been dying to find out since the cops showed up. I mean, I was glad they did when they did, but a few minutes longer and I might've already had my answers.

He wouldn't look at me, but also didn't let go of my hand as he dragged me to sit next to him on the curb. We were in the middle of nowhere near a large field. It was unclear where Dr. Shew and her cronies had been taking us.

"Yes," he said, after several painfully slow seconds.

"Why didn't you tell me sooner?" I was a little bit angry. If he truly had the dreams, he would know how essential it was to have someone to talk to about it. Someone to share the burden with. Someone who understood.

Finally he looked at me. His storm-gray eyes bright in the mid-day sun. Spring was in full force. "Because I didn't want you to figure it out until..." He trailed off.

"Figure what out?" I had no clue what he was talking about.

"I was afraid you'd be mad..." He stared at the ground near our feet. "I didn't exactly do as you asked."

My heart began to pound. "What are you saying?"

"You said I'm your knight in shining armor, but I don't exactly deserve that. At least I didn't."

"What do you mean?"

"I messed up so many times. I was selfish. I—"

It finally clicked. "That's impossible," I said aloud, but now it all made sense. He *knew* about Isabella and Mary. So either I told him everything about my dreams in this current reality that I didn't remember. Or...

I shook my head.

"That's impossible," I repeated, looking at him and waiting for confirmation.

"We weren't supposed to meet until that group meeting tomorrow," he said, still staring at the ground. "You *asked* me not to come until then."

My mind couldn't wrap around it. Not possible. "So, why did you come sooner?"

He finally looked at me again, then shrugged, and flashed that sly smile I knew so well.

It made me want to cry.

"Because you said you were in love with someone in *your* time," he said. "When we saved Mary you said there was someone else. I had to know who it was. I had to see if there was any way I could compete."

My face flushed. "I was talking about you," I said softly. "About Duncan."

"I know," he said and winked. "Guess I can stop worrying about Scott O'Neil."

"How? How was I seeing you here and meeting you there all of this time?"

"*Mysteries of the dreamers*, I suppose." He shrugged again. "Emily, there is something else I have to tell you. There is a chance that you'll forget all of this tonight. When we finally *meet* tomorrow, you might not remember anything about me."

"Forget you? Why would I forget you?"

"I do not know how it works exactly, but I change timelines too." He looked at the ground in front of us, then laughed. "I mean clearly! Otherwise I wouldn't even be here! I've been trying to keep track of where the... *other me* is." He paused and looked up at me expectantly.

"Oh! Are you asking me? Like where are you dream-wise?"
He nodded.

"You are... well, we saved Mary last night." It was a rare two-dream night of saving Mary, then witnessing Lucy's happiness.

He nodded again and looked back at the pavement. "After that I jumped *here,*" he said, waving a hand at the air, "which means my final jump will happen tonight in your timeline. It might change everything. Tomorrow is the moment when all our timelines intersect."

"When they intersect?" I asked.

He nodded. "You have two timelines, Emily, like two sides of a coin," he said, using his hands to illustrate. "One where we have never met and one where I have always been here... where you know me as Duncan. And after they intersect tonight, I do not know which reality you will wake up in tomorrow. I'm just hoping for one last strange time-travel loophole."

I didn't know what to say. *I promise I won't forget you*? I couldn't promise that. I knew what happened with timeline shifts and it utterly confused me too. I had no clue how they worked.

"Can I just say one thing before the rest of this day gets any crazier?" he said. "In case I can't talk to you again until tomor-row? Just in case?"

"Of course."

"I am sorry for what I said." He studied his hands. "Of what I implied."

"At the roller rink?"

He looked back at me. His eyes glistening. "I wasn't doing it for the *thrill alone*. I hate myself for ever letting you believe that. Emily, loving you, that's the thrill."

I didn't answer and did the one thing I'd been wanting to do since I finally knew who he was. That he was finally here. I threw myself into his arms, a little unsure what to call him now, so I breathed the first name I ever knew him by when I fell in love with him.

*Andrew.*

# epilogue

I wipe my hands on my jeans one last time as I walk up to the *kum-ba-ya* looking circle at the park. She's already here, sitting cross-legged in what looks like a guest of honor spot —which she absolutely deserves. The others eye her with awe and suspicion, which is probably why she stares at the blue book on her lap.

The *Lucy Walker* is what the world calls her. It's how I first came to know her—though not a soul knows my true origin. Nobody knows the truth about how long I've been in love with her.

She doesn't look up when I take a spot across from her.

And it's killing me.

*Will she remember me as Duncan? Or am I still Andrew, who she's curious to meet but still too angry and hurt to ever consider... ?* I shake my head. I've waited so long for this, but proposals don't happen at nineteen... no wait, I'm seventeen currently. Proposals don't happen at seventeen in this century.

"Thank you all for joining us," Dr. Williams, our facilitator says. She's a dreamer too, so she's the perfect psychiatrist to help young people like us. "And thank you to Emily Chandler who put this group into motion." There's an audible buzz around the circle when Emily's name is mentioned.

My eyes are glued to her, so I instantly notice the faint flush that colors her cheeks. She swishes her black hair forward and pushes her purple frames up the bridge of her nose in an attempt to hide her blush.

"I believe regular meetings with others," Dr. William's continues, "who experience the same struggles and trials will help everyone cope."

Irritatingly, Emily keeps her head down as the introductions begin. Dr. Williams instructs us to state our names and what we hope to gain by meeting regularly in the group. Most of the girls remark about how noble and brave Emily was when she learned she was the Lucy Walker. Some dreamed *they* would be the Lucy Walker—but admitted their plan for the money was less *noble*. The guys on the other hand look at her like they have other intentions. The jerk next to me makes an inappropriate comment.

"That's my *girlfriend* you're talking about," I hiss, with clenched fists. I should've planted myself next to her instead of giving her space.

"Duncan?" Dr. Williams asks, "is there a problem?"

I shoot another glance at Emily, who *still* won't look up. But the gesture answers my question. She doesn't know me.

"Call me Andrew, please," I say. There are the deep-blue eyes I know. "Duncan is my middle name, and I'd like to go by my first name in this group." I'd like to go by it forever now that she knows.

"Of course, *Andrew*," Dr. Williams says. "Is there a problem?"

"No problem," I say, then flash a smile at the confused expression on Emily's face. But I see the recognition there. And the deepening blush in her cheeks gives me hope.

I PRACTICALLY TRIP OVER MY FEET TO GET TO HER when the meeting is over. The half-hour meet and greet felt like *years*. Especially when Dr. Williams explained the one good thing that came from Emily's time with Dr. Shew: the *Rose Ritual.* And then she asked the rest of the group to explain their ways of coping. It understandably took some time, since most people's coping methods are more complex than mine—binging on junk food. A half hour turned into well over three times that. But Dr. Williams beats me to Emily despite my sudden clumsiness and hugs her in consolation.

*Right. Arianna.*

"I heard they finally found... the body?" Dr. Williams asks.

Emily nods, pulling back, then hastily wipes her eyes.

"Please come see me this week," Dr. Williams says. When she notices my hovering, she makes quick exit. *Thank you, Dr. Williams.*

Emily nods again, then turns to me. Her face instantly flushing again.

I smile at her.

"Andrew?" she whispers.

It's a punch to the gut. "Is that all you know me as?" I ask, reaching for her elbow to pull her further from the group. Thankfully she allows that.

She nods slowly but pulls her blue book close to her chest and attempts a smile. It's a devastatingly, depressing, *beautiful* smile.

I take a deep breath. "You don't know Duncan?" I'm a glutton for punishment. And for the first time *ever* since being Duncan, I want her to know me as him. Not as Andrew.

"No," she says, then quickly looks at the ground.

I am at a loss for words. My worst fear has come to fruition. All of that prep work, all of the befriending and *proving* that I was changed from all of those times we knew each other in my various pasts was all for nothing. I had repented of my various misdeeds and sins. I was trying to prove to her that I was worthy of her love again. *Duncan* was a better and reformed version of all of the *Andrews* she knew.

And I've been damn patient.

"So I guess I should call you Andrew 5.0 now?" she teases and it is all I can do to resist pulling her in my arms and kissing her, refusing to let go. *Ever. Again.*

But I resist and play along. "6.0," I correct.

"Right," she smiles, then looks back at the ground.

"And even though I'm here, in the twenty-first-century, I'd prefer it if you put the number next to my name when you say it."

That quickly brings her beautiful eyes back to mine. I itch to remove her frames so I can see them better. Other than her hair color, I can't fathom why she thought she looked *anything* like the selfish Genevieve. Emily is a thousand times more *gorgeous*, to use a word of my now-contemporary teenagers.

"You never met Andrew 5.0 ," I say. "But your Grandma Grace did." *Right before you were born,* I want to say, but resist.

Her pale pink lips form an *oh.*

"When I sold her that birdhouse."

"Roman numeral six?" She looks away, but I can't bear it and turn her chin to look back at me.

She jerks back like an electric shock, and I flinch away. Taking a step back.

"It's the only version of me you'll ever know," I say slowly and softly, praying that the words don't cause her to shy away the way my touch just did.

She stares at her book for what feels like another decade, before finding my eyes again. "But I will know Duncan," she says. Confusing me slightly. "I mean, the memories of you as Duncan."

I ball my hands into fists against my sides to fight the urge to pull her into my arms. But I don't resist the smile that forms instantly. "Yes, you will, eventually," I say. "How did you know?" The relief is instant.

"Lucy told me," she says. "She eventually remembered the

other versions of the fire." She pauses. "Even the one when you weren't there, when we died."

I nod. Now doesn't feel like the time to explain all of the confusion that comes when the memories come back. Luckily the ones that don't matter, the ones not actually in the current time-line sort of fade to black and white, so it isn't too hard to keep the current one straight. It's only disconcerting immediately after the time shift and when they initially begin to resurface.

Nope, not the time to explain all that.

But it gives me hope. She'll remember Duncan, eventually.

"Look, about Arianna..." I say. I'd be a horrible friend if I didn't help her through it. I was still changed. I was still Duncan, even if she didn't remember him.

As expected, tears well in her eyes. "Can we not talk about her right now?"

*She's pushing me away.* She doesn't want to talk to me about it. It's a devastating thought, but I must respect her wishes.

"It's just that you're here," she says, maybe seeing my fallen expression. "Finally. And besides that, Lucy and Carly will probably get the brunt of that emotion for a while. They are my best friends now that..." She trails off.

I nod. "I understand."

"Plus," she says, looking thoughtful. "I've definitely had help with that." She taps her head.

"Ah... your walker."

She smiles at the term. "Yes, my *walker.*"

"I know she was there when I ran from Dr. Shew, and it doesn't feel like she's gone."

When *she* ran. When she went through that *alone.* Every memory of me has been erased from her mind. I knew it was a possibility, but seeing it here firsthand feels like a punch to my gut. She doesn't remember me. Nothing. Not meeting in the graveyard for the first time, not the Sweethearts Dance, not sneaking into my room to retreive the Harker ring.

"Can I show you something?" She sounds suddenly nervous

as she holds up the blue book she's been clutching the entire time.

"Of course," I say, as she flips to a page in her book marked with a neon pink tag—the ones that lawyers and tax preparers use.

"A few weeks ago, I realized that anything written down in *any* timeline will survive a change."

I raise an eyebrow. That can't be possible.

"It's how Lucy was able to show me the letter your grandfather, Colin Harker, wrote about you only a few nights ago. Even though you aren't in that time anymore."

I feel my jaw drop.

"T-there are different entries about you that are from different timelines," she says.

"About me?"

She turns the page around to show me. "I wrote this last night and tagged it," she says. "*Before* I forgot about you as... *Duncan.*"


*March 11 -* ** *READ THIS* ** *Because tomorrow you might forget all about him. When you finally meet Andrew, give him a chance. I know, I know, you were hurt by what he did and said in the past, but in this time, he has been one of your best friends. He was your boyfriend for a time and you hope he will be your boyfriend again <u>very soon</u>. Anyway, just give him a chance, and when you have time, read back through this journal. He stars in it <u>a lot</u>. Oh! And he goes by Duncan.*


She closes the book and pulls it against her chest again. "So, I'm gonna read it," she says, staring at the ground again. "My memories might take time to come back, but at least I can read about them first." She shrugs, then awkwardly holds a hand out. "It's nice to meet you, Duncan."

## THE END

# letter to emily

*Dearest Emily,*

*Yes, I mean you, Emily Chandler. I know who you are. I know what you are. But I thank you. I thank you for being with my sister in her last moments. I thank you for taking over her lips. Her lips which never spoke a word in her entire life until that fateful day she ordered me off the ice.*

*Something strange happened. I have two memories of that day my sister died in the frozen river. I know which one really happened —the one when my sister did not speak. When I almost fell in myself and drowned. I know you were there with her for both.*

*I suppose that is the curse from being in a family of memory walkers. Even those of us who do not have the gift can sometimes remember when something was changed because of the choice of a walker.*

*By now, you must know that my grandson, Andrew Harker, is also blessed with the gift. Although he considers it a curse. His experiences have jaded him in a way. And I cannot say I fault him for that, but I am concerned. You see, he is planning something danger-ous, something I am not sure will even work, but I do not want him* to even try it because of what it might mean. For I will surely lose him if he succeeds.

I am sure you are aware of the power of wearing a talisman as you have been aware of walking Lucy more than once. I could see it in your eyes that first day we met. You can tell when someone is being walked if you know what to look for.

Andrew's talisman is especially powerful in that he has found a way to gain control in deciding who to walk.

It is clear that he has strong feelings for you.

I do not mean to cause you pain, but I feel that some of that love for you stems from his attraction to Lucy as well as the fact that you are like him.

I assume he has done the necessary research and preparation, but I am wary of his initial plans to drag you into a walk with him.

But bringing you into a specific walk with him will be his testing ground for what he plans next.

The future holds so much wonder for him, as anyone, and he declares that his feelings for you go beyond Lucy's pretty face. He plans to change his lineage and hop through time and get to you.

I am afraid of his failure or success. If he fails and becomes desperate, I fear what he will do. If he succeeds, then he will no longer be my direct grandson and will be obliterated from my life— and possibly my memory.

And if he doesn't succeed in hopping, he may erase his existence from all times.

Please, if you care for him at all, dissuade him from this. Stop him in any way you can.

Sincerely,
Colin William Harker

# Get three FREE short stories when you join Joanna's email list at joannareeder.com

# thank you for reading

Thank you for reading *Purpose In Her Dreams*!

If you enjoyed jumping into Emily's world and meeting Lucy, Andrew, and Duncan, please leave an honest review! Reviews are essential to indie authors like me.

# acknowledgments

First of all to my readers for reading this book! Thank you!

But seriously it never would have come to fruition without the support of my family. From my sweet husband who may not understand my need to tell stories but supports me anyway, and my crazy kids who are completely content to watch Netflix or nap for a couple hours a day so mommy can write. Also my parents, siblings, and extended family who have been my beta readers, emergency brainstorm session heroes, and for supporting me and encouraging me all of these years.

I also couldn't have done it without my amazing writer's group (Go Team Fellowship!) and critique partners, Jesse Booth and Aaron Herd who have helped me brainstorm, develop my stories to make them stronger, kept me motivated, and boosted my confidence along the way (you are my rock, Team Istari!).

Lastly, a huge thank you to my editor Katrina Beckstrand (editsbykb.com), who completely understood and visualized my vision for the *In Her Dreams* trilogy and helped polish them to make them all lovely and shiny.

# about the author

Joanna Reeder is a USA Today Bestselling author who takes readers time traveling through dreams, shifting into fantastical creatures, and tossed into Faerie. Her fantasy stories always have a dash of romance, leave readers turning pages long into the night, and eager to recommend them to their daughters and grandmas and coworkers!

When Joanna isn't writing, she enjoys bike rides and kayaking with her hubby and kids, vacations at the beach (with a book to read, of course!) and learning new songs on her blue electric guitar.

She's a believer in the paranormal (seriously, she has stories) and her motto is, "A Dr. Pepper a day keeps insanity away!"

If you love fantasy romance too, you can sign up for Joanna's weekly newsletter at joannareeder.com. You can also chat with her on Instagram @joanna_reeder.